DEAT

"Sharp writing and telling descriptions of family relationship... surprise and tension, propel this story to its shocking conclusion. Aficionados of crime-fiction-with-a-twist won't be disappointed… Marshall Keene has to deploy his investigative skills and no small amount of courage to exonerate himself and save his family."

—Dave Moores—

Moores is the author of several books. His latest novel is *Sparkles And Karim*

"Donna Kirk's novel holds appeal on several levels, above all the tense relationships between the central characters. Kirk deftly turns the conflict screws as the story progresses, exposing character flaws and corruption while suppressing information essential to the survival of Marshall Keene. Fast paced and evenly written, Kirk takes the reader on a ride through leafy Lakeville, exposing the seamy underbelly of crime in the 'Burbs."

—Michael Joll—

Joll is the author of several novels and short story collections. His latest is *Hacker*.

"Author Donna Kirk mines the dark depths of human relationships with a sure touch as unexpected hero Marshall Keene faces his demons and unearths a murderous plot. What he discovers is a dangerous sinkhole of blackmail, lies and abuse that threatens his wife and his unborn child."

—Barbara Stokes—

Stokes' work has been featured in Ontario newspapers and travel magazines. She recently completed *Death Scent*—a crime novel.

"…a well-plotted story with a host of engaging and diverse characters, especially the protagonist Marsh Keene whose at-times slightly taciturn and bitter personality (love his dialogue), hides a sensitive, wounded man. The author handles Marsh's new reality with great care and respect. Readers will enjoy riding along with him as he struggles to clear his name."

Shauna Clinning

Shortlisted for the 2022 Guernica Editions Prize for Literary Fiction, semi-finalist in the 2018 John Kenneth Galbraith Literary Award competition.

ALSO BY DONNA KIRK

Finding Matthew

a mother's memoir which chronicles the life of Matthew, born with multiple disabilities.

DEATH IN THE SUBURBS

A Novel

Donna Kirk

MiddleRoad Publishers

www.middleroadpublishers.ca

Making Literature See The Light Of Day

www.middleroadpublishers.ca

Library and Archives Canada Cataloguing in Publication

Kirk, Donna, author

Death In The Suburbs

Editor Ken Puddicombe

ISBN 978-1- 990765-39-1 (soft cover)

Front Cover design: kathryn.lagerquist@gmail.com

Back Cover layout: www.kenpud.wordpress.com

“Some people can’t figure out what I’m doing. It’s not a walk-hop, it’s not a trot, it’s running, or as close as I can get to running, and it’s harder than doing it on two legs. It makes me mad when people call this a walk. If I was walking it wouldn’t be anything.”

—Terry Fox—

(1958-1981)

DEDICATED

To Wheelchair Users, particularly Matthew, and Elisabeth, Freda, Peter. The world needs to learn more about *get-on-with-it* spirit.

Table of Contents

ACKNOWLEDGMENTS

Brian Henry, Dave Moores, Shauna Clinning, Mike Joll, Hannah McKinnon for their ongoing support and feedback.

Thanks to my family: husband Ed, son Joseph, daughter-in-law Crystal, and granddaughters Sloane and Reese. They listened to my chatter, the excitement of creating a novel, and the complaining.

Chapter 1

Monday, 5:00 p.m.

The January dusk pulsed with the flashing red lights of half a dozen cruisers. Ahead of me, a crime scene van swerved and parked. Two uniforms jumped out and opened the back doors. A night scanner on top of the van rose into position, ready to bring vivid clarity to what looked like an ordinary frozen mud field at the edge of a developing subdivision. For a journalist, this was like winning the lotto.

What do we have here? I felt my excitement building, forgetting about the cold beer I'd be cracking right about now if I were at home. *Please God, a murder.*

After parking my car at the side of the road and assembling my wheelchair, I approached the gathering of officers. Lack of snow this year made the short journey easier, my wheels bumping over frozen ground instead of getting stuck in ornery drifts and ridges of ice. Earl, a reporter from a competitive newspaper, stood twenty feet away. We seemed to be the only journalists amongst the officials. Crime in a suburban town like Lakeville was usually minor stuff and not worth the trip, particularly for the big dailies in Toronto. A cop I knew walked toward me. Out of respect for protocol, I held up my press card.

He waved it away with a smile that was more bared teeth than grin. "We can always count on you, Marsh."

"Evening, Jerry. Looks like this is a big deal."

"Body. We'll be here a while. Where's your sidekick?"

I tried to hide my joy at the news. "Munro's taking a few days off. Renovating his bathroom."

Jerry nodded. "Stay within the usual boundary. Hope you don't freeze your ass off."

I grinned. "I always obey orders, you know that."

There was no designated area for the press, but I knew what he meant. Don't wheel around and be a nuisance or you'll be turfed. He stepped aside, giving me permission to join my fellow scribe, then hurried away to deter some late afternoon walkers who had arrived at the scene. I was tempted to follow him, knowing he'd ask if they'd seen anything. But that meant leaving the allocated circle and risk learning nothing, so I headed over to the restricted area, a reasonable distance away. People at the scene were talking, but I couldn't hear what they were saying. I balanced my camera ready to take pictures. Earl and I nodded to each other.

"Fucking cold," he said.

"Yup," I answered. Journalists weren't the most communicative bunch, especially when a story was unfolding.

Christ. A body! And for the first time, a big story was all mine. Munro would be mighty pissed to miss this. I yanked off my gloves, unzipped my jacket, and dug my cell from a shirt pocket. I'd smashed a few phones attempting to text in frigid weather, so this one was attached to a cord around my neck. I texted Don, my editor, to let him know what was developing. My fingers were numb by the time I finished. More than my ass would freeze before this wrapped up.

The scanner flashed on, casting a glow that intensified the scene. Ahead of me, yellow police tape flapped in the breeze, encircling a small area beyond an embankment. A woman I recognized as the local pathologist-coroner crouched inside the enclosed area, half-visible behind a slight incline of frozen dirt.

Detectives and police stood in a haphazard circle, staring down at what I presumed was the dead guy. Or woman. Crime scene officers moved around, cameras poised, snapping pictures from different angles and gathering evidence into bags.

I glanced at Earl. "Wonder if the people who tipped off the cops are still here?"

He shrugged. "Dunno." He wouldn't tell me even if he knew.

My editor had old crony insiders who kept him informed of any local police investigations. He always passed any info on to his reporting team. I assumed Earl's editor did too.

We fell silent, focusing on the scene about 25 meters away. I raised my Canon 6D Pro Lens, an instrument I was proud of but still paying for, and took some shots. It was so cold I had to keep blowing on my hands. Later, Earl and I would be contacting the cops, trying to pry information loose. They were always guarded about releasing anything that would be of interest to journalists—instructed from day one of their training not to talk to the press.

"Couple of thugs reported missing in Hamilton two days ago," said my fellow scribe from behind his camera. "Maybe this is where they've been hiding."

He wasn't telling me anything I didn't know. We watched the proceedings in frigid silence punctuated by texting, ringing phones and stamping feet. My prosthetic feet and steel lower legs never felt anything of course, but my thighs had started to tingle. It took hours to scour a crime scene, so God knows how long the cops had been here. Long enough for word to get out. And long enough to have looked the scene over and place plastic markers randomly, wherever they suspected relevant evidence might be.

About forty-five minutes later, though in the cold it seemed much longer, forensics guys unloaded a stretcher from the van, a folded body bag on top. They ducked under the tape, pushing the gurney toward the coroner.

There were certain times when using a wheelchair had its advantages—like now. I got clear shots through the spaces created by officials shuffling around in front of me. Earl bobbed up and down, pointing his camera over their shoulders.

What looked like a man's body—judging by the size—wearing dark clothing and Doc Marten type boots was loaded into the black bag and heaved onto the stretcher.

"He's either in full rigor or frozen stiff."

Earl ignored my great pun.

Moments later, the two forensics guys pushed the gurney and its occupant to the van and guided their cargo inside. The scanner was switched off and lowered, the loading door clanged shut, and the men got into the front and drove away. Jerry and another cop got into a cruiser and followed. No need for sirens and flashing lights now.

"C'est tout," I said. Earl tucked his camera into a shoulder pouch and walked away.

Police dispersed, and those with flashlights switched them on—the field now in darkness. The coroner walked to her car, removed the protective clothing, stashed it in a bag and put it into the trunk.

Sporting a friendly smile, I wheeled over to her. She'd held her position for decades and had a reputation for ignoring any journalist who didn't treat her with deference.

"Hi, Dr. Carruthers. Anything you can tell me?"

"Good evening, Marshall. Police report will be out soon. That'll have to do for now, I'm afraid."

"You have my number just in case there's something you can share."

She smiled. "Yes, I have a drawer full of your cards."

"Have a good evening, Dr. Carruthers."

The police report would say *dick.* I'd wait until the autopsy was completed before visiting her office, if nothing solid turned up before then. Carruthers would be surprised if someone from our paper didn't show up.

Earl was talking to the police as they walked back to their cruisers. From his expression and the cops' headshakes, it was obvious they weren't in a receptive mood. I decided not to return to my car and stopped at the side of the road, pretending to be on my cellphone.

Two cops I didn't recognize approached and strode past, deep in conversation. The one speaking nodded. "Christ! Gotta be what, four, five shots to the chest?"

"Yeah. Maybe he's one of the local guys who was reported missing a few days ago."

They got into the closest cruiser and drove away. Multiple gunshot wounds— someone wanted that guy really dead. It should be fairly easy to find out who'd gone missing and if he was a known criminal. My gut told me I'd know his identity before long, and my gut is usually reliable.

Soon, only two cops remained to guard the scene. I wheeled over to my car and transferred into the driver's seat. In thirty-five seconds, my chair was dismantled and stowed behind me. Since I got the new wheelchair, I kept trying to beat the twenty-nine seconds suggested by the manufacturer. Today's time wasn't worth recording.

I sat behind the wheel and voice-recorded the names of the uniform personnel and the designations of others who were unfamiliar to me. I'd also recorded the conversation a few moments ago between the two cops, then sent the lot to Don. I started the car and headed back to the office— my editor needed to see my pictures of the crime scene, and he'd want to discuss the conversation I'd recorded just now between the two cops.

At the main intersection of the subdivision, I took a picture of the large sign advertising an idyllic lifestyle at *Whispering Pines*. The acres of property were bare of pines, or trees of any description, and no construction had begun. Places like this made me glad my wife Ann and I lived in an established part of Lakeville—even if my in-laws referred to our war-time neighbourhood as blue collar—a world away from their ritzy lakefront street, populated by bankers and lawyers.

There was a long night ahead, so I phoned Ann on the drive back to work. The call went to voicemail which meant she probably hadn't left the hospital.

"Hi, babe. You working overtime? One of the perks of being promoted, I guess. Call me when you can. Been a murder in Lakeville. I'll be at work for a while."

Five minutes later, my cell rang.

"Hi!" said Ann. "I was in a meeting. What's this about a murder—or is it your idea of chit-chat?"

I pictured her perfect smile, and the flawless Trinidadian skin that had knocked me out when we met seven years ago. "You're in a jolly mood! Guess your first day as charge nurse went well."

She laughed. "Today was one meeting after another. Tomorrow I can start to work on the changes I've been thinking about…tell me about this murder."

I gave her a summary of my sixty minutes at the scene. "I'm saving the graphic details for later."

"I don't like the sound of that. But a body in Lakeville! Great story for you right now."

"My big chance." But I had more important things on my mind. "No period yet?"

"I took another test today. Second positive in a row."

My heart did a little flip. After a miscarriage three months ago, we were both on edge. I wanted a kid just as much as she did and was afraid to get my hopes up again.

"Let's talk about you taking leave this time, Ann."

"I'd probably be better working."

No point in arguing right now. It wasn't as though I was going to win this one anyway.

"I'm seeing one of the gynecologists tomorrow."

"I'll come with you, if I can get away from work." The *Halton Register's* neon sign loomed ahead. "I'm just pulling into the parking lot. Let's talk later. Love you, babe."

I turned off the car and opened the door. It took thirty-two seconds to set up the chair, back to my average time, but still not good enough. If I got below twenty-nine, maybe I could appear in one of Medi-Chair's advertising videos. *Marshall Keene, wheelchair wizard.*

I propelled myself into the building, pulled up to the elevator and pressed the button. My chances of being able to go with Ann tomorrow were slim. We'd be working full bore on this story, plus finishing others that were already in the works. I'd practically be living at the office for a while.

What the hell was going on with the elevator this time? I stabbed the button again. And again. Why did the *Register* have to locate in an ancient building with one unreliable elevator? It wasn't as though I could bypass it and race up the stairs like most people in my office.

I kept thinking about the doctor's appointment. If I couldn't make it, Ann would go alone rather than ask her parents. Although my loyal wife had never said as much, her mother, Eileen, was a pain in the ass. Her appointments with various beauticians, fitness classes and social committees took priority—even above Ann. And His Honour Burton Young would have a full list of cases to preside over and could never take time off on short notice—although he'd probably love to accompany his daughter.

The elevator landed on the first floor and the door creaked open. I wheeled in, spun around and pressed the button for the fifth floor. Two people entered the building, rushed forward and squeezed in before the door closed. I recognized them as having an office on the same floor as the *Register.* We nodded and wished each other a good evening.

If Ann was pregnant, Burton would offer her money to stay home and take it easy, which would piss me off. He'd done that the last time and still insinuated the miscarriage might not have happened if she'd taken his advice. Maybe I could talk my wife into keeping our news from her parents for a while.

After visiting every floor on the way up just for good measure, the ancient device finally stopped with a bump and the doors jerked open. My two companions headed to their office and I spun down the hall to the newsroom.

Don, waiting at his office door, beckoned me inside. "Let's see those pictures, Marsh."

He had his hands on his hips. Don rarely congratulated anyone on a job well done, but you sure got a kick in the ass if something went wrong. The trick to a smooth relationship with him was ignoring his quirks, obeying orders and giving him what he wanted. I started by repeating what I knew.

He nodded. "We'll print those pictures in tomorrow's paper and hopefully we'll know more before then. Like if the dead guy's local or an import."

He also wanted the identity of the dead guy. Don smelled murder and so did I. The police report would be out soon. If it was murder, the cops would want to solve this rare local occurrence asap. There'd be an urgent appeal for information.

"I'll call the station and see if anyone's in the mood to tell me anything," I said.

Don nodded, but his eyebrows knitted together. I'd worked at the *Register* for four years and accompanied the senior reporter, Munro, on crime for the last two. Even though I'd learned to listen, leave my attitude at home, and record facts precisely, I had the feeling my boss was nervous about me handling a big story.

"Good idea. Munro's not here and you've made friends with some of the cops," he said.

He'd remarked on many occasions that he preferred not to deal with active-duty police. *The force today is just a bunch of youngsters playing cop.* Don had been in the newspaper business before today's batch of uniforms was born. He'd croak on the job before he'd retire.

"As soon as I have something print-worthy I'll let you know." I wheeled out of his office.

The last two people leaving for the day wished me a good evening as I rolled down the aisle. After pulling into my cubicle, I looked back at Don. He was already on the phone, and would spend the next few hours talking and writing. I'd be hard-pressed to offer him any information he wouldn't dig up on his own. But he'd expect me to write the story, then he'd edit the hell out of it before it went to print. I took out my cell, called the station and asked to speak to the duty cop.

"Wilson speaking."

"Marsh Keene calling, Hal."

"Hey, Keener, how's it going? Read your article last week about those portable wheelchair ramps. Hell of a good idea. Plenty of places around town could use them. What are they called again?"

"Easy Up Ramps. Thanks, Hal. I'm wearing a different hat today. Hoping you can give me some information."

"Like what?"

"Like the body at Whispering Pines subdivision."

"You and Munro working the story together?"

"Any info you can toss my way, like the police report? Munro's away. Don and I are working the story." There was a pause. Don wasn't popular at the station.

"Report won't say anything you don't already know, Keener." said Hal. "But here's your tidbit for the day. The dead guy was reported missing by his wife."

"By his wife? He's a local?"

"Could be. This might need your attention, Keener."

I frowned. Funny thing to say. "I overheard two cops say that he'd been shot in the chest multiple times."

"Keener, you have a keen nose for the police beat."

He expected me to laugh and I did. "What was the dead guy's name?"

"Nice try. You know the routine. Next of kin has to be notified."

I nodded to myself. The cops had to speak to the dead guy's wife. That meant they knew who the victim was—probably a local resident.

I thanked Hal again for the tip and started to construct the story. Plenty of bodies had been found in and around Lake Ontario in previous years. The cause was either suicide or mishap. But this was the first murdered body in the town of Lakeville in probably decades. I'd look up the stats and lead the article with that, grinning to myself that my colleague Earl hadn't heard the cops talking about the shots the stiff had taken.

After the opening paragraph, I added the information I'd learned at the scene, minus the tip Watson had given me. Didn't want to burn my bridges. His info would remain in my back pocket until I had facts to back it up. The story would be a question mark for now, but dead bodies always fascinated readers, particularly home-grown dead bodies.

I sent my story to Don, then checked my phone. There was a message from Ann saying she'd be working later than expected. I texted back saying I hoped she wouldn't be too late, already worried about this pregnancy. She replied saying *worrywart I'm fine…*

The on-line police report had landed in my in-box:

Halton Police Service are investigating a suspicious death in Lakeville. Police attended a subdivision where a man was discovered deceased. As foul play is suspected the homicide unit has taken charge of the investigation.

Just as I'd thought, the report was an appeal for information. The usual contact numbers were included after the three-liner. A local murder was a big deal. Upstanding citizens would be agitating to make sure their police force solved this asap.

I turned off my computer and wheeled past Don's office on my way out. It was now past seven o'clock. He beckoned me into his office and began talking before my wheels stopped turning.

"The murdered guy seems to be a local. To keep our crime beat section current, I've kept tabs on people sentenced for serious crimes in Canada, their bids for parole, and release dates." Don knew that I knew this. He hesitated, and looked me in the eye. "It seems that one of our home-grown bad boys was due to be released…you know who I'm referring to."

I sat in my chair and stared at him…then nodded. Probably a month ago, Ed Alexander, my legal advisor, had called. He told me that Allan Wright, the asshole who'd driven drunk nearly ten years ago, hit the car I was driving, killing my parents and my sister, and putting me in a wheelchair, was due to be released from prison.

Chapter 2

I nodded, spun my chair around and nearly collided with Munro. Don hadn't wasted time ripping him away from his reno project.

"Good timing, Munro," said Don. "Let's all go into my office."

Munro and I obliged. There was no invitation to sit. Good thing—the two chairs in front of the desk were piled to the tits with files. Don reached out and handed Munro a sheaf of papers. "Look this over while I talk to Marsh." Munro nodded, left the office and closed the door.

Don looked at me with a steady gaze. "Tell me about you and Allan Wright."

I didn't answer immediately, not sure what to say. "You know what he did to my family, Don." I told him about my recent conversation with Ed Alexander.

Don frowned. "All he said was that Allan Wright was *soon to be released*? He didn't say when?"

I shook my head. "He was calling from Europe. From a spa or something. He said he had health problems."

"Wright was released from the Kingston Pen last week."

Why hadn't Ed called me back to let me know the specific date? I felt stupid not knowing, and sat staring at my boss.

Don stared back, then spoke. "Your connection to Wright is a problem. Munro and I will handle the story from here."

"So, you've had confirmation that the dead guy in that subdivision was Allan Wright?"

Don nodded. I didn't doubt it. He'd been in the news business for decades and had acquired reliable, willing sources. Sources who were confident he knew what to print and what not to print. In this case, maybe someone with the ambulance service was in his back pocket. Don would never reveal his sources, or admit he had them. That's one thing I liked about working for a small publication—the boss was willing to take all the heat.

"So how is my connection a problem?" I said.

"You threatened him, remember? More than once. That won't be forgotten. The papers'll drag all that out again. Munro and I will handle the story. You can work on other things in the meantime."

"That was nearly ten years ago, Don. He'd killed my whole family and put me in a wheelchair, for Christ's sake. And instead of graduating from the Ontario Police College, I was in the hospital with both my legs cut off." I realized I was shouting, stopped and took a breath. "I sure as hell had nothing to do with his murder! My slant on this story would be something no other paper would have."

Don didn't even consider thinking about it. "We need an impartial account—for now, at least. I have a few assignments that need attention. You can work on them at home if you feel distracted here," he said, avoiding eye contact. "I don't care why Wright died or who killed him, but the optics of you handling this aren't good."

Meaning I could have killed Wright? And he didn't care if I had? Jesus Christ! Staying away from the paper would sure point things in that direction. My victim-impact statement and comments to the press years ago were no secret. Journalists had long memories; I could hear the buzzing around our office. *Where's Marsh? How come he's not at work? Remember that court case and what he said?* Vague half-truths would turn into solid facts.

Then it struck me. Don was ass-kissing the big boys who owned the paper and who owned him. He'd taken flack four years ago for hiring a disabled rookie despite insurance-risk concerns. My articles in various newspapers on disability had impressed him. When I started at the *Register,* I continued with what was considered my byline on disability. I also handled benign assignments for two years until one of the journalists quit and I started tagging along with Munro on local crime. My name on the Wright story could put Don in the hot seat. Really bad optics for him.

I gripped the armrests of the wheelchair to steady my hands. "Working from home doesn't cut it for me, Don. See you tomorrow morning."

I swung around, nearly crashing into the door frame in my haste to get out of there.

Calm yourself, Keene, and think this through. Deal with any fallout, and contact the union rep to find out if Don can force you to work at home.

No one had charged me with any crime…yet. Don would have to fire me to keep me away from my desk. And I'd be pumping Munro for every bit of information he dug up. I texted the union rep and, knowing him, he'd get right on it.

My mind raced during the drive home. If Ann was there, she would talk about her day as always, giving me time to calm down. She'd be surprised that I was home earlier than expected, and one look at me would tell her things had gone sideways. She'd want to know the whole story, particularly if the police wanted to interview me.

Rush-hour traffic was heavier than usual due to an accident, so I ducked in and out of side streets. Others had the same idea, particularly one guy driving an old black Toyota who managed to stay a few cars behind me. My cop instincts told me that one of Wright's cronies was tailing me. On the fourth detour, I lost him. The usual ten-minute trip had turned into twenty before I pulled into our driveway.

While I was trying to decide what would take less energy, walking into the house or setting up my chair, Ann came out and started down the ramp. I locked the car, told myself to get a grip, grabbed my canes and walked up to meet her.

"Hi, hon. I thought you were working late." She reached up for a kiss. "Marsh, what's wrong?"

I put one arm around her waist and we did our side-by-side walk into the house. "Tell me about your day first, I need a few moments to unwind."

I got a beer and a bottle of sparkling water from the fridge and shoved them in my pockets. Holding a glass full of ice, Ann followed me to our living room which also served as my office. We had to make every room count in our little war-time bungalow. Ann and I always sat on the couch to discuss our day. I leaned over and gave her more than just a hello kiss.

"Wow!" she said. "You're good. Guess you're not so tired after all."

I grinned and held onto her hand. "So how was your first day, Charge Nurse?"

She sighed. "Mostly meetings. Not my favourite thing." She poured the water into her glass and took a sip. "But I'll have to get used to it. The hours will be better, though. And no more weekends."

"You've earned it, babe. It'll be so nice to spend that time together. Especially if…" I squeezed her hand and we smiled at each other.

"Dad called."

I sipped my beer. "Oh yeah?"

"Why didn't you tell me Allan Wright was the guy who was murdered?"

Shit. My know-it-all father-in-law couldn't wait to tell his daughter the latest. Obviously, Burton had bloody good sources, too. Being a judge, he probably had access to all the latest criminal information. I tried to control my tone, not wanting her to know her father had pissed me off. Again.

"Don sent me to the scene, like I said, then I went back to the office to work on the story. The dead guy's a local and Don found out his name. I wanted to tell you myself, not over the phone."

She leaned closer to me, nodding. "Yeah, of course … I bet you don't know how to feel. But I'm not sorry he'd dead after what he did to you and your family."

"I haven't had time to take it in. But Don has."

She nodded. "And now you've got a big story to write."

It sounded so simple. "Don took me off the story. He doesn't like my history with Wright. He implied that I could've killed him."

"*What?*" She grabbed my arm, "That's ridiculous! What did he say?"

I repeated my conversation with him just before I'd left the office. "What would you have thought?"

She shook her head. "I don't think he meant that *you* killed him. That drunk killed your family and might've killed you too. If you wrote the story, people would really understand how drunk driving can change lives. They won't get that from an impartial article."

I nodded. "Good point. Too bad I didn't think of that. Don suggested that I work at home on other stuff for the next few days where I won't be distracted."

Ann's expression indicated she was as upset as I was. "Can he do that?"

I shook my head. "Don't think so. I'm waiting to hear from the union rep."

My wife looked at me for a few minutes, thinking. "Don wants to write this big story. It's like he's waving you away because he wants his name on it, but has to include Munro, the senior journalist. Why wouldn't he add a second story about your experience?"

"Yeah, I agree, but I know Don. He's made up his mind."

She swirled the ice around in her glass. "I still don't think Don meant that you killed him, that's nuts. You've said yourself that Don's…Well, you have several choice words for him."

"*Insensitive asshole* comes to mind right now."

"Yup." She gave me a half smile. "So, what're you going to do if the union guy says Don has the right to tell you to work at home?"

"I've made up my mind to go in anyway. Staying away will look bad when all that shit from the accident and the trial comes up again. And it will. I can't help thinking this murder is going to be a big problem for me." I decided not to tell her about the black Toyota following me home from work.

She squeezed my hand. "You journalists think too much. I guess you can't write the story for another paper."

"Not right now, but I like that idea." I leaned over and kissed her cheek.

"Anyway, I'm glad you got home in time to go to Mom and Dad's with me. Take your mind off things."

"What?"

She sighed. "I told you yesterday. We're having dinner at my parents tonight. I called Mom earlier and said you might be working late and I'd come alone."

"Sorry, honey, I forgot." Christ, this was the last thing I wanted to do. "I need a few minutes. Can you call and say we'll be there in about a half hour?"

"Sure, it's been a long day for me, too." Ann pulled out her phone and sent her mother a text. I jotted down the licence number of the black Toyota on a scrap of paper and shoved it in my desk drawer. Seconds later, Eileen texted her daughter back.

"Mom says everyone was glad to hear you'd be coming after all."

"Everyone?"

"She invited Aunt Nell, Uncle Frank and Jeanette. It'll be nice to see them."

"You're right, honey. It'll be fun to talk about Nell's latest plastic surgery."

Ann laughed. "She's a bit shallow, but she is my aunt. It won't kill us to be sociable." She tapped my arm. "You still like Uncle Frank, right?"

Burton and Eileen had imposed an uncle-ship on Frank, Burton's former law partner and best friend. "Yeah, he's a great guy. Sometimes I think your dad misses the law practice. Why didn't you ask me if I liked his dear wife?"

Ann frowned. "Marsh, please behave tonight, okay? Jeanette's all right, she's just...different." Ann looked at her watch. "I need to change first. We're late as it is."

"I really wish we could stay home. We must have some stuff in the fridge for dinner."

Ann shook her head. "I can't back out on my parents now. We cancelled the last dinner with them on short notice, remember?"

Conveniently, I hadn't. She stood and started pulling off her top. All I wanted to do was follow her into the bedroom. Instead, I went to the fridge and took out a couple of beers. Burton was a wine afficionado and I hated the stuff. We left the house. Ann stood beside me as I locked the front door.

"Is that beer stuffed in your pockets?"

"I bought one for Frank too," I said.

"You could just ask Dad to buy it for you."

Yeah, but I wasn't going to. He could've figured it out himself by now. Frank, his best friend, didn't like wine either. As we drove away from our house, I remembered the wheelchair was still in my car and decided to leave it there—Eileen would worry about the wheels marking her carpets.

Chapter 3

Even though the trip to Young's house on Lakewood Drive only took about ten minutes, Ann leaned her head back on the seat and slept. I drove around my in-law's neighbourhood for an extra ten to give her more time.

When we arrived at the gates to their property, I lowered my window and punched in the code. The wrought iron barriers swung open like a webbed clam, and for the millionth time, I wondered why Burton and Eileen had installed this pretentious entrance. The property, bordered on each side by rows of twenty-foot cedars, was accessible to anyone who had the muscle to push through. The lake behind the house allowed people to tie up at an old dock and walk into the backyard. The house and grounds had a security system that lit up like a runway at night, and sounded a three-beat honk that would have awakened hibernating animals.

What if there was a fire and my in-laws weren't around? I pictured firefighters blasting through the gates to perform heroics on the ugliest house I'd ever seen. Even my wife agreed with that.

Ann raised her head and looked around. "We're here already?"

Seconds later, we pulled up in front of the huge two storey house. The sweeping multi-columned front porch was a total disconnect from the rest of the modern architecture. It looked as though my in-laws couldn't agree—she wanted colonial, he preferred contemporary. The entire building, which resembled an up-ended shoe box with windows, was gleaming white.

I parked my old beater, a.k.a. classic Mustang, behind Nell's red Porsche which was lined up behind Frank's silver Cadillac. Burton would probably be pissed that I hadn't driven the dual-use SUV—hand controls for me, pedals for Ann—he'd bought us for a wedding present. I'd spent a fortune years ago having my Mustang converted to hand controls, and hated to give it up. We had a single-lane drive at home and it meant the first person to leave took the last car sitting on the driveway.

Ann and I got out of the car and before we'd taken many steps, my father-in-law, probably watching from a front window, opened the door and stepped out. He embraced his daughter. "So glad to see you, Sweet t'ing."

"Hi, Dad."

He nodded to me. "Marshall."

I nodded back. "Burton."

The evening was in full swing as we entered the double storey living room, or parlour as Eileen referred to it. The guests, all seated, stopped chatting and turned to look at us as though we were on exhibit.

Nell smiled and Frank walked over. He kissed Ann and shook hands with me. "Nice to see you kids." He smiled. "Evening would be damn dull without young people to liven us up."

Everyone else looked as though they'd been rudely interrupted. The bad feeling I'd had after my father-in-law's chilly greeting got worse. What had they been discussing before we entered the room? I smiled at Nell and nodded to Frank's wife, Jeanette. "Good to see you both again."

Ann chose a chair close to Nell, who leaned over and kissed her niece on the cheek. "Your mom and I are going on a spa weekend. We're thinking of investing in one not far from here. We'd love it if you joined us." Then she looked over at me, a coy smile on her face. "Could the groom stand to part with his bride for two whole days?"

Ann laughed. "We're hardly newlyweds after four years, Aunt Nell. Sounds like fun. Send me details. Just don't expect me to kick in money."

A spa weekend with Eileen and Nell? My bride would rather take an ice bath. She looked over at me and winked. It was news to me that her mother and Nell were interested in a spa. I wondered if Burton had known.

I would have preferred the straight chair he occupied, but propped my canes at the end of the couch and lowered myself into a cushion so soft, I thought my ass would hit the floor. Frank took a seat at the other end. "Still defending criminals?" I said.

He smiled. "Yup. Have to pay the bills and support my entourage."

I laughed. Frank frequently joked about all the money he shelled out for his two kids, one from each of his ex-wives. Jeanette glared and downed her glass of wine. "How many lawyers are working with you now?" I said.

"Only one, and I don't think he's a fit for the practice. I've hired and fired a few since Burton took the bench. Haven't been able to replace him."

Eileen walked into the room carrying a tray of things that were too big to cram into your mouth and would break into pieces if you bit into them. "Oh, glad you're finally here, you two. I saved the smoked salmon canapes for you, Marsh."

"Thanks, Eileen." I took two and balanced them on my lap. She pointed to little plates and napkins stacked on the coffee table.

"Marshy," said Nell, crossing her short, plump legs and tugging her elastic skirt. "I've never seen you walk with canes before."

"It's my latest trick." Why bother explaining—again—that the brain injury I'd sustained in the accident knocked my balance out of whack occasionally, particularly if I was tired, making the wheelchair necessary.

My wife gave me a warning look. "Marsh walks as much as he rides these days. He just got a new set of prosthetics."

"Why didn't you get those Blade Runner things?" said Nell.

"They cost more than I make in a year," I said. "But I'm buying lottery tickets." Not to mention the cost of therapy to get used to the things. She wouldn't ask about an electric wheelchair. We'd had that discussion before—battery driven mobility didn't appeal to me. I had my own personal charge and depended on that.

Eileen was still making the rounds with her hors d'oeuvres. Jeanette took one, gave it a second glance and placed it on a plate beside her.

Frank leapt from the couch and picked up a tray of wine glasses. "Let me help you, Eileen." I took a beer from my pocket and tried to lift the tab slowly. My wife frowned and accepted a glass of wine which she placed on a table near her.

Frank offered Nell a glass of wine. She smiled into his face. "Oh thanks, Frankie. I haven't finished this one, but it's my sister's house so I'm allowed to line them up." She giggled. Her fingers lingered over his as she took a glass.

Jeanette put her empty on the tray and took another without looking at her husband. She and Frank were polar opposites, and not only in skin colour. Years before, she'd paid me a compliment about my fair hair, saying what a job it was for her to maintain the same colour. Her over-bleached version hung around her shoulders in limp strands, and the black stuff around her eyes made her look like a raccoon. But her muscular body and exaggerated curves could make a man ignore everything else. I'd never met Frank's other wives and remembered Ann saying they were on the plump side.

Burton, his empty glass on a table beside him, refused another with a wave of his hand. One was usually his limit. Eileen placed the canapes on a table, grinned at Frank and took some wine. She was still steady on her feet, probably taking her hostess job seriously, at least for now.

The main course would be Trinidadian fare she ordered from a local restaurant. I hoped there'd be Pelau, a kind of meat and veggie dish flavoured with cardamom, cloves, cumin and coriander. There'd also be a selection of fish and shellfish.

Now that the canapes were served, Eileen could let loose and concentrate on the wine. Lately, she'd been drinking more than usual.

Frank returned to the couch after offering wine to everyone. I reached into my pocket and passed him the second beer. "Thanks buddy." He lifted the can and we said cheers. "Next time, I'll bring the beer." I stole a look at Burton. If he heard Frank's comment, nothing registered.

I watched Eileen float around the room, chatting, smiling and laughing. My beautiful wife shared her mother's lean body, glowing ebony skin and disarming smile, but that's where the similarity ended. Ann didn't inherit her knock-out personality from either parent.

Burton, usually gruff and unemotional, was a different man with his only child. He called her his *Sweet t'ing* and offered to pay for anything he thought would enhance her life. Like a better house before we were married, which we'd refused. Accepting the SUV had been a compromise.

All Eileen seemed to care about were her looks, clothes and the right friends. She never mentioned books she'd read, and Burton either went alone to plays and concerts or dragged us along. Ann referred to her mother as a fun-loving Trinidadian.

Burton's job at these social gatherings was announcing dinner and clearing the table once the meal was finished. When Eileen gave him the word, he rose from the fake antique chair. "Can we proceed to the dining room?" I could just picture *His Honour Burton Young* in court, banging his gavel, demanding order.

I picked up my canes and crossed the room to escort Ann to the table. When she took my hand, her skin felt clammy. She closed her eyes and sagged against me. Balancing on one cane, I caught her before she fell to the floor. I grabbed her wrist. Strong pulse, but her skin had lost its glow, and she was sweating. I bent down and put my arms around her. "Honey, what's wrong?"

"Sorry, Marsh," she whispered. "I felt dizzy when I tried to stand up."

The dinner guests halted in their tracks. "You okay?" said Frank.

Nell screamed, "Ann's fainted!"

In seconds, Burton was kneeling in front of his daughter. I would never have believed that a man with dark skin could look so pale. He took Ann's hands and patted them as though he was trying to awaken her from a coma, "What's the matter, Sweet t'ing? Shall I call an ambulance?"

Eileen wandered into the room, a dishtowel in her hand. "What's going on?" She looked at her daughter and shoved me aside.

"Dad, Mom, I'm okay. Haven't eaten much today. That's all."

"Oh, I know what's going on," said Nell, pushing her way into the circle that had formed around Ann. "You didn't drink any of your wine. Got something to share with us?"

"Let's call a doctor," said Eileen

"Today was Ann's first day as Charge Nurse," I said. "She probably didn't have any time for herself. And as soon as I got home from work, we rushed over here."

Burton looked at me with half-closed eyes.

"Please take me home, Marsh. I'm just tired," said Ann, loud enough for everyone to hear.

"Good idea," I said.

Ann stood and took my arm. Together we walked to the front door. Burton, Eileen and the rest of the entourage except Jeanette, followed behind us.

"Call me as soon as you get home," said Burton.

Eileen hugged her daughter. "Make sure you eat something, dear. Is Nell right? Are you pregnant?"

Ann ignored the question and promised to call later. We put on our coats without buttoning them and I opened the front door, never so glad to step into freezing winter air. The swirling wind blasted the crowd at the entrance and in seconds, they called a last goodbye and closed the door. I helped my wife into the car and hurried around to the driver's seat, my canes clicking on the cobblestones.

As I fastened my seat belt, Ann remembered she'd left her phone on a side table. I turned on the ignition and the heater before returning to the house. Burton already stood at the open door.

"Look after her," he said, handing me the phone. "Take her to the emergency right away."

I looked him in the eye. "I have always looked after my wife. And she *is* capable of making her own decisions."

He frowned, shook his head and stepped inside the house, shut the door and flipped the dead bolt. When I got into the car, Ann was sitting with her head back, eyes closed. I tucked the phone into her purse and seconds later, the gates opened automatically. We drove through—Burton was watching from inside the house.

Ann raised her head, said she was hungry, and suggested we stop and get Kentucky Fried Chicken and fries.

"Wow!" I said. "You've never wanted that stuff before."

"Been craving it lately."

She laughed when I asked if she wanted pickles too.

Fifteen minutes later, we sat at our table eating chicken from the carton. I made my wife some Camomile tea and had a cup myself, thinking it might quell the anger I felt for her father.

I grabbed a few fries. "Glad to see you're feeling better."

"I just had to get out of that house. They keep it so hot." She turned to look at me, and sighed. "There's something I need to tell you."

I said nothing, hoping my face looked neutral. I reached across the table for her hand.

"I was four months pregnant when Steven punched me and slammed me against a wall. A few days later, I miscarried." She sighed again, this time deep and ragged. "And since I lost our first baby a few months ago, I'm worried I'll never be able to go full term."

I knew the son-of-a-bitch was abusive, but hitting a pregnant woman? And hitting her hard enough to cause a miscarriage? Jesus Christ. "Why didn't you tell me this before, honey?"

"I couldn't, Marsh. I'm so ashamed. And embarrassed."

I gripped her hand tighter. "Why? You didn't do anything wrong."

She took a long time to answer. I poured more tea into her cup. She looked at me and shook her head, nearly in tears. "Why didn't I see the signs before I married him? I was so busy studying for my degree. We didn't know each other long enough—I realized that too late. He was jealous and possessive, but I thought that was flattering…and he kept pushing to get married. Not long after I knew he didn't love me—it was all about Dad's money and position. I feel so stupid that I didn't see it."

I sat quietly for a few moments. "When I went back for your phone, your dad told me to look after you. Now I get why he said that."

She shook her head again. "Dad's always been way too protective. I never told my parents that Steven was responsible for the miscarriage. All they knew was that he'd get into a rage and hit me and that's why I left him." She sighed. "He's gone now anyway. Dad made sure of that."

Yeah, by bribing him to bugger off and stay out of the country. Anderson got want he wanted—money. "He'll never hurt you again, honey." The words sounded lame, but Ann wouldn't feel any better if I yelled that I'd find the bastard and take his head off. We sat quietly for a few minutes holding hands.

"You agree I have a great gut instinct, right?" I said.

She nodded, but her frown asked where this was going.

"Well, my gut tells me we'll have a beautiful baby girl. I already have the name picked out."

Her face relaxed and she smiled. "Oh, Marsh, I never know what you're going to say next!"

"So don't you want to know what her name is?"

"Of course."

"Lucy Ann."

"I love that."

We finished our meal. I tidied the kitchen and Ann loaded the dishwasher. During the last hour, a few messages had come into my phone. The first was from Ed Alexander, the lawyer who'd represented me after the accident and sued Wright's insurance company.

Allan Wright's dead. Call you when I get back in a few months.

Shit. What if I needed legal advice before then??

The second message was from the union rep.

Don can re-assign but can't make you work from home unless your suspended for cause. F him.

I passed the phone to Ann. She read the text and we both laughed. A giddy laugh. I had a beer and she had more tea, then we packed it in and went to bed. Ann cuddled up to me and fell asleep quickly, as usual. I lay and listened to her breathe, and thought how lucky I was to have married a woman like her.

Seven years ago, Ann and I had been victims of trauma at roughly the same time. I was recovering in the rehab centre after losing both my legs, and she'd just left Steven Anderson to live with Burton and Eileen.

I'd hated my truncated body, and couldn't think properly due to severe concussion. I was forced out of my dream job as a police officer just weeks after graduation. I had no relatives and my friends didn't know what to say. My girlfriend deserted me. When I think back now, I pushed everyone away. I was angry and depressed and took my feelings out on anyone who tried to come close.

If I hadn't threatened to kill myself, I'd never have met Ann. After she and I got together, I told my colleague Munro we'd met on the psyche ward. I often wondered how she'd explained that to her own friends …

"So, how'd you meet your boyfriend?"

"He was one of my patients on the ward."

"Was it love at first sight?"

"Not until a year later, when I saw him at a night class."

I often imagined her parent's expressions when they heard about me, but I didn't want to think about their words. With a divorce from one loser under her belt, her new beau was a white guy with no legs, getting started in a career writing about disability and living off the proceeds of a lawsuit.

Ann had a quiet defiance I loved. We also shared the same determined resolve. I was attracted to her the first day we met on the ward. I also realized I was vulnerable, had no one, and she was my psychiatric nurse. When we met again by chance, a year later, she asked me to meet her for a coffee. After a year of dating, she moved in with me.

We'd both done well coping with our situations and moving on. I knew Anderson was abusive, and was surprised that Ann hadn't told me he'd likely been the cause of her first miscarriage. But I hadn't revealed everything either—the anger and low self-esteem that lessened only after years of counselling. We were both embarrassed by our imperfections.

The phone alarm woke me at seven-thirty the next morning. Ann had already gone to the hospital. I sent her a text, not really expecting an answer until she took a break at eleven. *Hi hon, hope you're feeling better.*

I strapped on the prostheses, headed to the bathroom, looked in the mirror and laughed. A red kiss was planted on my forehead. Ann had made the coffee, and put the newspaper on our kitchen table. I poured a cup, added cream, and sat to read the paper before heading to work.

The murder of Allan Wright occupied a decent sized column on the front page of the *Toronto Tribune*, which surprised me. He was a small-time hood. I read the headline again and decided the newsroom must have been short on sensation.

Career Criminal Found Dead Days after Release

Career criminal? Petty criminal wouldn't have had the same impact. And the alliteration was effective. The article gave little insight as to what kind of career this criminal was supposed to have had. Further along, it mentioned me. I sat up straighter.

...Marshall Keene, the young man whose family was killed by Allan Wright nearly a decade ago, was on the scene when Wright's body was discovered by police yesterday. Wright was released from prison last week after serving six years of a ten-year sentence for manslaughter and driving while under the influence of drugs and alcohol...

There was no mention that I was at the scene because I'm a fucking journalist.

...Wright had pled guilty to the charges facing him. Keene, a double amputee, confined to a wheelchair as a result of the accident, delivered a blistering victim impact statement at the end of the bench trial. Later, outside the courtroom, he shouted to journalists, "Allan Wright should be dead, instead of my family! He's lucky he'll be out of my sight for ten years!" Keene's lawyer then quickly wheeled him away..."

I slammed the paper down on the table. Who the fuck wrote this? Two guys I vaguely knew. And what was the point of the direct quotes? Obviously, a collaboration of previous stories and the police statement released yesterday, compiled by a pair of morons down at the *Tribune.* I was surprised they hadn't said *wheelchair-bound*, a phrase I hated slightly more than *confined to a wheelchair.* How about *uses a wheelchair,* assholes? *The Tribune* was printing my articles on living with disability. Obviously, they didn't read their own stuff. Bloody amazing.

They would've had to bang out the Wright story in a hurry before print deadline. The article ended by saying he'd left a grieving wife and two young kids. What about the fact that I'd been grieving for my parents and sister, Callie, for nearly a decade?

...Details of the murder are not being released. Police are looking for a suspect or suspects in Wright's murder.

Finding who offed Wright now became my mission. I gulped my coffee, ate a banana, showered and dressed. I assumed Ann hadn't read the article because the paper was still folded when I'd picked it up. Burton read the major newspapers. I wondered if she'd get a call from him.

I sent another text asking her what time her gynecologist appointment was today. I was pretty sure the doctor was right there in the hospital.

On the way to work, I planned a response to the *Tribune.* The events the paper printed had happened, but like many stories focussing on sensation, the content had convenient omissions, faulty sequencing, and an accusatory tone that irritated and scared the shit out of me.

I pulled into the lot, parked in my spot, and set up my wheelchair in what might have been record time, but was too preoccupied to bother recording it. Moments later, the elevator bounced open at the fifth floor. I didn't even think about what Don might say until I entered the newsroom and went past his door. Christ, all I needed was him on my back.

I needn't have worried. As I rolled by his office, he didn't look up. On my way down to my desk, one of his assistants handed me what I assumed were the stories he'd mentioned yesterday. I stopped to pour a coffee, then pulled into my cubicle.

One of the assignments concerned the extent of fentanyl misuse in the GTA. The other dealt with the controversial and illegal pop-up clean needle sites. He hadn't mentioned a deadline for either of the stories, so I decided to phone the editor of *The Toronto Tribune.* I was punching in the number when I saw Don coming down the aisle accompanied by two cops I recognized, Detective Sergeant Reese and Constable Christine Foss.

As soon as they reached my desk, Don turned and walked toward his office.

"Morning, Mr. Keene," said Reese.

Foss nodded.

"Good morning, Officers. What can I do for you?"

"Would you mind coming down to the station?" said Reese. "We'd like to ask you a few questions."

Chapter 4

I stood and faced the officers. "Am I being charged with something, Sergeant Reese?"

Instead of answering, Reese asked another question. "Allan Wright, the victim found dead at the Whispering Pines subdivision is known to you?"

"Yes." Okay, I knew where this was going.

"Am I being charged with something, Sergeant Reese?" I repeated.

He shook his head. "We'd like to ask you some questions, Mr. Keene."

I stood, facing Reese, not answering immediately. Might as well get this over with. They knew the history with me and Wright and had to check out my whereabouts in the days leading up to his death. I had a strong motive for killing him.

"I'll meet you there, Sergeant. I have some things to finish here first."

Like call the *Tribune*. The cops eyed me for a moment, then nodded and left the newsroom. I needed to get this interview out of the way. Ed Alexander was out of town and I knew not to talk to the cops without a lawyer. Frank was the only other lawyer I knew. It was a long shot, but I dialled his law firm and the call went to answer.

This is a message for Frank Veale. It's Marshall Keene calling. Can he call me, please? The police want to talk to me.

Colleagues who had been concentrating on their work while the cops were here, started to crowd around me.

"Marsh, what the shit's going on?"

"You don't have to talk to them, buddy."

"He will if he has any sense," said Munro. He handed me a print-out. "Check this out for future reference. Earl at the *Hamilton Advisor* found Wright's wife and tried to interview her. She wouldn't answer any questions and slammed the door on his foot."

"Thanks…why would they print that? She's a smart woman. I feel like slamming a few reporters myself right now."

"Yeah," said Munro. "I read the *Tribune* this morning. Complete assholes. Sorry about yesterday."

It wasn't his fault that Don snatched the story away from me. "No worries. We all have bills to pay," I said.

"Someone will be going to the coroner's office tomorrow. I'll let you know of anything important."

I thanked him and he headed up the aisle. Everyone else returned to their desks.

While I waited and hoped for Frank to respond, I called Paul Marchand, the editor of the *Tribune.* After listening to canned music for a few moments, he came on the line.

"Marsh, nice of you to call. I haven't heard from your group for a while. Got another article for me?"

"I'm nearly finished one about the lack of accessibility in Toronto buildings. But that's not what I'm calling about. I didn't like the tone of your front-page story this morning."

"We just wrote the facts, Marsh."

"Your writers fucked around with the facts, Paul. They didn't mention that I was at the crime scene doing my job yesterday, and they conveniently left out that one of Allan Wright's supporters threatened *me* seven years ago. My comments were made at a time of great stress. Your article was misleading and lacked integrity."

"You're certainly entitled to an opinion. Have a good day." He hung up.

This wasn't the first disagreement I'd had with Paul. Like Don, he was a hard-nosed editor and didn't care who he stepped on. Had I screwed up the charitable group's connection to the *Tribune*? I decided to find out. Although I didn't get paid as a spokesperson for *Able and Active*, the *Tribune* paid me for the articles. The new one Paul had asked for, *Unacceptable Accessibility,* just needed a quick re-read. I looked it over, sent it to him and included a YouTube video of my portable *Easy Up* ramps. A free plug would help.

Next, I composed a letter to the editor of the *Tribune,* slamming the story for what it was —shitty journalism—and emailed it in. I might as well dump all the cracked eggs into one basket.

My phone rang, Frank Veale, thank God. There was no hello. "I'm going into court. What's happened?"

"The cops were here at my office. They want to speak to me, probably about Allan Wright."

"Figured they would. I can meet you at the station in about an hour. My case here will go to remand."

"Thanks, Frank. See you then." Christ, what a relief, and what a lucky break for me. Until it was time to meet him, I forced myself to concentrate on one of the stories Don had assigned.

My boss wanted information on Fentanyl use in Toronto, but I knew the problem was a local one as well. I'd start with Lakeville then branch out. A few petty drug-related charges and arrests in our area popped up from an online search. The one I was looking for had happened a while back—a bust in a factory on Speers Road. I couldn't remember the details. After scrolling through a list on my screen, I read it had occurred nearly two years ago after a tip from an unnamed person or persons. Although a large amount of Fentanyl was seized, no arrests had ever been made. I wondered if the incident was territorial—one group of bad guys pointing to another group's stash to eliminate them. Be interesting to know who the squealer was.

My cell dinged. Ann was texting to say she was *okay, thanks.*

Stop worrying and meet me at two p.m. in the gyne's office at the hospital.

She gave me the location and the doctor's name. I replied saying I'd see her soon.

**

Fifteen minutes later, I sat waiting for Frank outside the police station. His Cadillac pulled up to the curb and stopped. Frank opened the door and sprang from the passenger's seat. He was dressed in a navy business suit, complete with white shirt and navy tie and no overcoat although it was January. "Okay buddy, we need a strategy," he said.

I started to fill him in and he held up his hand. "I read the article again coming over here. I'm also familiar with the statements you made six years ago, which is probably why the cops want to interview you. Don't offer any information. Just answer the questions unless I tell you otherwise."

This was a Frank I'd never met. Usually, his smile and eyes lit up his face. Today his dark clothing and black horn-rimmed glasses gave him an uncharacteristically stern look. We'd always met at my in-laws where he'd been relaxed and entertaining, the bright spot in their dull evenings. Too bad Frank wasn't Ann's father.

When we entered the station, a duty cop ushered us into an interview room. Grey paint was chipping off scarred walls. The chairs and table were chained and bolted to the floor. I guess the cops got tired of ducking when suspects heaved the furniture. The recorder, either a DVD or DC, was tucked into a recess in the wall. Why the hell was I sweating? I had nothing to worry about. Frank nodded as I activated the record feature on my phone and stashed it in my shirt pocket.

Sergeant Reese and a cop who introduced himself as P.C. Wood joined us and closed the door. I pushed a chair sideways so I could wheel up to the steel table. The two officers and Frank sat. Reese looked at Frank. "You're representing Mr. Keene?"

Frank nodded. "If needed, Sergeant Reese."

Reese turned to me. "Thanks for coming in, Mr. Keene. Allan Wright was found dead yesterday. You were at the scene. Why?"

"I'm a journalist. My boss asked me to cover the story."

"Where do you work, Mr. Keene?"

"*The Halton Register*."

"Don't you also write for the *Toronto Tribune*?"

"Not specifically." I looked at Frank. He nodded. "I volunteer with a group called *Able and Active*. We focus on issues facing people with developmental and physical disabilities. I write articles for them that are printed by the *Tribune.*"

"Don't you also have a side business?"

"I work for a company called *Easy Up*, as a sales rep. They manufacture portable wheelchair ramps." These cops had done their homework. "Can you tell us where you were on the night of January the fourteenth of this year?"

I hauled my cell out of my pocket, dialed back to that date then put the phone away. "That was a Saturday night. My wife and I went out for dinner."

"What time did you get home?"

"I don't remember exactly, probably around nine."

"Did you and Mrs. Keene eat alone?"

Mrs. Keene. Ann would love to hear that; she'd chosen not to change her name and I didn't have a problem with it. I was surprised Reese had made that assumption, but then he was close to my parent's vintage.

"Yes."

"Where did you have dinner that night?"

I gave him the name of our favourite restaurant, *Pasqualie's*. No doubt they'd check it out. Ann and I were well-known there.

"Where does your wife work?"

"She's Charge Nurse at Lakeville Psychiatric."

"Did you go out again after you returned home from the restaurant that night?"

"No."

"Was your wife with you the whole evening after you returned home?"

"Yes."

"Did you know prior to yesterday that Allan Wright had been released from prison?"

"No."

Reese paused before continuing. "Your lawyer didn't let you know he was being released?"

"Yes, he phoned and told me."

"But you just said you didn't know, Mr. Keene."

Frank turned to face the sergeant. "Mr. Keene said he knew Mr. Wright *was going* to be released. That doesn't mean he knew *when*. There's a big difference, Sergeant Reese."

Reese gave no sign of acknowledging Frank's statement. "Mr. Keene, did you have any contact with Mr. Wright while he was in prison?"

"No."

"Did Mr. Wright have any contact with you?"

"No."

"Did you see Wright or have any contact with him after his release from prison?"

I shook my head. This was all about those goddamn threats I'd yelled out years ago. Christ, I was glad Frank was here. Reese watched me, probably observing my body language. I looked down. My fingers were drumming the arm of the wheelchair.

Frank stood up and walked to the door.

"We may need to speak to you again, Mr. Keene," said Reese.

I looked at Frank, and didn't respond to Reese's statement.

Frank held the door open for me as we exited the interview room. Neither of us said a word until we were outside the station.

"Thanks, for coming, Frank. Reese was treating me like a suspect. Jesus." Without Frank it would have been two to one. Even though the second cop, who was there for back-up, had said nothing.

"He was fishing, Marsh. Reese is fully aware of your former case and your statements at that time. It's his job to check everything out." He smiled, "I bet Wright's wife killed him. She probably liked him better in jail."

I laughed. The Frank I knew was back.

"Actually, Wright's had plenty of scrapes with the law," said Frank. "They'll be looking at his associates. If police want to talk to you again, call me."

"You think they will?"

"Perhaps. Don't erase the recording you made today."

The silver Cadillac was waiting at the curb, exhaust curling skyward. I shook Frank's hand and thanked him again. "I can see why you didn't want me to go into that interview alone. You're billing me, I hope."

He smiled and got into the car. As it drove away, he lowered the window and waved. It had been years since someone other than Ann had gone to bat for me the way my parents would have. I looked at my watch. There was plenty of time to get some work done before meeting my wife at the hospital.

I wheeled over to the station parking lot where I'd left my car and thought about the interview while I dismantled the wheelchair. Knowing the cops were interested in me made me jumpy. At least I'd learned one more critical piece of information. Wright died on Saturday, January fourteenth, two days before he was found in the subdivision. And with multiple shots to the chest, the person or persons who killed him were mighty pissed off. Who were Wright's former associates and why had he been murdered? I sat in the car and added to my notes.

On the way back to the office, I thought about that day on the courthouse steps seven years ago. It occurred to me that there might be pictures in the newspaper archives.

When I rolled into the newsroom, an assistant told me Don wanted a couple of fillers written for print deadline that night. So much for working on the Fentanyl article. As I passed his office, he and Munro were inside with the door closed. Others were either busy at their desks or, I assumed, out for lunch. I wondered how long it would take people to come and ask me what the cops wanted, or if they would. For sure there'd been some talk amongst them while I was gone.

The two short pieces took me just over an hour to write and forward to Don. It had been years since I'd read what the *Tribune* had printed about Wright's trial. I had time to look at the old articles and logged onto the Toronto Public Library website. Seconds later, write-ups from the trial appeared on my screen. I saved everything for future reference. The last story detailed the final day of proceedings and included the picture on the steps of the courthouse—exactly what I was looking for. I'd forgotten how many reporters were there from the Toronto dailies and the smaller papers.

All through the trial, newspapers had made a big deal of the *tragic deaths* of my parents and younger sister, Callie, *innocent victims of an impaired driver and convicted criminal.* I had many requests for interviews from newspapers, all of which I turned down on the advice of my lawyer, Ed Alexander. He knew I was bitter and unbalanced. Now I realized he'd wanted to protect me from myself. But he hadn't been able to tailor my victim impact statement and prevent my rant outside the courthouse after the trial.

I zoomed in on the archive picture and the scene rushed back into my head. I had been in the middle of a journalists' scrum. Ed stood beside me, but Wright's lawyer was nowhere in sight. In the article accompanying that picture, a journalist asked me if I thought the sentence was fair and had justice had been served? I had been only too glad to respond.

That drunken murderer should be dead instead of my family. With his criminal history he should be declared a dangerous offender. Ten years is a joke. Wright's lucky he'll be out of my sight where I can't get at him.

Then I heard a voice behind me. "But *you* won't be out of sight, Wheel Man. You'd better watch your back!" Two other voices echoed the sentiment: "Well said, brother," and "Damn straight."

Of course, those statements weren't included in the article, and I'd blocked them from my memory—until now.

Journalists had pushed closer to me, thrusting their phones in my face. Before I could open my mouth, Ed whisked me away.

I had glanced back but never had a good look at those three guys, until now. It had to be one of them. They were the only people outside of my lawyer and I who didn't represent a newspaper. Who were they? No one had supported Allan Wright during the trial, not even his wife and two kids.

That old news report also quoted the most intense part of my victim impact statement:

You should be dead instead of my family. You killed three people and walked away without a scratch. And today, when the judge asked if you had anything to say, you just stood there. You couldn't apologize, show some remorse or take responsibility for what you did?

As Ed and I had driven away from the courthouse, he said he understood how I felt, but warned that the papers would be quoting all my statements. I was so angry and stressed I didn't care.

Wright had made me an orphan. He ruined my career as a cop, killed my little sister's dream of being a vet, and my parent's vision of a well-earned retirement. The old rage and despair hit me all over again.

I shook my head to dispel the feelings and refocus on those three men standing in the background. Two were strangers, but one seemed familiar. He looked about my age, with dark curly hair and a muscular build shown to advantage through his cropped, sleeveless t-shirt. A pack of cigarettes poked out of the chest pocket. Where had I seen him? This picture was taken seven years ago. He could have been at the gym where I had therapy, or one of the workers who'd helped with the renovations on my house, although that didn't seem likely. It would drive me crazy until I figured it out. I printed the picture.

I glanced at my watch. With only fifteen minutes to meet Ann, I saved the file and sped out of the office.

Munro followed me into the hall and we got into the elevator together. "How'd it go this morning?" he said.

"No big deal, but it shook me up. Thank God I had a lawyer with me. Cops have a knack of making you feel guilty."

The elevator stopped at the second floor and a woman got in, silencing us until we reached the ground floor. Munro followed me outside. "Let me know if you need anything or want to talk."

"Thanks buddy. I have a feeling I'm going to need you." We shook hands and he walked back into the building. It would be just like Munro to have told everyone in the newsroom to mind their own business and give me space.

On the drive to the hospital, I noticed that black Toyota two cars behind me. Same license plate. Had he been waiting in the *Register* parking lot? All I could see of the driver was that he wore a hoodie. What the hell was going on? I sped up, ran an amber light and zipped down a side street. I drove away from the hospital, not wanting to reveal my destination. After a few more turns into side streets, I was confident I'd lost him.

If I hadn't been going to meet my wife, I would've confronted him. Instead, I texted Frank. *I'm sending you the archive picture from the Tribune seven years ago. The dark-haired guy looks familiar to me. A car followed me home from work yesterday. The same one was behind me just now.*

As I pulled into the hospital parking lot Frank texted back. *Let's talk later.*

I responded: *Agreed*:

Chapter 5

All the parking spots on the ground floor were taken. I finally found a spot on the top which was open-air and cold as hell. An *Out-of-order* sign hung on the elevator. I'd have to roll down the ramps avoiding drivers who took the turns like formula-one wannabes.

As I approached the exit, Ann stood outside the garage. "Where'd you park? I didn't see your car on the first floor."

She frowned when I told her.

"I'll bet some of those people don't have handicap permits. I hope they get tagged."

"Don't sweat it, baby." I reached over to pat her behind. "What's that doctor's name again?"

"Sheila Wood. Fourth floor." She smiled. "You'll like her."

When Ann says I'll like something, she's trying to talk me into it. I just hoped this doctor wasn't a recent graduate and we were not her first clients. That thought left my head as soon as we entered the waiting room. I'd never seen so many pregnant women in one place. One sweaty-looking guy sat holding the hand of a woman who looked ready to deliver. Christ, that would be me soon. I started to sweat too just thinking about it. Chairs lined the walls but all were occupied. I managed to squeeze my wheelchair into the lineup.

Ann checked in with reception, stood for a few minutes, then sat on my lap. "I don't care what this looks like. I've been on my feet all day."

People came and went. "I wonder how long this is going to take," I said.

"Might be a while. Sheila is fitting us in as a favour. To speed things up I had the ultrasound this morning."

"You did? What did it show?"

She gave me a little hug. "I didn't look at it, silly. I wanted us to see it together. Basically, it'll show how far along I am and how the baby is developing. Stuff like that."

Five minutes later, a tall woman who looked about fifty, wearing a white lab coat over street clothes and a stethoscope around her neck, entered the reception room.

"Hi, Ann, and you must be Marsh. I'm Sheila Wood." She shook my hand. "Come with me, please."

I felt everyone's eyes on us. We followed Sheila down a wide hall lined with handrails, into an office. Ann chose one of the two chairs and I pulled up beside her.

The doctor sat behind her desk and smiled. "I've just had a look at the ultrasound. All good news." I didn't know what she meant, but sighed with relief anyway. Dr. Wood handed the picture to Ann.

"I can't wait to see it!…Oh Marsh, look..." She ran her fingers over the image.

"Wow! That's our baby?" It looked like some kind of fossil.

"Judging from this, you're in your fourth month," said Dr. Wayne.

"Really?" said Ann. "I must have conceived right after the D and C."

"But you thought you were only days late for your period." I said.

"After a D and C it's hard to know when your cycle will start again. I had spotting a few times over the last couple of months. I didn't think that was unusual."

Sheila looked at us and smiled. "It's very common."

"Ann had spotting before the first miscarriage," I said, feeling like a gynecological expert.

"I know you're worried, Marsh," said Dr. Wood, "but she's into her fourth month and that's a good sign. And the last showing was what, five, six weeks ago?"

I must have looked confused when Ann nodded. "Showing is the same thing as spotting, Marsh."

"How do we know the baby's alive?" I managed to check myself before asking what would stop it from falling out like the last one.

Dr. Wood stood and pointed to an examining table. "Hop up, Ann."

My wife knew the drill. She lay on the table and pulled her scrubs down, exposing her tummy and her small but definite bump.

"Come closer, Marsh," said the doctor.

I unhooked my canes from the back of the wheelchair and walked over beside Ann. The doctor bent forward and moved an instrument around Ann's belly, something that she called a fetal doppler.

Bump, bump. Bump, bump. Bump, bump.

Our baby's heart was beating through this small device. "Wow! Amazing!"

Ann lay on the table, tears squeezing out of her eyes. "Oh, I'm so happy! Our baby's finally real."

I could have listened to that magical sound for hours. I leaned over, kissed my wife and we both cried.

"Congratulations, you two!" Dr. Wayne let us listen to the heartbeat for a few more moments before turning off the instrument. "Now let's have a chat."

The doctor said that given the previous miscarriage and that Ann was thirty-five, she had to be careful. "However, many women are waiting until their thirties and forties to have children. Try and rest as much as possible, Ann."

I took the image and looked at it again. "Let's hope she gets a lot bigger."

Ann laughed. "This month he'll grow to the size of an orange."

I pictured an orange. No arms, no head, no legs. And that god-awful mottled skin. Jesus. I'd be a wreck before the kid was born. Thank God, we only had five months to wait. "He? We're having a boy?"

"Just a figure of speech," said Ann. "We should know in the next few weeks."

Dr. Wood confirmed our baby would be born around the end of June. We thanked her, made an appointment for Ann to come back in a month and headed down to the cafeteria to celebrate. We toasted each other with coffee and orange juice and split an old-fashioned plain donut, my wife's favourite.

"We're going to be parents, babe." We leaned over and kissed. I wasn't going to spoil our moment by telling her again how worried I was.

"Oh Marsh, I'm so happy! The next five months will fly by, you'll see."

Ann's pager went off. She had to get back to work and I should too. We hugged and promised to meet at home later. On our way out of the cafeteria, I noticed several people reading today's *Tribune*. Ann hadn't mentioned the story, and I was glad our conversation hadn't gone in that direction. We both needed to enjoy our baby moment.

Since it was late afternoon, there was no point in going back to the paper. I could work from home until Ann's shift was over, then we planned to visit her parents. She was dying to show them the ultrasound. There was really no point in trying to keep the pregnancy a secret. Ann, usually thin, was already showing, and Nell had guessed anyway.

Still no elevator in the parking garage. Slugging up five floors to my car in a wheelchair was a bloody good workout. I decided this would be the start of a new fitness initiative. Even though I exercised regularly, I wanted to be in top shape by the time Ann delivered. I wheeled up the ramps in record speed, pulled up beside my car, and dismantled the chair in thirty-two seconds—still not record-breaking. I stowed it and the canes in the back seat and drove back down the ramps, dreaming of the day we'd be leaving this hospital with our baby.

At the first stop light after leaving the hospital, I noticed the old Toyota behind me again. This time, four cars back. And this time, I didn't try to lose him. I obeyed the speed limit and stopped as soon as a light turned yellow. After ten minutes and more turns than I had to make, I was sure he was tailing me. A strip plaza was coming up on the right. I put on my signal and turned in, driving slowly so he could follow, and parked in front of a convenience store. I grabbed my canes and went inside. The front window was nearly covered with signs advertising Lotto draws, Red Bull and slushies. People actually bought that shit in January. Between the signs was a space large enough for me to watch the Toyota park at the end of the plaza.

I went to the reading rack and chose a family magazine, one that focused on birthing and parenting, then bought some Double Bubble, my favourite. I paid, put a piece of gum in my mouth, rolled the magazine and put it in my coat pocket. I smiled at the clerk and asked if I could use the washroom. Guys with canes are never refused anything. He pointed to the back of the store. Beside the toilet was the rear entrance. I used the washroom, went out the back door and walked behind the row of stores to the end of the plaza. As I walked along the side of the last store, I heard a car engine. After a few more steps, I was beside the Toyota, the motor running. I walked behind it and up to the driver's door. The guy was busy looking toward the convenience store and only turned to face me after I tapped on the window.

No way! Steven Anderson, my wife's bastard of an ex-husband! I balanced on the left cane, yanked the door open and grabbed him by the front of his jacket. The stench of his after-shave assaulted me. "What the fuck are you doing following me?" With my body against the car, I shoved him toward the passenger's side.

Anderson sneered. "You could be charged with assault for that, Crip."

"Go right ahead, asshole. See you in court."

He sat up and reached out. I moved out of the way before he slammed the door, then threw the car into reverse, barely avoiding me and someone passing behind him. The guy yelled and waved his fist. Anderson did a one-eighty and blasted away from the plaza. Stinking exhaust from his old crap-can flooded my nostrils.

When did that moron return to Canada? I knew damn well he'd never stay in the Caribbean. I walked to my car and drove home, making sure Anderson wasn't anywhere near me. Although it probably didn't matter—he'd know where we lived. The minute I got in the door I phoned Frank, the only person who could help me. I needed a sensible rationale before Ann got home. My call went to message but thank God he called back moments later.

"Marsh, what's up?" he said. "You sounded upset."

"I am. The car that followed me yesterday and again today was Steven Anderson." I told Frank how I'd confronted him. "After I drove away from that plaza, I realized we're powerless—he's in control."

Frank paused before commenting. "I don't know how long he's been back in Canada. You and Ann need to discuss this with Burton and Eileen."

My head buzzed. Ann's parents knew Anderson was here and didn't warn us? "Burton told you he was back? Did he ask you for advice?"

"I referred Burton to Gary Lund, the lawyer who works for me."

"I thought you didn't like him."

"He's capable of handling this, and he has to report to me, of course. Lund is efficient enough. Maybe I'm too demanding, but I can't seem to find a lawyer with the same drive since Burton left the practice." He paused for a moment before adding, "Your father-in-law could be a great help with this, you know."

"Don't see how. We piss each other off."

"In many ways, you and he are a lot alike."

Did he mean we're both irritating? "The only similarity I can see is that we love his daughter."

"Think about it." He put his hand over the phone, but I heard him tell someone he'd be right with them.

"Should I call you back?" I said.

"Nope, just closing the door." I heard him walk across the room and the squeak of leather as he sat in his chair. "Now tell me about that picture you sent. You recognized only one of those three guys?"

"Yup."

"This could be important. Let me know if you figure it out, but I'm guessing he was probably an associate of Wright's. Otherwise, why show up outside the court?"

"That's what I think too." I didn't have a lot of people in my corner, and was relieved to have Frank covering my back with this issue too. "Thanks. I really appreciate your help."

"You need to stay close to the police investigation on Wright. Let's ..."

Frank paused for so long I thought we'd been disconnected. Then I heard another voice in the background and Frank's angry reply. *I said I'd be right with you.*

"Sorry about the interruptions, Marsh. Call me anytime." Frank hung up.

I sat in my office, staring out the window. What the hell was I going to tell Ann? Had that son-of-a-bitch been following her too? No. She would've told me. I couldn't understand why her parents hadn't told us Anderson was back in Canada. They knew he was dangerous because Burton had asked Frank for help. There was only one way to find out. I'd talk to Ann first, then we'd speak to her parents.

I couldn't do anything more right now and tried to concentrate on work. Don had acknowledged the two short articles I'd sent him earlier and said he wanted a more detailed investigation of the fentanyl problem. He gave me the rest of the week to complete it. I also needed to start my research on the safe injection sites opening soon in Toronto—plenty to keep me busy. But getting kicked off the Wright murder story still pissed me off, and now Steven Anderson crowded my brain.

I got a Diet Coke from the fridge but had lost interest in working. I thought about the only bright thing in our lives right now and started surfing the net for cribs, carriages and those chest carriers, an efficient way to hold our baby while using my chair or the canes. There must have been about fifteen different types. I posted a blog on *WheelMaster*, my website, asking for advice from followers who were parents.

One way to improve my fitness was to use the canes more often. If I could ever afford *those blade runner things* as Nell had called them. and walk independently, I needed to improve my balance and endurance. I wanted to be a walking dad.

I was still daydreaming when Ann pulled into the driveway. Hours fly when you're in baby land. She came into the office moments later and looked at the site I had up on my computer.

She leaned in for a kiss. "Busy working, I see."

"How was your afternoon, honey?"

"Okay, I guess. My mind really wasn't on the job today." She smiled. "I couldn't wait to get home and change so we can go to see Mom and Dad."

I managed a smile. She looked me in the eye.

"You're worrying, aren't you?" She came over and hugged me. "The baby will be fine. I feel great this time. I'll go and change then we can leave."

"There's something I have to tell you. Steven Anderson has been following me."

She covered her face with her hands. "Oh my God! Are you sure?"

"A guy driving the same car tailed me three times in the last two days. At first, I thought it was one of those jerks who'd threatened me after Allan Wright's trial years ago." I pulled her onto my lap and told her how I'd confronted Anderson at the plaza.

"Marsh! That'll make him crazy. You don't know him like I do." Her voice was muffled against my neck. "Steven thinks I'm still his property." She shivered. "He told me enough times he'd never let me go."

"You'll never be able to forget how…brutal…he was honey."

She looked up into my face. "It never goes away even though I'm happy now—we're happy." She shook her head. "Just talking about him brings everything back."

My arm tightened around her and I swept a few strands of hair from her face. "Yeah, I still get flashbacks about the accident and the trial. I always worry that my head injury will kick in again." We sat in silence for a few moments.

"What was he driving?" she said.

"An old black Toyota," I quoted the license number.

She shivered. "I've seen a car like that lately on our street when I leave for work in the morning. I didn't notice the license."

"Did he follow you, honey?"

"I don't think so, but I didn't pay much attention. What're we going to do, Marsh?"

I wanted to call the police, but started by telling her about meeting Frank at the police station this morning. Christ, it seemed like days ago. She hadn't read the article in the *Tribune* and didn't mention that Burton had spoken to her about it.

"You were smart to call Frank. I need to read that article." She listened while I told her I'd discussed Anderson with Frank. "He's the best. So did he give you some suggestions about that, too?"

I let out a breath and shook my head. "He told me we need to discuss it with your parents. They know Anderson's back in Canada."

She bolted off my lap. "*What?* They *know* Steven's back? And they didn't tell me? Dad paid him to stay away. Why has he come back now?"

"He's had six years to blow his divorce settlement. I bet he wants more money."

She nodded and sat beside me. "You're probably right."

"It's too bad he wasn't charged with assault years ago."

"I know. I really regret that now." She sighed. "I begged Dad to get rid of him. Couldn't stand the thought of facing him again and going to court. I know you want to call the police, Marsh, but what can they really do? They won't arrest him for parking on our street—if it was him. And he'll tell them you assaulted him for no reason. Please, let's just leave it for now. I know my dad will handle it."

Anderson had never been charged with anything and we had nothing on him—right now. Years ago, Burton had swept the whole mess away by handing over a wad of cash and making him promise to bugger off to Trinidad forever. At the time, Burton had just been called to the bench and didn't need any embarrassing personal issues getting in the way. Maybe Don's suggestion about working from home would be a good thing.

I'd be able to drive Ann to work and back until that son-of-a-bitch was dealt with.

"We have to say something to your parents tonight."

"I know. But let's tell them about the baby first."

Soften the blow. Whatever she wanted, as long as we found out what was happening. It was ironic that Anderson was threatening us when Ann was in her fourth month of pregnancy again.

As soon as she'd showered and changed her clothes, we left for Young's. I drove away from our house slowly, watching for that black Toyota.

Chapter 6

"Do your parents know we're coming?" I said on the drive over.

"Sort of. I called Mom to make sure they'd be home. She wasn't going to say anything to Dad. I'll text to say we're on our way."

As we walked up the front steps, Burton opened the door. He always seemed to be watching, and like me, his office was at the front of the house. His face lit up when he saw Ann and he also managed to smile at me. "Well! Well! Come in." We draped our coats over the banister and followed him into the kitchen.

Eileen sat at the table, a glass in her hand. She saluted us, spilling red wine on her white blouse. "Oh, look what I've done. Silly me!" She dabbed at the spot with a napkin then looked up. "Nice to see you two."

Burton glared at her and shook his head. She glared back. I wondered if we'd interrupted a conversation about Anderson.

"You two had dinner?" said Burton.

When we said no, he invited us to share last nights' leftovers. Ann got plates and cutlery on the table while I hauled the food out the fridge—curried goat and Buss-up-shot roti. I loved these Trinidadian dishes, but my favourite was Eileen's Pelau, a chicken recipe that called for browning the sugar before adding the other ingredients. Of course, that had all been eaten the night before.

When Eileen was in the mood, her Trinidadian fare was amazing. Burton warmed each dish in the microwave before setting it on the table.

Before we sat down, Burton offered us wine. I accepted, knowing this was going to be a celebration, and as usual, there was no beer. Ann poured herself a glass of water and Eileen reached across the table for the wine bottle.

After we'd helped ourselves to food, Burton lifted his glass. "Thanks for coming over. We sure missed you last night. Glad you're feeling better, Sweet t'ing." The smile he directed toward Ann nearly persuaded me to like the guy. I knew at that moment I'd adore my own kid too. We all raised our glasses and drank.

Eileen in her kitten voice, said, "I think you've come to tell us something."

Ann smiled, put her fork down and took the ultrasound picture out of her purse. "You might be interested in this."

Burton took the image and looked at it. He removed his glasses and looked again. Tears came to his eyes. He passed the picture to Eileen. "I guess you were right."

"Well, I'm really not surprised," Eileen said. She looked at the picture and smiled. "I've noticed some changes in you lately. That dizzy spell last night reminded me of when I was expecting you. I'm happy for you both."

Burton, a broad smile on his face, stood and hugged us, then raised his glass. "Congratulations kids, this is the best kind of surprise. The moment I've been waiting for."

We toasted. "To our first baby and your first grandchild," said Ann.

"When's the baby due?" said Eileen.

"June. Only five months to go," said Ann. "I guess I got pregnant right after the miscarriage."

Burton stared intently at his daughter. "Will you take a leave of absence, Sweet t'ing?"

I knew this was coming.

"I'll think about it, Dad. I've just had a promotion, you know, and there are no more night shifts or weekends. The job will be a lot easier on me now."

Burton nodded, but I knew she hadn't heard the last of it. He'd offer to cover her salary if she stayed home until the baby was born, just like he did the last time.

We finished our meals and Eileen poured herself more wine. "You'll need a midwife." She reached for her iPad, nearly dropping it. "I'll start researching."

Ann frowned. "Thanks, Mom but I have an obstetrician and want to stick with her."

Eileen's long nails didn't stop clicking on the iPad.

Burton pushed his chair back. "Care to join me for a cigar, Marshall?"

What the hell could I say? I looked at my wife, then followed him out of the kitchen. He led me into his office—a huge man cave, and closed the door. It was also his smoking room, equipped with special fans that expelled smoke and odour. I wondered why he just didn't go outside like everyone else, and like the ground lighting outside, and the alarm system, high-priced gadgets were one of his quirks. They'd also installed an elevator while the house was being built ten years ago, to bring laundry and other stuff up and down. He took two cigars out of his desk drawer and snipped off the ends before handing one to me.

He'd probably bought them months ago when we'd announced the first pregnancy.

Burton took a lighter from his pocket, struck a flame and held his cigar just over the tip, rotating it slowly. "These things cost seventy-five bucks each and have to be properly lit." He blew on the end to make sure it was burning evenly before taking a puff.

From what I knew about cigar lighting, my father-in-law had executed a flawless procedure. When I tried to mimic his technique, I nearly burned my fingers. The cigar ended up half-lit and smouldered when I took a drag.

"Never smoked a cigar before, my boy?"

"Just the boys-night-out kind." I wondered how long this camaraderie would last.

As we smoked and talked about Ann and the baby, I felt almost relaxed in his company. This was not the time to bring up Steven Anderson, and Burton didn't mention the controversial article in today's *Tribune,* although he read the papers thoroughly every day.

"Your wonderful news has lifted my spirits, Marshall. Ann must have the best of everything. She has to stop working and take it easy. I'll cover her salary."

Back to the old Burton, but not back to the old Marsh. He was trying to soften me up before he had another chat with Ann. I decided not to challenge him. He must have sensed my reluctance to discuss the subject when I didn't answer.

"Eileen's father helped me out years ago. Without his support I would never have been able to afford law school or set up my practice."

Ann had told me that Grandpa Berresford, Eileen's father, had been dumping money from Trinidad into her account since she and Burton were married. And since Burton had never disclosed anything remotely personal to me, I decided to play along. "I guess you'll never forget his generosity."

He sighed. "Yes, I suppose you could put it that way."

The joy had gone out of his expression. I didn't understand the man. He wanted us to accept his offer, but was negative about the help his father-in-law had given him. Burton took a drag and blew the smoke up to where the fans were working overtime cleansing the air.

"Someday, I'll tell you about the Berresfords."

Clearly it wasn't a happy story and Burton didn't want to spoil the moment. This was the most personal conversation we'd had in the years I'd known him.

There was a knock, the door opened, and Ann stepped into the room. Eileen followed, a glass of wine in hand.

Ann stopped and faced her father. "Dad, there's something we have to talk about. Steven's been following Marsh."

I wondered if Ann and Eileen had been talking about Anderson. Burton let out a huge breath and stubbed out his cigar. I was happy to follow suit. Ann and Eileen sat on a small couch and I wheeled over beside them. Burton, behind his massive desk, must have felt he was in the hot seat.

He turned to me. "You're sure it was Steven Anderson who followed you and not someone connected to Allan Wright?"

My chest tightened and I felt my face redden. Why ask that when he knew Anderson was back in town? It took all I had not to shout *Frank said you'd be a great help.* Instead, I described the car Anderson drove and my altercation with him in the plaza. "Proof enough for you?"

"I'd hoped to handle the situation before anything like this happened."

"I'm presuming he's contacted you," I said. "Why didn't you tell us?"

He avoided my question. "Steven called and asked me for money. I refused and threatened to charge him with harassment and extortion." Burton looked at Eileen, who took a sip of wine and stared into her glass. "Then he called Eileen. She gave him money because...he threatened to hurt Ann. I called Frank immediately."

Ann leaned forward. "How long ago was that, Dad? And why didn't you tell us?"

Burton looked at his daughter and sighed. "About two weeks ago. We were going to tell you. Then you came over today with the great news about the baby."

That didn't explain why he hadn't told us as soon as Anderson started calling. "He's dangerous, Burton. Have you reported him to the police?"

"I'm discussing the next steps with Frank."

With Frank or with Gary Lund? "*My* next step will be to call the police if he ever follows me or Ann again," I said.

Eileen got up from the couch and walked out of the room. Seconds later, we heard a thump. Ann rushed out and I wheeled after her. Eileen lay face down at the bottom of the stairs.

"Mom!" Ann knelt beside her mother and took her pulse. "Are you okay?"

Burton emerged from his office. "What the hell's going on?" During the time Ann and I had been in the kitchen, Eileen had probably drained nearly a bottle of wine. God knows how much more she drank before we arrived or while Burton and I were talking.

Eileen opened her eyes, rolled over and sat up with Ann's help.

"Are you okay, Mom?" Ann asked again.

Burton, scowling, stood over his wife. "Should I call an ambulance?"

Eileen rubbed her head and looked around. "It's just a bump. I'll be fine. I don't know what happened."

"You might have a concussion. We're going to Emerge." Ann headed towards the kitchen. "I'll get some ice. Dad, please get the car."

"I'll take you," I called after her.

Burton yanked his coat out of the closet and went out the front door. Eileen and I stared at each other until Ann returned with a zip-lock bag full of ice. "Hold this on that bump. I'll get your coat." She looked at me, "Thanks for offering, Marsh, but why don't you go home? Knowing our hospital, this could take hours." She cut me off as I was about to object. "Honestly, we'll be fine."

I knew Ann wanted to handle her mother on her own, and she'd probably tell Burton to go home too after he'd dropped them off. So much for our first evening together as parents and grandparents-to-be.

"Okay, honey, but I'd really prefer to go with you." I held her close and kissed her neck. "Call me soon. I'll come back and pick you up."

"Thanks." She whispered in my ear, "I need to talk to Mom."

I escorted them to Burton's car and drove home. I hoped Ann would talk to Eileen about her drinking. Burton had been annoyed after she fell, and I wondered if Eileen drank every day.

I didn't notice that black Toyota anywhere. What a goddamn nightmare. Once inside my house, I pulled up in front of the computer. I'd never be able to sleep. There was no sense speculating on what was going on with Ann and her mother, so I forced myself to open *Fentanyl*, the file I'd saved, and re-read the articles.

The drug stash in that old warehouse on Speers Road two years ago was a big one— twenty kilos of fentanyl. After the raid, no suspects were found and the story died. Since then, there'd been nearly a dozen other small drug-related charges in our town leading to a few convictions. I searched the Toronto drug crime files. Same thing: a string of minor arrests that resulted in convictions, plus a couple of bigger busts with no arrests to date. Were the cops trying to net the big fish? I decided to base my article, *Tracking the Big Boys,* on that supposition. But I kept looking at my watch and couldn't seem to put any words together.

I phoned Ann and the call went to answer, so I sent a text: *Hope everything's okay. Call as soon as you can.* If my mother-in-law wasn't dying, she wouldn't be rushed through triage.

I still couldn't concentrate on the article. To put in time, I decided to have another look at that archive picture on the courthouse steps. I thought about texting Ed Alexander to ask if he remembered anyone supporting Allan Wright, but why bother? Even if Ed had noticed, what would that prove? I needed names.

I opened the file and clicked on the picture, which I re-printed, having left the original at work. Yup, I'd seen that curly-haired guy. I forgot names, but not faces. The other two dudes with him weren't familiar. The three of them dressed in cut-off tee shirts, exposing tattoos, one guy with a full sleeve, all looked about the same age. In fact, they looked close to my age at the time. In high school, we would have called them punks.

My gut told me to look through my old yearbooks. I unhooked the canes from the back of the wheelchair and walked down to our basement storage room. I might as well do something other than keep an eye on the time. The light was burned out, so I went up to find a new bulb. On the way back down, I nearly fell—canes and dark stairs aren't a good combo. After another trip up because I forgot my work satchel, I carried four yearbooks into my office and began looking through them, starting with my first year of high school.

Leafing through the books brought back people and stuff I'd forgotten. I wondered what all my old buddies were doing now, and particularly a few of the girls I'd had the hots for. The first three books yielded nothing. This was probably a waste of energy, but for old time's sake I went slowly through the last one, my graduating year. When I looked at that year's grade ten class photo, I found him: Julian Gilardi, the guy with full sleeve tattoos and dark curly hair. He was also listed as a member of the judo team, accompanied by a good-sized picture. The other two guys weren't in any of the books. Now what?

My phone rang. It was one a.m. "Hi, honey."

"As usual, the hospital was a zoo. Mom has a slight concussion. She needs to rest and take it easy. I've called a cab."

"Okay, I'll come to your parents' house and pick you up after you've got her settled."

"Marsh, I really need to stay with her tonight."

By my wife's short, terse sentences, I knew she was exhausted but determined. "Can't your dad look after her?"

"Marsh…please come by in the morning. Dad isn't in any mood to be a caregiver."

I knew when to let things alone, and this was no time to suggest they have a family chat about Eileen's drinking. "Okay, honey. Try and get some sleep. See you later."

I decided to try and get some sleep myself. Tomorrow would be time enough to dig deeper into Steven Anderson. Thank God I had Frank helping me with Allan Wright.

I pushed everything else aside and thought about our baby.

Suddenly, I was awake. Someone was running down the hall.

Ann burst into our bedroom. "Marsh! Wake up! There's a fire!"

Chapter 7

"Marsh! Wake up! The old cottage is on fire!"

Foggy from sleep, I sat up. "Cottage?"

"The old place beside my parents' house. C'mon, wake up!"

"It's on fire? How'd you get home?"

"Dad drove us." She sat on the bed. "He and Mom are in the front room. I called but you didn't answer."

"Forgot to charge my phone, sorry." I snapped on the prostheses and reached for my shirt and pants at the bottom of the bed. I grabbed the canes and followed Ann into the office. My in-laws sat on the couch in the dark, as far away from each other as possible. I flipped on the desk lamp. Burton wore an old tracksuit and a five o'clock shadow. Eileen had slipped a coat off her shoulders, revealing a shiny pink bathrobe. Her head wasn't bandaged.

"What the hell happened?" I said.

"We don't know yet." Burton ran his fingers through his greying hair and cleared his throat. "I mean, we know the old cottage caught fire. I saw the flames on my way up to bed, so I woke the girls, called the fire department and we cleared out."

Christ, a fire. That would make one hell of a story. "Are you worried about your own place?" I said.

"Our house and the cottage aren't that close together, but if the row of cedars between us catches fire we could be in trouble. That old wood place lit right up. Flames were shooting from the roof."

Ann put her hand on her dad's arm. "Let's have coffee."

He nodded. Eileen said she'd have a scotch. Ann disappeared into the kitchen and I sat in a chair facing my in-laws.

"It's a lucky thing I stayed up working on some stuff for Frank," said Burton, "Otherwise…"

I wondered what Frank wanted from Burton to keep him up so late. Hopefully it had something to do with putting handcuffs on Steven Anderson. "Yeah, I guess that old place wouldn't have smoke alarms," I said. "Wasn't it for sale a while ago?"

Burton nodded. "It used to be the gatehouse for the old mansion that was on our property, before the lot was severed. Why didn't you answer when Ann called?" I took the phone out of my pocket and put it in the charging unit behind me on the desk. "Why you kids don't have a landline is a mystery to me."

I didn't respond. We sat in silence until Ann returned carrying a tray with a steaming carafe, three mugs, cream and a glass of water. She poured two black coffees, and handed them to her parents. No sign of any scotch for Eileen and she didn't ask. I added cream to my mug. Ann took her water, pulled a chair over and sat beside me.

"Did you get a chance to talk to the fire department?" I said.

"We waited in the car until they arrived. I identified myself as the person who called 911, but they didn't say much, too busy getting ready to douse the fire. The police were right behind them. They said they'd be evacuating the street, so we left."

He took a sip from his mug, set it down and began pacing around the room. "I can't stop thinking about those cedars. They're old and dry. One spark could set them off."

I pictured the row of trees on fire, the flames travelling all the way up to the road and down to the lake at the back of both properties. That would make a fabulous picture for a story.

"Oh my God, I'm going to lose my beautiful house!" wailed Eileen.

Ann and I exchanged glances. Beautiful house was a matter of opinion. It if burned to the ground, what new architectural nightmare would my in-laws put up next?

Burton stopped pacing. "I can't just sit here," he said, even though he'd hardly warmed the couch. "I'm going back to make sure those idiots are taking care of things."

"Dad! You're not!"

Eileen looked up at her husband and managed a weak smile. "Just don't get in the way." All she cared about was that damn house.

"I'll come with you," I said.

"Marshall, *no*!" Ann's voice reached a decibel I'd never heard before.

"Honey, I can't let your dad go alone." Besides, a first-hand account of the scene could land me a frontpage story. "We won't be allowed to get close—you know that. I get why he needs to see what's going on."

"Oh, Marsh," said Eileen in her kitten voice. "That's so nice of you."

Ann glared at her mother, then at me and stood up. "Can we talk?"

I excused myself and followed my wife into our bedroom. She closed the door behind us. "Are you nuts? Just because Dad's compelled to go back there…"

I held up my hand. "Wait a minute. If my boss found out I didn't follow an important event because my wife didn't want me to, I'd be fired."

Ann sat on the bed with a thump and closed her eyes. "You're right. But what if your chair gets stuck or something? Burning bits can fly through the air."

"Come here, sweetie." She moved closer and we shared a quick kiss.

"Don't let Dad talk you into doing anything dangerous. It's crazy how much he cares about that ugly house." She reached into her pocket. "Here—take my phone. I'll use Mom's until yours is charged."

When we got back to the office, Eileen was sitting alone on the couch.

"Where's Dad?"

"Waiting in the car." Eileen pointed as if we didn't know where it was.

Burton's Jag XF purred in the driveway. He'd backed in so I could transfer to the passenger's seat straight from the ramp. I decided to use my wheelchair. I needed both hands to take pictures of the scene, not efficient with canes. Once the chair was stashed behind the passenger's seat, and I was belted in, Burton accelerated. He tapped the horn to acknowledge his wife and daughter standing at the window. I felt as though we were going off to war.

The car radio was tuned to the local news and sports station. An announcer talked about the fire but didn't mention Lakewood Trail and gave no details except to say the area had been evacuated and cordoned off by police. That wouldn't stop reporters from swarming the place. I just hoped we could get close enough for me to take some decent pictures.

When the newscast finished, Burton snapped off the radio and turned down the street next to Lakewood Trail. "We'll get onto my property here without being stopped." He pulled into an unlit park. To the west I saw flames. The glow illuminated children's swings, slides and a large splash pad, shut down for the winter. Burton parked the car beside a row of bushes and scrub trees and got out without a word. I opened the passenger door and assembled the chair in probably my fastest time but I'd never know. The air, heavy with chemicals, stung my eyes and throat.

"There's a path through here that leads to the side of my house." Burton pressed his remote-key fob twice—no beep—and shoved it in his pocket. "Just a short walk."

I knew about that path but was it navigable? I'd soon find out. Burton was right; this was probably our best chance of getting onto his property.

"Let's turn off our cell phones. We don't want anyone hearing them." He squared his shoulders and strode ahead. How would I be able to take pictures with a phone that was turned off? Why the hell did he think I'd come along?

The path was narrow. I had to navigate across branches and yank my wheels out of ruts in the frozen ground. Luckily, firelight filtering through the leafless trees made the job easier. This was one time I was grateful for the hours I'd spent in the gym working on my upper body. Soon we came to the row of cedars that separated Young's property from the public park.

Burton pushed through an opening in the hedge and held the branches aside for me. We came out only meters from his house. The fire eerily illuminated the stark white structure. Ambient lights under the eaves and on the ground gave the building a sinister appearance.

The scene was charged with hissing hoses, the smell of fire retardant and firefighters shouting. Two fire trucks were stationed in the cottage driveway and four flashing cruisers were parked haphazardly on the street in front. Even though the area had supposedly been evacuated, a small crowd hung back behind police tape. To my delight, the Totonto television crew was also barricaded from the scene.

Smoke saturated the air. I aimed Ann's phone and took pictures. From my vantage point, the tree-high flames looked as though they surrounded Young's house. The phone rang. I recognized my mother-in-law's number.

Burton, a few feet ahead of me, stopped and spun around. "You were told to turn that goddamned phone off!"

I ignored him, gave Ann a brief description of the scene and assured her we were safe. I promised to call back and rang off.

"Ann needs to know what's going on. She's had enough to worry about in the last couple of days."

Burton glared at me and headed toward the backyard. My wheels squeaked on the slippery half-frozen grass as I followed. We emerged out of the shadow cast by the massive house into the backyard, lit like a carnival by landscape lighting. I took a video of the firestorm, wondering how much closer we could get. The wood cottage, glowing like a Halloween lantern, crackled and swayed in protest.

Burton's fear had come true. The row of cedars that separated the cottage from Young's house had caught fire. One crew of firefighters drenched them, while another concentrated on dousing the cottage.

"Jesus Christ! I've got to make sure these people know what they're doing." Burton shouted and moved closer to the property line. I one-armed it up to him, my video still running.

One of the firefighters ran over to us. "This area is off limits! Go back up to the road!"

The cottage uttered a resounding boom and debris flew into the air as it collapsed. The firefighter yelled into his mobile, "Possible chemical explosion. Unauthorized citizens back here." He clipped the device onto his belt and ran toward the burning cottage. The Young's fire alarm went off, probably triggered by the explosion.

"Shit, this might be a drug fire," I said.

Burton ran back toward his own house. I pocketed the phone and pushed after him. Burning fragments flew through the air, chasing us and falling around us like fireworks gone berserk. The back of Burton's jacket caught fire. I pumped through the wet grass and lumps of soggy snow, stopping about a foot away from my father-in-law, who was bent over, frantically trying to remove his coat. Wheels locked, I leaned forward, pushed myself up and out of the chair and onto his back. He fell sideways with me on top of him. I rolled away. Burton got on his hands and knees, then stood. Our sudden collision had smothered the flames on his jacket. He finally managed to unzip it and throw it on the ground where it lay smouldering. I looked around for the firefighter, but he was probably with his team, concentrating on the cedars and on the flattened building that was shooting bursts of flame into the air.

"Christ almighty!" Burton stomped on his coat and felt the back of his neck. "Good thing you were here." He looked over at me. "Are you okay?"

Before I had a chance to respond, two cops ran across the floodlit lawn toward us, shouting over the screaming alarm, "Stay where you are!" They stopped and gave us the once-over—Burton, his tracksuit now muddy and wet, standing on his burnt jacket, and me, sitting on my ass a few feet away from my abandoned wheelchair.

"You're under arrest." One cop took handcuffs off his belt and walked toward Burton.

"Don't you dare come near me with those goddamned things!" Burton shouted over the noise. "I own the property you're standing on!"

"Guys, I'm a member of the press," I reached inside my jacket and took the press card out of my pocket.

"Keep your hands where I can see them!"

Burton flung his arms in a wild gesture. "You morons! I'm the one who called the fire department and the police in the first place. This is idiotic! I'll report you to your superiors."

The second cop, who so far had said nothing, stepped closer to me. "Long time no-see, Marsh." He turned to his colleague. "It's okay Mike. This guy's legit."

"Jerry!" I hadn't recognized him in the weird light. For the second time in two days, he waved away my press card.

Burton stood, fury in his eyes, looking back and forth between me and the cop.

"What the hell are you doing back here?" Jerry tried to guide the chair toward me but the wheels were locked and it scudded across embers that sparkled on the wet lawn.

I gestured to Burton. "This is Burton Young's property, he's my father-in-law. We're here to make sure it's being protected." Jerry helped me to my feet. "Thanks," I said, heaving myself into the chair. My butt was soaking wet and my face felt as though a rake had gone over it.

"I'll escort you off the property. The area's been evacuated." Jerry looked at Burton and pointed to the ruin next door. "And, as you can see, the fire is now under control. Do either of you need medical attention?"

"No, I think I'm okay," I said, putting a hand to my face.

"The only thing I need right now is to go in and turn off my goddamn alarm," shouted Burton. "Then I'm staying in my own goddamn house. And what's this about a drug fire?"

Jerry looked at me, then at Burton. "What makes you think the fire is drug-related, Mr. Young?"

"You are addressing *Judge* Young." Burton thrust his thumb in my direction, "My son-in-law told me."

Jerry stepped closer to me. "And how would you know that, Marsh?"

What the fuck. Burton had heard the firefighter, then heard my comment and jumped to conclusions. He walked over to Jerry, invading his comfort zone. "My son-in-law has a master's degree in criminology. And if he wasn't stuck in a wheelchair, he'd probably be your boss."

Had I been slapped or kissed? The heat from the fire and the blare of the alarm were getting to me. I wiped my face again, and my hand came away with specks of blood. If Burton didn't shut up, we'd both be down at the station—the second time in one day for me. Not good optics, as Don would say.

"Let's see some identification, please, *Judge*." Jerry snapped his fingers and held out his hand.

Burton searched his pants pockets, then picked up his burnt jacket and felt in those pockets too. He looked flustered. "It's probably in the house. I left in a hurry. I had to get my wife and daughter out. If you don't trust me, my son-in-law can go in and turn the alarm off and get my driver's license."

Burton wasn't thinking with his wig on tonight. Since when had he given me the alarm code? "You have the house keys, right, Burton? Maybe the other officer will go in with you."

Burton and Jerry's partner entered the house and lights automatically lit up the kitchen. In seconds, the alarm stopped wailing. Jerry and I watched them stride toward the front of the house, probably in search of identification, which seemed like a moot point now that the obvious owner had turned the alarm off.

Jerry turned to me. "So, what makes you think the fire is drug-related?"

I told him the firefighter had said *possible chemical explosion* moments ago and that Burton had taken it as fact. Jerry's expression said he either didn't believe me or I was hiding something.

"Who owns that property next door?"

I shrugged. "It was for sale a while ago. I've never seen any sign of life over there except for a groundskeeper. He's very efficient about taking away all the garden cuttings. Judge Young might know who the owners are." I knew damn well the cops would easily find out who owned the property, particularly if it was unoccupied.

"You seem to have noticed quite a bit," said Jerry.

I eyed him. "It's my job to be observant."

"So, how did you manage to get through our security?"

"Judge Young parked his car in the kids' playground on the next street over." I pointed. "We came through that woodlot." The area was dark and foreboding now that the fire had died down.

Jerry looked at me, nodding slowly. "Un-huh. You came through those trees, in the dark, in that wheelchair."

I stared back, saying nothing.

"Why didn't *Judge* Young identify himself to the officers on the street as the homeowner?"

"My father-in-law does things his way." And this time, I was happy to go along with his way. I had pictures and a video of the fire that no other reporter would get. I pulled Ann's phone out of my pocket and sent the video and photos to Don.

"Maybe the Judge has something to hide, like his ownership of that property next door," said Jerry. "Maybe he was trying to make sure something got destroyed."

Christ, I was glad Burton wasn't around to hear that unlikely speculation. But Jerry's words made me think. How much did I really know about His Honour Burton Young? Everyone had secrets.

Chapter 8

Burton stuck his head outside the back door and announced he was staying put. Jerry asked me to wait a few minutes while he went inside. "I'll drive you home after I've spoken to the judge."

"Sure. Take your time, Jerry." Had Burton given any thought as to how I'd get home?

The scene next door had calmed. Firefighters were still busy, but the sense of urgency was gone from their voices and actions. They were probably grateful for the landscape lighting on Burton's property as they moved around putting out small blazes that shot out of what was left of the cottage, now collapsed in a smoldering heap. The whole area smelled like charred wood, and what I presumed were fire retardant chemicals perhaps mixed with other substances—the aftermath of an exploded drug lab. I wheeled closer to the property line, took pictures and sent them to my boss. They'd make an excellent contrast to the raging blaze of a few minutes ago.

Ten minutes later, Jerry emerged from the house. I pointed to the plastic bag in his hand. "You got the security tapes?"

"Yes," he said.

We'd just started to walk toward the front of the house when my phone rang. I knew it was Ann.

"Marsh, you promised to call me back! What's going on? Are you okay?"

"Sorry, honey. We got kind of busy. Your dad and I are fine. The cottage fire is out. A police officer is driving me home."

"Why? Is Dad staying there?"

"Yup. See you in a few minutes. Tell your mom I'll drive her home."

"Mom decided to stay here, but thanks. We're sleeping on the pull-out in the office." That meant Princess Eileen was sleeping in our bed. The couch just wouldn't cut it.

"Was mom and dad's house damaged?" said Ann.

"Nope. Firefighters did a damn good job of getting that fire under control."

"Glad you're on the way home. I've been worried." She made a kissing sound and hung up.

As we reached the driveway at the front of Young's house, Jerry pointed to a squad car parked on Lakewood Avenue. The gates opened. True to form, Burton was watching from inside the house.

On Lakewood, police were holding back about twenty spectators. I grinned watching the guys in the news van trying their best to film the scene from a distance. Maybe a raise would be in order for my brilliant and dangerous coverage. *Reporter Risks Life and Limb to Film Treacherous Fire.* Maybe you're suffering from smoke inhalation, Keene, this was the sort of drama and excitement expected of a reporter.

"Your face looks pretty sore. Should I take you to the hospital?" said Jerry.

"No thanks. My wife's a nurse. She'll fix me up."

Jerry opened the car door, watched me transfer to the passenger's seat and dismantle my chair. He opened the back door, placed the sections on the seat then got behind the wheel and fastened his seat belt. "Doesn't take you long to take that chair apart."

"Just over thirty seconds," I said.

He started the engine and we drove away. "Your father-in-law said you came through the woods to avoid being stopped."

"Yup." I told you that already, buddy. You'll see us and anyone else who was prowling around when you look at the security tapes. "If you hang a left just up here, Judge Young's car is in the park." I pointed to the side street.

"That's already been confirmed."

Of course. These guys check everything. I decided to sit quietly and let Jerry talk. No sense in re-fuelling the fire. But Jerry didn't say anything. Except for the occasional squawk from the police radio, which he ignored, the only conversation was me giving directions to Ortona Street. I texted Don to make sure he'd received the video and the pictures. Within seconds, he confirmed and asked for the story, ASAP. I wondered if he ever got a full night's sleep.

Jerry pulled into our driveway, got out and retrieved my chair. He stood beside the cruiser and called headquarters. By the time he finished speaking, I was in the wheelchair.

"Appreciate the lift," I said. Jerry nodded, got back in and drove off.

Ann was waiting at the front door when I rolled up the ramp. She hugged me and held the door open. "You smell like smoke, Marsh. I just spoke to Dad. He says everything's under control. He'll be here in the morning with breakfast." She stood back and looked at me as I entered the front hall. "Oh my God, your face is cut. And what happened to your jacket?"

I couldn't sugar-coat this. "You were right about things flying around. The cottage…went up all of a sudden, but they got it under control in jig time."

"Marshall, you're making this sound casual. What happened? I want the reality version. You can tell me in the bathroom. I need to look at your face."

She didn't like what she saw. "How did this happen, Marsh?" She started wiping my face with antiseptic lotion. Stung like hell.

I gave her a rundown of the events and showed her the pictures and the video.

"You jumped on his back? Is he hurt too?"

"I think his hands and the back of his neck are a little sore."

"I don't suppose he thought about getting checked out either?"

"I don't know, honey."

"Luckily, your face is more scratched than anything," she said, applying something else that stung. "Any idea what caused the fire?"

Burton hadn't told Ann about the possible drug connection. "Too early to know. Who owns that old place?"

She shrugged. "Don't know. Dad was thinking of buying it a while ago when it was up for sale. It's never looked lived-in to me. Probably bought by someone planning to tear it down and rebuild."

Maybe Burton did buy it. Owning the lot next door made perfect sense. I looked at my watch; it was four a.m. "Let's get some sleep."

Ann took our extra bedding out of the closet and we pulled out the sofa bed. I threw sheets over the mattress and tossed pillows on top. We undressed down to our underwear and lay facing each other, cuddling under a Hudson's Bay blanket. I reached out and put my hand on her belly. "Please don't go in to work tomorrow."

"I'm one jump ahead of you, worry-wart. I've already called in sick."

I held her close and we kissed goodnight. "Hope your dad doesn't show up too early." As usual, Ann fell asleep as soon as she closed her eyes. I lay listening to her breathe. I'd forgotten to ask if she and Eileen had talked about her drinking, or Steven Anderson, while they were waiting. I knew Don wanted an account of the fire and I couldn't sleep thinking about it. I slipped out of bed, transferred to my chair and pulled up in front of the computer. Ann didn't even stir.

An hour later, I emailed the story to my boss. I gave the street name where the old cottage was located, something my boss would expect. Don might figure out that my in-laws lived right next door and edit my piece to include that detail—something beyond my control.

I lay down beside my wife, hoping to get a few hours sleep before breakfast arrived.

**

Bright sunlight streaming through the blinds woke me. My cell said 9:35 a.m. and Ann wasn't beside me. I snapped on the prostheses, grabbed my canes and walked down the hall toward the bathroom.

Eileen and Ann were in the kitchen talking. She called to me, "Glad you got some sleep, Dad's on his way."

"Be with you in five," I said. "Can you bring me some clean clothes, please?"

After my shower, Ann came in with underwear, pants and a shirt. She applied a fresh layer of antiseptic cream to my face, then sat on the edge of the tub. "How does your face feel?"

"Itchy." I winked. "Want to help me get dressed, baby?"

She wagged a finger and lowered her voice. "Mom's just outside that door. Tonight, I'll help you get undressed."

"Deal."

She tilted her head. "But you have to do whatever I command."

I licked my lips. "Think about where you want me to start."

She got up to leave the room, but I motioned for her to come close. "The cops will probably want to talk to me again," I whispered. "And most likely they'll have a few questions for your dad."

She frowned. "Why?"

"They think we had another reason for being there last night."

"That's ridiculous. Dad was only trying to make sure his house was okay."

"They were probably going to arrest us until one of the cops recognized me."

"Really?"

I nodded. "They didn't know your dad. Dressed in a tracksuit, stomping on a burned jacket, I guess they thought he was going to rob the place or something." I didn't hide a grin.

"Not funny, Marsh." She looked me in the eye. "Do you think the same thing would have happened if he was white?"

I let out a breath. "Ann, he was full of attitude and tried to throw his weight around. He kept opening his mouth to change feet." I told her the firefighter had shouted to his team that the explosion could have been drug-related and Burton made a point of asking the cop, then said I'd told him.

She thought for a moment, shaking her head. "He's been really touchy lately. There's something bugging him. Besides my ex-husband, I mean."

"Speaking of your ex, did Eileen mention anything when you were at the hospital?"

She shook her head. "No and I didn't bring it up. She was embarrassed enough. And before you ask, we did talk about her drinking. She just said she was trying to work through some stuff."

"Oh." By drinking? Ann always stood up for her mother. My gut told me much more going on with Eileen.

We heard Burton calling out on his way down the hall, "Breakfast everyone." I gave Ann a pat on the butt and she went to join her parents.

I finished my morning routine, joined everyone in the kitchen and greeted my in-laws. Burton looked exhausted, but wore a business suit, and was clean shaven. His right hand and the back of his neck looked professionally bandaged. Eileen sat at the table with some kind of green goop on her face and announced she was trying out a new line of face products. I hoped that crap wasn't all over our sheets. Neither one commented on my face, and I wondered if Eileen had noticed her husband's bandages.

Ann and I set the table while Burton opened take-out containers from Lizzie's, an organic restaurant in town. I smelled smoked salmon, my favourite.

"Mom, if you want to wash that mask off, we're about to eat."

Eileen picked up a purse the size of carry-on luggage and went into the bathroom. When she emerged five minutes later, the goop had been replaced with slimy-looking cream. She reclaimed her chair, frowned at her paper napkin and put it on her lap. It had been a while since she complained that we never used the linen ones she bought us.

We helped ourselves to salmon, rye toast, croissants and fruit salad. "Thanks, Burton. This looks great." I poured coffee into our mugs.

"Yeah, Dad, thanks, it's a real treat."

Eileen looked at her husband. "What happened to your hand?"

"Just a little mishap. A nurse at the hospital fixed me up. Anyhow, the important thing is that our house escaped any damage."

Christ. Both spouses getting medical treatment at the same hospital only hours apart. I wondered if they'd wondered about spousal abuse.

"Oh," said his loving wife, reaching for some smoked salmon. "I'm so glad our house is okay."

Ann and I exchanged glances.

"Your face looks better this morning, Marsh," said Ann.

Burton looked at me and gave a cursory nod.

"Anything else happen after I left last night?" I said.

"Nothing really," he said. "I walked around to make sure everything was okay. Then I went into the house and turned up the ventilation system, although I didn't smell any smoke inside. I think the cops and firemen stayed out there all night. I fell asleep just before dawn."

"How does the house smell now?" said Eileen. "You know how bad my allergies are."

He glanced at her but didn't answer.

"You're welcome to stay here for a few days if you want, Mom." Ann looked to me for confirmation. Anything I said would sound phony as hell, so I just nodded and reached for a chocolate croissant.

"Did the cops take your security tapes, Burton?" I said, although I knew the answer.

"Yes. Be interesting to see if anyone was prowling around last night."

"Besides us, you mean?" His expression said he didn't think my comment was funny. "Did they ask you who owns that property next door?"

"Yes, of course." He glanced at Eileen who had just applied lipstick and was examining her teeth in a compact mirror.

"So, Dad, who owns it?" Ann put her fork down and looked at Burton. "You were thinking of buying it at one point, weren't you?"

"I did buy that property. I wanted to have some control over what happened right next door to me."

I nearly choked on my croissant. A perfectly reasonable explanation, one that I'd already considered. Why the hell didn't he admit this earlier? Ann looked at Burton, her eyes wide. "Oh," was all she said.

I wondered if it was news to Eileen. Her eyebrows rose slightly, but her expression remained deadpan.

"So did anyone live there, Burton?" I said.

"No. I kept the gardener on who was looking after the place before I bought it. I let him use the boathouse to store his fishing gear plus the use of the old boat and motor. When you mentioned something about a chemical fire, Marshall, I realized I should have paid more attention to that old cottage. Maybe it was being used as a drug lab."

He's had time to think about that, I thought "The cops will look into it, Burton."

He nodded and didn't comment. Probably wishing he'd kept his mouth shut last night instead of blowing off steam.

Eileen snapped her compact shut and dropped it in her purse. "We really should be going, Burton."

"Mom, what's the rush? Dad's hardly eaten anything. More coffee, anyone?"

Burton looked at his watch. "I still have some time before my first case."

We slid our mugs over and Ann topped them up. Eileen put her hand over hers as though she was refusing a glass of wine.

"Taking the day off work too, Marshall?" said Burton.

"Sort of. I may go in later. I was up until five writing about the fire." Ann didn't look surprised. I guess she knew me.

"You wrote about the fire for your paper?" said Burton and Eileen almost in unison, their voices higher than usual.

I nodded. "I didn't identify you as next-door neighbours, if that's what you're worried about. I have to stay in my boss's good graces, you know."

My second attempt at humour tanked. Burton sighed, but it sounded more like a huff. "Well, it won't take people long to figure out where that fire was, and it won't be lost on them that my son-in-law wrote the story." His voice got louder. "I would have thought you could have had the good sense to declare a conflict of interest in this case."

Ann sat up straight and looked at her father. "I don't get it, Dad. Marsh has to do his job. What's the big deal? Plus, if he hadn't been there last night…"

At that moment I would have bought my wife a colossal diamond if she wanted one.

"The *big deal* is," said Burton, "that I've already had to *deal* with colleagues asking me about Wright's murder and my son-in-law's connection to him. They all read that article in yesterday's *Tribune*." Glaring, he stopped to catch his breath. "Now, he's written about a fire on my property next door."

A fire on a property that you've kept quiet about, until now. Burton seemed to have forgotten I'd saved him from serious burns, and probably from a big hassle with police. He was bloody lucky I didn't write about that. It would've made a good story. *Irate judge proves that sometimes the law really is an ass.*

I couldn't help shooting back. "I didn't like that *Tribune* article either, Burton. But there isn't a goddamned thing I can do about it, except try and find out who killed the son-of-a-bitch that murdered my family. Then I can finally be rid of Wright, and clear up any ridiculous speculation. And you might as well know that Frank is helping me."

Burton rose from his chair, wiped his mouth, and tossed his napkin on the table. Eileen stood, and they hurried into the front hall, collected their coats, and were out of the house before another minute passed. Ann and I sat in our seats, stunned.

My cell phone dinged. I took it out of my pocket and saw a text from Paul Marchand at the *Tribune* then read it to my wife. *Your article Unacceptable Accessibility will headline this weekend's Disability Section.*

"One less person mad at me," I said, surprised Ann hadn't told me off for shouting at her dad. "Plus, a nice cheque will be coming my way."

"I'm not mad at you, Marsh." She reached over and took my hand. "I don't know what got into Dad. I don't understand why he didn't tell us about that property. I wonder if Mom knew he bought it."

"Good question."

"I still think there's something else bothering him." Ann sighed and her shoulders slumped. "Sometimes he gets moody if a case isn't going well, but I don't think that's the problem. It's no secret that he and Mom aren't getting along. They were never great together, but now they're fighting all the time. Her drinking makes everything worse. She never drank like this before."

Why the hell wouldn't they separate? Eileen had money—Burton had hinted at it yesterday when we were smoking our cigars in his office. And, she and her sister were buying a spa. My gut told me again there was plenty about my in-laws I didn't know.

We busied ourselves tidying the kitchen and putting the leftover food in the fridge. Ann went back to bed and I lumbered into my office to text Don that I'd be in tomorrow. With the all-nighter I'd put in for the paper, there'd be no problem. Then I called Munro.

"Hey, how's it going?" I said.

"Great article and pictures of that fire, Keene. I heard your in-laws' place is next door—did it get damaged?"

The location would never have been a secret for long. Soon Burton's name would be associated with that property. The cops had probably done a title search as well. "No, they were lucky. Been to the coroner's office yet?"

"Don went this morning. Wright took five shots to the chest. One went through his heart. He didn't die where they found him, not enough blood at the scene. He'd probably been dead for more than twenty-four hours before he was dumped in that subdivision. No mention of where the real crime scene is."

"Any thoughts on why he was murdered?" I said.

"Good question. Who'd he piss off so soon after getting out of jail?"

"Maybe the killers were pissed for a long time and just waiting. I need to find out who and why. That *Tribune* article made me look bad." Some would think *I'd* been the one waiting to off the bastard.

"Yeah, I don't blame you. I'd dig into it if it was me. But anyone with half a brain will know you didn't have anything to do with Wright's murder."

I thanked Munro and told him I'd see him tomorrow.

I decided I had to do a record search on Gilardi, the guy I'd recognized in the newspaper picture, and on Allan Wright, although I already knew he'd been convicted of drunk driving before my car accident. I reminded myself that I had to ask Frank about what steps to take next regarding Steven Anderson. Things were heating up.

I sent a text to Earl, asking for Mrs. Wright's address. Even though he'd struck out with her, I had to give it a shot. I told him I wasn't going to the police or the paper with any info she gave me. I'd make it personal between her and me. Maybe she'd have some sympathy for that approach and not slam the door on *my* foot.

With a million thoughts running through my head, there was no point trying to work. I was exhausted and decided to join my wife for a nap. It seemed like I'd only closed my eyes when Ann's phone rang and I heard her pick up.

"Oh, hi Dad..." She looked at me and raised her eyebrows. "You're not bothering us...That's okay, I could tell you were stressed...Sure, come over, I'll throw something together for dinner." She rang off and shook her head.

"What's up?" I said.

"He sounds terrible but wouldn't tell me over the phone. I could hardly hear him. He apologized for this morning."

"Really?" That's a first, I thought. "What time is it?"

"Four o'clock. He's coming over."

Christ, what now?

Chapter 9

Fifteen minutes later, Burton pulled into our driveway. I abandoned my workstation and answered the door. He nodded to me, took a drag from his cigarette, tossed it onto the driveway and entered the house, smoke streaming from his nostrils.

Ann hurried down the hall, hugged her dad and led the way into my office, "Let's sit in here where it's comfortable."

Burton, over six feet tall, always carried his head high, eyes focused beyond the immediate, as if he possessed an authority inaccessible to most people. Today he slumped, his eyes half-closed, his skin grey.

"I'll make tea," I said. Ann needed a few moments alone with her father. I watched them walk into our living room slash office. I had no energy for more family angst. Why didn't they go to the kitchen so I could continue to work?

Like a good husband, I boiled the water and steeped the tea. Ann came to help carry the tray back to the front room. I leaned close to her. "Has he said anything?"

"No," she whispered. "He's just sitting staring out the window. Said he wants us both to hear what he has to say."

Ann led the way back to the office. She poured the tea, handed a mug to her father and one to me. "Okay, Dad you look as if somebody just died. What's going on?"

"I don't know where to begin," he said, shaking his head.

He just sat and looked at us for a few moments, then cleared his throat. "For the first time in my career, I called in sick. Another judge is handling my case load today. And probably tomorrow too."

This was serious. Ann and I exchanged glances.

He looked down at his hands. "I'll start with the first thing that happened."

I knew how Burton valued order—there would be no hints along the way—and we wouldn't hear the punch line until the end. But by the look of him, this could be an all-bad news scenario.

He took a sip and put the mug down. His hand shook and tea spilled onto the table in front of him. "This will probably come as no big surprise to you. Your mother and I have decided to divorce."

What? That was it? No lead-up?

Ann's eyebrows shot up then came together in a frown. "You're right, Dad. It's not a surprise. But I kept hoping that you and Mom could work it out."

Burton sighed. "Someday we'll tell you the whole story."

Ann's frown deepened. "So, where's Mom? Why are you telling us by yourself?"

"We had an argument about the cottage property. She was annoyed that I didn't consult her before I bought it. I think she went to meet Nell at that spa they're interested in."

Did Eileen know Burton was here telling us about their breakup? Ann was used to her parents' disagreements, but I could see she was upset. When would Eileen get around to telling her only child?

Ann looked at her father. "The spa in Newmarket they were talking about?"

Burton nodded.

"I really don't blame Mom for being annoyed about the cottage property. Why didn't you tell us you'd bought it, Dad?"

"Everyone would have found out in time," he said. "It wasn't my story to tell."

Ann frowned. "That's weird. What do you mean?"

Burton sighed, took an initialled handkerchief from his pocket and wiped his face. "I bought it for Frank. He was going to repay me after…" He covered his face with his hands. Sobs shook his body.

Ann moved closer to her father and grabbed his arm. "Dad!"

Burton held up his hand. "Please, let me finish. Frank wanted that property because he was planning to leave Jeanette. He was having an affair with Nell. I think they were going to fix up that old cottage and live in it."

What the …? Why would that make Burton cry?

Ann's eyebrows shot up. "Wow! I had no idea."

Burton continued before we could comment further. "Today, after your mother left to meet Nell, I tried to contact Frank about the fire, but he didn't answer. I must have left five messages. An hour ago, the police called. Routine questions about last night, I thought."

Ann's hand covered her mouth. "Oh my God, is mom okay?"

He nodded. "Yes, I presume so. It wasn't about her." He closed his eyes and took a deep breath. "Frank was found dead in his office this morning. The police are calling it a homicide."

Jesus Christ! "*Frank*? What happened?"

Ann gasped, hurried over, and threw her arms around her father. "*Uncle Frank? Why?*" She sat close to Burton, her hand on his arm.

He wiped his eyes and shook his head again. "God only knows. The police wanted to talk to me in person, of course, and I told them I'd be here. I hope you don't mind. I just couldn't face the interview alone. They'll be here any mom—"

The doorbell rang, followed by a knock. "Halton Police." I'd been so distracted I hadn't seen a car pull up. Perfect timing. Thank God Burton managed to tell us before the cops did.

I wheeled out of the office and opened the front door. Two officers stepped into the hall, Detective Sergeant Reese, who had interviewed me about Alan Wright only two days ago. Frank had been with me during that interview. Reese was accompanied by a cop I'd never met. He introduced him as Detective Robert Brown, probably from homicide. We shook hands and I led the way into the kitchen where there'd be enough chairs for everyone. As we passed the office, I beckoned for Ann and Burton to follow.

The officers accepted Ann's offer of tea. This would be a preliminary interview to learn about Burton's relationship with Frank. We got more mugs and boiled the water again. The cops, sitting across from Burton, offered their condolences.

"You were law partners with Francis Emmerson Veale, Your Honour?" said Reese.

"That's correct."

I presumed Burton would follow the advice Frank had given me and not offer any information. I knew damn well he wouldn't disclose what he'd told us about Frank's plans. I looked over at my wife, wondering what effect this terrible news would have on her, and on our baby.

Reese leaned forward. "You're no longer law partners with Mr. Veale, why is that?"

"I was called to the bench seven years ago. I gave up the partnership at that time."

"Have you had contact with Mr. Veale since you ended your partnership?"

"Yes, of course. We're–were–close friends." Burton accepted the fresh mug of tea I handed him. "Thank you, Marshall." He looked Reese in the eye. "Sergeant, as you can imagine, I am overcome by Mr. Veale's death. I cannot imagine who would harm him. However, he was a criminal lawyer and a damn good one. He also had his share of losses. Clients can be bitter. That is an avenue you should explore."

The two cops thanked Ann as she passed them steaming mugs then turned their attention back to Burton. "What can you tell us about Mr. Veale's private life?" said Reese.

Burton assumed his usual imperious posture. He waited so long to answer I wondered if he was going to ignore the question.

"My former partner was married to Jeanette, his third wife. He had two children, one from each of his previous marriages. I can attest to the fact that he paid alimony and child support faithfully. He loved his children and saw them often."

His Honour Burton Young was well above a couple of police officers in the food chain. Would Reese and Brown be cowed by Burton's dismissive attitude and status?

Besides Frank's affair with Nell, what else did Burton know about him? My mind drifted back to the phone conversation with Frank yesterday, and the angry voice I'd heard in the background. Who the hell *was* that? Did it factor into his murder?

"What was Mr. Veale's relationship like with, did you say, his *third* wife?"

"Frank never discussed personal issues with me."

The cops' deadpan expressions didn't indicate whether they accepted that statement.

"Who were Mr. Veale's friends? Did he golf? Play any sports?" said Reese.

Burton's eyes darted away from Reese, then back again. "He didn't follow sports. Frank is…was, a busy man. With two ex-wives and two children, plus a thriving practice, I don't think he had much time for friends."

"You just said he was your best friend."

Burton had said they were *close* friends. The cops were putting words in his mouth.

"We got together several times a year for dinners in each other's homes."

"And were those social occasions?" said Reese. "Were others invited?"

Burton nodded. "Occasionally my daughter and son-in-law, and my wife's sister joined us."

Ann and I were always included in the dinners at Young's house. In fact, our attendance on those occasions was more like a command performance. We'd never been invited to Frank's house. He and Jeanette lived in the country in a renovated farmhouse. It was news to me that Burton and Eileen ever went there.

"As his best friend, you must know what Mr. Veale did for fun? You can understand, Your Honour, we have to look into every aspect of his life." When Burton didn't react, Reese continued. "There were a few brochures on his desk from Woodbine Racetrack."

I had to give Burton full marks—his gaze never wavered. "Mr. Veale enjoyed horse races occasionally."

Occasionally? Wow, that was a beaut. Frank was always talking about what he'd won or lost, mostly lost, on the horses when we met at Young's. Maybe he'd gotten in too deep.

"Did he own a gun?" said Reese.

"Not to my knowledge," said Burton. "How did Mr. Veale die?"

"We can't discuss those details at this time, Judge."

Burton would find out easily enough and they knew it. Why not tell him? They might learn something from his expression and body language. I wished the cops would leave so I could start writing down the questions that were popping into my head. Frank's death changed a lot of things. We all lost a good friend. I'd lost a mentor in my mission to find out who killed Allan Wright, and Ann had lost a man she loved enough to call *uncle*. Burton was stuck with the property next door and any potential fallout.

My mind was racing. Had Frank been able to prod Gary Lund into doing anything about Steven Anderson? I hoped Burton would be in the mood to talk later. Like it or not, we had to figure this out. We owed it to Frank.

"And I suppose you're not at liberty to tell me if your boys saw anything on those security tapes I gave them last night?" said Burton.

Reese shook his head. "Do you know who owns the property next to you, Your Honour?"

"I presume you mean to the east, Sergeant? The park on the west is owned by the town."

Reese nodded. "Yes, the property that burned."

"I am the registered owner of twenty-twenty Lakewood Drive. I told your officers last night."

He did? Not when I was around. Maybe he told Jerry's sidekick when they went into the house.

"Was the cottage occupied?" said Reese.

"No. I was eventually going to tear it down. I bought the land so no one could build beside me."

Ann took a gulp of tea. What was she thinking?

"The grounds not destroyed by the fire looked well kept," said Reese.

"I hired the gardener who'd worked for the previous owner. Didn't want the place to look deserted and attract undesirables." Burton shifted in his seat. "How long before the Fire Marshal's report comes out?"

The cops looked at each other. "Probably a few days."

Arson, misfortune or drug lab? My money was on drug lab.

Burton hadn't volunteered that the gardener had access to the boathouse. And the cops didn't think to ask. I decided to look around later and see if there was anything inside beside a boat and maybe fishing tackle.

Reese looked at his partner. They pushed their chairs back. "Thanks for your time, Your Honour, Mr. and Mrs. Keene."

Burton stood and shook hands with the two cops.

"We may need to talk to you again," said Reese.

We? Detective Brown hadn't said a word. For sure Burton wasn't a suspect in Frank's murder. With Burton as the registered owner of that burned cottage, the cops had no way of knowing Frank's intentions.

"Anytime," said Burton. His expression told them they'd better have good reason to bother him again.

I accompanied Reese and Brown to the door and wished them a good day. Reese didn't respond, although his mouth stretched into a terse grin. They walked down the ramp, got into an unmarked car and drove away.

When I returned to the kitchen, Ann was crying, her head on her dad's shoulder. Burton, now sitting straighter, his expression haggard, stroked her cheek. "Sweet t'ing, there's nothing we can do about it. I'm just as upset as you are. Let's concentrate on you staying healthy and delivering a healthy baby. That's the most important thing right now."

I felt sorry for the guy. His wife had checked out on him, and so had his close friend —in the most horrific way. Plus, a yet unexplained fire on his lot next door had to be dealt with.

"Your dad's right," I said. "We have to hang in. We're all in shock. You and I are going to figure it out. Right Burton?"

He looked at me and nodded slowly.

"I still have that bottle of Scotch you gave me. Please stay for dinner. We have left-over salmon thanks to you, and I'll throw a salad together." No sooner had I spoken than I thought about Eileen and Nell. Someone had to tell them about Frank. I poured the scotch and handed my father-in-law his drink.

"Thanks, Marshall." He took a sip, closed his eyes and leaned back. "You two are all I have left."

Ann leaned against her father. "Have you told Mom and Nell?"

Burton opened his eyes. "I tried to call, but her phone's turned off. I'll have to drive to that spa."

He made no effort to move. Ann and I looked at each other. No way would either one of us allow Burton to go alone.

"In a way I'm glad she's not answering," said Ann. "It would be terrible to hear this news over the phone. Particularly for Nell."

I knew what my wife was thinking. "Honey, you can handle dinner," I said. "I'll drive up to the spa and talk to Eileen and Nell."

Without hesitating, Burton spoke. "I'd be so grateful if you would, Marshall." He signed, took a deep drink and brought the Scotch bottle closer.

I asked for the name and location. Ann got her purse and handed me a brochure that Eileen had given her. I punched the address into my cell. The drive would take about forty-five minutes. I had trouble believing that Eileen hadn't already known about the cottage and its hidden agenda. Didn't sisters tell each other everything?

But how the hell was I going to tell them that Frank had been murdered?

Chapter 10

On the way to the spa, I called Burton. "I think this is worth mentioning. It's about my last conversation with Frank yesterday. Someone was in his office and they were arguing, but the other voice was muffled. Frank must have covered the receiver when he yelled at whoever it was. I didn't say anything in front of the cops today. They weren't there to ask me questions."

I heard Burton breathing on the other end. "Frank's a shouter and he's been under a lot of pressure lately. It's probably nothing, but thank-you, Marshall."

Case dismissed. He knew Frank better than I did. I asked him to put Ann on the phone. She assured me that her father was staying until I returned from the spa. She was the only person I really cared about.

As I drove, I thought about the last few days. First, the murder of Allan Wright, convicted more than once for DUI years before he went to prison for killing my family. After researching criminal profiles, I'd learned he was also a suspected drug dealer, but that wasn't proven and no associates were named. A corresponding bleeding-heart article suggested he'd found Jesus in prison—apparently his wife's influence.

I grinned to myself. Maybe Jesus realized what an asshole he was and struck him down. I had to talk to Wright's wife. Maybe she'd tell me who his visitors were when he was in the can. That could be a starting point.

I'd forgotten to check my messages when I left home and pulled over. Journalist's number one rule, stay current. Only two caught my attention—Earl had answered my text. He told me Celine Wright lived in the Ontario Housing Complex off Third Line in Lakeville.

I thanked him. Every journalist in the country knew about my affiliation with Allan Wright, and for sure Earl had read the articles in the *Tribune*. Now I owed him a favour.

The second was confirmation that my Certified Plate Search had been received. I'd paid eighteen dollars to have the plate on the black Toyota checked out. Turn-around time was fifteen days. Slow as hell, but proving the plates were stolen, and when they were stolen, might be my only way of getting the cops to pick Anderson up.

I was sure someone was helping Anderson. I was convinced there was a bigger picture.

My mind flipped back to the newspaper picture outside the court after Allan Wright's conviction. Burton, in his capacity as judge could access juvenile records. The guy I recognized, Gilardi, had been supporting Wright. Maybe that association still existed.

Events were coming into focus. I just had to figure out the order of business. Frank had suggested that Burton could be a big help. I decided to honour that advice.

Canada's Wonderland came into view. I was getting close to my turn off. The huge rollercoaster, Yukon Striker, my favourite ride, was closed for the winter along with all the other attractions. I pictured taking my daughter there when she was big enough. The line-ups would be no problem for us. People who used wheelchairs never had to wait, and sometimes got to ride twice at no extra charge.

Ten minutes later, I pulled into the New Life Spa and Wellness Centre. The parking lot was jammed, probably because two large banners bookending the entrance proclaimed the grand opening. On a Wednesday. I was out of touch with the spa crowd.

The only place I could find to park was in a no-parking area. There were no designated handicapped spots. I slapped my sticker on the dashboard, assembled the chair and headed to the entrance of a weathered log-cabin-style building. No ramp, just stairs. The place looked old and probably had been ignored as far as the new accessibility regulations were concerned. At least there were railings along the short staircase.

I grabbed my canes and started to climb the stairs, then thought better of it. All I needed was someone walking off with my wheels. What the hell would people do who didn't use canes—get bumped up the stairs backwards by their companion, presuming they had one? A small person like Ann could never manage.

After a trip back to the car to take the chair apart, stow it, and listen to some moron who chewed me out for parking where I did, I was in no mood to dish out sympathy to my mother-in-law and her sister.

I climbed the stairs that led to the front door and the huge porch which spanned the length of the building. Nearly out of sight, at the end, I noticed a ramp leading down the side of the building. What the hell? Why was it all the way down there?

I yanked open the massive wooden door and entered a large reception room. The place smelled fresh and clean, like our bathroom after my wife took a shower. To the left, through open double doors, a large restaurant and bar was filled with people holding wine glasses. Eileen and Nell stood behind a podium facing the crowd. Eileen, mic in hand, was speaking. I walked closer, but didn't enter the bar.

"We thank you again, ladies and gentlemen for attending the grand opening of our New Life Spa." Eileen loved socializing, holding the floor and being the centre of attention. Today her welcoming words sounded flat, her smile plastic, and there was something else amiss I couldn't put my finger on. She passed the mic over to Nell. "My partner would like to say a few words."

Her partner? They really were the owners. I wondered what Burton thought about that. I watched as Nell began her message of thanks. Her face, usually full of dimple-cheeked grins was serious and drawn, her eyes puffy. The chubby hand holding the mic shook. She wore a dark skirt and jacket minus the usual red scarf or colourful adornment that enhanced her panache. No flashy jewellery, black shoes instead of her usual killer heels, often shiny red.

Eileen, the queen of match, always dressed in monotone, including her handbag and shoes. Today was no exception, except she didn't carry her snazzy outfit with energy. No saucy tilt of her head when she addressed the crowd, and she stared vacantly while Nell spoke. I realized the other element that was missing—their melodic Trinidadian voices sounded flat.

I knew that they knew. How did they find out?

After Nell delivered her few short sentences, Eileen took charge. "Enjoy the refreshments, ladies and gentlemen and have a good evening. Don't forget to book appointments while the opening specials are still available. Tours of the facility will start in ten minutes."

The mic squawked as she replaced it on the stand and flicked it off. As soon as Eileen and Nell stepped away from the podium, they were surrounded by people offering congratulations. From the bits of conversation I heard, many of the guests were from Toronto. This was a spa with a difference—overnight stays, all-organic dining room, and any kind of beauty and wellness service you could wish for. Maybe the booze was organic too.

Guests followed Eileen and Nell into the main entrance which was soon jammed. Everyone talked at once. I walked closer and caught Nell's eye. She nudged Eileen and whispered to her. After socializing with the crowd for a few moments, they walked my way. Nell threw her arms around my neck, nearly knocking me over. "Oh my God, Marshy. Thanks for coming to the opening."

"Hello, Marsh," said Eileen. "Let's go into the office."

She started across the room. Nell took my arm and we followed. Eileen stopped in front of what was probably the private office behind a long, smoked glass wall. She unlocked the door and we entered.

"I guess Burton sent you," said Eileen.

Wow. She just rolled up the welcome mat Nell had put down. I wondered if Burton would ever get around to revealing the full story about his relationship with Eileen and her family.

"Hello to you too, Eileen," I said. "Actually, I offered to come. Mind if I sit? It's been a long day."

Did she blush? I hung my canes on the back of a chair. Nell sat beside me. Eileen sat behind a desk at the end of the room. I turned to face Nell.

"You're welcome, Nell. Why didn't you tell us you were spa owners?"

Nell's eyes darted to Eileen.

"I'm sure Burton has told Ann we're separating," said Eileen. "This opportunity came up. I wanted to have a focus."

Burton had said they were divorcing. "He told us about an hour ago. But that's not the reason I'm here…"

Nell started to cry. "Oh, Marshy. You came to tell us about Frankie."

I nodded. "Your phone was off, Eileen. Burton was too upset to make the trip, but wanted to make sure you heard about Frank from one of the family."

"That's so thoughtful of you both, Marshy," said Nell, crying openly. "Burton was so good to Frankie and me…"

"Be careful what you say, Nell," said Eileen.

"Careful about what? That Burton bought the next-door cottage for Frank? Sorry Nell, but Burton told us about that property. Ann and I are the only ones he could talk to."

Eileen scowled, her lips tight.

"That's okay, Marshy." Nell covered her face with her hands and her shoulders shook. "Oh, my Frankie…his bitch of a wife killed him."

Eileen put both hands flat on the desk. "Nell! You don't know that. Frank was…"

"Frank was what, Eileen? You don't have to tell me, but if you know something I'd advise you to speak to the police. They've already interviewed Burton. This *is* a murder investigation."

Eileen extended her hands toward me, as if suddenly asking for compassion. "We're so upset over…Frank's death. It's devastating, and what with the opening of our spa and all."

Why the sudden change in attitude? Did she have something to hide? Nell sat sobbing into her hands.

"Ladies, it's been a terrible shock to everyone. I've been rude. Sorry."

"That's okay, we're all upset, Marshy." Nell shook her head, "I couldn't believe it when Gayle called me this morning."

"Was she the one who found him?"

Nell nodded. "What a terrible thing to see. She's not young you know, been his secretary since he started practice. The shock might've killed her."

"Did she tell you anything else?"

Before Nell had a chance to answer, Eileen spoke. "Nell, it's probably best if you don't say anything more. We'll have to talk to the police at some point."

Nell looked at Eileen, then back to me. "But maybe Marshy can help. You won't write about it, will you?"

"This is family stuff. You have my word. Ann is devastated, too. She thought of Frank as her uncle."

Eileen crossed her arms. "You wrote about the fire, Marsh."

So that's what she was pissed off about. "I didn't know Burton owned that property. Like Ann said, I was doing my job." But I would have written about it anyway.

I handed Nell some tissues and she blew her nose. "Frankie and I were close, you know. He was very unhappy with his wife."

Eileen gave her sister a warning look.

"That was obvious to me at the dinner party on Monday night," I said.

"Is Ann okay?" said Eileen.

Did she mean to change the subject, or did it suddenly occur to her that she should ask how her pregnant daughter was?

"She's very upset, of course. Burton is staying with her until I get back."

"I'm glad she didn't come with you. Let's hope she can hold onto this baby. I had a terrible pregnancy when I was carrying her, and was glad when it was over."

Nell smiled through her tears. "We're all so happy to have our beautiful Anny. And, Marshy, congratulations," said Nell with a smile.

Eileen managed a smile too.

Nell sighed and shook her head. "Frankie loved Anny as much as he loved his own kids. This will be terrible for them."

I'd never ask Nell about her relationship with Frank, and couldn't imagine she had anything to do with his death. She was obviously in love with him and claimed that *his bitch of a wife* was responsible. I remembered Frank joking with me yesterday that Allan Wright's wife probably killed him. Police would look at Jeanette Veale for sure.

"Did Gayle call to tell you Frank had…died?" I said.

Nell nodded. "He was working on something for me. I had an appointment with him tomorrow morning. I guess she was informing all his clients."

That sounded lame. But maybe Frank had helped with the spa purchase even though he wasn't a real estate lawyer. Why didn't Gayle call *me*? I'm one of his clients too. But my name probably wasn't in his appointment book.

I decided to try again. "Just so you know, Nell, Burton and I have agreed to look into who did this…did Gayle tell you anything else?"

Nell nodded and took a deep breath. "She went into his office, saw him lying on the floor and said there was lots of blood. She knew he was…gone, and called 911."

"I spoke to Frank late yesterday," I said. "There was someone in his office who sounded angry. Maybe Gayle would know who that was."

Nell shook her head. "Gayle told me she was off work yesterday. Dental appointment. It could have been anybody. My Frankie was very good about mentoring junior lawyers you know. And he always had a waiting-room full of clients."

"You're asking a lot of questions, Marsh," said Eileen.

I nodded. "Like I just said, Eileen, Burton and I agreed to get to the bottom of this."

She looked at me for a moment, then stood. "Nell and I will be back in Lakeville tomorrow morning. I'll walk you to your car."

I'd been dismissed. I didn't blame her for trying to protect her sister who needed guidance right now. Although Nell was the eldest, Eileen was more cunning and seemed to control the relationship. I wondered how long it would take the police to find out about Frank's affair. They'd speak to Nell just like they'd spoken to Burton.

Nell stood up to hug and kiss me goodbye. "Oh, Marshy, I know you and Burton will find out who did this."

Eileen escorted me out of the office into the reception room. People were still wandering around, drinking the free wine and eating the free goodies. Eileen smiled and nodded to everyone. We left the building and she watched me walk down the front steps.

Eileen pointed. "There's a ramp over there, you know."

"Yes, I saw it after I'd taken my chair back to the car. I'm not sure it's legal having it so far from the front entrance. You could have made the space for the stairs much wider; the ramp could have run alongside."

"A ramp won't get much use. We wanted it out of the way."

Meaning that people with disabilities didn't visit spas, or that spas were only for able-bodied people? I couldn't find the words to say goodbye, descended the stairs and walked to my car. When I drove past, she was standing at the door, staring into the distance, talking on her cell.

Chapter 11

I sped from the parking lot, spraying dirt and gravel in my rush to leave the whole scene behind. Why couldn't Eileen at least have called Ann after she found out about Frank? Then I decided she probably didn't want to give her daughter that kind of news over the phone. The same reason I drove to the spa to tell Eileen and Nell. I was glad to have a forty-five-minute drive to calm down.

Finding out who killed Frank would be a priority. As for my investigation into Allan Wright, I'd be on my own figuring out who offed him and why. Then there was Steven Anderson, chugging along like the dirty caboose at the end of a long train.

I decided to wait a while before phoning home, hoping Eileen would do the right thing and call Ann. I knew she'd tell me right away. For once, my instinct was right. Ann called about ten minutes later, just as I was pulling onto the 400 Southbound. "Hey honey, I'm on my way home."

"Mom called and told me you'd just left." Ann's voice was flat.

"You okay?"

"Just tired."

"Is your dad still there?"

"Yes."

"Is there something you're not telling me?" Christ, all we needed now was to lose the baby.

I could hardly hear her. "I'm okay. Just so upset."

"I'll be home soon. Maybe take a few days off work and get some rest?"

"I've already called in and booked off until Monday."

"Smart move. I'll go in tomorrow and tell Don the same thing. Can I pick anything up?"

"I guess that means you're hungry." I knew she was smiling. "We're just going to order Chinese. You want Peking duck?"

"Whatever you want," I said. "Can't wait to get my arms around you."

We said *I love you*, and hung up.

Every damn thing had piled up on us. I had to grip the wheel and force myself to pay attention to the road. Somehow, this jumbled heap would get sorted out, but protecting Ann and the baby came before anything else.

The phone rang again a few moments later and scared the shit out of me. It was my boss. At seven o'clock at night. The guy never stops working. "Hey, Don."

"Marsh. Guess you've had a busy day."

"Yup, it's been a long one. What's up?"

"Frank Veale, Judge Young's former law partner." His tone said *Why the fuck do you think I'm calling*? "What d'you know about the murder?"

"Only that Frank's dead. Cops have spoken to my father-in-law."

"Were you in on that interview? What was your take?"

I heard Don take a drag on a cigarette. I thought about telling him I wasn't there, but he'd know it was a lie. "Tough one. Conflict of interest."

"You didn't have any trouble writing about the fire on Lakewood Drive last night."

"A story about a fire is a bit different than the murder of a close friend, Don."

"Even though the fire was on property owned by Judge Young, who just happens to be the former partner of the dead guy?"

Christ, he was a ball-breaker. "You can believe this or not, but last night I didn't know who owned that property." And with that stupid statement, I'd just given him ideas. I knew how his journalist's mind worked.

"Interesting. I'll see you in the office tomorrow, Keene. See if you can come up with something useful." He hung up.

First, he wanted me to work from home; now, he wants to make sure I'm coming to the office.

I drove past farmlands, frozen and serene this time of year. The seasonal repetition of a farmer's life would get to me, but right now I could use a little routine. The next few days would be filled with people pumping me for information, hiding information, or lying when I asked for information. The cops held their cards close in murder cases, and I hoped His Honour Judge Young would get some privileged intel.

Collaborating with Don wasn't an option unless I agreed to write the story of Frank's murder, even though he'd probably dig up a lot of the stuff I wanted to know. I could have told him over the phone that I'd decided to work from home, but I preferred facing him. And I wanted to talk to Munro in person. He'd know everything Don knew and wouldn't suffer any backlash from writing the facts. Yesterday Munro had promised to help, and I hoped he'd share everything that had come in.

Even though Burton and I had agreed to work together, I couldn't count on him one hundred percent. His personal issues would weigh him down, and like his wife, he might not trust me. I wondered why Eileen had been insistent that Nell not say too much this afternoon. What were they hiding? On the way up to the spa when I was thinking things over, I'd had a brilliant idea. I'm sure it was about Eileen and Steven Anderson, but I was damned if I could remember. When I pulled into our driveway thirty minutes later, my brain was still numb. I was starving and dying for a beer.

The take-out arrived as I was setting up my chair. I paid the guy, set the bag on my lap and wheeled up the ramp. The food was burning my legs by the time I got into the house.

Ann and Burton came into the front hall when they heard the front door open. He took the bag to the kitchen, and Ann sat on my lap and wrapped her arms around me.

"That was a long four hours," she said. "I'm sorry you went all that way for nothing. I wish Mom had called sooner."

I held Ann close and kissed her neck, cheeks and forehead. "The trip was actually worthwhile. We can talk about that later."

Her body felt tense. She seemed more stressed than when I left a few hours ago. "This will all get sorted out, honey." Lame remark, Keene.

She gave me a weak smile and grabbed the right wheel. I grabbed the left, and together we rolled up the hall into the kitchen.

We all seemed buried in our own thoughts as we moved around setting the table and organizing the food. Everyone helped themselves and sat down to eat. I broke the silence by asking for drink preferences. Ann was happy with water. It surprised me when Burton said he'd have a beer.

"Bottle or glass?" I said.

"Bottle will be fine." When I handed it to him, he looked at the label. "Is this one of those craft beers?"

"Yup. Brewed right here in town. Hope you like it."

He twisted off the top and took a sip. "Very nice."

"I didn't think you ever drank beer, Burton."

He smiled. "Used to drink a lot of it in university—the only thing I could afford." He took another sip. "And I must say this is a big improvement over the stuff we had then." For a few moments he concentrated on his food before putting his cutlery down. "Thank you for going to that spa this afternoon, Marshall."

"No problem."

He sat looking at us as though he wanted to say more. Finally, he spoke. "I know this isn't the best time to talk about what happened to Frank, but as soon as we've eaten, I need to get home and take care of a few things."

I'd nearly finished my first helping. Ann had just pushed hers around the plate.

"That's okay, Dad. Marsh needs to know the details."

The food in my mouth wouldn't go down. What details?

"Frank was stabbed."

I swallowed the half-chewed chicken ball. "Christ. Who told you, Burton?"

"A reliable source. It appears that Frank had returned to the office to get some work done and surprised someone who was ransacking the place."

"What the hell for?" I said.

"I can't understand why anyone would stab him," said Ann.

"I guess you don't know if he put up a fight or what the murder weapon was?" I said.

Burton shook his head. "They think it might have been the letter opener he had on his desk although it was clean. When Gayle, the office admin, found him the next morning, there was no sign of a break-in."

"Letter opener? Sounds spur-of-the-moment to me. Someone wanted something pretty important. I can't imagine Frank would keep money around. I wonder how many people had keys?" I said.

Burton answered immediately. "Gayle, Lund, the cleaners and the management company all had keys. The wall safe was open and papers were strewn all over the place."

I thought for a few moments, then mentioned my last conversation with Frank again. "He ended our call suddenly. Nell said Gayle was off work yesterday. Maybe Gary Lund was there and heard the conversation."

Burton shrugged. "Good point. I need to call him anyway. Find out what he plans to do about Steven Anderson. But to get back to Gayle, why would she call Nell?"

"I asked that question too. Apparently, she had an appointment with Frank tomorrow and Gayle was calling to cancel."

Burton's eyebrows went up. "Really?"

"Yeah, I didn't believe it either. When you talk to Lund, you could ask who was on Frank's appointment list for the day, although maybe Nell's name wouldn't be on it. Be good to know who his current clients are, too." Lund could be a good source of information, but the cops would see him as a suspect, along with Gayle and anyone else close to Frank, and they'd be cautioned about talking about the case.

I looked at my wife. "As soon as I got to the spa, Eileen tried to keep Nell from talking."

Ann didn't hesitate to cover for her mother. "I guess Mom didn't realize Dad had told us about the affair."

I nodded. "You're probably right about that, honey." I wondered again if Burton knew his soon-to-be ex-wife and her sister owned the spa. It wasn't up to me to pass that on.

"Women stick together," said Ann. "I think Gayle called Nell to tell her that Frank…had died. I bet she knew about the affair and didn't want Nell to find out the hard way."

Burton and I looked at each other. "Really?" he said.

"Yes, really." said Ann. "Secretaries know these things."

I still thought Eileen and her sister were hiding something, and I intended to find out what.

"It seems to me Gayle is the person you should be talking to," said Ann.

"I agree." Burton rubbed his chin. "There's so much to think about."

"I'm wondering if Frank's death had anything to do with the fire," I said.

Burton nodded. "That's been going through my head too. Both events happened in the same night. Maybe even around the same time."

“I think we should take a look at that boathouse of yours, or have the cops already been there?”

“No. Good point, Marshall.”

“Have you spoken to Jeanette, Dad? I think you should visit her and offer your condolences personally.”

He gave a faint smile. “You’re both on point here. I’ve been thinking about her too. I have to say something to the woman.” He stood and gathered our empty plates and took them to the sink. “Gotta be on my way, kids. Let’s sleep on all this and we’ll talk again tomorrow. We’re a good team. Frank would be honoured.”

By the time we’d said goodbye to Burton, tidied the kitchen and locked the house, it was past ten o’clock. Ann and I headed to the bedroom.

“I know I promised to help you get undressed tonight darling, but I’m too tired,” she said.

I watched her undress and slip a nightie over her head, our growing baby adding to her beauty. The filmy thing was just transparent enough to tease me.

“That’s okay, honey. I’ll take a rain check.” Even though I was worn-out, I could have found the energy if she’d been game.

**

When I rolled over the next morning, the clock said four minutes past eight. Ann was still beside me. We’d slept a solid seven hours. I snapped on my prostheses and headed into the kitchen to turn on the coffee machine. First things first.

Ten minutes later, I sat in front of my computer, mug in hand, reading today’s *Tribune* online. Frank’s murder took up one section of the front page. The article summarized what Burton had already told us and focused on the dangers of being a criminal defense lawyer. I supposed we were meant to conclude that one of his unhappy clients had committed the crime. That pissed me off. Although it was an angle that shouldn’t be ignored, they were telling readers what to think. Just like their article yesterday inferring I could have killed Allan Wright because I’d threatened him years ago. Would I get a response from my complaint? Unlikely. Today’s story concluded by saying Frank left a grieving wife and two grown children.

I shut off the computer and headed for the shower. When I was dressing in our bedroom, Ann opened her eyes and yawned. "You going in to work?"

"Yup."

"I thought you were going to take some time off."

"I am, but I need to talk to Don first." I sat on the edge of the bed and leaned over to kiss her goodbye.

"Mmm, you smell so nice." She pulled me close and started to unbutton my shirt. Before I knew it, the shirt was on the floor and I was lying on the bed.

"Ow!" she said. "Every time you lie beside me with your legs on, you kick me."

I pulled her closer and kissed her neck. "Sorry, hon, getting into bed with you makes me forget everything else."

"Oh?"...She giggled... "And?"

I didn't respond right away.

"Well, wheel master, are you all yack and no shack?"

I held her face in my hands. "Actually, sweetheart, I'm afraid of hurting the baby."

"It's perfectly okay for people to have sex during pregnancy, but I know what you mean." She lay quietly for a few moments. "But that doesn't mean we can't have some fun." Her hand found me. "And you can't go to work like this, big boy."

I removed my prostheses and everything else that would get in the way. Then I lifted Ann's nightie over her head.

**

Twenty minutes later, we had a quick shower together. I retrieved my shirt from the floor and got dressed again. Ann got back into bed and I brought her a cup of tea.

"Great start to the day." She smiled when I kissed her good-bye. "I should be home soon, maybe in time for lunch. Then I'd like to go over to your dad's and take a look inside that boathouse."

"The boathouse? Oh, for clues about the fire." She smiled, straightening the duvet. "I may still be here when you get home."

"Well, I hope so, honey," I said. "Where would you go?"

She laughed and waved goodbye.

Neither of us had said anything about Frank. We had a lot to consider—the fire, Steven Anderson, and now, who killed Frank, and I had to prove I didn't kill Allan Wright. I was glad we'd shared some private moments together.

I locked the door behind me and headed down the ramp. After stashing the chair in the back of my car, I looked up and down the street. No black Toyota. But that didn't mean Anderson wouldn't be back, or wouldn't use a different car to stalk us. From Ann's description, he was a control freak and hated that she'd moved on. Just thinking about him made me realize how powerless I was. Jerks like Anderson don't give up.

On Monday night, when I'd returned to the house to get Ann's phone, Burton had told me to look after her. He knew damn well Anderson was back in town. It pissed me off all over again that he and Eileen hadn't said anything. They might not have known he'd caused her first miscarriage, but they sure as hell knew how dangerous he was.

I thought about turning around and sending Don a text, telling him I'd decided to take him up on his offer and work from home. Instead, I sped through the streets, anxious get my business over quickly and get back home.

My wife's parting words shook me. *"I may still be here when you get home."* I knew she'd meant she might still be in bed, and I also knew she was joking. She couldn't stay still for long and would be up getting something to eat, making sure her dad was okay, or doing things around our house.

And she'd be the first one to tell me I worried about stuff before it ever happened. I took a deep breath and pulled into *The Halton Register* parking lot.

Chapter 12

When I wheeled past Don's office, he and Munro were inside having a confab. Don waved me in. Munro dragged a chair out of the way and I pulled up beside him.

"We're just swapping information on the Veale murder," said Don. "What have you come up with?"

"Only what's in today's *Tribune*," I said.

He slid his reading glasses down on his nose, "Are you onboard, Keene?"

I looked at him before answering. "I can't work this story, Don. Besides being a conflict of interest, Frank's death has been a terrible blow to my family. But I'd like to know what you've heard."

Don didn't comment. He swivelled, his back to us.

"I'll take you up on your offer to work at home for a while, Don."

"When did I make that offer, Keene?" he said to the wall.

I looked at Munro, who raised his eyebrows. "Monday."

I felt like adding: *When you took me off the Allan Wright murder, claiming you wanted an impartial viewpoint.* Don had a sharp memory. I knew he recalled that conversation and what he'd implied.

"I need time, Don. Frank was a close family friend."

He turned to face us. "Take a long weekend, Keene. I want that Fentanyl article Tuesday morning. Then you can work on the pop-up needle sites story."

"Thanks."

He didn't say anything more. I was dismissed.

I nodded to Munro, left the inner sanctum and went to my desk, wondering what, if any, new information they had on Frank's murder. I checked my emails, stalling for time, waiting for Munro to finish with Don. I called Frank's law office and left a message for Gary Lund. "This is Marshall Keene. I'm...was, a client of Mr. Veale's. Can you please get back to me on an urgent matter?" I left my contact info, hung up and wondered if Burton had asked Lund to keep on looking for Anderson.

Five minutes passed before Munro returned to his desk. Seconds later, a text from him dinged into my phone. *Meet you outside.* Munro probably wanted to discuss things he didn't want others to hear, or speculate about. I stuffed a few things into my work bag and wheeled down the aisle past Don's office. He was on his phone.

Outside, the asphalt was slippery. My wheels slid and skidded as I made my way to the car. I hate ice and thought about inventing winter tires with studs for wheelchairs.

I transferred to the driver's seat and set my stopwatch. Might as well try to beat my record time dismantling the wheelchair. But I couldn't concentrate and dropped one wheel. It rolled toward Munro who was approaching, his eyes on his cell. Just in time, he looked up and instinctively covered himself. Then at the last second, did a neat side-step and grabbed the wheel as it rolled by. I nearly fell out of the car laughing.

"Glad you're finding this funny, Keene. I still have a life, you know." But Munro was smiling. He handed me the wheel then walked around and opened the passenger door. "You sure it's safe to sit in this old crap can?"

"Nothing's safe around me." I meant to be funny but realized it was the truth. I finished folding the chair and stashed it behind me.

"Yeah, your family is having trouble dodging the bullets. You deserve a few days off."

"Did Don say anything after I left his office?"

Munro nodded. "I think you may have hit a sympathy bone. Didn't know he had one."

"So, what did he say?"

Munro started playing with the seat controls. "It's amazing that these still work."

"For Christ's sake!"

He looked up and grinned. "Don would never want to appear soft or sympathetic, right?"

"Right."

"After you left, he spoke to the wall again. He said I could pass on any developments in the Veale case. He didn't say to whom, mind you. Maybe he meant the office cleaners."

I laughed. "He's a strange cat. So, is there anything new?"

Munro shook his head. "Standard stuff so far. They're looking into Veale's gambling, going to question the wife. I heard she was his fourth. That true?"

"Third…I don't like the woman, and from what I saw the last couple of times we were together, I don't think Frank did either. Now he's dead."

"A killer wife would be too obvious…but worth thinking about. Considering he's a criminal lawyer, there's lots of possibilities. Maybe one of his unhappy clients paid him a visit."

"Yeah. We've all thought about that angle. Looks to me as though the murder was a spur-of-the-moment thing." I thought about mentioning a possible connection to the fire, but didn't want to reveal the reason Burton bought the property.

Munro nodded. "Yeah, we heard he was stabbed with a letter opener. I guess you already know that."

I nodded.

"Sounds like the killer grabbed the first thing that would do the job," said Munro. "Veale was a prominent lawyer. The cops won't share much, but Don's network might come through." Munro got out of the car, then leaned back in. "I'll keep you in the loop."

He shut the door and walked toward the building, whistling the same tune as always, one I could never identify. Munro had been married for over twenty-five years. His kids had grown up and were on their own. From our conversations since I'd worked at the *Register*, I knew he was content—proof that a dedicated newspaperman could have a good life. I thought about my wife and our baby, fastened my seat belt and headed home. Glad we'd have a few days together.

Moments later, I opened the front door. "Hi honey."

No answer. Heart pounding, I started down the hall. Ann came out of the kitchen and walked toward me, phone to her ear. She ended the call and kissed my cheek.

"Had to weigh in on an issue at work," she said. "What did Don have to say? You look worried."

"It's all good. I'm off till Tuesday."

"Great!" She looked me in the eye. "But something's bothering you. What's going on?"

I felt stupid talking about this now. "I hated leaving you this morning."

"That's so nice, honey…why?"

She knew me well. "Frank's murder will get sorted out. But Anderson's behaviour scares me. I can't get him off my mind." I didn't mention Allan Wright, my third albatross.

She nodded. "He *is* scary. But I don't think it's about me now. Money was always the most important thing to him. I spoke to Dad today, he said he'd get Gary Lund to handle it."

I didn't comment.

"You're not convinced," she said. "I know Steven got off easily when we split up, but now he knows Dad means business."

"We still have to be careful." Ann didn't want to think about how relentless her psycho ex could be. Burton had promised to take care of the situation, *again*, and that's all Ann needed. But she was right about one thing—Anderson wanted money. I wished Gary Lund would call me back. If I heard something solid from him, I'd feel more comfortable.

"You still want to go over to Dad's? He'd love to see us."

**

Burton was standing on his porch smoking when we stopped in front of the house and got out of the car. The air was stale, and the flattened cottage looked like oversized lumps of charcoal. How long it would be before the neighbourhood smelled fresh again.

Burton had said there was no odour inside the house, but being a smoker, his sniffer probably wasn't working right. He smiled, dropped his cigarette and stepped on it. I counted three butts on the ground, so maybe he'd been out there for a while. He shook hands with me and hugged Ann.

"I have a message from the Fire Marshal's office." He pulled out his phone. "The cause of the fire is still undetermined. They're considering faulty wiring or a creosote explosion. They'll be conducting a more thorough investigation."

"So they don't know, Dad."

Burton nodded. "Right. And now there'll be more people crawling over my property."

"What about arson?" said Ann.

"Or drugs," I said, remembering the firefighter shouting about a possible chemical explosion.

"Let's hope it wasn't drugs," said Ann.

"The place was empty. Anything could have been going on," I said.

"The police and the fire department have to rule everything out," said Burton. "I would have thought a drug lab would have been obvious. Faulty wiring gets my vote. And the Fire Marshall's Office hasn't told me what they're looking for."

I was about to ask Burton about his gardener when Ann asked another question. "Have you heard from Mom?"

"She and Nell are coming back from the spa today. The police got in touch and want to talk to her."

"You mean, Nell?" said Ann.

He nodded.

"Do you think the cops know about the affair?" said Ann.

"Mom didn't say, Sweet. But it won't take them long to find out."

"Do you think Nell would tell them about that?" said Ann.

"She'd be smart to because Jeanette sure will, and it'll make Nell look bad," I said. "The woman wronged and all that sh…stuff. For sure the cops have spoken to her at least once by now." I pointed to the ruin next door. "I wonder if she found out about their plans and burned the place down."

"Five seconds ago, you were talking about a drug fire. Now you think Jeanette might be an arsonist?" said Ann.

"Got to consider every angle," I said.

"Unlikely on both counts, kids," said Burton. "The gardener would have reported any unusual behaviour to me. He worked here long before I owned the property. Remember I told you the deal with Frank was verbal? No paperwork had his name on it. I phoned Jeanette this morning to express my condolences and offered to visit. She couldn't get off the phone fast enough, but managed to thank me for calling."

I imagined the conversation between cultured Burton and coarse Jeanette. I bet he was relieved to avoid the duty visit. Mrs. Veale the third could easily have known Frank's plans with Nell. Was she pissed enough to burn the place down, and then go to his office and kill him?

"Jeanette didn't like any of us," I said. "That was more obvious than ever at your place last Monday. The cops will take a real close look at her."

"I hope so," said Ann. "I never understood what Frank saw in her."

"Had to be her body. She's really built."

Ann rolled her eyes. Did Burton smirk?

"About that agreement you had with Frank," I said. "Maybe he wanted to hide things from more than just Jeanette."

"Like who?" said Ann.

I shrugged. "Tax department, creditors, who knows?"

Burton didn't comment, and changed the subject. "You wanted to look at the boathouse, Marshall?"

"Sure, for what it's worth." I unhooked my canes; the terrain being too unpredictable for the chair. We followed Burton across the property line and started toward the lake.

"What's the gardener's name?" I said.

"Douglas Lancaster."

"He kept an eye on the cottage for you too?"

Burton nodded. "I hired him to look after everything. I didn't want to be bothered with day-to-day stuff like that."

"Does he know about the fire?"

"I sent an email telling him not to bother coming around until further notice," said Burton. "The whole place will have to be bulldozed."

"Including the boathouse?" I said.

"No, that can stay. I own the boat and motor. The gardening tools and other stuff in there belong to Lancaster. He'll probably want to come and pick them up, so I'll wait a few days before changing the padlock."

"Did Lancaster use the boat?"

Burton nodded. "He took it out occasionally to go fishing."

Since there was little snow so far this winter, the path from the fallen cottage to the boathouse was visible. A few piles of soggy garden debris lay on the property line between Burton's house and the cottage.

"Guess he wasn't as efficient as he could have been," said Burton. "This stuff is left over from last fall."

Burton produced a set of keys and unlocked the boathouse—it was exactly how he'd described it—old tin boat in the slip, equally old motor attached to it, banged-up oars inside, along with a red gas tank. Ordinary tools lay amongst the seasonal gardening stuff.

"Looks like the gardener also used this place to store tools. Was he a handyman too?"

Burton shrugged. "No idea."

Ann looked around. "I haven't been here in years," she smiled. "Time to confess, Dad…I used to come here with my friends and smoke pot."

Burton's expression was serious, but his eyes smiled. "What makes you think I didn't know?"

Her eyes opened wide. "You never said anything!"

"No point. I knew where you were and who you were with. You've forgotten the lecture I gave you about driving after drinking alcohol or smoking pot."

"No, I haven't, Dad."

They left the boathouse, arms around each other. Burton hung the padlock in place, snapped it shut and we started back to the house. The ground was slick from the dousing it received two days before and my feet slid. I reached out with my left cane, and instead of gaining purchase, it sank into a pile of garden clippings. I lost my balance and toppled over into the decaying heap.

"Shit!"

Burton and Ann turned, came back and grabbed me under the arms. "Smells like it too," she said as they hauled me to my feet. They both knew better than to ask if I was okay, knowing how much I hated a fuss when something like this happened.

"Thanks," I said.

Ann picked up my canes and handed them to me.

I looked down to make sure there was no ice underneath me. "What's this?"

Something that looked like a wallet lay in the pile of leaves and clippings I'd disturbed. I bent over and picked it up. It had been there awhile; the leather was soiled and half-frozen. "Christ! It's full of money."

Ann and Burton moved closer to get a better look. I hauled ten soggy one hundred dollar bills out of the wallet. "Wow! Wonder how long it's been here?" I handed the money to Burton. "There's something else here." I removed a piece of paper and unfolded it. "Looks like a receipt."

Ann and Burton leaned in. *Grant's Storage*, we said in unison.

"There's no name on it, though, just something that might be a customer number," I said. "It's dated October last year."

"Anything else in there?" said Ann.

I spread the billfold open. "Nope."

"Odd," said Burton. "I don't like this."

I stood looking at the receipt. "Maybe it belongs to the gardener. I wonder where the money came from?"

"Or what it was for," said Burton. He handed the money back to me. I put it and the receipt in my jacket pocket along with the wallet. We all got sticks and poked around the piles of leaves. All we found was a dirty, wet garden glove.

"I think I'll go over to Grant's and check it out."

"They won't tell you anything," said Burton. "Customer confidentiality."

What the hell, it was worth a try. Nothing else was lighting up my screen.

**

Ann was happy to stay with her father while I went over to the storage joint. She probably didn't want to watch me make a fool of myself. Ten minutes later, I parked in Grant's lot. A sign saying, *Auction Today,* covered the front office window. I undid my seat belt and sat in the car, thinking.

I retrieved my canes from the back seat, got out of the car and walked into the office. A crowd had gathered inside, making it difficult to reach the counter. A fifty-something man, wearing a shirt with *Grant's Storage* embroidered on the pocket, shouted from behind the counter: "The contents of Unit 207 will be opened for viewing in five minutes. Please proceed to unit 207. I'll be right with you."

People started moving to the door. I trudged up to the clerk, receipt in hand, my feet dragging with each step. His eyes focused on me for a second, then he sighed and glanced at his watch. "Can I help you, sir?"

I handed him the receipt. "Can you please check and see if I've paid my bill this month."

He looked at me as though I was a sore on his ass. "You can check your status online, sir."

"Don't have a computer."

He blew air out between his lips. "I need two pieces of identification." He held out his hand.

I leaned the canes against the counter, searched my pants pockets thoroughly, and repeated the process. The shirt pockets came next. "Dang it all, I must have left my wallet in the car. I'll just be a sec."

I dropped one of the canes, and after several tries, managed to pick it up. He frowned and looked at the watch again. I turned and started toward the door, dragging my right leg.

"Hold on, sir," he said and shouted to someone in the back. "Glen, take over the counter. I have to start the auction." He turned back to me, "Someone will be right with you." He rushed out to join his customers at Unit 207.

Glen emerged from a door behind the counter. The red peach fuzz on his cheeks and the latest mushroom haircut told me he must have been all of seventeen. "How can I assist you, sir?"

I turned and took two slow steps back the counter, dragging my feet. I handed him the receipt. "Your colleague was going to give me a printout of my account."

Glen took the receipt and started punching in the number code. "Hmmm, unit 109…Mr. Lancaster?"

"Yup."

"This account is paid up for six months." The printer hummed and two pages landed in the tray. He handed me the receipt and the two printed sheets.

"Thanks," I said. My exit was slow and deliberate. No sense in ruining my image. I needn't have bothered—when I glanced back, Glen was texting.

I got into the car and took a close look at the printouts. The account was in the name of Gregory Lancaster. Burton had said his gardener's name was Douglas Lancaster. Who the hell was Gregory? A brother? A son?

Chapter 13

My wife and her father listened to my adventure at Grant's Storage. Ann laughed. "You should have been an actor, Marsh. I'm glad I wasn't there—I would have blown the whole thing."

Burton looked at the printout. "Gregory Lancaster? Douglas is certainly old enough to have a son, but I've never seen anyone else here with him. Could be a brother, too, I guess." He handed the printout to Ann. "I think we should go and take another look inside that boathouse. Then I'll call the police to come and pick this up."

"Good idea." I handed the wallet and the money over to him. "They should have this too."

"What do you think is going on?" said Ann.

I shrugged. "Can't be sure, but this Lancaster guy is worth looking into. I looked at Burton. "How long has he been working for you?"

"Since I bought the property about a year ago. The cottage hasn't been lived in for years." He settled back in his chair. "Shortly after Eileen and I built this house, the couple who lived next door moved and the property went on the market. A developer bought it and he hired Lancaster to cut the grass. The developer wanted to knock down the cottage and build at least three houses. Long story short, the neighbours, including me, objected. It took years, he lost the fight and put the property on the market. As I've told you, Frank was interested, and had his reasons for not wanting another asset in his name. So, I bought it until he could pay me back. I figured if his plans didn't work out, I'd end up with a great piece of property."

"You didn't think Frank would end up with Nell?" I said.

Burton sighed. "I've known him since law school. Let's just say he's had many relationships. But I never dreamt he'd be murdered." He paused and shook his head. "To get back to Lancaster. He seemed to be doing a decent job. He comes to my door for cash each month. Other than that, I don't pay much attention to him. I have no idea where he lives."

"I've been researching for an article on illegal drugs in the GTA. Along with cross-border activity, there's a history of drug trafficking on this lake," I said. "This property is the perfect set-up."

"Really?" said Ann. "Why?"

I counted on my fingers. "One, a possible chemical explosion was suspected as the cause of the fire, and the Fire Marshal's Report is inconclusive. Two, the secluded lake access, and a boat and motor used exclusively by Lancaster, who's had the run of the place for years. And three, we found a wallet full of cash and the storage locker in the name of Gregory Lancaster."

"What do you think, Dad?"

"We certainly have to check it all out." Burton pushed himself away from the table and stood. "Let's go down to the boathouse before it's too dark. I'll bring a couple of flashlights. First, I want to get another padlock out of my office."

"I'll stay here and figure out something to eat. Do you think Mom and Nell will come for dinner?"

Before Burton left the room, he looked at his daughter and half-smiled. "I don't know, Sweet t'ing."

"I'll send a text," said Ann.

For once, I hoped Eileen and her sister would show up. Nell was so transparent. I'd love to see her reaction to a possible drug connection. Frank had always complained about a lack of money. Was he involved in anything illegal?

As soon as Burton returned with the flashlights and the padlock, we headed down to the boathouse. The temperature had dropped and the path to the lake was more slippery. My fake feet behaved this time and I got down to the boathouse without making a jackass of myself. Burton removed the old padlock and we stepped inside.

The place had the same damp, cold smell. There's nothing more inhospitable than a boathouse in winter. Burton turned on both flashlights and handed one to me. Shelves along one wall held bags of lawn fertilizer, weed killer and a few cans of bug spray, most likely left over from the last gardening season. The bags were unopened and the bug spray smelled like bug spray. The handyman tools and gardening stuff didn't look disturbed since this morning.

I shone my light on the boat. "Would you hear that motor from your house?"

"I was just thinking about that," said Burton, pointing his beam in the same place. "Probably not if I was in my office at the front. But I remember seeing the boat out on the lake last summer."

"Was Douglas Lancaster in it?"

"The guy had on an old red cap, grey hair sticking out. He always wore the same hat, so it could have been him. Sometimes he was alone, and a few times I saw someone else with him. The boat was always full of what looked like fishing gear."

I looked around. A couple of fishing rods were stashed in one corner. What looked like a tackle box, sat on the floor. I checked it out. Sure enough, it contained spare line, a reel and some lures and loose hooks, all well-used. I focused my attention on the boat again, knelt, stretched out one cane and hooked the red gas can. Burton knelt and grabbed it.

"Feels half full," he said, placing it beside him.

I shone my light inside the boat. "Take a look. There's damp mud on the bottom near the motor. The rest of the dirt is dry and there's no dust mark around the can. Looks like the boat's been used recently. Do you ever take it out, Burton?"

"Wouldn't dream of it. All this stuff came with the property. I haven't been in this boathouse for years."

"It would be easy for someone to use it this winter, and for other boats to dock here. There's no ice build-up around the shore."

Burton nodded. "Why the hell didn't we think of that this morning?"

"We're looking at things with different eyes now," I said.

My cell rang. I yanked it out of my pocket. "Marshall Keene," I said.

"Gary Lund calling. You said you were a client of Mr. Veale's. I didn't find your name in his appointment book, Mr. Keene."

"Frank's a friend of mine. He was doing me a favour. Can I call you back, please?"

"Whatever's convenient, Mr. Keene." Lund hung up. His tone told me he really didn't care if I called him back or not.

Burton had been training his flashlight around the boathouse. He flicked it off and turned to face me. "That was a call you probably needed to take. I'll go on ahead and help Ann with the dinner." If he had any idea who the caller was, he gave no indication.

"Thanks, Burton."

I took pictures of the boat and the surroundings before we left the boathouse. Burton put the new lock in place, then headed to the house. I followed him up the path until I was on his home property where the ground was more level. Just ahead of me, he entered the house through the back door.

I pulled out my phone and called Lund.

"Gary Lund."

"Mr. Lund, its Marshall Keene calling back. Thanks for taking my call."

"What can I do for you, Mr. Keene?"

"I was a client of Frank Veale's. He was helping me with a problem. But I'm calling about something else. Frank referred my father-in-law to you about my wife's ex-husband, Steven Anderson."

"Your name doesn't ring a bell, Mr. Keene."

"Like I said, Frank was a friend. He'd just started helping me before he died."

"Who is your father-in-law, Mr. Keene?"

"Judge Burton Young."

"Surely you understand lawyer/client confidentiality, Mr. Keene."

"Of course, I do, Mr. Lund. Please hear me out…"

He butted in before I could continue. "First I need to understand which issue you need help with, Mr. Keene."

"Frank and I had just gotten started. I called him Tuesday morning and he met me at the police station an hour later. He was killed that night." Christ that sounded good. I raced on before he had a chance to interrupt again. "I'll handle that issue on my own. It was just between Frank and me, anyway."

"And obviously, the police, Mr. Keene." This guy's imperious attitude was pissing me off. "So, you want to discuss the matter you claim Judge Young sought my advice on. I remind you, Mr. Keene, I cannot discuss another client's business."

"I don't expect you to, Mr. Lund. I'd just like you to please listen."

I took his silence as permission to carry on. "Let's suppose that Judge Young asked you to look into Steven Anderson, my wife's ex-husband. And let's suppose that Judge Young told you that Anderson had demanded money from him and my mother-in-law, Eileen. Judge Young could also have told you that although he refused to pay, Eileen gave Anderson money because he threatened to hurt my wife, Ann."

"Go on, Mr. Keene."

"Anderson followed me three days in a row, and on Tuesday I confronted him and threatened to call police. When I told my wife, she said the same car was on our street a few times when she left for work in the morning." That was a bit of a stretch. She'd said the old Toyota might have been there. I paused, out of breath.

"And…"

"When Anderson was married to Ann, he beat her when she was pregnant. The baby died."

I heard him take a deep breath. "I see."

"My in-laws don't know the cause of that miscarriage, Mr. Lund. My wife didn't tell them. Although they did know she left him because he was abusive. Anderson was never charged with assault seven years ago, something my wife now regrets. At the time, my father-in-law gave him money to go away, thinking that would be the end of it. Ann and I are expecting our first child soon."

"What's the purpose of this call, Mr. Keene?"

"I want to make sure you know all the details, Mr. Lund. I don't want Anderson anywhere near my family."

For a moment there was silence on his end. "Thank you for the information, Mr. Keene." He hung up.

Did he believe me? He gave no hint that he knew about Anderson. Couldn't he have been more pleasant? I remembered Frank saying he'd had trouble hiring lawyers after Burton left the practice. He said none of them were a good fit. Now, with Frank gone, I had no confidence that Anderson would be dealt with, and I had to rely on Burton to make sure Lund carried on with his wishes. At least I'd be working from home until Tuesday morning and could make sure Ann was safe. After that, I'd have to figure something out, like suggesting she tell her dad the truth about the miscarriage, and ask him to step up his game with Gary Lund. Either that or tell my father-in-law the whole story myself.

I looked up and Ann waved to me from the kitchen window. I pocketed my phone and started up the path to the house.

When I came in through the kitchen door, she was at the stove stirring something. I could smell meat cooking in the oven. "Why were you standing out there for so long? Who were you talking to?"

No point in lying. "Gary Lund."

For a moment the name didn't seem to register with her. Then she frowned. "Why?"

"Where's your dad?"

She stopped stirring and put the spoon down. "He's in his office talking to the police."

"The cops are here already?"

"Marsh, what's going on? Why did you call Gary Lund?"

"I had to, honey. Burton has supposedly called him about Anderson, right?"

"Do you doubt that Dad spoke to him?"

"No. But Burton doesn't know the whole story, does he?"

"What are you getting at?"

Burton came into the kitchen just as I was about to tell Ann that if no one knew about the miscarriage, how would Lund know how serious our situation was.

"Ah, here you are, Marshall," said Burton. "The police want to talk to you."

I looked at my wife with a what-the-hell-can-I-do expression and followed Burton into the office. The officers were Detective Sergeant Reese and P.C. Wood, the same cops Frank and I had seen on Tuesday.

"Good afternoon, Mr. Keene," said Reese.

I nodded. "Officers."

Burton didn't offer chairs and the four of us stood facing each other. Thank God this little chat was his call, on his turf.

Reese held up the paperwork from Grant's. "We'd like to confirm a few things, Mr. Keene. You were the one that got this from Grant's Storage, correct?"

"Yes." I wondered what they thought about interviewing me twice in as many days on two separate issues.

Reese held up the wallet and the cash. "You found these items in a pile of garden debris?" His words held an unspoken doubt.

"That's correct." I knew damn well if Burton and Ann hadn't been with me, Reese would never have believed the story.

"Thank you, Mr. Keene." He looked at Burton. "And thank you, Judge for your insight and for bringing these items to our attention."

Reese's last comment sounded genuine. Burton must have expressed an opinion as to what he thought was going on, and I wondered if the name Lancaster was known to police. I mentally added Douglas and Gregory Lancaster to my criminal enquiry list.

Reese and Wood left the room and Burton followed. He said goodbye at the front door. When I heard it close, I joined him in the hall.

"That's it?" I said.

Burton frowned. "It's just the beginning, I'm afraid. Now they'll send a crew to scour the boathouse and comb through that ruin."

"What kind of reaction did you get when they saw that stuff?"

"They looked at the wallet and the cash, then read the printout. Their interest picked up when I told them Douglas Lancaster was my property maintenance man. They wanted to know how long he'd worked for me, where and how we found the wallet. When I told them, they asked me to repeat what I'd said. Wood took notes."

"I bet they raid the storage locker. I'd love to see that."

"They'll have to get a warrant of course, and they'll have to get another one to search my boathouse."

I nodded and started walking to the kitchen, but he hadn't finished talking. "Ann looked unhappy a few moments ago. What's upsetting her?"

I turned to face him. "Maybe you should ask her, Burton."

He glanced at me and I thought he was going to say something else. If so, he changed his mind and walked ahead of me. When we entered the kitchen, Ann looked up from her phone. "Mom's just sent a text. Nell's going to talk to the police tomorrow. They're staying at a hotel here in town. They'll have dinner there."

Burton didn't comment and neither did I. Ann was pissed off at me for sure, and she'd be really pissed when I told her what I'd said to Lund. Plus, she was probably disappointed that she wouldn't see her mother. It wasn't surprising that Eileen didn't want to sit around the family table with her soon-to-be ex-husband.

"Time for a drink." I walked to the fridge. "Want anything, hon, Burton?"

I opened the fridge door. My choices seemed to be iced tea or Diet Coke. Burton walked over, started rummaging around and yanked out a Miller Light. My least preference, but it was a beer.

"Nell brought these over a while ago. I put them in the fridge this morning."

Ann wanted iced tea and Burton cracked open a bottle of Chardonnay. I proposed a toast to the success of the investigation and it occurred to me I should have made that plural. I reached over and squeezed my wife's hand, but there was no return squeeze.

"How long until dinner, honey?" I said, making an attempt at conversation. "Anything I can do?"

"About twenty minutes," she said without looking at me. "I guess you could set the table when the time comes."

Burton turned to his daughter. "You're unhappy about our separation, aren't you, Sweet t'ing?"

"In a way, I am, Dad," said Ann. "But…" she didn't finish her thought.

"Speaking for myself, I'll always be here for you. I'm so looking forward to the baby. I can't wait to be a grandfather."

Even though Ann's eyes filled with tears, she smiled at her father. "I just wish all this was over and we could get back to normal again."

And I couldn't wait for dinner to be over so we could go home. Burton's cell phone interrupted my thoughts.

"Judge Young speaking…Yes, Mr. Lund…Please repeat that…I see …" Frowning, Burton got up from the table and walked away. Seconds later, we heard his office door close.

Chapter 14

Ann swung around, her body facing me. "What did you say to Gary Lund?"

I turned to her, our knees touching. "I told him you lost a baby because of Anderson's abuse."

She glared at me. "You told him that? Why?"

I leaned closer to her. "Somebody has to do something about Anderson. I told him your parents didn't know. He was insistent about lawyer/client confidentiality and never even acknowledged that Burton was a client."

"So what? I confided in you, Marsh. It wasn't up to you to tell anyone."

"I don't see it that way."

Our discussion ended when we heard Burton approaching. He looked at each of us, sighed, and then sat in the chair he'd left moments earlier, his face grim. "Well, I've got more bad news." He refilled his wine glass, took a couple of sips and stared into space.

Ann looked at me, then broke the silence. "What did Lund say?"

As usual, Burton took his time getting to the point. "I guess I haven't told you much about my conversations with him."

Ann sighed. "No, you haven't, Dad."

"Frank advised me to contact him a few weeks ago when your mother told me she'd paid off Steven Anderson," said Burton. "So, I called and told him about the recent threats and filled him in on the terms of our past agreement. I gave him the phone number I had. We talked about some options and came up with a plan. Days later, he reported back that he'd spoken to Anderson and invited him to come into the law office on the pretext of discussing a new arrangement."

"What was that?" I said.

"Lund was going to tell Anderson he was facing charges of extortion, punishable by a fine and jail time." Burton grabbed the wine and topped up his glass. "Anderson never showed up and his phone number is no longer in service. I put a detective on him right away."

I nodded. "He was smart enough to realize he was walking into a trap. That conversation with Lund sent him underground."

Burton nodded. "He's violent and manipulative, but he's not stupid."

"What's happened since?" said Ann.

"The car Anderson drove was found in a mall parking lot. It's been towed to a wrecking yard." He looked at Ann then shifted his gaze to me. "The plates were stolen."

Proof of Burton's speedy old-boy network. I'd wasted eighteen bucks on the plate search, but knowing now that those plates were stolen was a hell of a lot better than waiting two weeks. "Was it the same car he had seven years ago?" Why didn't I think of that sooner?

Ann and Burton both shook their heads.

"Someone's helping Anderson. It sure sounds like *he* has a plan," I said. "I guess Lund has no idea if he's even driving now?"

"Or where he is," said Ann.

"That's right." Burton shook his head. "I thought I'd seen the last of him."

Ann had said the same thing yesterday. How could they be so naive? Burton was the ultimate cash cow. "Anderson won't give up easily."

Burton nodded. "Afraid you're right, Marshall. I know he left the country seven years ago and came back last year. I've put a second detective on it. Maybe between the two of them and Lund, they can find him. I called the police, told them that he was back in Canada threatening us and I wanted to press charges."

Finally, thank God. "I'd love to know where he got that car—maybe it's stolen too."

"Good question. I don't like any of this. You're right, Marshall, Anderson has a plan," said Burton.

Yup, a long-term strategy to hit up the ex-in-laws as soon as his cash was gone. What was the original settlement? I didn't see how a second detective would do much good if the first one struck out. "I'm glad to hear you've spoken to the cops." What did Burton tell them? I looked at my wife. "Ann and I really appreciate it."

"Help me get dinner on the table," said Ann, not looking my way.

Since Burton didn't jump to his feet, I assumed she meant me. I did what I was told.

**

An hour later, on the drive home, I pulled over to the side of the road a block away from our house and undid my seatbelt.

My wife turned to me. "What are you doing?"

"I want to talk about Anderson before we get home."

She sighed and turned to face me. "Okay."

"If you wanted your dad to step up his plan to find Anderson, why didn't you tell him about the miscarriage?"

"How do you know I haven't?"

I felt my eyebrows rise.

"I told Dad yesterday," she said. "Why couldn't you trust me to tell him?"

"Why didn't you tell me?"

"It was a personal issue between me and my parents, and I knew Dad was talking to Lund. Do I have to get your approval before I talk to them?"

"That's not fair, Ann. We're in this together, I'm trying to help. You could have told me."

Now she was shouting. "And it's not fair that you walked all over me. You don't get it, do you? It was up to me to tell that story. You should have spoken to me before you went blabbing to Gary Lund."

I nodded. Although I felt like saying I was sick of everyone pussyfooting around Anderson.

Her voice got louder. "Do you think I'm stupid? That I don't know how dangerous Steven is?"

I reached for her hand, but she brushed me away. "You said it was all about money, not about you. There are three of us to consider now, Ann, and I couldn't be sure Burton had done anything about that jerk."

"Well, you didn't find out a whole lot by talking to Lund, did you?"

I shook my head.

"So why didn't you just ask Dad what he'd done about Steven?"

Good question. "I should have. Your dad and I seem to be getting along better now. I didn't want to rock the boat." I hated to admit that my father-in-law intimidated me, that he felt I wasn't good enough for his daughter.

She thought a moment then took my hand. "Okay. Maybe you and Dad are getting along better because you're both more willing to see each other's point. Just promise you'll discuss stuff with me first."

"I'm sorry. I was worried that we wouldn't agree."

"Then we'd have to compromise."

"How do you spell that?"

She sucker-punched me on the arm.

**

The next morning, I sat drinking coffee and thinking about the events of the last few days. Before we left Lakewood Drive last night, Burton mentioned he'd make sure to be around when the police searched his property and the boathouse. He might get some useful information if he asked the right questions.

Right now, the only puzzle I could sort out was digging into the murder of Allan Wright. Ann had gone to the hotel to drink herbal tea with her mother. I think they'd planned to have a massage and some other kind of treatment, so that gave me plenty of time to find Wright's wife and try to convince her to talk to me.

**

The community housing complex where Mrs. Wright lived was a block away from the subsidized apartment my family had lived in many years ago. Dad's pay hardly covered the bills. Mom cleaned other people's houses and took in sewing. I took any job I could get to pay for my clothing and Callie babysat to pay for hers. When my grandparents died within months of each other, my parents used their small inheritance for a down payment on the war-time house Ann and I lived in now.

I parked in a designated handicap spot and assembled my wheelchair. The complex stretched out in front of me, townhouse after townhouse. Curtains hung haphazardly in some windows while other windows had no coverings at all. The area had that stale, desperate appearance I remembered. Maybe that was unfair. It *was* winter and everything looked grey and stationary. But from memory, even long after the snow had gone, few people bothered with flowers or took an interest in their own small patch of grass.

I wheeled along the block, mindful of the slippery sidewalk, looking for Mrs. Wright's unit. Number 275 was the last one in the row, situated beside a playground. A few women stood around watching half a dozen preschool children playing on swings and slides even in January. Two boys sat in the frozen sand pit, bashing the surface with toy shovels.

I wheeled up to the unit and rang a worn-looking doorbell. I didn't hear a responding chime, so I knocked on the door and waited. After a few minutes, I knocked again. From the playground, someone called out.

"Who are you looking for?"

I swung around. A woman was walking toward me. "I'm looking for Mrs. Wright."

"You're a newspaper reporter, aren't you?"

"I'm not representing a newspaper. This is a private matter."

"Private? What'd you mean?"

"Do you know Mrs. Wright? I'd like to speak to her. My name is Marshall Keene."

She looked at me, squinting as if to put me into focus. "I know who you are. And you're lying, you're a reporter. I read the papers. Leave me alone." She turned to walk away.

I raised my voice and spoke to her back. "I work for the *Register,* Mrs. Wright, but I'm on a leave of absence right now because I have to find out who killed your husband. If you talk to me, I won't be writing about our conversation. You have my word."

She turned, clutched a threadbare black coat around her and walked back. Her hair, mostly grey, was gathered behind her head. I remembered a discussion I'd had with my lawyer at the time of Wright's bench trial. Allan Wright would have been about be forty now, and Mrs. Wright could be the same age, maybe younger. But she looked older than Eileen, who was nearly sixty. I wondered how my mother-in-law would look without the continuous pampering a woman of her stature could afford.

Mrs. Wright gave me another long, hard stare. She took in my wheelchair. Her eyes lingered on the prostheses exposed below the hem of my pants where they connected to my shoes. Another woman walked out of the playground and stood beside us. "You okay, Celine?"

She nodded and turned back to me. "You of all people would be glad Allan was dead. Why would I trust *your word?* And what makes you think we're going to have a conversation, anyway?"

I wheeled closer to her. "I'm just hoping, Mrs. Wright, more than I've hoped for anything in a long time. An article in the *Tribune* a few days ago made me look like a suspect in your husband's murder. I had nothing to do with it. I didn't even know when he was getting out of prison." I raced on, knowing I had a small window with this woman. "Yes, I threatened him years ago. Please understand I was ill at the time. Hated the world, but I didn't kill him."

Celine Wright gave me a hostile stare. "Yeah, I read that story. It made sense to me."

"That's why I'm here, Mrs. Wright. A lot of people might agree with you. I need to find out who actually killed him. I need to keep my job and support my family. I just want to ask you a few questions and I promise you'll never see me again."

"And how do I know you aren't lying? You'll write about this because you're a journalist and you have to make money. You just said so yourself. That other guy that came around wanted a personal story. He was pushy and rude and I slammed the door on him—he probably gave you my address."

"You have no way of knowing whether I'm lying, Mrs. Wright. Please understand this is a personal issue with me. I haven't been charged with a crime, but I need to clear my name. I did get the address from that reporter, he's one of my colleagues, no point in lying about that."

The two women looked at each other. The second one pointed to the playground. "Marlene is watching the kids for you. At least this guy's not the cops. They won't look too hard to find out who killed Allan. Remember what we talked about yesterday."

Celine Wright nodded to her companion.

"Anyway, he's stuck in a wheelchair. Somebody like that couldn't kill anyone."

I ignored her ignorant supposition, and hoped the sympathy card she'd unintentionally played would work. She hadn't noticed the canes attached to the back of my chair. Like most, she assumed people who use wheelchairs can't walk, have no life…I took their silence as permission to carry on, and looked at Celine Wright. "Your husband served his time, then someone who was probably waiting for him to get out…murdered him."

Celine Wright sighed heavily. "Allan's death was a terrible shock. Things will be tough without him. While he was there, he accepted the

Lord Jesus Christ as his saviour. It was the happiest time of our lives, and gave me great hope." She paused and looked past me. "Two days after he got out, he was killed. I don't see what I can do for you." Celine Wright's eyes filled with tears and the other woman put an arm around her shoulders.

I pulled the picture of Gilardi and his two buddies out of my pocket. "Do you recognize any of these men? I know this picture was taken years ago."

The companion, who'd been silent said, "Can't hurt to look Celine, if that's all he wants. Might help get some closure."

Mrs. Wright nodded and took the printout out of my hands. The other woman moved closer and they both looked at it.

Celine seemed to shrink inside her threadbare coat. "The police didn't have this picture when they were around a few days ago. Where did you get it?" The bravado had gone from her voice.

"It was taken on the courthouse steps years ago after your husband's trial." I leaned closer and pointed. "You can see me talking to reporters. Those three guys are the ones I'm interested in. One of them threatened me. I didn't see them during the trial, and wondered who they were and why they were outside the court that day." I didn't mention I hadn't seen her or their kids supporting Wright at the trial either. It says a lot about a man's family if they don't turn up at his trial.

Celine Wright narrowed her eyes and looked at me. "They were friends of Allan's. I didn't like them and told him not to bring them around our kids."

"Why didn't you like them, Mrs. Wright?"

She thought a moment. "They were up to no good in my opinion. Didn't have jobs."

"Where did your husband work? Before the accident, I mean."

"He was part-time security at Mason's. But there was never enough money, even with me babysitting." She shook her head.

I pointed to the picture. "Do you remember their names? Is this Julian Gilardi?"

Her eyes darted around and she lowered her voice as she spoke. "Could be. These people are part of Allan's past. He's gone and I have to get on with my life."

"Do you know who the other two are?"

She pursed her lips and nodded slightly. "Like I just said, I have to move on."

"Can you please tell me their names?"

She shook her head and again, her eyes searched the complex.

"Was your husband involved in illegal drugs? Did the police ask you that question?"

"It's a mortal sin to speak ill of the dead, Mr. Keene. And what good would it do to dig into that again?" She took her companion by the arm. "We have to get back to the kids. It's time for their snack."

"Thank you for talking to me, Mrs. Wright. Here's my card if you decide to share anything else."

She looked at the card and stuffed it into her pocket. The two women walked away and I watched them rejoin the others in the frozen playground. Three children ran to her and she opened her arms to them.

As I rolled along the walkway, Celine Wright's companion stood against the fence watching me. Like my mom, Mrs. Wright lived from day to day to make ends meet. I wondered if Gilardi and the other two were paying for her silence.

Chapter 15

I sat behind the wheel staring at the parking lot of the Ontario Housing complex. Celine Wright had said her husband was part-time security at Mason's before he went to jail. As far as I knew, Mason's was a plumbing supply outfit not a security company. I pulled out my phone. Google gave an address at 1750 Speers Road.

I scrolled through my notes. If I was right about the numbering, that was also the address of the warehouse the police raided two years ago. A load of Fentanyl had been discovered. I heard police had suspects, but no evidence had been found to make arrests.

Ten minutes later, I pulled into 1750 Speers Road, an industrial plaza. A big sign above the door of the first unit read, *Mason's Plumbing Depot.* I thought the place that had been raided was a warehouse; this looked like a storefront. I set up my chair and wheeled from one end of the complex to the other. Beside Mason's was a store selling hot tubs and next to that, an outdoor furniture and bar-b-que outlet. Seven other small businesses completed the row.

I wheeled around to the rear of the complex. All the units were deep, with loading doors on the back of each one. I decided to go into Mason's and ask a few questions, and rolled around to the front. The door swung open when I pressed the handicap button. Places with appropriate accessibility always gave me a good feeling.

The inside resembled the front office at Grant's. A small reception area with a long customer counter was manned by a fifty-something man wearing a denim shirt with *Mason's Plumbing* embroidered across the pocket. Various types of plumbing equipment lined the shelves behind him. "How can I help, sir?" he said.

I smiled. "Did you people move? Thought you were somewhere else before."

He returned my smile. "You're absolutely correct. Used to be down the block at 1800 Speers. Moved into this space last year. Better location for us and a bigger warehouse out back."

I extended my hand. "Marshall Keene. I'd like to talk to someone who's been employed here for a while."

"David Mason." We shook hands. "I've been with the company from day one."

"Pleased to meet you, David. I work for the *Halton Register*. I'm writing an article on the drug crisis in the GTA and surrounding area." I pulled out my press card and showed it to him. "I came to this location thinking it would be abandoned."

The customer-friendly smile left David's face. He ignored my I.D. "We moved in last year."

"Wasn't there a drug bust here a few years ago?"

Like Celine Wright, he looked me up and down. "I don't feel comfortable about reporters showing up and digging into the past history of this building. I own *Mason's Plumbing Depot*. My business is doing well here."

Had other reporters tried to talk to him in the past? I shoved my press card back into my pocket. "I can totally understand your concerns. My article is about various aspects of the drug problem, not about specific names and locations, Mr. Mason. I'm interested in businesses that hire or have hired security companies to guard their premises during off hours."

"Ask your questions. I'll decide if I want to answer."

"Fair enough." I pointed to the security sticker on the front door. "Do you have an alarm system or do you hire security guards?"

"We have an alarm system."

"In your previous store, did you have security guards?"

He nodded. "Triple A Security. They're out of business now."

"Were they the only security company you used?"

He nodded again, shifting his weight from one foot to another. "I got rid of them years before we moved here."

"You weren't satisfied with their service?"

"Alarm systems are hassle-free compared to dealing with people." He looked at me before continuing, as if choosing his words. "Anyway, what does this have to do with your so-called article about drugs?"

"I have a theory, Mr. Mason. I think security guards can fill in their time with other things. Like dealing drugs."

His eyes didn't meet mine. "I wouldn't know."

"Do you remember the name of the guard who worked at your premises? Was it Allan Wright?"

The hostile expression on his face deepened. He took a breath and his tone was sharper. "I thought you weren't going to be specific. Question period is over, Mr. Keene, I have work to do." He walked over to the door and pressed the automatic opener.

I wheeled to the open front door. "Thanks for talking to me." I wondered if he'd fired the security company because of Allan Wright. Maybe I was totally off base. But as soon as I'd mentioned working for *The Halton Register* and the drug bust, he shut me down. Probably just like many people, he hated reporters.

I went back to my car and googled local security companies. There was no listing for Triple A, so I guessed David Mason was right about them being out of business. However, Advanced Security was three blocks away and claimed to have kept Lakeville safe for twenty years. Maybe they'd remember Triple A.

When I pulled into their lot, I had to leave my chair in the car. There was no ramp. Three concrete stairs led to the front door, not a good omen. I grabbed my canes, walked in and after waiting about three minutes, rang a bell for service. Seconds later, a man who looked to be about twenty opened a door behind the front desk and stepped into the room.

"Sorry. Out back talking to the boss."

"No worries. I'm hoping you can give me some information."

He tilted his head and looked me over. "Sure."

"Do you know of a company called Triple A Security?"

"Nope. But I've only been here a while. I'll go ask. Triple A, you said?"

Before I could answer, he'd gone back inside. Almost immediately, an older man came through the door.

"You asked about Triple A?" The ends of his bushy grey moustache twitched when he talked.

"That's right, sir. I can't seem to find an address for them."

"You won't. They went tits up. About five, six years back, I think. Why?"

I introduced myself and told him I was gathering information for an article on the drug problem in the GTA. I assured him that no names or businesses would be quoted. I showed him my press card and explained my theory about drugs and the security guard business.

He laughed. "Yeah, you'd be right about Triple A. Small outfit with dodgy employees that worked cheap. Company had a poor reputation."

"Oh? What would give a security company a bad or good reputation?"

"Like our ad says, we've been in business for over twenty years. We specialize in construction sites. Never wanted to look after small individual businesses scattered all over the place."

"Sounds like a good business plan." I was about to repeat my question, when he carried on.

"Yup. We keep at least two guys on each job, more if it's a big subdivision. Another guy drives around at night checking all our sites. They're also in constant communication and I'm on call twenty-four seven."

"So why did Triple A have a bad reputation?"

He took a deep breath. "Well, I can only speak for Advanced Security." His chest puffed out. This guy loved the sound of his own voice. "We screen our employees thoroughly and like I just told you, we know exactly what's going on at all times." Even though he professed to know only about his own company, he finally threw in his oar about Triple A. "They seemed to hire a bunch of bad actors and turned a blind eye to the goings on." He chuckled. "Or maybe, like you say, it was part of *their* business plan."

"Would those *goings on* include criminal activity? Can you be specific?"

He rubbed his chin. The mustache shifted from side to side. "No, nothing as you say— specific. But we heard plenty of rumours, like guards smoking pot and dealing drugs on the job. Industry gossip gets around you know, Matthew."

I didn't give a shit what he called me as long as I got some information. "Do you know of any businesses that hired Triple A?"

He shook his head. "Might have, but can't remember now. Wait a minute .... the gossip started when one guy got rid of them—Tripple A, I mean. Rumour went around that the guards were dealing drugs on the job. Had quite the operation going. We found out about it because they lost their license over it—Tripple A I mean."

"And you don't know the business owner who fired them?"

He shook his head. "Can't remember. All I know is that I took a damn good look at all our own guys after that."

"Do you know where the Triple A office was?"

"Hmmm." He gave the stash a twirl. "Somewhere around here. Not this street though. Pretty sure it was Speers Road."

The front door opened and two guys in work clothes entered. Mustache came out from behind the counter, greeted them then looked back at me. "Good luck with your research, Matthew."

"Thanks, you've been very helpful."

Ten minutes later, when I turned onto our street, I was surprised to see Ann's car parked in the driveway. God, I hoped she hadn't brought Eileen back with her. I had no time for small talk. I set up my chair, wheeled up the ramp and went into the house.

On my way to the kitchen to grab a beer and rummage around for something to eat, I called out to Ann.

"I'm in here," she said from the bedroom. She was in bed, under the covers. Not like her at all.

My heart pounded. "Honey, are you okay?"

"Yup. Fine. That massage made me feel sleepy. Thought I'd take advantage of my time off and have a nap."

Christ, I'd be a nervous wreck before this baby was born. "Can I make you some tea?"

"Mmmmm, that would be nice."

Ten minutes later, we sat in the front room. I decided that tea would be better for me than beer. I needed to start setting a good example for our daughter.

Ann sat with her legs stretched across my lap. "What've you been up to all day?" she said.

"Everything seemed to be at a stand-still, so I decided to see if Mrs. Wright would talk to me. She lives in the Ontario Housing Complex off Third Line."

Ann sighed. "How did it feel to be back there?"

"Total Deja Vu. A small playground's been added, but the place looks even more run-down. I passed our old apartment building and looked up. My mom put blue curtains on the windows. They were still there, but hanging at odd angles. I realize now that we were at what they call *below the poverty line.* There were folks worse off than us in that building, and we heard rumours of bad things happening. Funny how things like those curtains remind you of all kinds of other stuff."

"Want to talk about it?"

"Nah. Even though we didn't have much I don't remember being unhappy. My parents worked hard. I didn't realize we were poor until we moved away. Guess that says a lot."

Ann smiled. "I envy you, Marsh."

"You envy *me*?"

She nodded. "My parents were never happy. Their marriage was a sham."

"What do you mean?"

"It was all one-sided. Mom married Dad so she could stay in Canada. She actually lied about being pregnant. I wasn't born until Dad was nearly finished law school."

Christ! I couldn't imagine Burton towing the line like that. "What did your dad do when he found out?"

Ann shrugged. "Got over it, I guess. He was in love with her. Plus, Grandpa Berresford paid for his law school and all their living expenses too."

This was the *help* Burton had referred to. It sounded like old man Berresford owned him. That's why Burton had been so ambivalent. But decades later, he bribed Steven Anderson to get the hell out of Ann's life and stay out.

"Okay, I'm trying to piece this together. Burton meets Eileen, falls in love. She really wants to stay in Canada and tells him she's pregnant. Her father agrees to put Burton through law school and foot all the other bills if they get married. It's the longest pregnancy in history and you aren't born for a couple of years."

"Yup. That's it."

"So why would Eileen lie about being pregnant? Why was she desperate to stay in Canada?"

Ann drew in a big breath and let it out slowly. "Mom got into trouble in Trinidad when she was young. Hung out with the wrong crowd. Drugs were involved. I don't know the whole story, but I think Grampa had the charges dismissed. He sent her here to go to school. She hated it, dropped out and got a job in a bar. That's where she met Dad. And you know the rest."

"This was nearly forty years ago, right? How long have you known about it?"

"I heard them fighting when I was in high school. I asked Mom, but she just said it was all in the past…there's more, Marsh."

Jesus. More family secrets. "Why didn't you tell me before?"

"It all happened so long ago and people can change. I didn't want you to think bad of Mom…I wish I had told you."

"So why are you telling me now?"

She jabbed her toe into my stomach. "Just listen and you'll find out. It's all about Dad giving Steven money if he went back to Trinidad after our divorce."

I nodded.

"I can only guess," she said, "but I bet I'm right about this. Steven was scary angry when we split up. His family knew my grandparents. They were high society. I knew his parents were pleased when we married. I think they would have been embarrassed when he came back divorced so soon after the wedding, and God knows what story he told them. They probably dug around looking for some dirt and found Mom's old brush with the law that Grampa had covered up.

"Then Steven came back to Canada and didn't get any more money out of Dad, but Mom paid him off. He threatened to tell the Law Society that Judge Young's wife was a former drug dealer."

I snorted. "I wonder if the Law Society would've paid any attention to old shit that happened decades ago in another country. But Anderson's threat would sure be enough to scare Eileen. No wonder she paid him off. I thought he threatened to hurt you?"

"He did. Mom didn't tell me the other part until today."

"I'm guessing Eileen decided to come clean and tell Burton she'd paid him off."

"Yeah, she realized it would never end and told Dad. I guess they had a huge fight. He called Frank. Now Lund is handling it."

I shook my head. "Your ex is after money and he'll figure out another way to get it. And now he knows the law is after *him.* I'm sorry I jumped the gun and talked to Lund. I just didn't believe that your dad was taking the whole thing seriously enough. I really wish I'd known all this."

"I didn't know Steven had threatened Mom about that old stuff in Trinidad, either."

"I can understand why she told Burton, but why did she tell you?"

Ann sighed. "I wondered that too. Mom and Dad have decided to divorce, and maybe she thought he would tell me. I think she's embarrassed, and I guess she wanted me to learn the whole story from her."

"Did she and Nell come to Canada together?"

"No, Nell's only been here for about ten years. Came after her own divorce. Believe it or not, Nell wasn't the wild one when they were kids."

"She's taking big chances now."

"There's something else, Marsh."

"Wait a minute. I need a beer before you dump any more family secrets on me. You want more tea?"

She shook her head. Minutes later I was back with a beer. "I'm guessing your ex-husband's threat wasn't the only thing Eileen told you today."

Ann nodded. "Mom made me promise I wouldn't tell. But I don't want to hide things, especially now. I'm telling you, and Dad needs to know too. Nell is going to the cops with it anyway."

"What the hell is it?"

"Remember we said that Frank might have been killed because he got into trouble gambling?"

I nodded.

"And remember we heard that the safe in Frank's office was open?"

"Yeah."

"Nell told Mom there was money in it—hundreds of thousands. It was for Frank's gambling debts. He was supposed to meet someone and hand it over to them."

"Jesus! That's huge, he was really into big-time losses. When the cops got there the safe was empty and Frank was dead. Did anyone else know about the money?"

"I don't know. Mom didn't say and I didn't think to ask."

"Did Nell go to the station to talk to the cops?"

Ann nodded. "She was already there when I met Mom at the hotel."

"I'm surprised Eileen didn't go with her."

"I think she was dying to go. I got the impression Nell wanted to talk to them alone."

Good for Nell. "I'd love to know what questions they asked."

"Yeah, me too. But I'd never ask. Maybe she'll talk to Mom." Ann sat quietly for a few moments. "Now I want to hear about Mrs. Wright. Did she talk to you?"

Ann listened while I described my morning poking into other people's business.

"Poor woman," said Ann. "She sounds scared. You did well getting her to talk as much as she did. I think the fact that she's into religion helped."

"Yeah, but I'm sure she was still holding back."

I moved on to my chat with the owner of Mason's Plumbing.

"He's probably hiding stuff from you too," said Ann.

"Yeah, that's what I think. If I owned a business and hired a security company to guard my premises, I'd go over there once in a while to check up on them. I guess he did and saw Wright dealing drugs. He was the one who mentioned Triple A Security, but when I asked him about Allan Wright he clammed up. And Celine Wright said her husband worked at Mason's."

"That fits. You're so good at asking the right questions. I could never do that," said Ann.

Ann meant I was nosy. "I still have no proof."

She wasn't as interested in the second guy, even though I made his facial hair dance for her. "Glad you got confirmation from Mr. Moustache that Triple A was a shady company," she said. "He was so talkative. Guess he had nothing to worry about." She smiled and wiggled her feet, my signal to give them a rub. "Good work though, Matthew."

I laughed. "Yeah, it was an interesting morning. I'll have to figure out how to nail down more info about Allan Wright and that guy Gilardi." I drained my beer.

She smiled. "I'd hate to be the one you were tracking down."

"What d'ya mean, baby? I'm always tracking you down."

We still had the weekend together. Monday it was back to work for her. It was nice to sit down and talk, even if it was about our worries. Ann looked at her watch. "I'll go and see if there's anything for dinner, or if I have to shop."

I watched her walk away. My cell rang. Unknown caller came up on the display. Ann ignores those calls. I always pick up. "Marshall Keene speaking."

"It's Celine Wright calling."

Chapter 16

I thought Celine Wright would never want to talk to me again. Calm down, Keene, she probably wants to officially add you to her shit list.

"Thanks for calling, Mrs. Wright."

"I've been thinking about our conversation this morning, Mr. Keene." Her voice had an edge. "Tess said the cops won't look too hard to find who killed Allan. She hated him. But I think they will because that's their job."

Tess? I presumed she meant the woman who had joined us. "I agree, Mrs. Wright. But it may take a while. It'll be an open case until they find the…person responsible."

She sighed, and her tone softened. "Your family is um…gone and you're stuck in that wheelchair because of Allan. I was rude to you this morning. I'm sorry."

"You needn't apologize, Mrs. Wright. I'm sure you're tired of people prying into your business. You're not responsible for what your husband did."

"Thanks, Mr. Keene." I heard the snap of a Zippo, then inhalation, and presumed she lit a cigarette. "After the kids left this afternoon, I went to my church. I always see things more clearer when I talk to our Lord."

Whatever worked for her. I was just glad she was reaching out.

"The Lord made me see that this is *our* business, mine and yours. He sent you to me this morning. I want to do my part to make up for what happened to you and your family."

Nothing you can say will make up for my loss, lady. "I appreciate the thought, Mrs. Wright."

"About that picture you showed me this morning…I won't be able to face myself and our Lord until I tell you what I know."

There was such a long pause, I thought maybe He had intervened and changed her mind.

"Yes?" I said, anxious for her to continue.

After an intake of breath, I assumed she'd taken another drag. She started talking immediately and I pictured smoke coming out of her mouth and nostrils as she spoke. "Before Allan went to prison, I never knew much about what he did when he left the house. It was easier not to ask questions. Our children were in school then. Allan's known those three men for years. They're all no good if you ask me. He was fired from his job because of them."

"At Mason's? He was a security guard there?"

"Yes. He worked for a security company—can't remember the name now—but he was a night guard at Mason's."

"So why was he fired?"

"He said those guys framed him, but Allan didn't always tell the truth."

"Framed? Did he say what for?"

"No. But he must have been scared because he disappeared for a while after that."

"What made you think your husband didn't tell you the truth?"

"Even though there was barely enough to keep us going, Allan always had money for booze and other things. When I asked where it came from, I never got a sensible answer."

"Do you think your husband was involved with drugs?"

She hesitated. "That's what I thought even though I had no proof."

"Could those men have been his partners?"

"I think so."

"Do you know their names?"

"You asked me if one of them in that picture was Julian Gilardi. I only ever heard him called Gilardi. The guy in the middle was Jacobs, I think, or something like that, and GL was beside him. I'm pretty sure his name was Lancaster because I heard Allan talking to him on the phone a lot and called him by both names. They visited him in jail and I got the feeling Allan didn't like that."

GL as in Gregory Lancaster? Fucking bingo. Maybe. "Did you mention those names to the police, Mrs. Wright?"

"The cops asked me who Allan's friends were." Her laugh was nervous. "I lied and said I didn't know."

"Are those guys threatening you, Mrs. Wright?"

"They came around to ask how I was doing. Said they were just checking on me. It wasn't a friendly visit. I know they don't care what happens to me, and probably just want me to keep quiet."

"When did they visit? After Allan got out of jail?"

"Yeah, just after. I don't know the exact day. Then Allan went missing. The last few days have been a blur. But I'll never forget Monday night when the police came around to tell me they'd found Allan's body."

"Do those guys ever phone you, Mrs. Wright?"

"No. They just came by in person." She took another drag and coughed. "I've told you all I know, Mr. Keene."

There was nothing more effective than an eyeball-to-eyeball threat. "Thanks for calling. You've given me something to work on. Please call again if you think of anything else."

"Be careful, Mr. Keene." She hung up.

The woman was scared, with good reason. Interesting that she was visited by those guys just before Wright's body was found. My thoughts went into overdrive. Did they kill him? Why? They'd supported him years ago on the courthouse steps after the trial. Had something turned sour while Wright was in jail? I suspected the cops knew who those three guys were before they questioned Celine Wright, and knew she lied when she denied knowing them.

I punched in 411 Lakeville on my computer and looked up the names Gilardi, Jacobi and Lancaster. There were no local listings for Gilardi and Jacobi, and a few for Lancaster. It would probably be a waste of time calling them. Those guys most likely didn't have landlines and their phones would be burners. On impulse, I looked up Mason's Plumbing and called the number.

"Mason's Plumbing Depot, David speaking."

"Mr. Mason, it's Marshall Keene calling. Please don't hang up on me. I need some information, then I'll leave you alone."

"I have nothing to say, Keene. I told you that this morning."

"I just heard some interesting things from a reliable source. Stuff the cops might find useful in a current investigation. Help me out so I won't steer them in the wrong direction."

"I know who you are, Keene. That story in *The Tribune* the other day didn't make you look so good. This is all about that dead guy, Wright, isn't it? You lied about writing an article."

"I actually am writing that article, Mr. Mason. *You* weren't honest with me this morning. And yes, this call is about Allan Wright. I need to know who killed him."

David Mason said nothing. At least he didn't hang up.

"In your old location on Speers Road, you were involved with Wright and his cronies in drug trafficking," I said. "Things got hot, so you pretended to fire Wright and moved your sideline business to another location. But that was busted and by some miracle, you were never charged."

I had to hold the phone away from my ear. "If that's your so-called reliable information, it's bullshit! Stop hassling me or I'll…"

"You'll what? Call the police? You knew damn well Wright was into drug trafficking. The cops would probably be very interested, especially since you moved your plumbing business to a location that was busted two years ago." I could hear him breathing hard on the other end. "I talked to other business owners in your area. They remember the name Triple A Security and the stories about them turning a blind eye to certain things. The stink from shit like that doesn't fade in a hurry."

"Okay, Keene. But you've got it wrong. Yeah, Wright worked for me. Never liked him. I got suspicious and came around at night to see what was going on. He was dealing drugs out of my warehouse, but I was *not* involved. That's the truth. I called Triple A Security, blew the whistle and installed a security system."

"Guys were dealing drugs out of your warehouse at night and you just shook your head and said tut-tut? That doesn't make any sense, David. You got a reason for not calling the cops, like a previous record? You didn't want them nosing around?"

He blew out so much air I thought he'd entered a wind tunnel. "I hadn't been in business long and didn't need the hassles. And yeah, I have an old conviction. It wasn't for drugs, Keene, but you probably know that, too. And for your information, I got a good price for this location and a long lease. I knew it was the place that was raided and so what? I needed more space and this was perfect."

"Who were Wright's associates?"

"I don't know. Noticed a couple of guys hanging around. They disappeared in a hurry when they saw me. Couldn't identify them. It was years ago anyway."

It's amazing what people will tell you if you push the right buttons. I thanked him for the confirmation and hung up. Maybe he'd call the paper and complain about me. I didn't give a shit. I was on a roll.

Ann was talking on her phone when I went into the kitchen. "That was Nell," she said after the conversation ended.

"How is she? Any mention of her interview with the cops?"

Ann nodded. "She's sad, Marsh. She said the police recorded everything. They were really interested when she told them about the money, and asked all kinds of questions about Frank's gambling and who that money was for."

"Let me guess. Nell said she had no idea."

Ann nodded. "Right. Then they asked her if she knew why the security inside Frank's office wasn't working."

"Video inside his office? Jesus. He must have been worried about something to have that installed. What did Nell say?"

"She didn't know about any security. Why would she?"

"I wonder how long it was busted and when it was installed. What about cameras outside the building?" I said.

"They weren't working either."

"That could have all been deliberately disabled," I said. "Those cops knew it wasn't working, they just wanted to get Nell's reaction. Did they give her the third degree about her affair with Frank?" I wondered if she threw Jeanette under the bus.

"She said they asked a lot of questions about her and Frank. She's tired and just wants to go to bed. We really can't push her, Marsh. The police are working on it anyway."

"She might talk to me at some point. When I was at the spa, she said I could help."

Nell only saw the good in people, but today's probing might have opened her eyes a little. Who hated Frank enough to kill him? Could Nell be the next victim? I decided to wait for a while until she'd had a chance to mull things over before I spoke to her.

"Dad called," said Ann. "We talked about the money in Frank's safe. I'm glad he knows about that."

"Did you tell him?"

"No. I don't know how he found out. Does that matter?"

"Maybe not. He probably heard from one of his sources, or maybe Nell called him. If so, info is leaking out."

I got a drink from the fridge, went back to my office and thought about everything I knew about Frank's murder. There was no forced entry. Either the killer had a key, or Frank let him or her in. Or did Frank surprise someone who knew about the money and was trying to steal it? The safe hadn't been broken into, did the thief know the combination? Maybe Frank already had the safe open when the thief and potential killer showed up.

The cops were on it, and I'm sure Burton would be dogging their every move. Frank was his best friend. Plus, Burton seemed to be getting information from his own high-powered friends. Those legal boys looked after each other.

I felt like a guy learning to juggle. All the goddamn balls were landing on my head. I decided to catch the one with Allan Wright's name and run with it. Right, Keene, how are you going to keep your nose out of all the other stuff swirling around you?

I told myself it made sense to find out who'd killed Wright, keep my reputation and my job. Don might fire me if I didn't press the send button on that Fentanyl article before Tuesday. Then of course, there was my wife's ex-husband...I'd concentrate on the things that impacted on us.

Ann went to bed early, and I sat in front of my computer. I had half the Fentanyl article written and couldn't concentrate. I decided to amuse myself by calling all the telephone listings for Lancaster, asking for Gregory or Douglas.

I had a few hangups, but everyone else told me I had the wrong number. I knew Burton had contacted Douglas Lancaster in an email after the fire. I'd ask if he had his telephone number as well.

**

The next morning, Munro called. "I've got more on the Wright murder. I told you he took five shots in the chest, right? And that he didn't die where they found him."

"Yeah, you did."

"Whoever killed him was really pissed," said Munro.

I remembered being that mad. "Seven years ago, when I read my victim impact statement, I told Wright that killing my family was like shooting *me* in the chest," I said.

"Ironic how shit like that comes back to haunt you. I totally get that you have to find out who killed the bastard…here's the latest. Carruthers found some fibres on his clothes. Could have been from inside a car, I guess, she didn't elaborate."

"Well at least we know the time of death, and that the scene was a second location." I said. "If he was shot in a car, whose was it?"

"Good question. On another note, the cops will be searching that burned-out property your father-in-law owns. Frank Veale was his law partner, right? Do you think they're connecting the fire to Veale's death?" Munro never took off his thinking cap.

"Frank and Burton stopped being partners when Burton became a judge. I think the fire department are still trying to pin down a cause. But interesting point—maybe that fire *was* connected to Frank's death."

A source had told Munro about the property search. I wondered if Burton had received the same information, even though he probably suspected the search was going to happen. Munro hadn't mentioned anything about the storage locker, so I guessed he hadn't heard about that. We promised to be in touch and rang off.

I hated keeping my thoughts from Munro, but didn't want to speculate. And I couldn't imagine that anyone would find out Burton had bought that property for Frank. His name wasn't on the deed.

If I had something definite, like Frank being involved with drug dealing because he needed money, I'd fill Munro in. He'd keep it quiet. My notion that Douglas and Gregory Lancaster were connected and involved with something illegal needed solid proof. I wondered if the cops had decided the locker at Grant's was worth searching. Burton might know, and if he did, would he tell me?

Ann came into the office to kiss me goodbye. She was meeting her mother at an exclusive baby store, even though we'd spent hours online looking at every imaginable second-hand baby thing.

"You're not going to buy anything yet, are you, hon?" I said.

"Just looking. I need to actually see all the different manufacturers—find out what the best brands are."

Just like going to a dog breeder to look at the puppies. No such thing as coming home empty-handed.

I kissed her. "Try not to have too much fun, honey. And don't forget to text me when you get there."

Ann wasn't listening. She was stuffing a bunch of flyers into her purse.

I watched her practically skip down the ramp. My old beater was the last car in the driveway. Ann hopped in, started the engine and backed onto the street. I smirked. Eileen would cringe seeing her daughter drive up to an exclusive store in that old piece of shit.

I settled in front of my computer. Now I'd have uninterrupted time to look into those guys Celine Wright had confirmed were Allan's friends: Gregory Lancaster, Gilardi, and Jacobi—she'd called him Jacobs. I logged on to the *Register* to take advantage of their various information sites. I told myself that the info could be used for a future story about crime in Lakeville.

But I couldn't concentrate. I felt so alone now that Frank was gone. What if Allan Wright's killer was never found? What would happen to me and our family? I'd be branded as the revenge killer who got away with murder.

First, they'd have to prove it.

Chapter 17

I shook off feeling sorry for myself and took stock of what I knew. Both Celine Wright and David Mason had confirmed that Allan Wright was doing dangerous things. Celine mentioned Gilardi, GL or Lancaster, and *Jacobs*, but I was sure she'd meant Jacobi.

My gut told me to keep trying to connect the Lancasters with local drug dealing and the murder of Allan Wright. Celine had confirmed that Wright's three companions, who she never liked, had visited him in prison. She'd also said that Wright hadn't appreciated the visits. Were the police any closer to connecting those three to the murder of Wright?

I thought about the wallet and the money I'd found on Burton's property, and my visit to Grant's Storage. Had the cops followed up?

Munro had told me Wright wasn't killed at that subdivision. He'd also said the coroner found fibres on the body. Wright must have screwed up big time for him to be dead two days after being released from prison. Maybe payback for an old quarrel?

I decided to go to the cops with the picture I had. Even though it was decades old, it proved that the four amigos were a team from way back.

Homicide would search Burton's property again, including the boathouse this time. That could happen today. I decided to show up and try to talk to them, guessing that my tip about the storage locker had produced results. I had a personal interest in Allan Wright, which I hoped would be more credible to the police than just a nosy journalist looking for a story.

Would the cops lean on Celine Wright again for information? With those three morons running around the community, that possibility bothered me. I felt as though I was betraying her trust. I'd honour my promise and never mention her name in any of my articles. But I would write about it—I had to clear my name.

I refocused on the article Don wanted about drug use in the Greater Toronto Area. Were Wright's companions involved in that bust on Speers Road a few years back, the place Mason's Plumbing now occupied?

David Mason was probably safe from scrutiny, not that I gave a crap about him. He wasn't admitting all he knew.

My mind switched to Frank's gambling and his murder, convinced the two were connected.

Finally, I remembered the idea I'd had driving up to the spa. Did Eileen and Nell know Frank was in some kind of trouble? Nell might have confided in her sister. Eileen kept cautioning Nell to be careful what she said to me that day. I reasoned that someone else must have known about the money. Otherwise, the person or people Frank owed would just show up at the office and collect. No need for murder.

That would be obvious to the cops too. I hoped Nell would decide to talk to me. At the spa she'd said I could help, but maybe Eileen had changed her sister's mind.

How many people knew about Nell's relationship with Frank? Jeanette for sure. Nell was convinced she'd killed him. And, of course, Eileen and Burton.

Frank loved to live on the edge. He had money problems, but still bought expensive toys in the form of antique cars housed in a building near his renovated farmhouse. His beneficiaries would be the kids from his previous marriages. Jeanette would factor in somehow too.

I refocused on Frank's safe. How much money was in there? Nell had said *a lot.* She was wealthy, and her idea of *a lot* could be *huge* in my reality.

Thinking about money reminded me of Steven Anderson. He had an agenda for sure. He'd been so visible lately, and for the last day or so, invisible. That worried me. Abusers never give up.

I phoned Ann. She was probably getting pissed off with my constant calls, but I couldn't shake the feeling that Anderson would pop up at any time. When I'd spoken to her earlier, she said Eileen was only ten minutes late getting to the baby store. My call went to message.

"Hi! honey. Just heading over to your parents' house," I said. "I think the cops will be searching the cottage property and the boathouse today."

**

When I arrived at Young's, a forensics vehicle was parked in the cottage driveway, along with two cruisers. I opened Burton's gates, drove through, and parked close to the house. I wheeled up to the front door and before I could ring the bell, Burton answered with his phone tucked under his chin, and motioned me inside.

"Thanks, Gary. Give me an update later," he said and ended his call. "Let's go into my office."

I followed and he closed the door behind me. He turned on the ventilation system and lit a cigarette. Eileen was gone and I wondered why he didn't smoke anywhere. He must have read my mind.

"Force of habit," he grinned. "When the baby comes, I don't want the house smelling of smoke."

"Appreciate that, Burton." But his clothes always smelled like cigarettes. I hated the thought of him holding our baby.

Outside his office window, I saw hazmat guys poking around the burnt ruin. The cops were serious to have those guys on board.

I pointed. "I figured they'd be having another look at your property. Hope you don't mind…"

He smiled a half-smile. "Not at all. Glad to have company, Marshall."

"Have you had a chance to speak to them?"

He shook his head. "I thought I'd wait until they finished, but we can both go over." He took a drag of his cigarette. Smoke streamed out his nostrils. "That was Gary Lund just now. I've decided to press both harassment and extortion charges on Anderson. Trouble is, he seems to have disappeared."

"Do you know if anyone searched that Toyota?"

Burton nodded. "My detectives went to the scrap yard and found nothing in the car. The plates were stolen. I may have mentioned that—there's so much going on, I forget what I've told you."

I took a deep breath. "I don't like this, Burton. Did you know who Anderson's friends were? When he and Ann were married, I mean." My wife and I had never discussed the social side of their marriage. I never wanted to feel a personal connection to that moron.

Burton shook his head. "I asked Ann that question too. I thought he could be staying with a friend since he came back. She said he didn't have any friends when they were married, just some guys he worked with at the gym. He never brought them home, and she didn't know their names. And before you ask, my detectives went to the gym he belonged to and turned up nothing."

What could I say? For the millionth time I wondered why my beautiful wife had married that asshole. But my thoughts were cut short, Burton was in the mood to talk.

"They met at the gym. But I guess you knew that. I think Ann was impressed with his knowledge of how the body works, or something like that. Being a nurse, they had things in common. She was so busy studying to upgrade her qualifications, she didn't have time to meet other men. That's my theory, anyway.

"She didn't know Steven well enough before they decided to marry." Burton stared out the window. "Eileen said he came from a *good family* in Trinidad."

The parallel between father and daughter struck me. How well did Burton know Eileen before he'd married her? She'd lied, and coerced him into marriage. Did he know that I knew? I also knew Ann wouldn't have married Anderson unless she loved him. I hated that my wife had once loved a jerk like him.

Then she'd married me, a legless White guy in a wheelchair. How could her parents not think she'd made another mistake? I shook myself to ward of the bad karma.

"You cold?" said Burton. "I keep the temperature lower now. Eileen liked it too hot for my taste."

I smiled. "No, I'm fine. Do you have Douglas Lancaster's phone number?"

Burton's eyebrows migrated toward each other. "Why?"

I grinned. "Ann and I don't need a gardener. I'd like to find out if your gardener is connected to Gregory Lancaster." I told Burton what I wanted to do.

He nodded, took out his phone and gave me the number. "Might work," he said.

I pressed *69 on my cell and dialled. A male voice answered on the second ring.

"Doug Lancaster."

"Hey Doug, it's Gil. Greg with you?"

"*Gil?*"

"I need to speak to Greg. Like now. He's not picking up."

"He's not here. What's so important?"

"It's about Al. Giving Greg a heads up. The cops'll probably want to talk to him. And you too, now that I think of it."

I heard an intake of breath. There was silence on the other end for a few seconds.

"Go fuck yourself." Lancaster hung up.

I pressed *69 again and called the number back. My call went to message. I repeated the conversation to Burton. "Do you think he's calling Gregory now?"

"Could be. You certainly caught him off guard." Burton grinned. "Now it's my turn to try something." He picked up his phone and punched in a number, and had to press re-dial a couple of times before someone answered.

"Good afternoon, Douglas. It's Judge Young speaking...Fine thanks...I'm calling to let you know I found a wallet near the boathouse with a lot of money in it...well it's certainly not mine either...did you give the key to anyone else?...Police officers are here searching the property right now, so I'll just hand it over to them."

Burton smiled and put his phone down. He lit another cigarette and put his feet up on the desk.

"Bloody fantastic, Dad," I said, then snapped my mouth shut and stared at him.

He placed his cigarette in an enormous ashtray. He uncrossed his legs, stood and reached out. We shook, and he placed his other hand over mine for a few seconds.

"Can't remember when I had such a good time."

He settled back in his chair, a wide smile on his face.

"What the hell did Lancaster say to you?" I felt as though my eyes were still bulging out of my head.

"As the Limeys would phrase it, he was gob smacked. You gathered of course, that he didn't admit to owning the wallet. Didn't admit to anything and stammered when I mentioned the money and key. He coughed when I mentioned the police. Like all good suspects, he's worried that they will test the wallet and money for prints."

"I wonder if they'll find any prints besides ours?"

Burton shrugged and extinguished his smoke with a mighty stab, stood and gestured toward the door. “Douglas Lancaster has no criminal record. His prints won’t be on file. But Gregory has a juvenile record.”

I nodded. Burton was digging deep, and passing on exactly what I wanted to know. He’d never tell me how he knew and I didn’t want to know.

“Well, my boy,” he said, “let’s wander over there and see if we can learn anything.”

Burton followed me into the hall. The doorbell rang before we reached the front entrance. I wheeled up and opened the door. Detective Sergeant Reese and the homicide cop who’d accompanied him two days ago stood on the front porch.

Chapter 18

Burton ushered the two cops into the living room. He sat on a chair and waved Reese and Wood to the couch. I pulled into the space opposite. That way, I could see everyone without swivelling my head like a spectator at a tennis match.

Burton didn't offer any refreshments. Once again, I liked his modus operandi. The cops had come to him and he was in control. "Well, officers, I presume you have information regarding the fire on my property."

Reese cleared his throat. "It appears the fire was caused by faulty wiring. The Fire Marshall's office just confirmed that. We need to ask you some questions about your boathouse."

"The fire and the boathouse are two separate issues?"

Reese nodded. "We're going on that supposition. Who had access to that boathouse besides yourself?"

"My gardener, Douglas Lancaster. I mentioned to you that he had a key. He stored his gardening tools and his fishing equipment there. He also had use of the boat."

"You used the past tense, Your Honour. Is no one looking after your property now?"

Burton stared at Reese before answering. "What's left of the cottage will have to be bull-dozed. I'm waiting for the Fire Marshal to give me the okay. I told my gardener not to come back until further notice. I also asked him to pick up his tools before the padlock was changed. Which he hasn't done. And just to be clear, I have a separate landscape company looking after my home property."

Reese nodded. "Why did you change the lock on the boathouse?"

Burton eyed the cop for a moment before answering, "After my son-in-law found the wallet and the receipt for Grant's Storage, securing the boathouse seemed like the prudent thing to do. What's your interest in my boathouse, Sergeant Reese?"

Reese ignored the question. "We'd like more information."

"I've told you all I know."

Undeterred, Reese continued, "You said your gardener, Douglas Lancaster, had use of the boathouse for his tools and the boat for fishing excursions. When did he take that boat out?"

Burton pushed his glasses up on his nose. "Usually at dusk. Best time for fishing, I'm told. He once brought me a huge salmon, so I had no doubt he was fishing."

"Did he go out every night?"

"I have no idea. My wife and I aren't home every evening."

"On the occasions that you did see the boat go out, how many people were in it?"

"Sometimes one, sometimes two."

"Was one of the occupants Douglas Lancaster?"

Burton thought a moment. "I presumed it was Douglas. He always wears the same hat. I don't know who was with him. I never saw more than two people."

"How long did these fishing excursions last, Sir?"

Burton shrugged. "Can't help you there. I've heard a boat coming in several times long after dark."

"Was this recently?"

"Last summer or fall, probably. During the day I'm in my office at the front of the house and don't always hear lake activity. In summer we sit on the porch at the back, to take in the lake views, of course."

"What time do you go to bed, Mr. Young...er...Your Honour?"

"Around midnight. I sometimes take a stroll around my property before retiring during the nice weather." Burton leaned forward in his chair. "Did your people find drugs in my boathouse? Was there a drug operation on my property? I'm aware that you've found Fentanyl in that storage locker, Sergeant Reese. The one my son-in-law tipped you off about."

One of Burton's sources must have told him about the raid on the locker, and he was giving me credit for it in his round-about way. He wasn't afraid to let Reese know he was following police activity.

"As you can understand, Your Honour, we don't discuss ongoing investigations."

"You have my security tapes. Anything interesting on them?"

Reese was probably wondering who was in charge here. "The tapes will be returned to you."

I took advantage of the pause and pulled the now well-worn picture of Lancaster junior and his two buddies from my pocket. I wheeled over and handed it to Reese. "This may be of interest to you."

Wood leaned toward Reese and they both looked at it. "Why would we be interested in this?" said Reese.

I pushed back, out of their space. "It was taken on the courthouse steps the last day of Allan Wright's trial seven years ago, and published in the *Tribune* the next morning. You can see me in the foreground talking to reporters. One of the three guys in front of me yelled that I'd better watch my back. I'd just told a reporter that Allan Wright was lucky he was going to prison where I couldn't get at him. I regret that comment now of course, but you can imagine how upset I was then."

The cops held the picture closer, looked up at me then at the image.

"I've done my homework," I said. "Those guys were friends of Allan Wright. They visited him in prison. Wright was found dead only days after he got out."

"We're aware of Mr. Wright's companions." Reese took a deep breath and let it out slowly. "You seem to have more than just a passing interest in the case."

No shit. "Wright was responsible for killing my whole family. The *Tribune* insinuated that I'm a potential suspect in Wright's death in an article they published a few days ago. I need to know who killed Wright and why."

"We're also aware that you've spoken to Mrs. Wright," said Reese.

"I'm worried about her safety, Sergeant Reese. She felt guilty that her husband killed my whole family, and identified those three guys for me. They called on her just before Wright's body was found. She knew damn well it wasn't a friendly visit." The cops were probably aware of that, but I had to try and protect Celine Wright.

"What're you getting at, Mr. Keene?" said Reese.

"She's frightened and feels threatened. She might know more, but is afraid to talk. I'll tell you what I think, Sergeant Reese, for what it's worth."

Reese and Wood exchanged a glance. "Go on."

"I've uncovered a connection between Allan Wright and those three men in that picture. They were more than just buddies." I leaned toward the cops. "Remember that drug bust on Speers Road a few years ago?"

They responded with slight nods.

"Before he went to prison, Wright was into drug trafficking. I found out that he was a night security guard for Triple A Security. It's a boring job with long hours. Why not sell drugs to make the time pass?"

Burton sat still in his chair, a slight smile on his face. Reese, his eyes half closed, looked as though he was listening to a bedtime fairy tale. Since there was no objection, I carried on.

"Wright was caught dealing drugs by a business owner. I've spoken to the guy who caught him. He said Wright had accomplices, but he didn't know who. I assume the accomplices didn't work for the business owner, and he didn't call the police for reasons of his own, so Wright and his boys didn't suffer any consequences. Maybe they relocated to the building on Speers Road—the one you raided a few years ago. Maybe they changed locations a few times before they got there. Drug dealers have to stay on the move."

The two cops sat looking at me. The only things moving on their faces were their eyelids.

"Long story short, drug dealers can have disagreements. Mrs. Wright said she often heard her husband quarrelling with someone over the phone. He called Gregory Lancaster by name." I paused to take a breath.

"Who, in your opinion were Wright's other companions?"

"Besides Lancaster, the other two are Julian Gilardi and a guy named Jacobi. Don't know his first name."

If Reese and Wood recognized the names, they gave no indication.

"Wright drives drunk, kills my family and goes to prison. The three guys pay him a few visits on the inside. Maybe they have disagreements over the distribution of money. Mrs. Wright told me she had a hard time making ends meet after her husband went to prison. Maybe there's a longstanding grudge amongst Wright and his buddies."

Reese looked at his watch. Wood shifted in his seat. Burton sat like a statue.

"Here's my theory. Wright feels powerless and thinks he's getting screwed as far as money is concerned. He's not the brightest and spills to one of the inmates that the Speers Road building is the new drug headquarters. The inmate gets a perk for repeating the story to jail authorities, who pass the info on to the cops. Speers Road gets busted and drugs are seized. Either Wright was not stupid enough to mention names, or you guys couldn't link Lancaster and his buddies to the bust."

Reese's eyebrows went up.

"Here's another theory. Mrs. Wright told me her husband found Jesus after he went to prison, and it was the happiest time of their lives. Imagine that. He's in jail and it's the happiest time of their lives. Mrs. Wright also said she had high hopes for the future."

Reese and Wood sat perfectly still. They were paying attention.

"Wright in his new state of grace, feels he's doing the right thing by coming clean about the drug operation. It's kind of like kicking his former colleagues in the balls in the name of the Lord. The three amigos know damn well who talked and decide to get rid of Wright as soon as he's out because they're still in business. They also know that you guys never found anything connecting them to the Speers Road raid, and are probably arrogant enough to think you're not on to their game."

"You should write a novel, Mr. Keene," said Reese.

"I'm not quite finished, Sergeant Reese. After the Speers Road fiasco, Douglas Lancaster starts working for my father-in-law." I nod to Burton. "Daddy Lancaster knows what son Gregory is up to, and the private lakefront location is the perfect venue for the drug operation. Then the cottage burns down and I stumble upon that wallet and receipt."

"Are your musings going to appear in Monday's paper, Mr. Keene?"

Of course, he'd think that. It also made *me* think I was on to something. Reese either saw me as a lame-brained journalist, or was worried I'd blow the angles they were working on.

"Not until this murder is solved, Sergeant Reese, and there's solid proof that I had nothing to do with it. And then the story will be a personal article about why it was important to me to find the killer. The names of people who've given me information won't be disclosed."

Reese nodded, and looked as though he believed me.

Burton jumped in. "Are you finished asking questions?"

"For now," said Reese. He and Wood stood. Burton had more to say.

"There's one more matter I'd like to discuss—Frank Veale, who was very important to me. We were close friends and law partners before I was called to the bench. How is that murder investigation going?"

Reese and Wood slowly lowered themselves into their seats again. "We're looking at several angles—Mr. Veale's personal life and his financial status."

Why did Burton bother asking? The answer was straight out of the cops' *Tell the Public Bugger All* handbook.

"I presume *personal life* would include interviewing his wife?" Burton threw in his hook again. He knew it would come up empty. When there was no answer, he stood, they stood, and he ushered them to the front door. I wheeled into the kitchen, hoping to find a beer in the fridge. On the bottom shelf, a six-pack sat chilling. I took one and twisted it open.

Burton came into the room, grabbed a bottle of red from his wine rack, popped the cork, and poured himself a glass. He sat at the table, shoved a chair out of the way, and I pulled in opposite him.

"You really *should* write a novel," he said, laughing.

I smirked. "I had nothing to lose, and wanted to see their reactions. If they thought I was a suspect, they'd have arrested me by now."

"You're not a suspect, and your scenarios made sense. Do you think the police missed connecting those three guys to the Speers Road operation?"

"Probably not. They just couldn't pin it on them."

"No fingerprints anywhere in that warehouse? Lancaster and Gilardi both had records."

Once again, he'd passed on information I wanted to know. I took out my cell and pulled up the article on that drug bust. "It doesn't say anything about prints. They were all probably smart enough to wear gloves and maybe they got lackeys to handle the drugs. The cops sure found a load of Fentanyl."

"I think this operation could be bigger than we think."

"I agree." I sent him the article. "It sounds to me as though they were running an in-and-out operation. First, or maybe not even first, it was David Mason's warehouse at night, then the Speers Road building fits in there somewhere, and now that storage locker probably via your boathouse. Maybe there are other lockers too."

I lifted my beer and we toasted.

Burton filled in the blanks once again. "Police got a few sets of fingerprints, some handguns and twenty-two calibre bullets, plus drugs when they raided that locker last night."

This whole scenario involved Burton's reputation. I didn't blame him for pulling in all the favours he could to deflect the missiles coming his way.

The guns and bullets he mentioned pointed to serious criminal activity. "Wright was shot with twenty-two calibre bullets. They'll be trying to match them up with one of the handguns. If those prints belong to Lancaster and his buddies, that'll put paid to the whole goddamn thing. If they can find them, that is." I nearly said they could be hiding with Steven Anderson, but kept quiet. That would be a very unfunny joke.

"I wish I'd paid more attention to my gardener," said Burton. "It was short-sighted of me to presume that this neighbourhood was immune to criminal activity."

"You had no reason to suspect anything. And, no one's been arrested yet."

"Even though the police would never admit it, you've been a great help in this case, Marshall." He looked at me. "You realize that I've got…connections…and what I've disclosed to you is to be kept confidential...my reputation's at stake."

"Of course, Burton." It was on the tip of my tongue to call him Dad again. But twice in one day might be too much for us both.

"The hazmat guys probably found traces of drugs in the boathouse, and maybe in the boat as well," said Burton. "Otherwise, why go on about how often it went out and who was in it?"

"You're getting as bad as me," I laughed. "Would Lancaster and the boys take that boat out in the winter?"

Burton rubbed his chin. "The lake never freezes over around here, we're in a protected bay. There's some ice close to the shore, but any good drug dealer could handle that problem. Plus, people fish all winter long on this lake. If my boat went out lately, I didn't hear it."

"I think the cops were damn happy to have a reason to get a search warrant for this property."

Burton nodded. "Now that I think about it, they've probably been keeping an eye on Lancaster Junior and his buddies for a while. The father didn't have a criminal record, and now it looks as though they've been able to connect him with his son, who does." He took a sip of his wine then swirled the red liquid around in the glass. "I've been talking to Nell. She called yesterday after her interview with the police."

That surprised me. She must have been closer to Burton than I thought. "Oh? She spoke to Ann last night, but didn't say much."

Burton nodded. "She's finally getting smart. I got her a lawyer for the interview."

More news. "Do you think she's a suspect?"

"No, but a person of interest as far as the police are concerned. Everyone close to Frank is. She didn't like hearing that from me, though." Burton sat and seemed to be thinking. "She had a solid alibi the night Frank was murdered."

Was she at the spa with Eileen? I didn't know if they'd gone the night before their opening event or early in the morning. It was Burton's story to tell. I'd learn more if I just shut up.

"You've had great insight into your issue with Allan Wright," said Burton. "What are your thoughts about Frank?"

That was the prize-winning question. "I keep returning to something Frank said. I thought he was joking at the time, but now I'm not so sure. I think I told you."

"Refresh my memory."

I took a gulp of beer. "When I met him at the police station on Tuesday, we were talking about the article in the *Tribune* that morning. Frank agreed it didn't do me any favours. He encouraged me to prove I had nothing to do with Wright's murder. I started speculating about who could have killed him."

Burton shifted in his chair. I knew he was aware of some of this, but I wanted his perspective on the whole conversation. "Frank said, *Wright's wife probably killed him. She liked him better in prison.* Then he laughed. At the time, I wasn't aware that Frank and Nell were planning to…be together."

Burton put his glass down and nodded. "I see what you mean. Nell is convinced that Jeanette killed Frank. I know she said the same thing to you at the spa. And she also told the police."

"So did Frank think his wife was going to kill him?"

He let out a long, ragged breath. "This was his third marriage. He cheated on each former wife with the next one. I can't believe any of them killed him. But he also knew that Jeanette was angry. He'd said as much to me."

"So do you think his luck ran out and she actually killed him?"

"It's one possibility. The gambling issue is open to question, too."

"But why would someone who's come to collect a gambling debt kill Frank? Wouldn't he have to report back with the money? If he ran off with it, he'd be as good as dead."

Burton nodded. "Maybe the person who came to the office that night wasn't the one Frank owed the money to."

"Yeah, that's what I think too. Who else knew about it?"

"Beside Nell you mean?" said Burton. "Maybe Jeanette and other employees in his office."

I took a deep breath. "Maybe money wasn't the reason Frank was murdered. I'd be willing to bet that Nell had nothing to do with it. She's distraught and loved Frank from what I could see."

Burton nodded. "Nell didn't kill him. But the police will keep questioning her. There's a good chance Jeanette knew about the money. It was two hundred thousand dollars, you know."

"*Wow*! Two hundred k! Nell only told Ann it was *a lot*. Frank had a serious problem. Maybe Nell would be interested in that kind of cash."

Burton shook his head. "I doubt it. She's a wealthy woman. Ann never told you that their dad, old Berresford, has been putting money in both his daughters' accounts since they left Trinidad? Enough to make them independent. He had a big position in the oil and gas industry and could easily afford it. Nell was at the spa the night Frank was murdered. That alibi has been checked out."

"I wonder where Jeanette was that night. I haven't heard that she's been interviewed. For sure, the cops would have asked her some questions."

"Didn't I tell you? When I called her and offered to come over after Frank died, she said the police were coming. She told me it was for routine questioning. I know they've interviewed her again since."

"What about Gary Lund and the admin, Gayle? What do you know about those two?"

Burton nodded. "I've been thinking about them."

Chapter 19

"Has Gary Lund mentioned anything more about Frank's death?" I said.

Burton shook his head. "We've had conversations about Anderson, but since the police spoke to him and Gayle, he's been very guarded."

"I guess the cops gave them a thorough going over. Probably told Gayle to keep her mouth shut about what she saw when she found the body." I looked at my watch. "It's time to go home and find out what the shoppers couldn't live without."

Burton smiled. "Can you give me five minutes? I want to go over a few things and write them down."

Being a note-taker myself, I knew what he meant. Things were clearer after discussing them with someone. "Sure. I bet Ann and Eileen are still out anyway."

But I had trouble believing my own words. Ann was tired lately, and I knew she could only stand so much of her mother. I was tempted to phone her, but decided against it. In a few minutes, I'd be on my way home.

Burton went into his office and returned with a thick yellow pad and a fountain pen. "I told you that I called Gary Lund the morning after the murder. He said he'd talked to Frank after dinner the night before." As he spoke, Burton wrote things down in point form. "Frank was going into the office to do some prep work for the next day. But according to Nell, he was meeting someone to hand over the two hundred thousand to pay off the gambling debt."

Burton began each point with initials. I assumed they represented the person who had given him the information. He put his pen down and looked at me. "So, who got the money? And who knew about it? The safe was open and the money was gone. Frank was found stabbed to death with the letter opener."

"It must have been one hell of a letter opener," I said.

"Had a very sharp edge. I think I mentioned it was mine originally."

I pictured Frank struggling with his killer. "It's a damn shame the outside cameras weren't working," I said. "Negligent, actually, on the part of the law firm. There was probably some interesting traffic coming and going that night."

"Every camera was in good working order when I was there," said Burton. He picked up his pen. "Gayle came into Frank's office Wednesday morning, saw the open safe, found the body, and called 911. Then she called Lund. Then Lund called me. There was no sign of a break-in, although papers were all over the floor. Later on, Gayle called Nell to cancel an appointment she had with Frank that day."

Did the lovers make a habit of meeting there? Maybe a little action on the couch in Frank's office?

Burton read over his notes. "The people who could have keys are Gayle, Lund, the cleaners and the management company. Most likely Jeanette, maybe Nell and probably past employees who never handed in their keys."

"Do you have a key, Burton?"

His eyes darted toward me, then back to the page before he answered. "Yes. I told the police when they called that morning. It's the same one that opened the door when Frank and I worked together. He never agreed with me that locks should be changed periodically."

Burton probably thought the place had gone to rat shit. I brought up my last phone conversation with Frank the day before he died. "Who could have been so angry? It sounded like a man's voice. I got the impression Frank needed to take care of the situation right away because he told me I could call anytime then hung up. When I went to the spa, Nell told me that Gayle had been off work on Tuesday so she wouldn't have seen anyone coming into the office. But where was Lund?"

Burton wrote rapidly, answering my question. "In court. The session went on well past the dinner hour."

He prefaced this information with letters I couldn't read. This was the third different set of initials he'd used. His sources were probably people high up in law enforcement, who looked after each other. If Burton assumed Munro and I exchanged information, he was right.

"I've tried to find out who was in Frank's appointment book leading up to the day he died," said Burton. "I asked Gayle and she mentioned a few names. The police have taken everything from the office. Even if we had access to the records, how much time do we have to check everything out?

I'd love to have another chat with Gayle. I'd also like to know how friendly she was with the women in Frank's life." He thought a moment, then continued. "The police have most likely shut her down, but that won't stop me from sorting things out my own way."

"I wonder if there were any other women in Frank's life besides Nell," I said.

"Good point." He laid his pen on top of the pad, which was now covered in orderly script. Point after point, all neatly recorded down the page in black ink. "After you write that novel, you could consider going to law school."

Was this another back-handed compliment? Journalism wasn't a good enough career? He walked me to the front door. Get over yourself, Keene. Burton is just being Burton.

He put his hands on my shoulder and gave me a paternalistic pat. "Thanks for your insight, today."

The complacent feeling I'd felt after Sergeant Reese and Officer Wood left had turned to fatigue. Be nice to get home, talk to Ann and recharge my battery before finishing that article for Don. Two blocks from our street my phone rang. Ann. Had she and Eileen bought so much baby stuff she had to break the news gently over the phone first?

"Hi, hon," I said.

Her voice quivered. "Marsh, where are you?"

"Honey, what's wrong?"

"Steven's been here."

"*What?*" I sped up and skidded around the last turn, the SUV swayed left and then right before I regained control. "He's gone?"

"He just left. Where are you?"

"Twenty seconds from the house. Are you okay? Stay on the phone."

I remembered my own words. *Abusers never quit.* I charged past the last couple of houses, sped into our driveway and stopped inches from the old Mustang, grabbed my canes and hurried up the ramp. Ann opened the door and threw her arms around my neck, nearly knocking me backwards. Before we went into the house, I took a look behind me. No strange cars were on the street.

Ann clung to me. Somehow, we managed to get to the couch without falling over. I sat and she lay in my arms, shaking and sobbing. I could feel our baby between us. She held me so tightly it was impossible to see if that bastard had hurt her. I knew she had to cry it out before I could ask questions, and cursed myself for not being here, or calling earlier.

With my lips on her ear, I whispered, "Okay, honey. I'm here now. I'll never leave you alone again. This is my fault." I stroked her hair and kissed her face over and over. Finally, her crying lessened and she lay with her face against my neck. I reached for a box of tissues and handed them to her. I wanted to call the police, but first I needed to know what had happened.

Finally, she spoke, her head still pressed against me. "Oh God, Marsh."

"Honey, I have to know. Did he hurt you? Should we go to the hospital?"

She looked up at me and shook her head. "No, he didn't touch me. He's more scary now than he ever was. The look on his face. His crazy eyes. I ran behind the couch but he didn't come after me. I thought maybe he had a gun this time."

"Did you see a gun?"

She shook her head. "He had on a parka and never took it off."

"How did you get rid of him?"

"My phone rang. I told him it was you. Thank God, he didn't grab it and check. He just told me to turn it off. His parting words were: *You've ruined my life. You and your family are going to suffer.*"

"We have to do something about this, Ann. You know that, don't you?"

She blew her nose and nodded.

"Tell me exactly what happened…you okay with that?"

She nodded again and put her head on my chest. I tightened my arms around her.

My cop training clicked in. "Can you start at the beginning? Try not to leave anything out. Even the smallest detail." I shifted my body, hauled the phone out of my pocket and turned on the record feature. I placed it on the side table, and waited for her to talk.

She took a deep breath. "I'd just gotten home and was coming out of the bathroom. He was standing in the hall. I forgot to lock the front door. I knew right away he was in one of his rages."

The son-of-a-bitch was following her. But she'd been driving my old crap can—maybe he thought it was me. She was about four months along when he'd caused the miscarriage years before. As if reading my thoughts, Ann placed a hand on her belly.

"I remembered how those rages started. He'd work himself up by accusing me of stuff that was totally nuts, like cheating on him, like plotting to kill him. I learned not to bother denying everything because that made him worse."

"So, what happened next?"

"He glared at me and said: *I know the cripple isn't home. He's at your dad's house.*"

The bastard had been tracking us. I knew damn well he hadn't disappeared. Ann stopped talking and leaned her head against my shoulder. "Take your time, darling," I said.

When she shivered, I grabbed a blanket from the end of the couch and wrapped it around her.

"Now I understand why you always want to know where I am, Marsh."

"We're going to get him. Then you'll never have to worry again." I had to get her back on track. "Did he say what he wanted?"

She sniffed and blew her nose again. "He didn't ask for money, if that's what you mean. He just said, *I'm getting even with you, your high and mighty father, your snobby bitch mother and your useless husband. But first you all need to sweat until I decide it's time.*"

"Those were his exact words?"

"I'll never forget them."

What was he planning, a mass murder? Drive around and pick us off, one by one? Killings like this had happened before this crazy fuck thought of it. He'd come here today just to torture Ann. Like all abusers, he was a coward and made sure I wasn't home before he terrorized her with his plan. I had to form a plan of my own.

My head spun and I felt like I was going to puke. I had to call the cops. Ann couldn't go back to work until this monster was caught. *I* couldn't go back to work either. Where was he hiding out? How in hell was I going to find him?

"By any chance did you notice if he was driving?" I said.

"I knew you'd ask me that. We were still in this room when he left, so I saw him getting into a car. Not the old Toyota he had before. This one was old-looking too, but it was a faded blue colour with a bashed-in fender. Might be a Honda. I didn't see the plate."

"That's great, honey. You've done well. That fender? Was it front or back, passenger side or drivers?"

She thought a moment. "He was facing north, so it was the passenger side. But I can't remember if it was front or back."

I hugged her tight. "Brilliant detective work, baby."

She shuddered. "The phone ringing seemed to make him stop and think."

"Let's see who called," I said. Whoever it was probably saved her.

She reached into her pocket and handed me the phone. "Unknown number," I said. "Probably a telemarketer. I'll never curse them again."

Ann sat up, but leaned into me and gripped my hand. "I just want it to be over. We can't stay in this house, Marsh."

I went to get her something to drink before we decided what to do next. I had to move a six-pack of *Stellas* out of the way to get at our filtered water. Be nice to drink them all, but I needed a clear head, so I poured myself a glass of water instead.

First, we decided to call Burton. He was incensed and frightened at the same time. He said he'd put an emergency call into Gary Lund and the two detectives he'd hired. I said I'd call the police and report the threat, even though Ann would have to tell the story all over again. I was confident Burton would pull in more favours owed to him if it would help catch and convict Steven Anderson.

Because the Young's house had a security system to beat all security systems, Ann and I accepted Burton's offer to pack up and stay with him. The place even had an elevator, so I'd have no problem getting to a bedroom if I didn't want to use my canes. I wondered if Eileen would decide to come back when she found out what had happened. I packed up my computer. I'd never be able to sleep tonight. Might as well work.

I'd told the police to meet us at Young's, and they were there when we arrived. My father-in-law had his judge's hat on and controlled the proceedings. Two officers whose name tags said Grant and Wetmore, took notes while Ann told them about Anderson's threats. She repeated the horror story like someone just going through the motions, pausing only to close her eyes once in a while and take a breath. When I thought she'd finished, she looked at me. "Oh, there's something I forget. Steven was still wearing his wedding ring."

Jesus Christ. I'd like to rip the thing off his hand and shove it up his ass.

"Perhaps he's remarried, Mrs. Keene," said the cop.

Ann shook her head, not bothering to tell him she was still Ms. Young. "We had the rings custom- made. It was the one I gave him."

The crazy bastard hadn't let her go, and wouldn't until he was forced to.

The cop nodded. "Is there anything else we should know?"

Burton cleared his throat. "I'm trying to proceed with charges of extortion against Steven Anderson," he said, after explaining what he thought precipitated today's threats. "I pressed charges a few days ago and should have reported him much sooner, but I never thought he was this dangerous."

Bull shit. He knew bloody well Anderson was dangerous seven years ago. Burton didn't want any public embarrassment back then. He figured throwing money at the guy would solve everything. I looked over at Ann. She was staring at her father, lips tightly closed.

"Is this the first time your ex-husband has physically threatened you, Mrs. Keene?" said one of the cops.

Ann slowly shifted her gaze to the cop. "He was abusive throughout our marriage. That's why I divorced him."

"Was your ex-husband ever charged?"

Ann shook her head.

The cop turned to Burton. "Were you aware of the abuse, Your Honour?"

Burton looked straight ahead, not responding. No one moved or said anything. I wondered who would break the silence. Finally, Ann spoke. Her voice was even and controlled. She looked one of the officers in the eye. "I kept that part of our relationship from my parents."

The cop looked from Ann to Burton, who was staring at his hands. I felt like jumping up and slamming one of my canes down on his flawless mahogany coffee table.

After a few more questions the cops stood, promising to investigate the matter, offering no guarantee that Steven Anderson would be found. They made it clear that if he was found, Ann would have to personally press charges to bring him to justice. Burton ushered them out and I hustled Ann upstairs before I was forced to speak to him again that night.

We got ready for bed in silence and lay beside each other. The guest bedroom was at the back of the house. The night had turned stormy, and I could hear waves crashing into the rocky shore. My heart hammered inside my chest and I wondered if Ann's did too. And what about our baby? Was emotional stress harmful to a fetus?

I realized we'd had no dinner and offered to go down to the kitchen and rummage around in the fridge. Personally, I wouldn't be able to swallow one bite. Ann shook her head, telling me that she'd had a late lunch. She took my hand.

"I'm here, honey," I said.

"I love you, Marsh."

I felt like bawling. Not now, Keene, keep it together. I rolled on my side and took her into my arms. "You know what, Ms. Young? You're the bravest, smartest woman on this planet. And the most beautiful. I adore you. If I had any energy, I'd jump your gorgeous bones."

She snuggled into me and fell instantly asleep.

Chapter 20

What the hell was I going to do?

My first priority was keeping Ann and our baby safe. Anderson knew the blackmail game with his former father-in-law was over, and was cunning enough to realize the proposed meeting at Frank's office was a trap. Abusers always have to be in control. Countless dead girlfriends, wives and ex-wives were silent witnesses to the rage of freaks like him. Thank God the cops were finally on board with a more detailed picture.

I'd counted on Burton's help, but after his performance earlier, I couldn't pretend everything was okay. Why the hell didn't he tell the police he knew about Anderson's abuse? It was probably embarrassing for him to admit he'd paid him off years ago to get out of Ann's life. His Honour Judge Young had the biggest ego I'd ever bumped into.

I got out of bed, put on my prostheses and pants, grabbed my canes and walked to the end of the hall. Lights still lit up the main floor. I started down the stairs. Most likely Burton was smoking in his office with the door closed.

Halfway down, I stopped. What are you going to do, Keene, burst into the office and tell him he's a coward and that he betrayed his daughter? There was no way back from the conversation I wanted to have. I hesitated, and heard a door open. Burton walked into the front hall, shutting off lights behind him. He stopped at the bottom of the staircase, put his hand on the rail and looked up. His glare dared me to make the next move as I stared down at him. Then he frowned. His eyes focused on something behind me. I turned.

Ann stood at the top of the stairs. "Marsh?"

No one moved and no one spoke. Then Ann came down and stood beside me. She took my hand. I transferred both canes to the left hand. Together we turned and trudged back up, walked to the bedroom, closed the door and climbed into bed.

"I really want to go home to our own house in the morning," she said, tucking her head against my chest. "But I'm afraid of what Steven will do next."

I stroked her hair. "Yeah, I know. I'll figure something out."

I lay beside her, my mind jumping from rage at Burton, to panic at our life-threatening situation. When Ann finally fell asleep, I got out of bed, took the cards the cops had given me out of my pants pocket, went into the hall and dialled one of the numbers. My call went to message. *It's Marshall Keene calling. My wife and I are going back to our own home in the morning. Please have officers patrol our street on a regular basis.*

Lame, Keene. My gut told me Anderson would still be watching. Would seeing the cops drive by send him a message? Nope. I had to figure out how to stop him.

**

It seemed like I'd only fallen asleep when Ann nudged me and got out of bed. It was barely dawn. "Let's go," she said. "I want to be at home where it's just us."

Burton wasn't around when we left a short time later. It took a few minutes to brush the snow from the SUV, and by the time I finished, the inside was warm. The snow removal service had been at work during the night, so it was easy to navigate the driveway and open the gates even though about ten centimetres had fallen. On the drive home, rooftops and trees sparkled as the sun rose. We were the first car on the side streets, carving a fresh path through the powdery snow. Despite the peaceful scene, my mind was in chaos.

Our driveway didn't enjoy the luxury of Burton's plowing service, but tire tracks had already made channels in the snow. Ann and I looked at each other.

"Wait here." I got out of the car and made my way slowly up the ramp. I looked back. Ann was holding her phone. Tucked into the front door was a police officer's calling card. I smiled, called to Ann and waited for her on the front porch.

I'd have to do something about the snow. Years ago, when I was too stubborn to ask for any help, I cleared the driveway once by strapping myself into my chair to stop from falling out. Reaching down and throwing snow sideways damn near finished my back. From then on, I'd paid a kid, but it was usually a while before he got to me. For now, I'd put salt down and let the snow ugly itself away. The sun might be warm enough to co-operate. We went inside and made coffee and tea.

"Thanks for not saying anything to Dad last night."

"You showed up at the right time, honey. I'm glad you did, but I don't know where we go from here."

Ann didn't answer right away. "With Dad, you mean? I have to sort out my feelings first."

Yeah, I'll bet she did. There was no doubt about how I felt, and Burton would get the message when he woke up to an empty house. He needed to explain to Ann, at least, why he didn't tell Officers Wetmore and Grant the truth about Anderson's abuse. Best for me to back off and let her take the lead with her father.

The big issue was our safety. Cops driving by our house once in a while couldn't guarantee anything. I felt weak and shaky. Maybe some breakfast would help. I took a piece of the toast Ann had made and passed her the plate. "What do you think we should do about Anderson?"

She sighed and looked at me. "We have to get on with our lives. I'm going back to work tomorrow and you're going back on Tuesday."

"But–"

She held up her hand. "Just hear what I have to say. We can't stay at home worrying and waiting for something to happen. I did that for too long. You can drive me to work and pick me up. Thank God I don't have to deal with shifts anymore."

"But—"

Her hand went up again. "I'll call my supervisor and tell her the situation. Suzanne knows about Steven anyway—I had to take time off when I miscarried before..." Ann put her hand on her belly and took a deep breath. "She'll alert the security team at the hospital. This isn't the first time someone has been afraid of a former spouse showing up."

I'd feel better if one of those security guards followed her around all day and then came home with her at night. "That makes sense. And I'll park the car and meet you in the lobby after work."

Ann was right. We'd go nuts caged inside the house all day waiting for Anderson to make a move. And I trusted her co-worker, Suzanne. She and Ann had been friends long before I came around. "I'm going to call some security companies and push for a system to be installed tomorrow morning, with cameras attached to our phones."

"Good idea." She hesitated. "Marsh…Mom gave me some money for the baby. We could use that instead of putting the security system on plastic."

"Oh?" I hated it when her parents gave us money.

Ann sighed. She didn't need an argument from me. "I couldn't refuse. She really wants to help."

Pick your battles, Keene. There were worse things. "Yeah, okay, honey." Spending the money on a security system *would* be for the baby. There'd be no family if Ann and I were found murdered. I started to sweat thinking about what could happen and how.

"Did you and Eileen buy anything yesterday?" I said, trying to hide my anxiety. "I don't see any parcels around."

She shook her head. "I couldn't decide what I wanted. That's why she gave us money."

"How much?"

"Five thousand."

"Christ! We could outfit triplets with that kind of cash."

"You'd be surprised, Marsh. The baby furniture and clothes will cost thousands." Ann smiled and her eyes shone as she listed off various things she wanted.

**

We spent the rest of the day keeping busy with household stuff. At least Ann did. I finished the article on Fentanyl and sent it into Don in time for Monday's paper. Then I made some notes for a bigger story on criminals who run drug operations, which would tie into the pop-up needle sites Don wanted me to write about. If the Lancasters were arrested, I had front row experience.

I called a bunch of alarm companies and left messages to call me back Monday morning, ASAP. I decided to accept the one that could install right away—everything had to be up and recording by Tuesday.

In the afternoon, we relaxed in the front room. Ann scrolled through pictures of baby stuff. I kept trying to tell her about the wonderful second-hand sites I'd found. Just when she was willing to look, her phone rang.

"Hi! Mom…Honestly, I'm fine. Who told you?…Oh. How did she find out? Have you spoken to Dad?…I don't want to stay in a hotel, Mom.

Marsh is having a security system installed tomorrow before we go back to work. You and Nell are at the spa?"

Finally, Ann hung up and gave me a *what-the-hell* expression. "Mom hasn't been talking to Dad. Nell told her about Steven."

"Who told Nell?"

"She called Dad to find out if he'd heard anything more about funeral arrangements for Frank. It's a week on Tuesday since...he died. That's when Dad told her."

"I thought there wasn't going to be a funeral."

"Frank wasn't a churchgoer, but Jeanette was brought up in the church. Anyway, the body was released yesterday. Dad was talking to Gary Lund and he said there'd be some kind of service but didn't know when."

"I bet your dad called Lund to light a fire under his ass after we spoke to the police. He's paying him and those two detectives and wants action. They're probably all running around talking to anyone who had anything to do with Anderson."

Ann nodded. "I love the way you put things together. You should have been a lawyer, Marsh."

"Your dad said that to me yesterday."

She sighed. "I can't decide what to do about him." Her eyes filled with tears. "He hurt me, Marsh, just sitting there and saying nothing. It made me feel so…insignificant."

I put my arm around her and she leaned her head against my shoulder. "I know him—he's so stubborn. He'll never make a move if I don't talk to him first. Maybe he doesn't even realize he hurt me."

Hurt her? He fucking trampled over his daughter who'd suffered terribly and was still suffering, thanks to him. "I'm going to suggest something you won't believe."

She looked up at me, eyes wide.

"Leave it for a while," I said. "Your dad's a thinker. He knows damn well he hurt you. I don't understand either why he just sat there. He knows he has to make it right."

She managed a smile. "Wow! Coming from you, Mr. Instant Potato. I thought you'd be telling me to go over there screaming and pounding on his desk."

"I guess you read my mind last night." I didn't mention that her dad had plenty of time to think now that he was on his own after more than forty years of marriage, his only daughter wasn't talking to him, and his best friend had been murdered.

Ann nodded. "I think you're right. I'll wait for him to make the first move. But I know you, Marshall Keene. You won't ask Dad for help now, and you'll do something about Steven besides install a security system."

I sighed. "I want to talk to anyone who knew him. You can help with that. Start thinking of people I could contact. Why do *you* think he come back to Canada?"

She looked at me, not answering. We'd previously discussed that life could have turned sour for him in Trinidad. Maybe he was in trouble with the law. We knew he'd asked Burton for money and was refused.

"Someone has to know who he hangs with," I said. "I'll go to that gym and ask questions. The bastard's got to be somewhere close because he's sure keeping an eye on us."

The people who knew him other than Ann were Eileen, Burton and Nell. I had never wanted to ask about Anderson. Someone had to know where he got the new-old-wheels he drove around town yesterday. I'd visit the junkyard. Maybe he'd been there and bought that Honda.

"You must have a picture of him somewhere, honey."

She glared at me. "You must be kidding. I ripped them all up ages ago."

Stupid question, but I could ask Eileen. She might have kept at least one picture of her daughter's wedding. I knew they'd gone all out—expensive dresses, tuxedoes, big church ceremony, country club reception. If I was going to ask people about the guy, I needed his picture to flash around.

**

When I looked out in the morning, the sun and the salt I'd put down yesterday had done a reasonable job on the driveway and the ramp—only a few centimeters of shrunken slop left. Luckily, it hadn't been cold enough to freeze, and I had no trouble navigating the streets at seven forty-five a.m. driving Ann to work.

I sat in the SUV and watched her walk into the hospital, taking note of every car parked within my sight line. No old blue bashed-up Hondas, and I was the only guy sitting in his car. Moments later, Ann texted to say she was on the ward.

I was eager to get home and start phoning security companies rather than wait for callbacks. On our street, all the neighbours who went out every weekday had left, and no strange cars were around. I parked in our driveway and started wheeling up the ramp. There was an envelope under one of the windshield wipers of the old Mustang. My heart thudded in my chest.

I grabbed the envelope, opened it and took out a typewritten sheet. *Need help with your snow crip?* There was a phone number. I called it—no longer in service. Only one person had ever called me *crip*—Anderson. I started to sweat. That envelope wasn't there when we left half an hour ago.

Ann's ex was getting bolder. I looked around. There was a public walkway directly across from us. It cut between two houses and led to a cross street. Why hadn't I thought of that before? The town had already cleared most of the snow, and I made my way along easily. My wheels added to the footprints coming and going from both directions.

Anyone could park a car at the end of that walkway and walk through to our street. Nothing blocked the view from one end to the other. Anderson could have seen us coming and going while he sat in his car. I imagined him watching our activity for weeks now. He knew our routine. If I'd only looked in that direction, I might have seen him. My heart raced again.

By the time I got back to the house, my fingers felt as though they were frozen around the wheels, and my hands stung with salt from navigating through the slush. I poured a coffee and wrapped my throbbing fingers around the mug. I wanted to call Ann to make sure she was okay. She'd know by my voice that something was wrong, so I texted her instead. *hi honey you okay.* I pressed the send button then realized she'd wonder why I asked. I'd just driven her to work.

Concentrate on what needs to be done right now, Keene. I decided it might be worth speaking to a few neighbours to find out if they'd noticed who delivered that envelope this morning. But the security system had to be installed immediately. I started calling companies, and luckily my first choice promised to be here at noon. I guess the guy was thrilled that I wanted every goddamn feature they offered which included the latest smart panel, Wi-Fi doorbell camera, door and window contacts, interactive integration and guard response, whatever the hell all that was. The feature I liked best allowed us to view secure videos in real time on our phones. I wondered how long it would take the installer to explain all this shit, and how long it would take us to avoid tripping the alarm ourselves.

Thanks for the five grand, Eileen.

A text dinged into my cell. Ann. *what's going on are you okay*

She knew something was up. But I had to know she was still safe. *just a little spooked still alarm company coming.*

She must have been waiting for my answer; I got an immediate reply. *good re alarm calm down security here is in the know see you later in lobby.*

She was safe at work. Now I had to make sure she was safe at home. Even though I was confident Burton had told Gary Lund about Anderson's latest threats, I wanted to speak to him myself. I needed to make sure His Honor had relayed every detail. My call went to message.

"Mr. Lund, its Marshall Keene. I presume Judge Young told you Steven Anderson came to our home and threatened to kill my wife and family, including me. Can you please call me? It's urgent."

I hauled out the cards that Detectives Grant and Wetmore had given me. I couldn't remember which one I'd called early this morning, and dialled Grant's number.

"Grant speaking."

I recognized the voice. He was the one who'd said very little, probably the junior officer.

"Detective Grant, its Marshall Keene. I'm calling to follow up on our meeting at His Honour Judge Young's house on Saturday." I was pissed off at Burton, but I didn't mind making use of his name.

"Detective Wetmore is in charge of that investigation. I forwarded the message you sent earlier to him. I'll have the desk connect you."

I thanked him and seconds later Wetmore picked up. I explained who I was.

"Yes, I got your earlier message, Mr. Keene. An officer has been by your house. I presume you are there now."

"Yes—"

He interrupted me before I could explain why I was calling again. "I understand that His Honour Judge Young also has two private detectives trying to find Mr. Anderson."

"That's up to Judge Young. So far, they've struck out and so has the lawyer he hired. I have more faith in a police investigation. I'm calling because I got a message on my windshield this morning from Steven Anderson. He's still watching us." I read him the note.

"It doesn't sound particularly threatening to me, Mr. Keene, just insensitive. Are you sure it's from Mr. Anderson?"

"Have you forgotten he followed me home from work last week?" My voice was so loud I was glad no one was home to hear me. "I didn't mention this to you, but the son-of-a-bitch called me *crip* when I confronted him. He's the only person who's ever used that word. And, just to reconfirm what I told you at Judge Young's house, Anderson knew I wasn't home on Saturday, came here and threatened my wife. Threatened to eliminate all of us. He must be watching from the public walkway across from our house. Please check that out."

"Please calm down, Mr. Keene. I've recorded everything you and Mrs. Keene told us and I'll add this incident to my notes. We'll take a look at the public access and keep patrol cars on your street."

"Thank you." My voice returned to a more normal level. "I can't remember if Ann, my wife, mentioned that Anderson's still wearing the wedding ring she gave him. They've been divorced for seven years. He's obsessed with her. Please don't forget that he told my wife he was getting even with the whole family and we'd have to sweat until he decided it was time."

"We agree, he's dangerous and this is a serious situation. I spoke to His Honour Judge Young and assured him that we're trying to locate Mr. Anderson. He has no criminal record. We know he entered Canada six weeks ago..."

He was going to add something but thought better of it. Did he have to be more careful because a judge was involved? "Have you been able to get an address for Anderson, Officer Wetmore?"

"We can't divulge any information, Mr. Keene."

Did that mean they had the bastard's address? And that if he gave it to me, he thought I'd go and fucking kill him? Anderson had probably put false information on the custom's form when he entered Canada.

"One more thing," I said. "My wife is expecting our first child. Years ago, Anderson beat her. She was pregnant at the time and lost the baby. That incident was the only one she kept from her parents, but they knew he was abusive."

"Why wasn't this reported to the police years ago?"

"You need to ask Judge Young. Here's my number again." I gave it to him along with my email address. "I know my wife mentioned this yesterday, but did you make note of the car Anderson was driving on Saturday?"

I heard pages turning. "It was an older model blue Honda with right front bumper damage. Plate unknown."

He asked me if there was anything more. When I said not right now, he told me he'd be in touch and hung up. I was willing to bet my new security system I'd never hear from him again. Maybe not from Burton, either.

Time to get my shit together and track the bastard down myself.

Chapter 21

While I waited for the security company to show up, I called my next-door neighbour, John Reynolds, a widower and retiree who'd lived on Ortona Street for over fifty years. In the summer, he sat for hours on his front porch, watching everything that went on in the neighbourhood. I'd sometimes have a beer with him and learn who couldn't pay their mortgage, whose property was a disgrace, and who was rumoured to be putting their house on the market. In the winter, he hid in the house watching the news channel. John recognized my voice right away.

"Must be rough getting around right now, lad," he said. "How's the missus? Time you two had a family."

After exchanging a little small talk, I got down to business. John hadn't noticed anyone on my property this morning and didn't receive any offers to remove his snow. "But I seen an old blue Honda in front of your house on Saturday. The car was probably ten-twelve years old. A guy ran down your path and drove off in a real hurry. Meant to call you. Forgot about it until now. Sorry."

John had worked for the Ford Motor Company for forty years and knew his cars. I was glad someone beside Ann had seen Anderson's Honda.

"You didn't happen to see the plate, did you?"

"No, son. Eyesight's not as good as it used to be. Couldn't even tell you if it was local. But the car had a smashed front bumper on the passenger's side. Even I could see the car was rusted out."

When I asked what the man looked like, John said a hood was pulled over his head. "That guy bothering you? Doesn't like something you wrote in the paper? Being a reporter can be dangerous, what with you stuck in that chair and all."

That phrase usually annoyed the crap out of me. But I knew old John was one of my biggest fans. My parents had been a great help when his wife was putting up with Alzheimer's. He was overcome when my family was killed. John had looked out for me in his own particular fashion ever since. I learned to ignore his ill-chosen comments.

"We'll have a beer together when I can talk about this," I said. He'd never know my version of the events would be an adaptation he could spread around the neighbourhood. Knowing John, he'd be sure to throw in that he'd helped solve my problem. Maybe even saved my life.

I thanked him and phoned two other neighbours who were usually home during the day. No one had noticed anyone earlier and like John, hadn't received any snow removal offers. When I asked about the old Honda, the responses were negative too.

I phoned Nell. She started to cry. "Marshy, I've been meaning to call. It's so good to hear from you, I feel so lost without my Frankie." She sniffed and blew her nose, then rambled on in her usual breathless fashion. "Thank God I've had the spa to keep me busy. Eileen told me that Steven actually came to your house and threatened Ann. Oh my God, what are you going to do?"

I asked if she had a picture of him, then answered her question. "I've got a few ideas. I guess Eileen told you we've spoken to the police. But I can't sit back and wait for them. I'm feeling totally isolated."

"What do you mean?"

I gave her a brief version of the events since Anderson's visit including Burton's lack of disclosure to the police. I was confident Nell knew about the abuse, but didn't mention the previous miscarriage. I told her we'd left Burton's house and hadn't spoken to him since Saturday night. "I was counting on his help. The two detectives he hired haven't found Anderson, and it doesn't look as though Lund has done anything useful either."

"Burton's too proud for his own good," she said. "I'll do anything to help my Anny. Just say the word. Can we meet for a coffee?"

"I'm at home waiting for a security system to be installed. Can you come over?"

"A security system? Good move. I'd love to see you. Can't stay long, though, I'm testing out a new masseuse at the spa later. I'll bring coffee. Double cream, right?"

"I'm surprised you remember that. Thanks, Nell, see you soon." I didn't want to prolong the conversation. She was much more animated in person.

"See you in ten."

I knew Nell's ten minutes would be more like an hour. She and Eileen both operated on West Indies time. Thirty minutes later, the doorbell rang. Two guys from *Safe and Secure Systems* walked in carrying coffee, creamers and donuts. They'd brought an extra coffee in case I wanted one. I thanked them, took the coffee, and chose a honey crueller.

They went over the whole house and gave me excellent advice about the features I should choose. Because it was a bungalow, I decided to have the main rooms wired and security cameras in multiple locations. To hell with the cost—Eileen was paying. They thought I was overdoing things, but I ignored their suggestions on where I could cut corners. After I signed the contract, they got busy installing, and by the precise way they went about the job, I knew they couldn't finish in one day. With Anderson lurking, I hated the thought of leaving the house until the system was up and running.

I'd just finished my coffee when Nell arrived with another x-large. After drinking that I'd be as wired as the house. Thank God she didn't bring any donuts. The guys were working in the front room, so we sat in the kitchen.

Nell took off her coat and hung it over a chair. I'd seen her only a few days ago at the spa, the day we heard that Frank had been murdered. She looked more drawn and anxious. Her hand shook as she passed me the paper cup. "Marshy, thanks for asking me over."

I wheeled up and hugged her. "Nice to see you. You're welcome anytime, Nell. Thanks for the coffee."

Her eyes filled with tears. She reached into a gigantic purse, brought out a pack of tissues and sat sobbing for a few minutes before looking up. "Sorry to be such a downer, but I can't talk to many people about Frankie. Who wants to listen to the *other woman*? I won't be able to go to the funeral, whenever it is. No way that bitch would ever let me come."

"I'll find out when it is—probably soon, now that his body has been released. You should go to the funeral with Eileen. And Ann and I will talk to you anytime about Frank. Why don't you stay here with us for a while?"

"Thanks for the offer. You're a love. But I'm going to the spa—plenty to keep me busy there. You'll feel safer with a security system, Marshy. Glad to hear you called the police about Steven. They should've known years ago."

It always took me a few minutes to get used to Nell jumping from topic to topic. When I was first getting to know her, *Marshy,* irritated me. Now, I'd think something was wrong if she didn't call me by her pet-name. Ann usually was Anny and sometimes she referred to her sister as Eileeny. I'd never heard her call my father-in-law anything but Burton.

"I understand that you feel isolated, Marshy. And like I said, I'll do anything to help Anny. She's still not talking to Burton?"

I shrugged. "Maybe she'll phone him from work today—that isn't what I want to talk about. I asked if you have any pictures of Anderson. Ann burned the ones she had, and I'd rather not ask Eileen."

I'd forgotten Nell's musical laugh. Of the two sisters, she was the charming one. "I've got *millions* of pictures on my phone. I hope I still have some of Steven." She poked around for her photos and started thumbing through them as we talked.

"What did you think of him?" I said.

"Steven? I didn't get to know him all that well. Only saw him with Anny at Eileen and Burton's house, maybe four or five times before the marriage was over. He was a good-looking guy, into bodybuilding in a big way. Wore clothes that showed off his muscles. He talked about himself a lot."

"What was your impression of him as a person?"

She frowned. Her super-sized diamond rings sparkled as she twirled a heavy gold bracelet on her wrist. "He wasn't smart enough for Anny—too fond of himself. She had a great career and he was a personal trainer. I don't know what she saw in him, other than–you know."

The image of that moron having sex with my wife made my gut ache. "What did Burton and Eileen think?"

Nell shrugged. "Eileen seemed to like him at first. He came from a society family back in Trinidad. Burton never said anything to me one way or another—but then he wouldn't, I guess. I wasn't surprised when Eileen told me Steven and Ann had separated."

"Did you ask why?"

She shook her head. "You don't know my sister like I do. Never ask personal questions. I was going through a separation at the same time, so wasn't paying much attention to anyone else. A few weeks ago, Eileen told me that Steven phoned asking for money—that's when she told me they'd divorced because he beat Ann. I'm sure you know Burton is trying to have him arrested." She reached over and touched my arm. "Marshy, please don't tell Eileen I told you any of this."

I wondered if she knew the extent of Steven's abuse. "Whatever you say stays here, don't worry, Nell. Can you think of anyone else who knew him or might know where he is?"

She shook her head. "You could try the gym where he worked. That's all he talked about, so he must have made friends there. Frankie told me he'd never liked him, but didn't let it show. He wouldn't have wanted to hurt Anny. I remember at the family gatherings Jeanette was nice enough to him."

Frank had trusted and confided in Nell. I wondered how long they'd been having an affair.

"What do you mean Jeanette was *nice enough?*" I said. "In a social kind of way or flirting with him?"

"That cold bitch? I can't imagine she'd ever flirt with anyone. She just didn't seem to sneer at Steven, the way she sneered at everyone else."

It would never have occurred to me that Nell could have noticed something as subtle as that. But she was right, *sneer* was the perfect descriptor for Jeanette's demeanour.

"A couple of weeks ago, Frankie told me that Steven attempted to blackmail Burton and Eileen. I never let on that I knew. Frankie told me he thought Anny wasn't happy very soon after they got married. He said Steven always talked about himself as though he was really important and never gave his wife credit for anything."

"Frank said that?"

She nodded, pulled another tissue from the pack and blew her nose. "I think about everything we said to each other in those last few weeks, and re-live every minute we spent together." She cried again, then apologized.

"Thank you for telling me all this," I said. "Frank was my friend. I can only imagine how tough his…passing must be for you."

She blew her nose again and continued. "Yes, it is, but I want to help Anny," she repeated. "I feel guilty for not guessing she was so unhappy back then. Frankie's opinion of Steven made so much sense when I thought about it. He was good at sizing people up, you know. I guess that's why we got along. I'm a talker and he just sat back watching and listening."

She put her phone down. More crying and nose blowing. The poor woman. I could see how she and Frank complemented each other. Nell collected herself and started talking again.

"He also said that before Anny married Steven, she'd always been excited about life, that she was a happy person. Talked about what was going on at her work and other stuff she was interested in. She had a great way of letting you in, if you know what I mean. Not long after they were married all her stories stopped. Steven did all the talking about wealthy clients who insisted on having him as their trainer.

"Oh, and another thing—Frankie said that a few months after Ann and Steven were married, she started wearing different clothes. Long sleeves and pants instead of the more stylish stuff she usually wore. Stuff that showed off her figure. Frankie thought Ann looked tired all the time."

All this information gave me a clear picture of the jerk. Anderson seemed to put himself out there, but never talked about any friends or anything personal. It was as though he wanted people to know only what they could see—the muscles, the so-called good looks, the superiority attitude. I wondered if all abusers were like this. Nell was still talking. I asked her to repeat what she'd said, afraid I'd missed something important.

She leaned closer to me. "I just said that Steven had threatened Eileen about stuff that went on in Trinidad years ago. He said he'd hurt Anny if she didn't pay. I can't go into the Trinidad thing, Marshy. It's better left alone."

"That's okay, Nell." Too bad she wouldn't go into it. I wondered if her version matched Eileen's.

"Anyhow, that's when Frankie recommended Gary Lund, and Burton agreed to give him a try."

I'd never seen the true Nell because I never bothered to look. She'd always seemed rather silly. Beyond the glitz and flamboyant personality she had an innocence and charm. And depth. Who else had I misread?

"What do you think of Gary Lund?" I said.

She wrinkled her nose. "He's dull. Boring clothes, boring voice. I think Frankie was giving him one last chance to help Burton find Steven before getting rid of him." She thought a moment. "Gary's one of those people who never looks you in the eye, you know?"

I nodded. I wondered if Lund knew he was standing on the edge of the unemployment cliff. Did he kill his boss, hoping to run the law practice? And steal the money while he was at it? That seemed too obvious and outrageous. I remembered Frank saying he'd had a hell of a time hiring good lawyers after Burton left the practice. I told Nell that Frank hadn't hesitated to meet me at the police station last week, hoping my own confidential disclosure would keep her talking.

"That would be my Frankie. Drop everything to help someone."

"He was very observant too. Why the hell didn't Burton and Eileen see the changes in Ann?"

"People don't like bad stuff, Marshy. Easier to pretend everything's okay."

That certainly summed up my in-laws. But now, Burton was starting to acknowledge the ugly side.

One of the security installers poked his head around the corner and asked a question. Instead of looking at me while I told him what he wanted to know, his eyes focused on Nell. She was glamorous and possessed a presence that invited glances. But, how much of our conversation had he heard? He managed to look my way before disappearing down the hall.

Nell picked up her phone and started scrolling again. "I don't know what you plan to do with the pictures, but please be careful. Oh… I nearly forgot, Frankie mentioned that Anny had called him just before she and Steven separated. She told him about the abuse and asked what her rights were. He advised her to leave right away, tell her parents what was going on and worry about the legal stuff later. She moved in with Burton and Eileen just before their first anniversary. About a year later she met you, Marshy." She smiled and patted my hand. "We're all so happy about that."

I smiled back. "Thanks, Nell." I wondered who was included in the *we*.

Did Nell know Ann was pregnant again? I decided not to mention our baby. She'd go on and on about how wonderful it was. I needed to keep this conversation on track.

"I just know you'll find Steven and have him arrested," said Nell. "You're so smart, Marshy…I just hope you won't forget about who killed my Frankie."

"No, of course not. Start thinking about anything unusual that might have happened before his death. Things he may have said about people he associated with, or maybe something strange that you didn't understand." We talked about the angry voice I'd heard during our last conversation.

"It was probably that bitch yelling at him. Oh God, I'll never forget when Gayle called and told me Frankie had died. We had a date that afternoon. She'd always let me know when Jeanette was coming to the office so I wouldn't bump into her." She looked down and twisted the tissue in her hand. "She killed him, Marshy. That bitch killed him."

I didn't mention, again, that the voice I'd heard was a man's—or point out the obvious–that the police hadn't arrested *that bitch*. "Who else knew about the two hundred grand in Frank's safe?"

Nell couldn't let go. "She knew Frankie and I were in love. I'm sure she went through his phone. She accused him of spending money on whores and horses."

Wow! Talk about a woman scorned. The poet who coined that phrase had Jeanette in mind. "Did she know Burton had bought the cottage for Frank and that he planned to live there with you?"

I wondered if this question would catch Nell off guard, but she answered immediately. "I know Burton told you, and I was glad he didn't say anything to the police. That bitch knew—she had ways of finding out."

My thoughts swirled, there were too many unknowns, ifs, and suppositions. The police were looking into Frank's gambling as a possible motive for the murder. If the people Frank was indebted to didn't get their money, someone stole it. Like Lund? Or Jeanette? Or someone entirely different?

"Do you know for sure that the two hundred K was for a gambling debt?" I said. "And how'd Frank get his hands on that much cash?"

"Yes, for sure it was. Frankie mortgaged the house and sold a couple of his antique cars. Jeanette knew about us and she knew he was tight for money. When they separated, she'd get nothing. I think she went to his office, killed him and broke into the safe."

"When the police interviewed you, did you tell them you thought Jeanette killed Frank?"

Nell nodded. "They said they were looking into many possibilities."

It didn't sound to me as if they were convinced about Jeanette's guilt. "If she took the money, what about the people expecting to be paid off?"

"I guess they'd be out of luck, Marshy. What could they do? Frankie was gone."

I loved her simple logic. *Money lender goes to Frank's office as arranged. Money isn't there and Frank is dead. That's that.* Something came to mind that I'd thought about a few days ago—Nell's safety. "Did you ever go to the races with Frank?"

She smiled and then sighed. "Yeah, we had some fun times there. He was treated like royalty."

"Who treated him like royalty? Can you remember any names and what they looked like?"

"Frankie never introduced me to anyone at the track. It was just him and me spending quality time together, you know. We had free drinks and food and a private box."

Who the hell was Frank connected to at that racetrack? Obviously, he was a big player. I knew absolutely nothing about horse racing and its underbelly. "Did you bet on the horses, too, Nell?"

She tilted her head and gave me a coy smile. "Sure, Marshy. That's the point of going, isn't it? I had my share of wins and losses, too. I took a picture of Frankie with a horse he liked to bet on. You'll love it."

"Did Frank pay for all the bets?"

She nodded. "My Frankie was such a gentleman."

"If all the bets were paid for upfront, how did he get into debt?"

She lowered her voice. "Side betting, Marshy. And just so you know, after I found out, we stopped going to the races."

With her obvious wealth, she might be a target if the debt was still outstanding. That didn't seem to have occurred to her. And maybe Frank didn't owe money to loan sharks, just guys at the track he hung out with. "Did you mention all this to the police?"

She nodded, stopped scrolling and looked up. "Oh, here's a picture of Anny and Steven. It's on their wedding day…sorry."

I couldn't look at it. "Can you send it to me, please?"

"Sure. I'll keep looking for others. I'm sending the one of Frankie, too."

Christ, did I have to look into the ins and outs of horse racing now? Who were Frank's buddies at the track when Nell wasn't around? I couldn't take on Frank's murder all by myself, and hoped the cops were working their asses off to find his killer. I was confident that Burton would be too.

"Have you asked Burton for advice? I'll do all I can, Nell, but I think he's a better bet than me."

"Yes, I've been speaking to him…I need all the help I can get."

"If there's anything he tells you that I should know, can you pass it along?" I said.

Nell nodded. If she knew we weren't talking, she never let on. The second installer came into the kitchen. He too made a point of looking at Nell before turning to me and asking his question. I dismissed him with a wave of my hand and said I'd be right with him. He disappeared down the hall.

Nell looked at her watch. "Look at the time! I have to get to the spa." She stood and put her coat on, having trouble pulling the sleeves over all her jewellery. I accompanied her to the door.

"You know Marshy, everyone close to us is hurting. You and Anny, Burton and Eileeny, and me. We're family. We all need to stick together right now." Nell hugged me, then walked down the ramp and got into her car. She waved and blew me a kiss as she drove away.

I returned to the house and gave the guys the information they wanted. They were finished in our front room, so I pulled up to my computer, turned it on, and stared at the screen, thinking about next steps.

Lund still hadn't called me back. I checked my phone just in case I'd missed a message. Nope. I took a look at the picture Nell sent. Seeing my beautiful wife in a frothy dress smiling up at that beefed-up loser was like driving a knife into my heart. No goddamn way was I going to use this picture. As I was heading to the kitchen, my phone rang. Munro.

"Hey, buddy, what's up?"."

He got right down to business. "Giving you a head's up.. Don's grapevine says police are planning a raid."

Chapter 22

"Hang on a minute, Munro."

Someone was coming toward my office. I turned away from the computer and pushed forward into the hallway. The *Safe Secure* guy nearly ran into me.

"Another question?"

"I just want to double-check the location of the two motion sensors in the hallway."

I thought I'd made that clear earlier. "One facing the front door and one facing the kitchen."

He nodded and went back to work. I rolled into the office and closed the door, unwilling to be the source of their afternoon's entertainment. Was he wondering why I wanted this security overkill in a little bungalow in blue-collar land? Maybe he thought I was a drug lord protecting my stash.

I put the phone to my ear again. "Sorry, Munro. Having a security system installed. Okay, man, what are the details?"

He laughed. "Got your attention, eh, buddy? Don found out that cops from homicide and drugs have been working on what they call *Operation Red Wave*. Tomorrow morning they'll be doing a sweep of some areas around the GTA, probably their usual time of four am."

I whistled. "That's huge. Thanks."

Don and Burton were about the same age and had played their respective roles for decades. Just like Burton, Don was well regarded. He knew what to print and what to hold back.

Munro didn't have to tell me this was confidential, or who he was referring to. I could hear traffic noise in the background. He'd gone outside to call me. I thanked him again and we hung up. I also said a silent thank-you to Don—he was being true to his word to keep me informed.

I hoped like hell Lancaster and his friends were big enough to be included in the sweep. That homicide was involved was huge.

My conversation with Burton came to mind. He'd said the police had found Fentanyl, fingerprints and twenty-two calibre bullets in the storage locker.

I nodded to myself. Surely Lakeville would be included in the police raid and specifically, Douglas Lancaster's residence.

My thoughts swivelled back to the chat with Nell and her relationship with Frank. I opened the picture she'd sent of him at the racetrack.

The photo showed Frank standing in the winner's circle. A mud-spattered jockey sat on the horse, a garland around its neck. Frank stood on one side holding the bridle, and three guys dressed in suits and ties were on the other. Everyone was smiling, including the horse.

Could Frank have owned the horse, or been part-owner?

Interesting that Nell never met any of Frank's racing buddies. I wondered about sending the picture to the cops, then immediately decided against it. Nell's rich. If Frank still owed big money, that could make her a target. I decided to forget about any possible ownership of that horse, too. No one knew if the right people got the money Frank owed.

Nell sat with me this morning, speaking freely about Anderson and everything she knew about Ann's relationship with him. Then she made a point of asking me not to forget Frank's murder. I felt obliged not to let her down. I couldn't help feeling that all the events surrounding Wright, Frank and Anderson were somehow connected. Weird. Also, unlikely.

As far as Frank was concerned, it was all about the two hundred k. If the people he owed were paid off, why was he dead? Had Burton thought that too?

Nell was convinced Frank's wife, Jeanette—*that bitch*—stole the money and killed him. And, she'd said as much to the cops. For sure, they'd have questioned Jeanette. They always look at the spouse, particularly when money is concerned.

The night of Young's dinner party, Nell flirted with Frank and Jeanette was openly hostile. Maybe Jeanette was pissed enough to kill him. I told myself the cops didn't have proof or she would have been charged by now.

I was spinning in circles. The more information I learned, the more confused I felt. Get organized, Keene.

First, I was working the scene where Wright's body was found. Next, Frank was found murdered. Then, Steven Anderson surfaced again.

I needed to make sure my name wasn't associated with the murder of Allan Wright, and I'd like to get closer to whatever happened to my friend, Frank. Anderson had threatened our lives, and I didn't think those two cops, Grant and Wetmore, were taking him seriously. I had to find that asshole before he decided it was time to come around again.

I reminded myself that Ann and I were on Burton's shit list. I needed his help. Like Don, he was well respected and had access to information. Was it up to me to extend the olive branch?

I rolled into the kitchen to get something to eat. The Safe Secure guys were at my table eating a late lunch.

"How's it coming along?" I said. "You going to finish up today?"

The one who seemed to be in charge, glanced at his buddy. "We'd have to stay late. Have to ask the boss."

"Do that, please. I'd like to be up and running tomorrow." I'd bought every goddamn feature the company had to offer. They should be able to accommodate me.

The men looked at each other and nodded. I detected a *What's going on here* expression. I took an apple and one of Ann's Diet Cokes from the fridge and returned to my office. I grabbed my phone, pressed *69 and called Grant's Storage. A guy picked up on the first ring.

"Grant's, Glen speaking."

It was the kid I'd spoken to a couple of days ago. I hoped he was no good at voice recognition.

"Halton Police calling," I said, and muttered a name. "Following up on locker number 2017. What street address to you have for the owner listed as Gregory Lancaster?"

"Can you verify the account, officer?"

"Just a sec." Shit, think things through, Keene. I shifted through the pile of papers on my desk, knocking the Diet Coke and my jam jar of pens and pencils on the floor looking for the copy I'd made before giving the print-out to the police. "Here it is, account L7-78934."

"L7-78934..." I heard him punching the number into the computer. "We have 342 Maple Street, unit 101."

A townhouse, not far from here. I thanked him and hung up. How much time could I do for impersonating a police officer? I grabbed a handful of tissues, mopped up the coke, and crammed all the stuff back into the jar.

If the cops were raiding Lancaster's place tonight, I was going to be there. I'd probably have to hang around out of sight for hours, but this could be the breakthrough story of my career—a major crime sweep. *And,* I'd have the scoop and the photos. Christmas.

But first, I needed to pick my wife up from work.

**

Ann was waiting in the hospital lobby. Even though it was quitting time for most people, the joint was buzzing. People in wheelchairs with drip bags and oxygen attachments were being pushed in all directions. Every seat in the cavernous room was filled with folks drinking coffee, reading papers or sitting back with their eyes closed. A few kids chased each other, laughing and making the place feel less like an institution.

I approached my wife who was talking to another nurse. I always used my canes in places like this, unwilling to be a full-time member of the international wheelchair club. Ann stepped forward to meet me.

"Hi hon, this is Nancy. She's a nurse on maternity…Nancy, this is my husband, Marsh."

I leaned my right cane against my body and shook Nancy's hand. "Nice meeting you."

Nancy smiled. "I hear congratulations are in order. I hope I'm on duty when your baby's born."

I smiled back. "Not long now."

After a few more pleasantries, Ann and I headed for the parking lot. If Anderson was hiding behind pillars, he was doing an excellent job of it. Maybe he'd been by our house today and had seen the security truck. He'd be changing his game, but to what? My eyes swept the back seat as we got into the car.

After Ann and I exchanged our *How was your day* questions, she told me Burton had called. That was a first—phoning her at work.

"Dad told me Frank's celebration of Life is Wednesday at St. George's Church."

She didn't mention whether he'd offered any explanation for his behaviour last Saturday, and I didn't ask.

"Burton could have easily texted you. Glad he called instead." At lease he'd made the first move.

Ann smiled. "That's what I thought too. He wants to pick us up so we can go together."

"Sure." I reached for her hand. "I didn't think Frank was a church-going person."

Ann shook her head. "He wasn't baptised in a church. When his parents were alive, religion was important to them. I guess Jeanette's decided to honour that."

Christ, I hoped St. George's wasn't hoping for a big donation from Frank's widow. "Do you think his former wives will come to the funeral?" I said, curious to see them.

Ann shrugged. "They were on good terms, so why not? His kids will for sure."

We pulled into the driveway. The *Safe Secure* truck was gone. Maybe one guy went to get coffee and something to eat, but no, when we entered the house, they'd both left.

Ann's hands flew to her face. "Marsh, *they left the house open!*" She grabbed her phone out of her purse. I knew what she was thinking.

"Assholes!" I said under my breath. My heart pounded. "We talked earlier about finishing tonight. I told them I'd be out for a while and they said *see you later.* I assumed that meant they'd be here when we got back."

I snatched my canes off the back of the wheelchair. "I'll check the house. Get ready to call the police." I started walking down the hall.

Ann stood at the front door. "Marsh! Wait! What will you do if Steven's in there? I'm coming with you."

And if he was, he'd be hearing our hysterical voices. "*No*, you're not! Stay here and get ready to dial if I yell. I'll do this floor first."

I went into my office. Even though the *Safe Secure* guys had attempted to clean up, debris still lay around. The closet was barely big enough to hold our spare bedding and some work supplies, let alone a big dude like Anderson, but I checked anyway. There were no other places to hide in that room. I returned to the hall and checked the tiny spare room, our bedroom and bathroom, yanking open the shower curtain.

The kitchen was clear as well. It was an open space and no one could squeeze into the broom closet, but I looked there too. There were footprints on our back deck, hopefully from the security guys. The prints looked like the boots they wore, and cigarette butts lay on the deck. Anderson, the health nut, would never smoke. I locked the kitchen door. Before descending to the basement, I secured the side door too. Ann called to me.

"Marsh! Keep talking. I need to hear you."

"Yup, okay, honey."

At the top of the stairs, I turned on the lights. Our basement was fully excavated but unfinished. Thanks to Ann's sense of order, the boxes of stuff we couldn't live without and never opened since we moved in, were undisturbed against one wall. Both the bunker-slot windows were intact.

"Marsh?" By the sound of her voice, she was at the top of the stairs.

"All's good. Going into the furnace room now. Get ready to dial." How ridiculous. If Anderson was down here, I was setting myself up. I got ready to balance on my left cane so I could strike out with my right.

I opened the door to that small enclosure and switched on the light. The furnace took up most of the space. I led with my cane and poked into the space before going behind the furnace. No one. I flipped off the light, closed the door and started back to the main floor.

"Everything's good. Coming back up now."

When we met at the top of the stairs, Ann was still clutching her phone. We hugged, took off our coats and headed for the front closet. *Christ!* The realization that I'd forgotten to check there must have shown on my face.

Ann took my coat from me, opened the closet door, and hung our coats. "I already looked here."

**

Ann always showered and changed her clothes after work. As soon as she went into the bathroom, I took my phone out of my pocket and called *Safe Secure*. Someone answered even though it was after the universal five o'clock quitting time.

"*Safe and Secure Systems*, Brian speaking, how can we bring your family peace of mind?"

"For a start, Brian, you can tell me why your two installers have gone for the day and left my house unlocked while I was out."

"Sorry sir. Where are you calling from?"

I gave him the address.

"I'm looking for that installation order, sir. Who was your salesman?"

"I spoke to Stan this morning."

"Stan? Please give me a moment…ah…here it is." He repeated the address. "Did they finish the job?"

"They weren't finished when I left forty-five minutes ago. I told them I'd be back soon. They said, see you later. We'd discussed finishing tonight and I assumed they'd got the go-ahead to do that."

"Who was working that install, sir?"

"Danny and Fanny, how the hell should I know? They didn't introduce themselves and I didn't take note of the names on their I.D. Don't you have them listed on your paperwork?"

"Um…yes…It says here, Hank and Bill. Sorry sir."

"So, what's the deal? Are they coming back tonight to finish the job?"

"I can't answer that question, sir."

"Well, who can? Put me on to one of your managers."

"The manager has left for the day, sir. I'm just answering the phone."

"Well then, Brian, get in touch with someone, and *please* have them call me. Like now."

"I'll see what I can do, sir. Have a *Safe Secure* day."

Had I been speaking to a person or an A.I. robot? I felt like taking my canes and smashing everything in sight. Instead, I sat on the sofa, closed my eyes and took deep breaths.

That put paid to going to Lancaster's tonight. I just had to hope the police would raid that house. While Anderson was still on the loose, I wouldn't leave Ann alone.

She came into the office, rubbing her hair dry and smelling delicious. Her housecoat was loosely belted at the waist and I knew she was naked underneath. Usually, that made me horny.

Ann stopped rubbing and looked at me. "Who were you yelling at?"

She listened quietly as I told her. "This is my fault for hiring a company that could come immediately," I said. "They can't have been busy, which also means they're probably incompetent. The good news is that I haven't paid them a cent."

Ann nodded. "And the house is a mess—there's bits of whatever lying all over the place. I can't believe how much dust they raised." She looked around the room. "I thought about something else while I was in the shower."

"What?"

"I want to go downstairs. Come with me?" she said.

"Sure." We walked down the hall, I turned on the basement lights, and we descended together. Ann stood in the middle of the room and opened the door to the furnace room for a few minutes before closing it.

"Thanks, I feel better now," she said and we returned to the main floor. "There's no trace of that awful aftershave he always wore. I didn't smell anything on the first floor either."

I'd forgotten that stench the day I'd confronted him. I didn't mention that there had been no smell after he'd been here a few days ago, either. She'd probably been too upset at the time to notice.

"Let's go into the front room and calm down before dinner," I said.

After Ann got dressed, she cuddled up to me on the couch. "So, what else have you been doing today?"

I told her about my conversation with Nell and how distraught she was. Then I summed up the thoughts I'd had about Wright, Frank and Anderson. She listened carefully and agreed with my rationale.

"Sounds like you got a lot done today. I'll get you a beer. You've earned it."

When she went to the kitchen, I picked up my phone and ordered Chinese. We'd eat sitting on the couch and watch whatever she fancied on T.V. for the rest of the evening. It wouldn't be Grey's Anatomy—those phony medical shows pissed her off. And it wouldn't be the Raptors either, damn it. Most likely, a documentary or nature show.

Even though we enjoyed our evening together, I still felt uneasy about the house being left open, and I know Ann did too. Neither of us mentioned it. No one from *Safe Secure* called me back. I re-checked every window and door before we retired for the night.

Ann turned to me as we undressed. "I've been thinking. You went to a lot of trouble phoning that storage locker to get Lancaster's address. You didn't mention why…so, why?"

She slid a filmy nightie over her head.

I looked at her for a long time before answering. "I found out that the cops are raiding some locations tonight. It's not certain they'll hit our area and Lancaster's house."

She tilted her head. "You left that out when you were telling me about your day. I think you should go, Marsh."

"No way."

"I know a way," She said.

Chapter 23

Ann didn't want to stay here alone, particularly without the security system. I took off my prostheses and got into bed beside her.

"What did you have in mind?"

She turned toward me. "You said that raid would probably start at four? I'll set the alarm for three-fifteen. We get in the car and grab coffees, then go to the address on Maple Street and wait…simple."

I took a deep breath. "Okay…let's say the raid is a go. Lancaster might not be alone. I think he's into drug trafficking, and there could be shooting. He's got nothing to lose. The cops would shoot back."

She lay quietly for a few moments. "That's the worst thing that could happen. You said yourself you're not sure the cops will raid that house." She sat up. "I know you really want to check it out. I'm more afraid of staying here alone than going with you. Besides, we won't be able to get close if there's a raid. I know that from the other raid you and Munro were at. There was no shooting then and nothing happened to you."

"Yeah, I remember that. But when I told you about what could have happened, you nearly shit an eggroll."

"Very funny," she lay back with a thump. "Sometimes you can be a jerk."

"Mea culpa," I said.

That raid was a few years ago, just after I started accompanying Munro on police investigations. I'd have taken any risk to help get the big story and prove my worth as a journalist.

Ann was right—I wanted to check out Lancaster's house just in case there was a raid. "I could drop you off at your parent's house, then go on to Maple Street."

"No thanks. Dad still hasn't mentioned a word about…you know."

I did know. She was waiting for him to apologize, or at least explain himself. "Let's forget it, honey. It's not worth the risk."

She lay quietly for a few moments, then sat up. "I have an idea. We set the alarm clock, you drop me off at the hospital, then go on to see if there's a raid."

"Drop you at the *hospital*?"

"I've wanted to see the nightshift in action since I took over as Charge Nurse. My quarterly report's due soon, and this is the perfect opportunity to check that everything is going according to plan…so that's decided then." She reached over me and set the alarm.

There was no point in arguing. I leaned close and saluted. "Yes, captain."

Her plan appealed to me. But we'd be leaving the house empty, and if Steven Anderson was watching, we could come home and find him here. When she fell asleep, I turned off the alarm. She didn't even stir.

**

For the second time in less than a week, my wife nudged me and told me to get out of bed. This time, the alarm had already awakened me.

"What's going on?"

"It's three-fifteen, Marsh. Let's go."

Go?…Then I got it. "I turned that alarm off."

"Yes, I know. And I turned it back on."

She grabbed my arm. "Marsh, I really want to do this for you. And, I need to drop in at the hospital unannounced. Let's go. It's our last chance to do anything impulsive before the baby's born."

She had a point. I wondered if she was making up the part about her report. It didn't matter—she'd be safe at the hospital, and if the cops raided Lancaster's house, I wanted to be there. Win, win.

Although Ann didn't say anything about danger, I knew it was on her mind. Most likely I'd sit in the car for a couple of hours watching a neighbourhood fast asleep. Then I'd go back to the hospital and pick her up, drive home, we'd get ready for work and drag our asses around all day.

What the hell, it was worth a try. Like she said, it was our last chance to be impulsive. We'd laugh about this, years from now. But we didn't laugh about the real reason for this complicated plan—Steven Anderson. He could be watching the house, waiting for an opportunity for Ann to be alone so her could kill her. Didn't he say he'd pick us off one-by-one? He'd probably driven by and noticed the Safe-Secure trucks out front. He wouldn't know they hadn't finished the job.

I snapped on my prostheses. We pulled on some clothes, I grabbed my canes, and we headed for the front door.

"Got all your stuff?" said Ann.

I nodded before realizing it was so dark, she probably couldn't see me. "Yup," I said, and picked up the carrying case loaded with my camera and night lens attachment. We locked up and left the house. No strange cars were on the street, and when I went out of my way to cruise the street at the end of the walkway, there was no sign of the old blue Honda.

After getting coffee at a twenty-four-hour drive thru, I drove to the hospital and waited at the bright-as-day front entrance until Ann was safely inside. She waved before getting on an elevator. Even at that time of the morning people were coming and going, cars arrived and left. An ambulance pulled into the emergency bay, lights flashing.

I drove to Maple Street, arriving before 4:00 a.m., and parked my SUV across the street, a few doors down from Lancaster's house. The streetlights seemed brighter than usual, and I moved my car out of the glare. The standard in front of townhouse 342-101 cast its light on the lawn and driveway. The old complex looked dreary. Roof shingles buckled and curled. Tongues of paint hung from pillars. Porches sagged. The streetlight two doors away blinked on and off, as if issuing a warning. Stop…Stop …

I attached the night lens to my camera, leaned out the window and took some pictures. A black pick-up was parked in Lancaster's driveway. Why the hell hadn't I asked Burton what kind of car his gardener drove? Would Ann recognize that truck? Deep inside the house I thought I saw a light.

I grabbed my canes and was ready to get out and take pictures of the license number when the front door opened. I switched to video mode and stayed put. A man hurried out, the hood of his parka fell back and his red baseball hat flew through the air and landed on the frozen lawn as he ran toward the truck.

Under the glare of the streetlight, I could see his head above the cab. I'd seen Douglas Lancaster many times at my in-law's house—it was the same guy. The vehicle lights flashed, he got in, started the truck with a roar, and sped down the driveway. The distinctive Ram insignia glinted under the streetlight as he turned and gunned it down the street. I leaned out and followed him with my camera, capturing the whole sequence.

"Someone must have tipped him off," I said to myself. "He didn't even lock the house."

I started my car, threw it into gear and followed the Ram. Light standards passed by at dizzying speed. Maple Street was long and winding, with only a few side streets intersecting along the way to the main intersection, a stop light. Cars with overnight parking permits lined one side of Maple, an old, narrow, one-way street. I stayed behind Lancaster, but not close enough for him to lean out and shoot with any accuracy if he had a gun. I heard sirens behind me. Cops, late to the party, joined the chase and were closing in on me.

I'd lost my bearings and couldn't judge how far it was to the main intersection— presuming that was Lancaster's goal—the side-streets being mostly Cul-du-sacs. The cops were right on my bumper and there was nowhere to pull over. The cruiser behind drove up on a lawn and back onto the road, nudging in just ahead of me. The frantic convoy raced on.

Moments later, the cruiser swerved, then hit the Ram broadside as Lancaster attempted a sudden left turn onto a side street. I was able to slam on my brakes and pull into a driveway on my right, only yards from Lancaster and the cruiser. I threw my gear into park, grabbed the canes and camera and jumped out the passenger's side door—my car the only protection between me, Lancaster and the smashed Ram.

Then I noticed the reason for his attempt at a quick turn. Ahead on Maple Street, a barricade announced *Road Closed,* and behind that, huge road vehicles were parked for the night.

For seconds the scene froze. Cruisers had screeched to a halt, sirens screaming and lights flashing. Then cops jumped out and doors slammed. Using one cane to keep me steady, I trained my camera on Lancaster's bashed-in Ram and got a clear view of him exiting the passenger side, gun in hand. He leaned over the cab and shot into the cruiser that had hit him. No officer was visible. Perhaps he'd jumped out seconds earlier, and joined his colleagues who squatted behind their vehicles.

One cop shouted: "We've got you covered, Lancaster. Step out with both hands in the air and drop the gun."

Lancaster popped up from behind the Ram and fired at the cops. They returned fire. Lancaster kept ducking down and popping up to shoot. This was turning into a shootout, and I knew Lancaster was anxious to get away. For sure he'd seen my car pull into that driveway.

A cop yelled. "Private citizen. Stay down and remain where you are." He was telling me I'd put myself in a dangerous position and to stay the hell out of the way.

The sound and the frequency of Lancaster's shots changed. He'd switched to something more powerful than the gun I'd first heard. After more shots back and forth between him and the cops, he fired in my direction, hitting the ground in front of my SUV.

"Okay, Keene, step out where I can see you," he said. "Hands over your head."

He wanted to get control and knew damn well the cops wouldn't shoot an innocent man. I put my camera and lens beside me on the gravel. I figured Lancaster was planning to take me hostage and make his get-away in my wheels. Shit. If I hadn't been there…but if I hadn't been there the cops would have missed Lancaster who was barrelling down the street before they arrived.

I glanced at the cruisers parked haphazardly on the street, and at the cops crouching behind them, guns poised.

"*Keene! I said step this way!*" Lancaster's voice came out in a high-pitched scream. "If I have to die, you're dead too! This whole goddamned thing is all your fault."

My eyes darted to the cops. They seemed to be taking up new positions. Did Lancaster sense this?

I was his only opportunity to escape, and emerged from behind my SUV, extended my right hand above my head, cane reaching into the night sky.

"Good boy, keep your right hand in the air," yelled Lancaster and walked toward me.

My phone vibrated. It must be Ann. Who else would call at this hour? She was probably wondering if anything was going on. With one arm in the air I wobbled, slipped and nearly fell on the frozen driveway.

"Keep that hand up," Lancaster shouted, moving closer.

I did as he ordered. Lancaster stopped only feet away. We locked eyes. A sudden noise on the street made him look away, and he pointed his gun in that direction.

Balancing as best as I could, I took a few steps back and launched my right cane. The twirling, wobbling missile smashed into his shoulder with just enough force to knock him off balance.

Lancaster fired. The bullet went wild, over my head.

More shots were fired. Lancaster fell.

I fell too. Guns drawn, officers rushed forward, surrounding him. Two ran over to me. With their help, I stood.

"You, okay?" said one.

I nodded. "Yeah, thanks. Lost my balance."

They ran and joined the group around Lancaster. I leaned on my cane, watching and listening. One cop seemed to be in charge, speaking into his mobile.

What seemed like only seconds later, an ambulance came through the side street, lights flashing, no siren. The scene was eerily quiet. The group around Lancaster spoke in hushed voices. He must be dead. No one was bothering with the cruiser that hit his Ram, so that cop must be okay.

I looked around. Porch lights were on, but people stayed inside their houses. Gunshots in the middle of the night tend to alert a neighbourhood.

The ambulance turned and backed as close to the Ram as possible. Attendants opened the rear doors, extracted a stretcher and wheeled toward the group.

I couldn't see what was going on, the throng was too tight. One officer came over to me holding the cane I'd thrown moments before. He handed it to me.

I thanked him. Wouldn't it be considered evidence?

The officer pointed. "Back up and leave on that side street."

It was the second command I'd received, and this one I'd gladly obey. The cops knew I hadn't recorded my last interaction with Lancaster. They'd also achieved their goal and got their man—happy ending, just like in the cop shows.

But their body cams would show my moments of fame. Not my business what happened to those recordings.

I was about to walk back to my SUV, when the officer handed me his card. "Come to the station tomorrow to make a statement—your version of what happened tonight."

Shit. I knew this was a possibility, and took the card. But I also knew I was not obliged to make a statement. "I need time to think about this."

Lame, Keene. "After I speak to my lawyer." I added, "Journalists have the right to gather news, officer. Am I under arrest?"

When the cop shook his head and walked back to the group around Lancaster, I returned to my SUV, picked up the camera equipment and got in. Once I'd backed down the drive, it was a tight squeeze passing the twisted Ram, all the debris, the crowd of cops and the ambulance.

I started down the cross street when I remembered the phone had rung, pulled over to the side, and checked out the call. Ann. I called her back. No answer. She'd probably turned her phone to silent, her usual practice on the ward. I sent a text. "All's good. On my way."

I looked at my watch—just after five a.m.—and sped to the hospital. Ann would be exhausted. I couldn't remember if she had the day off tomorrow. I parked illegally in the circle drive at the front entrance, making sure the handicapped sign was visible on my dash. The parking lot would be nearly empty, but I didn't want to waste time making my way through the garage, a good distance from the entrance. My stumps were throbbing and I wished I'd brought the wheelchair.

I rode the elevator and identified myself outside the psyche ward. A nurse opened the locked door, reminding me that patients here were prisoners twenty-four hours a day. When the nurse saw me, she smiled.

"Marsh! What can I do for you?"

I must have met this woman, but I was damned if I could remember her name. "I've come to pick Ann up. Will you tell her I'm here?"

She frowned. "Ann? Come in while I check the schedule."

I frowned too, stepped inside the ward and followed her to the nurse's station, a glassed-in fortress. She unlocked a door and went in. It swung closed with a decisive click. I knew Ann wasn't on today's schedule—she'd come to check up on them—didn't this woman realize that?

The nurse looked up and shook her head. "I haven't seen her. She's not on tonight, Marsh."

I felt weak and leaned against the railing that surrounded the nurse's station. "But I dropped her off her over an hour ago" …My thoughts raced. Had that crazy bastard Anderson followed us to the hospital? Had I been too focused on going to that goddamn raid to notice any cars behind us? I remembered watching her enter the hospital before I drove away. She'd turned and waved.

The nurse was at my side again. "You okay, Marsh?"

Another nurse entered the ward and approached the station. "Hi Marsh! Looking for Ann? She's lying down in the staff room. At least she was before I went on my break."

I nearly collapsed with relief. "Thanks. Lead the way." I followed on wobbling legs. I didn't remember meeting this person either. It was probably common knowledge that Ann Young was married to a white guy who walked with canes and sometimes used a wheelchair.

Another key opened the door to the staff room. Sure enough, my beautiful wife was asleep on one of the couches. She sat up when her colleague said, "Your husband's here, Ann."

"Hi!" she said as I collapsed beside her, my canes clattering to the floor. "Are you okay, Marsh?"

All I could do was nod.

"You look exhausted. Let's go. I'll drive home." She took my arm.

"Why didn't you answer my text, Babe?"

"You sent a text? Oh, sorry. I was tired and fell asleep. I called but you didn't answer. So did anything happen?"

I let out a breath. "Yeah. They got Lancaster. I'll tell you about it tomorrow." Then realized it was tomorrow and had been before we left the house.

I didn't dare sleep while Ann drove us home. Anderson could be waiting.

Chapter 24

The doorbell woke us just after nine a.m. By the time I'd written the story and sent it to Don, I'd slept for maybe a couple of hours. He knew the raids were happening and would expect a thorough report. The story was strictly from a bystander's point of view. My encounter with Lancaster before he was shot remained hidden. I'd told Ann a shortened version, confident that my part in the action would never be revealed by police.

After the bell rang again, I vaulted into my chair wearing only shorts and a t-shirt, wheeled up the hall and opened the door. Two workmen stood on the front porch.

"Mr. Keene?" said the taller one, his eyes glued to my legless body. "We're from *Safe and Secure Systems.*"

Not the same guys as yesterday. "Wait here while I throw on some clothes." I closed the door, locked it, and sped back to the bedroom. "It's the installers," I told Ann.

"Check their ID," she said.

"I plan to." Which was maybe on the paranoid side, but I didn't give a damn.

Ann went into the bathroom to get ready for work, even though I'd tried to convince her to take the day off. I put on my prostheses, a pair of pants and a shirt, grabbed my canes and walked up the hall. When I opened the front door, they looked me up and down, probably wondering where the legs came from.

"Sorry if we woke you, Mr. Keene."

"Let's see your identification."

They handed over I.D. cards. The pictures were better than the passport variety, good representations of the cardholders. I took my time looking at each one before handing them back.

"I asked to speak to your manager last night," I said. "I had no idea what the hell was going on, or if anyone would show up today."

The taller guy, the only one to speak so far, took a step forward. "Stan Granger," he said, holding out his hand. "I'm the manager. I apologize for the confusion yesterday, Mr. Keene."

I shook his hand, then ushered them both into the house. "I wasn't confused, Mr. Granger, I was totally pissed off."

He nodded. "I didn't hear what happened until after midnight. Didn't like to call you then." He started to go into the specifics of why his company screwed up but I cut him off.

"How long will it take to finish this?"

He thought a moment. "Mind if we take a look around? I need to see how much work was done yesterday."

We spent the next fifteen minutes looking, and discussing what was needed to finish the job. The short guy tagged along, eyeballing everything, saying nothing.

"It looks pretty good so far," said Stan. Shorty nodded.

"I'll believe that when I see the system running properly. How long will it take you to finish?"

"We'll be here until late afternoon, maybe longer. If we're done before you get back, I'll set the alarm. You can call me when you're on the way home and I'll meet you here."

"Fair enough…this house is *not* to be left unattended today until the job is complete. And no one is allowed in until we get back."

Stan nodded.

"There's a damn good reason we're having this system installed."

"Yes, of course, Mr. Keene." I wondered if the two bozos from yesterday had told him about my conversations with Nell and Munro. I handed Stan my business card. "Here's my phone number. My wife and I won't be back until dinner time at the earliest. Make sure you call me when you're finished."

Stan nodded, gave me his card and pointed to a number. "That's my cell. Call any time. I guarantee you'll be one hundred percent satisfied, Mr. Keene. We're offering you a ten percent discount, with no payment for the first thirty days." He nodded to his companion. "Bernie and I are going out to the truck to bring in some equipment before you leave for the day."

Once they returned with their supplies and were busy inside the house, I drove Ann to work. She hadn't mentioned the raid again after I'd told her the basics last night, and I sure as hell didn't bring it up. I was confident my paper would print a vanilla version of the events. They didn't need hassles about one of their journalists impeding police business.

Ann yawned. "I feel better about those two guys. That nonsense with the security company yesterday made me nervous. I couldn't help thinking they weren't a real company and that Steven had something to do with it. I'm so paranoid right now."

Yawns are catching. I reached over and took her hand. "I thought the same thing, honey. There's been so much crazy stuff lately I don't trust anybody either." I still wasn't sure about *Safe Secure* but kept my thoughts to myself. At least I got a discount and didn't have to pay for a month.

I went into the hospital lobby with Ann, put my arm around her and gave her a real kiss.

"Marsh! We're not at home, you know!"

"Yeah," I grinned. "Too bad." But she *had* kissed me back. I promised to be waiting in the lobby at the end of her shift.

Instead of going directly to the office, I drove to Lancaster's house to see if anything was going on. The snow on the front lawn had been trampled. A couple of cruisers and a forensics van were parked in front, and a cop stood guard at the door. Probably plenty of others were swarming around inside. They must have struck gold to call in forensics. That brought a smile to my face. A television crew wandered around in front, filming and talking to neighbours who were anxious to have their two minutes of fame. I parked the car, grabbed my canes and walked over to the throng, eager to hear the chatter.

"Is there dead bodies inside?" said a kid with a backpack who should have been at school.

"The guy was never around during the day," said a woman who was well past retirement. The dog at the end of a leash she held looked about the same age.

"We knew he was weird, didn't we, George?" said a middle-aged woman next to me. "All that coming and going in the middle of the night."

A reporter moved closer and stuck his phone in her face. "What did you think was going on?"

The guy beside her, presumably George, nudged her arm. "No comment," he said.

They walked to the townhouse connected to Lancaster's and went inside.

I approached a guy who had just come out of Lancaster's house carrying a couple of evidence bags. He headed to the forensics van. I held up my press card.

"I'm from the *Halton Register.* Anything you can share? Like what's inside those bags?"

He shook his head. "No comment." It was a popular phrase this morning. He stowed the bags inside the van, closed the door and locked it.

"You guys investigating a homicide?" I said, thinking about Wright and where he might have been murdered.

Mr. Forensics looked surprised, then shook his head before going back inside.

I snapped a couple of pictures of the activity, got back into the car and drove past my own house. The *Safe Secure* van was still there. I stopped in front, decided not to go in, and texted Don and Munro that I was on my way.

When I wheeled into the pressroom, Don beckoned me into his office. Munro was already there.

"Welcome back!" Munro grinned and punched my arm. "Just saw the video you sent. Fantastic, buddy!"

"Great reporting, Keene," said Don. I wondered what their comments would have been if they'd seen my dance with Lancaster.

Don handed me the lay-out for the story, and actually thanked me for staying up and writing it. "That'll be in tomorrow's paper including the pictures and a link on our website to your video. Munro went over to Maple Street early this morning. I guess he just missed you."

No wonder Don was pleased. Our paper would be featuring an important story at the same time as the big dailies. Breaking news had usually broken days before our next issue was due. And, no publication would have a link to my video on their website.

I don't think our smiles could get any bigger. Even Don's mouth was slightly turned up at the corners.

"Any details about the city-wide sweep?" I said.

"It was called *Operation Red Wave,*" said Don, as if he hadn't already told us. "The latest count indicates more than six locations around the GTA were raided. Drugs, guns, stolen property. Big operators who are all connected."

I hadn't forgotten Lancaster's son, Gregory, and asked Don if he'd heard of any local arrests. "Dozens of guys are in custody." He got up and closed his office door.

I wondered if Don had heard the full story from his sources, namely, my personal interaction with Lancaster, and that I could have had my head blown off. If so, he didn't let on. I asked if he thought I could be charged with interfering in police business for the video.

"I doubt it." Don winked. "They don't need the aggravation, but that's just my guess. There's probably going to be an announcement on TV tonight. This looks like a big success, and the police force will want taxpayers to know their money is being well spent." He paused and looked at us both. "Gregory Lancaster was arrested inside the family home last night. I'll keep you posted."

I wondered if Gregory's two sidekicks, Gilardi and Jacobi were arrested too. We thanked Don and left his office. As I made my way to my cubicle, several colleagues came over and congratulated me.

"Great work, Keener!"

"Way to go, Wheel-Master."

That felt damn good, and I thanked them.

But there was still Steven Anderson—I couldn't leave Ann alone anytime in the future until something was done about him. I called Gary Lund. He hadn't returned my call from a few days ago. Gayle, the office admin answered and put me through to his voice mail. I hung up without leaving a message.

Now I didn't have a choice; I'd have to ask Burton what was going on when he picked us up for the funeral tomorrow. Lund would be there and I wanted to see what kind of relationship he had with my father-in-law.

Don, Munro and I spent the rest of the day checking in with various sources for any updates on the raids, and finalizing other stories for tonight's deadline. In early afternoon, the police issued a statement that they'd be holding an information session on the six o'clock news. I asked Don if I could watch from home. I gave him the details about our problems with Anderson and the security company.

"Sure. You've had plenty to deal with lately, Keene. I hope the cops catch the bastard. Go home and grab a beer. Let me know your take on that press conference."

I had another hour before meeting Ann and decided to visit the gym where Anderson had worked years ago. Even though Burton's detectives had struck out, there might be different people in the gym today and maybe someone remembered him. The joint was called *Fitness Perfection Inc.,* located in an industrial plaza about five minutes from my office.

Right away, I didn't like the place. The name matched Anderson's narcissistic personality. So did the neon lights, flashing above the entrance, *perfection=fitness, perfection=fitness.* I grabbed my canes and walked in. It was an ego thing for me; I wasn't perfect, but I could still look fit.

I opened the door and felt as though I'd stepped into enemy territory. This was not my kind of gym. The place was a wide-open room lined with mirrors and crammed with vicious looking equipment, guaranteed to punish every muscle in the body. People hefted weights, their bare arms, clean-shaven chests and six-packs bulging. They'd never heard of a dress code. A heavy smell of sweat and last night's beer hung in the air. There wasn't a woman in the place. Go figure.

After seven years, would someone remember Anderson?

A semi-circular reception desk was off to one side. The guy standing behind it looked like a bald Tarzan except he wore cut offs instead of a loin cloth. Thank God.

"Here for an assessment, sir?" said Tarzan in a high squeaky voice. He walked over to me and stuck out his hand, twice the size of mine. "I'm Roberto, manager of *Fitness Perfection.*" His grip was as loose as a child's and instead of grasping my hand he shook my fingers.

"Matthew Kelley," I said. "I'm hoping you can help me."

"That's what I'm here for," he said with a wink and a smile, showing two rows of teeth that resembled Chicklets. He looked me up and down. "What do you bench? We got a promotion going on right now. I'll waive the assessment fee."

I shook my head. "Thanks, but I'm trying to locate an old friend. He worked here a while ago before he moved to Trinidad and we lost touch. I heard he was back."

"Oh?" Roberto looked disappointed. "What's your friend's name?"

"Steve, Steve Anderson. Big into body building. He's the one that got me interested in fitness."

"Steve…Anderson. Name doesn't ring a bell. I've been here three years. You said he worked here? How long ago was that?"

I scratched my chin. "Oh-h-h, let's see. Probably about five, six years ago, I guess. Maybe longer."

Roberto shook his head and pursed his lips. "Before my time, I'm afraid."

When Burton's detectives had come in looking for Anderson, I wondered if Roberto had been on duty.

He looked me over. "You interested in getting back to the gym? If you book an initial appointment with me, you also get two free sessions on any of our equipment." He smiled, flashing the dazzling teeth.

"Appreciate it, Roberto, but I have a gym membership. I just wanted to find Steve and thank him."

Again, the look of disappointment. Then he brightened up. "I might be able to help with that." He pointed. "See that guy on the bench press?"

Which one? There were at least four men grunting over impossible weights, spotters hovering. I followed him. He stopped beside a huge guy lifting a hell of a lot more than the average 135 pounds. By the size of his physique, he worked out for hours every day.

"Hey, Trev, when you're finished, I have a question."

"Three more sets to go," said the spotter without looking up.

We watched while Trev grunted through the sets, his companion saying: "Push through, man. You can do it." Then, "Great work, bro." The spotter racked the weights.

Trev sprang to his feet. "Thanks, buddy" He looked at us. "Be with you in a sec."

He dried himself with a towel, gulped water from a plastic bottle, then walked over. Every muscle was massive, his thick neck evolved into a head that looked like a tiny afterthought. A pencil-thin red moustache was the only hair visible. He stood, ape stance, facing us. "You had a question?" At least Trev had a normal voice.

"Sorry to interrupt your workout," said Roberto. "You've been around here a long time. Do you remember a guy called Steve Anderson? He worked here maybe six years ago."

Trev nodded slowly. "Yeah." The look he gave me was none too friendly.

Roberto gestured in my direction. "This is um, sorry sir, I forgot your name."

"You know Steve?" I said, an expectant smile plastered on my face, ignoring Roberto.

A hint of a smile appeared on Trev's face. He nodded. "Stevie could press his own weight. He's one of the best builders I ever met. Hard core." His cold stare returned, along with a frown. "How'd you know he was back in town?"

I hadn't mentioned anything to Trev about Stevie being back in town and I was sure he hadn't heard my conversation at the front desk with Roberto.

Roberto's eyes darted back and forth between us. "I'll leave you two to talk," he said and hurried back to the front desk.

I stuck out my hand. "A mutual friend at physio told me."

"Trev Martin." His handshake was firm but not killer. "You look like you've spent a few hours in the gym yourself, buddy. What'd you say your name was?"

"Matthew Kelley. I'll never forget Steve. He got me started after my accident. We lost touch after he moved to Trinidad."

Trev's expression softened. "He stopped by last week, but he's just here for a short visit. Said he was leaving soon. Came in to see if anyone he knew was here. I'm the only oldie-goldy still hanging around." He smiled revealing his own perfect teeth.

"How the hell is he?" I took a breath. "Still married to that gorgeous girl? You got his number?"

Trev's face clouded over. "Bitch dumped him, that's why he went to Trinidad. You didn't know that?"

I tried to keep my face deadpan, given the bitch he'd referred to was my wife. I shook my head. "Geez, too bad. We didn't talk that much about personal stuff. He just concentrated on getting me mobile. I'd love to work out with him again, get some fresh pointers."

Trev's eyes shifted to my canes. He moved closer and lowered his voice to a whisper. "He's a…private guy. I can't give out his number."

"Yeah, I get it. Tell him I was asking after him. Be great to have a beer together sometime." I turned to leave.

"You said your name was Marty?"

Whatever. I nodded.

Trev walked back to the bench and picked a phone up off the floor. He came back and stood beside me, scrolled, made a selection and seconds later someone picked up. "Hey, Stevie?…It's Trev. I got an old friend of yours who wants to talk to you." He handed me the phone.

My hands were sweating so much, I was afraid of dropping it. It never occurred to me that I'd actually be talking to the bastard. I looked down at the display which still showed the number he dialled. Probably a burner. I held the phone to my ear. "Surprise, Stevie. It's Marsh." I looked at Trev and smiled. I had great teeth, too.

For a few seconds there was silence on the other end. All I heard were strange sounds in the background. Then he spoke. "Hope that new security system keeps you safe, Crip."

My heart bashed against my ribs. "I'll find you, asshole. It's just a matter of time."

Anderson laughed and hung up. I handed the phone back to Trev. "Thanks."

Trev got right in my face. "Who the hell are you? What's going on?"

I moved in closer, our noses nearly touching. "Ask your buddy, *Stevie*. He'll tell you who I am. But he won't have the balls to admit why he left the country."

Chapter 25

I got the hell out of there. The wind pushed the door and it slammed behind me. How close were Steven and Trev? I'd just laid down a challenge. Two against one were never good odds. Like Steven had implied, I'd need more than a security system to keep us safe.

How long had I been in that overkill sweatshop? I looked at my watch—fifteen minutes. It seemed much longer. I still had time to visit the junkyard where the cops had towed Anderson's old Toyota.

The place, called Scrap-Car, was on the way to the hospital. I entered the property through gates that were opened from inside the compound. The enormous yard piled helter-skelter with the corpses of dead cars, resembled heaps of broken smarties. A guy came out of a little shack and walked toward me. I rolled down my window.

"Lookin' for parts?" he said.

I shook my head, grabbed my canes and got out of the car. I handed him my press card. "No, I'm hoping you can give me some information."

He looked at the card and grinned. "Well at least you ain't the cops. I'm John."

"Marshall Keene. Do you still have a black Toyota that was brought in by police a few days ago?" I gave him the license plate number.

"Yeah. She's over there." He pointed to a bunch of dismembered cars. I looked closely and saw the Toyota, off to one side. "Cops told me to let them know if anyone asks about it. You're the only one so far."

"Do you remember hearing them say anything when they brought the car in? Like who owned it?"

"Nope."

"Have you seen this guy?" I swallowed my pride and showed him the picture Nell had sent of Steven and my wife on their wedding day. I covered Ann's likeness with my thumb.

He peered at it and shook his head. "Nope. And I'd know. I own the place." He grinned. "Sometimes even sleep here."

"Mind if I take down the VIN number?"

"Knock yourself out. If nobody claims it soon, the cops'll give me the go-ahead to sell the parts."

They had probably gone over the vehicle before bringing it here. I wondered if the car had belonged to Trev Martin. But Burton said the plates were stolen and maybe the car was too. Anderson didn't have a police record, so fingerprinting wouldn't help. The police needed to know that Martin could be a possible owner.

John followed me as I walked over and jotted down the VIN. For my own satisfaction, I took a picture of the inside and outside of the car. I shook my head. "Why was it left in a mall?"

John reached over, released the lever and lifted the hood. "Engine blew. This piece of shit ain't goin' nowhere. Why waste money on a tow? When they find the owner, he'll have to pay."

"Do you ever sell any of your cars?"

"Naw. Just the parts. They're pretty much done when they come to me."

Assuming Anderson had bought the Honda he was driving now, where did he get it? Even if I found the dealer, they wouldn't give me the purchaser's address, which could be a fake anyway. And maybe Anderson stole the car. Too many unknowns, Keene, move on.

I thanked the scrap dealer and continued on my way to the hospital. Ann wasn't in the lobby so I sent her a text. Within seconds, I got a reply. *Be down in five.*

I called Gary Lund while I waited. He was in a meeting and reception put me through to his voicemail. Might as well have a little fun.

"It's Marshall Keene calling. I just visited *Fitness Perfection,* where Steven Anderson worked, before he went to Trinidad. I got his telephone number from a member there, Trev Martin, who's been in touch with him. Maybe the black Toyota belonged to Martin. I'll call the police and give them an update. See you at the funeral tomorrow." I didn't give Lund the phone number. He'd have to call me back to get it.

Next, I called Burton. He didn't answer either. To break the ice before he picked us up tomorrow, I gave him the same information and included the phone number.

I called the police for strikeout number three. My call went to answer, and I repeated the information about Trev Martin as the possible owner of that Toyota and hung up.

A text had come in while I was on the phone. It was from Munro and said, *call me.* He picked up on the first ring, and started talking.

"Police caught two guys named Gilardi and Jacobi, buddies of Greg Lancaster. Don already told us they'd hauled Greg in. There were so many arrests the cops probably won't mention names tonight, except maybe the big players in Toronto."

"Wow! Thanks, Munro."

"Welcome," he said, and hung up.

Munro knew that the names he'd mentioned were *my* big players. I wondered if Burton had received the same information from his sources. If he didn't mention anything, I wouldn't break my colleague's confidence.

**

Ann and I got home about twenty minutes before the six o'clock news started. I hadn't heard from *Safe Secure* all day. They were still working in the kitchen, and said they'd be finished in about an hour. When I asked if anyone had come to the house while we were out, they both shook their heads.

I ordered pizza for dinner. While Ann went to get a beer for me and a pot of tea for herself, I phoned Detective Wetmore to see if he'd received my earlier message about Trev Martin. He was off duty and his voicemail box was full. I called his sidekick, Detective Grant. When he picked up, I gave him the information plus the telephone number I had for Anderson. He said he'd discuss it with Wetmore and hung up. No thanks or appreciation for my hard work. Journalists are nuisances and meddlers.

Ann and I sat down with our drinks just before the evening news started. The talking heads smiled and wished viewers a good evening. A red and white banner floated across the bottom of the screen announcing *Breaking News.* The female anchor took the lead, and I turned on my VCR.

"We begin tonight with breaking news. Early this morning, police conducted a series of raids throughout the Greater Toronto Area. Operation Red Wave has been in the planning stages for months and included officers from the GTA, Halton and Peel Regions. We'll be speaking to Inspector Eric Strathy, head of Toronto Integrated Guns and Gangs Unit." She paused and spoke to someone off-screen. "Do we have the connection?"

The screen switched from the anchor to three men standing in front of a freestanding microphone. The guy in the middle stepped up to the mic. I recognized Strathy and presumed the others represented Halton and Peel Regions.

Strathy, a no-nonsense, bulldog of a cop who had probably just met the now antiquated height requirement, grabbed the stand, tilted it toward him and cleared his throat. He looked left and right as if to acknowledge his colleagues.

"I'm Inspector Eric Strathy. My fellow officers and I are pleased to report the successful execution of a months' long investigation called Operation Red Wave. Early this morning, our team executed search warrants for vehicles and residences in the Greater Toronto area and Halton and Peel Regions. Drugs, weapons and stolen property were seized in pre-dawn raids.

"Twenty-eight people are now in custody facing charges of theft, possession and trafficking of illegal weapons, trafficking in illegal substances, and murder. We have also seized more than three hundred and fifty thousand dollars."

The scene shifted to a table beside the officers. The camera panned, revealing packages labelled fentanyl, cocaine, cannabis, MDMA and ketamine, along with stacks of bills. An array of various guns and ammunition lay in front of the drugs and cash. I wondered if the guns Lancaster had used were in the pile.

Strathy appeared on screen again. "We estimate the street value of the drugs to be four to six million dollars. This indicates the substantial level of drug and gun crime in this city and adjoining counties. With these arrests, we have broken a long-standing, widespread drug and illegal weapons ring."

He paused to look at the two men beside him again, still staring straight ahead, hands clasped in front.

"This investigation has resulted in murder charges in the death of Mr. Allan Wright, whose body was discovered last week in a suburban subdivision. Thanks to a tip from a citizen, Gregory Lancaster of Halton Region, has been charged with the murder of Mr. Wright. Douglas Lancaster, father of the accused, was killed in a police raid early this morning, in the Halton Region. Multiple charges have been laid in the Halton region and in Greater Toronto, which include weapons offences and importing illegal substances for the purpose of trafficking."

"Yes!" I yelled and pumped my fist. "Thank God!" I grabbed my wife in a bear hug.

"Marsh! Did you know about this?"

"Some of it."

She nodded and I toasted Ann's cup of tea with my beer. She wouldn't ask what I knew, or how I knew.

"That's great!" she said. "I bet those guys were caught because you found that money and that print-out from Grant's Storage. Why wouldn't that cop give you credit for it?"

"They'd never mention a tipster's name. It would be like me revealing a source," I said.

"Well, I know you're the hero in this."

We hugged again and turned our attention back to the anchors. They thanked Strathy and went on to other news. Our doorbell rang. "That's probably the pizza. Can you get it?" I said. "There's money in my jacket pocket. I have to call the office."

Don answered immediately, then got Munro on the line for a conference call. Once the three of us were connected, he congratulated me. Sort of.

"Keene, I suspect that tip Strathy referred to came from you. You've had a pickle up your ass about that Wright guy, and you were right on the money."

I wondered if he realized he'd just made a great pun, but didn't interrupt. Praise from Don was rare.

"Good work," he continued, "I want the full story of your accident, Wright's trial and his release from jail. People will love reading about the saga of one of my reporters. Work from home if you want, but I need it on my desk before the next publication."

That was the longest speech I'd heard Don make. "No problem, boss. I'll get right on it." But it was hard to enjoy the moment when I was so tired. All I could think about were the hours of work ahead of me.

"I'll handle everything else till you get it done," said Munro. "And congratulations, buddy. Frigging fabulous work."

Don's voice all but cut him off. "Have a good night," he said, and everyone hung up.

Munro would stay at the office to finish up the raid details until Don was satisfied. Now I'd finally get to tell the full story of my connection to Allan Wright. I needed to get on it. Frank's celebration of life started at noon tomorrow and I had to be there.

While I was talking to Don and Munro, Ann had come in with the pizza. She put two slices on a plate and handed it to me. "The security guys want to go over the system with us."

"What? Now? Shit, I forgot about them. That could take a while and I've got a story to write. Can you handle it and tell me how everything works later?"

Ann frowned, slightly annoyed. "Yeah, I guess so. But I'll call you if I need to." She left the room and closed the door behind her. Those guys would be shaking their heads. After all the noise I'd made about installing the system, I wasn't going to be around to learn how to use it.

I pulled up to my computer but couldn't concentrate. Where was Wright murdered? My guess was inside Lancaster's house, maybe one of the reasons forensics was there. I also wondered if stuff Wright had handled was inside that storage locker, and maybe other stuff relating to Burton's property. Probably Gilardi and Jacobi were lackies to papa Lancaster and his son, Gregory, who probably reported to others higher up.

Good sum up, Keene, but it's speculation. I turned my thoughts to organizing the story for Don. I planned to go back to the car accident seven years ago, when Wright drove drunk, plowed into us and killed my family. How crazy and desperate I'd felt, particularly at the trial, the threats I'd made to Wright, and the warning his supporter, maybe Gregory Lancaster, had shouted on courthouse steps.

I heard Ann thanking the security guys and closing the door behind them. She came into the office. "It's as easy system, but I made them go over it three times. I made up a code—you have to memorize it. I want you to set the alarm before you come to bed."

We went into the hall and she repeated the code a few times before showing me how to arm and disarm the system. So many beeps meant it was set. More beeps meant it was off.

We were getting back to our pizza when her phone rang.

"Hi Dad...Yeah, great news for Marsh...Okay thanks, see you then...Yeah, he's here." She handed me the phone.

"Hi, Burton, I guess you got my message." Ann looked at me with raised eyebrows.

"Yes. You were very persistent about the Lancaster bunch," said Burton. "What a relief to hear they've been charged." I presumed he'd seen the news and knew Douglas Lancaster was dead.

"I guess that takes some pressure off you," I said. Burton's reputation would no longer be in doubt now that it was clear, to us at least, that Douglas Lancaster had taken advantage of his goodwill in offering the boat and boathouse.

"And to respond to the message you left," said Burton, "the detectives I hired asked around at the gym but didn't speak to Trev Martin. I've directed Officer Wetmore to interview him immediately."

I wondered if Wetmore had saluted on the other end of the phone. Burton was still miffed because he was so formal.

"Gary Lund hasn't answered my calls," I said. "Can you ask him to give me any updates?"

There was silence at his end for a few seconds. "I'll speak to Lund. I told Ann I'd pick you both up around eleven-thirty tomorrow."

"Appreciate it, Burton. See you then."

Ann went to bed, knowing I'd be up late working on another article.

**

Hours later, I stretched and decided to go for a walk around the house. The article was finished. I wanted to check it once more to make sure I didn't sound like a whining victim. Don would cut and re-write any stuff he didn't like anyway.

I was hungry and realized I'd hardly eaten any pizza. I grabbed the left-over slices and went into the kitchen to zap them. After a few bites, I tossed them into the garbage. Microwaved crust tasted like cardboard. I rummaged in the fridge and took out two of the hard-boiled eggs and a handful of carrot sticks we always kept handy. I ate leaning against the counter, thinking about Frank's celebration of life. Who'd be there? I put my phone on charge, ready to take pictures.

It was well past midnight when I finished checking the piece and sent it to Don and Munro. Ann was taking the day off tomorrow for Frank's service, so maybe we could sleep in.

I walked to the bedroom then remembered Ann had asked me to set the alarm. What the hell was the code? Why hadn't I written it down? She'd be so pissed if I screwed this up. I remembered her saying it would be easy to remember the number because all the digits added up or something like that.

"Shit."

I was usually so good with numbers. I closed my eyes and tried to visualize the sequence I'd punched in a few hours before. The code started with the number one, I was sure. Yeah, one, for the year we'd dated before moving in together. Then the next number was four, for how long we'd been married, then five because four and one equals five. But what the hell was the next number?

"Crap."

Okay, if they all added up, it had to be the sum of one, four and five which would be ten. So, 14510. I wrote that on my hand. What if I was wrong? The goddamn thing would make a series of error sounds and wake Ann. Then she'd kill me.

What the hell. I punched in the number. The keypad chirped a happy tune and the red light came on, letting me know the system was armed. I got ready for bed and climbed in beside my wife. She sighed and moved close.

My brain wouldn't shut off. I started thinking about my phone conversation with Anderson today at the gym and that sound I'd heard in the background. What the hell was it? Where was he?

Chapter 26

Burton parked on the street in front our house. Luckily, I was sitting in my office going through emails when the Jag stopped at the curb. It was apparent he wasn't coming in. I texted him, saying we'd be right out, and called to Ann.

"You ready? Your dad's here."

She rushed down the hall. "He's fifteen minutes early. Why wouldn't he just come in? If he's still sulking this'll be a long day."

I left that one alone, grabbed my canes and put on my jacket. "You go out honey, and I'll set the alarm."

Ann sat in the front with Burton. I got into the back and wished him a good morning. He said hello without turning around, put the car in gear and headed to the church. Frank's Celebration of Life was probably the reason for Burton's sombre mood.

As we approached the church, I realized it was a good thing we were early. Even though it was a cold January day, a large crowd had congregated outside. Frank, only in his late fifties, was well-liked and had a good reputation—the joint would be packed. The parking lot was filling up too. Burton chose a space and we all got out of the car. No one had said a word since I'd wished him good morning. Ann took my arm and we walked to the front of the church.

Burton excused himself. "There's Gary Lund and Gayle up ahead. I want to talk to him."

He called out, and Lund turned, his expression none too joyful. Burton was in no hurry to catch up, and Lund stood waiting. His smooth dark hair was combed straight back, his trendy black coat fit perfectly. Black leather gloves graced his hands. All he needed was a bowler hat and a walking stick. Even though Ann and I were right behind, I couldn't hear the conversation. Burton seemed to be doing the talking. Lund, his head down, nodded a few times. Gayle looked straight ahead.

Police presence was palpable. A couple of cruisers idled across the street from the church, exhaust floating for seconds before disappearing. Two uniforms inside each car. I told Ann I wanted to mingle outside with the crowd for a few minutes, took out my phone, shut off the sound, and pretended to text while I took pictures of people talking in little groups.

Burton and Lund walked up the steps together and disappeared into the church. Gayle followed. I didn't see anyone else I recognized. Eileen and Nell weren't there, but they were last-minute people.

The undercover cops were obvious—three loners wandering from group to group. Frank's murder was high-profile, and to my knowledge, nothing of value had been uncovered.

Ann and I made our way up the ramp at the side of the front steps—easier for me than navigating slippery stairs with my canes. As we reached the entrance, organ music filled the silence. I started to sweat and took a few deep breaths. Ann looked up at me and squeezed my arm tighter. I hadn't been inside a church since the funeral for my parents and sister Callie seven years ago. We paused before going in.

Ann whispered, "You okay, Marsh?"

I nodded.

"We should sit with Dad. I don't see him."

I pointed. "Up there, close to the front. Gayle and Lund are with him. You go up, honey, I'll stay back here."

Ann shook her head. "I'd rather make sure you're okay."

She knew I was afraid of having a panic attack. "No, no. Burton needs you today. I'll be fine if I sit in last pew." I wanted to rub shoulders with Lund, but this wasn't the time. Plus, from the back, I could get the hell out without disturbing the whole congregation.

We heard familiar voices behind us. Nell and Eileen had just come in together.

"You and your mom go and sit with Burton. I'll ask Nell to sit with me."

After whispered greetings and a hushed conversation between mother and daughter, they joined Burton. Nell and I slid into the last pew. She rummaged in her bag and brought out a pack of tissues. She pulled one out and dabbed her eyes. "Oh, Marshy. Thanks for sitting back here with me."

"Glad you decided to come, Nell."

I took out my phone and again pretended to scroll through messages. I looked like a total jerk, but it was more important to get shots of strangers when they walked up the aisle. Maybe one was Frank's killer. Sometimes those sickos got a thrill watching the grief they'd caused. Like an arsonist hanging around after he'd set a fire.

The undercover cops walked in—one sat across the aisle from us, one sat mid-way and the third, close to the front. Ten minutes later, an organist started playing *How Great Thou Art,* my mother's favourite hymn. The congregation rose to its feet. Nell bumped one of my canes, but I grabbed it before it clattered to the floor.

The minister appeared in the entrance holding a Bible and walked to the front of the church. Directly behind her, funeral parlour employees guided the gurney carrying Frank's shining black casket, draped with red roses. Jeanette followed, wearing a black suit. The jacket ended at the waist and the tight, short skirt gave everyone a great view of her well-rounded ass. A black veil covered her face.

Nell whispered, "Get a load of the grieving widow."

Jeanette looked at us, her eyes fixed in a cold stare. As she continued walking, her head turned to maintain the gaze for a few seconds.

Behind her, two young men, who I assumed were Frank's kids, each linked arms with a woman, presumably Frank's ex-wives. The kids, boys in their twenties, wiped their eyes and looked straight ahead.

Nell leaned close to me. "Harry and James. Great kids who loved their dad. I've met the mothers, too. Nice women who stayed friends with Frank after the divorces."

I couldn't remember if Burton or Ann had told me that his ex-wives had each worked for him. But I knew Jeanette had. The exes were somewhat plump, but still attractive in a made-up, bleached-blond way.

The casket arrived at the altar and the minister turned, made the sign of the cross then walked to the pulpit. Jeanette sat in the front pew with two women I didn't recognize. Were they family? I knew very little about the widow Veale. Frank's kids and ex-wives slid into the opposite front pew. Two men shifted along to make room for them.

I stared at Frank's coffin, but instead saw Callie's—pure white, decorated with painted flowers, an enormous spray of pink and white roses on top, cascading down the sides. The urns containing the remains of Mom and Dad stood on pedestals on either side of Callie, protecting her.

My parents had talked about cremation being more environmentally friendly. I remembered how Callie and I laughed the few times we'd heard that discussion. When I had to make those terrible decisions, I couldn't destroy my eighteen-year-old sister's body. She was so bright and had barely started to live. I wanted to give her every chance to come back.

I felt weak. Tears poured down my face. A box of tissues was wedged into the hymn book rack and I grabbed a handful. Nell looked at me and gripped my free hand.

"Oh God, Marshy." She sobbed. "I know you miss Frankie too. We were going to have such a great life."

Even though Nell didn't sense my private grief, I'd have run out, gasping for breath if she hadn't been beside me. I forced myself to stay and listen to the eulogies. Harry and James came up together and took turns speaking about their father. Although half-brothers, they were lighter-skinned version of Frank, both tall and slim with short black hair. The boys cried openly, holding onto the pulpit for support. Their messages were ones of admiration for a father who had loved and guided them. They each told a few funny stories that brought out the Frank I knew—a fun-loving joker who enjoyed a good time.

A man about the same age as Frank came up next. He introduced himself as Mike Willis, saying he'd known Frank since high school. He spoke about the struggles they'd faced as teenagers.

"Frank and I hated that we were expected to like each other just because we were the only black boys in the school. For the first two years of high school, I couldn't stand him. And he avoided me. Maybe I was jealous because the girls loved him."

Some people in the congregation laughed. Watching Mike's face, I wondered if this was meant to be funny.

"Then in grade eleven, we were both on the school basketball team. Frank was the most unselfish player. He always seemed to be in the right position to help his teammates. We started to hang out. When I got to know Frank, I realized he was a natural leader. The real bonus for me was that after being with him for a while, the girls started to like me too."

Everyone laughed, including me and Nell. Some people clapped. I wished I could have seen Jeanette's face, but all I could see was the back of a stiff, resolute figure, clad in black. Mike Willis paused to collect himself as he expressed his love for Frank and their long-standing friendship. Before going back to his seat, he went over and hugged Jeanette. Then he walked toward a white woman, a few rows from the front and offered his hand to her. Three children sitting beside her stood as he approached, then they all sat. The kids, a delightful mixture of the two parents, looked to be in their teens. The woman leaned toward Willis and their lips touched briefly.

I turned my attention to the front of the church. Burton stood behind the pulpit.

"Ladies and gentlemen, family, friends and colleagues, my name is Burton Young. Frank and I were close friends, and law partners for ten years."

Burton looked down, his shoulders shaking. He pulled a tissue from his pocket and wiped his eyes. Then he continued, his voice low and weak.

"Life can be cruel. Circumstances change. Choices and decisions are made that you disagree with. But the last thing you expect is the murder of your best friend. I'll never be able to accept that."

Everything was still all about Burton. His wife had moved out, his relationship with his only child was rocky, the criminal activity on his lot next door made him look bad. The cop near us sat up straighter when Burton had started to talk. Was he a suspect? Nell looked at me and raised her eyebrows.

While Burton continued talking about his relationship with Frank, who was, as far as I was aware, his only friend, I watched my wife and her mother. Ann's head was lowered and her shoulders were hunched forward as if she was shrinking into herself. Eileen sat up straight, her head turned to the opposite wall. Mother and daughter had not moved to close the gap between them where Burton had been sitting. Lund and Gayle sat by themselves at the end of the pew.

I looked at my watch. We'd been here for just over a half-hour. It seemed much longer. Burton talked about what a great law partner and friend Frank had been, and how successfully he'd carried the practice since Burton had been called to the bench. I knew he'd throw in his status as a judge. Then I mentally kicked myself—*attitude is everything, Keene, so pick a good one.*

I couldn't see expressions from the back of the church, but people seemed restless, coughed, shifted in their seats, the pews creaked.

My mind wandered to my conversation with Don this morning. He'd make some changes to the story I'd sweated over last night. I scrolled through my emails; he hadn't sent anything back yet. This was one time I wished I worked for the *Toronto Tribune* to see my personal account of Allan Wright and the details of the raid in a major newspaper.

Burton thanked everyone for paying their respects to Frank. He left the pulpit, nodded to Jeanette, and returned to his place between Ann and Eileen. After a prayer and the committal of the body, the minister announced that the family would be hosting a reception downstairs in the church hall.

Nell sighed. She leaned over and whispered, "Should I come?"

"Why not? You were a friend of Frank's. You don't have to talk to Jeanette."

The congregation stood while the minister walked down the aisle, followed by the casket, Jeanette, Frank's kids and ex-wives. Frank was going to be cremated and the private interment would take place at another time, an enormous relief to me. I couldn't have stood beside an open grave.

Nell and I joined Ann, Burton and Eileen downstairs in the church hall. I didn't see the undercover cops. Along one side of the room, a long table was loaded with sandwiches, coffee, cold drinks and desserts. I was starving. Ann filled two plates, one all desserts—she knew me—and carried them to a table. Burton, a coffee in hand, joined us and sat beside Ann. Eileen and Nell were speaking to Frank's kids and their families.

I looked at Burton. "Gary Lund and Gayle didn't stay?"

He shook his head. "It's a workday. Gary will be calling you."

Damn. I wasn't going to have my ten minutes of fun asking Lund questions in front of Burton. I'd eaten only two of my sandwiches when Ann patted my hand.

"We should go over and pay our respects to Jeanette."

She was with the two women who sat with her during the service. As we approached, Jeanette stood and moved away from the table. The black veil had disappeared. Her straw-coloured hair was pulled back from her face. There were no smudges of mascara around her eyes, and the neon-pink lipstick was perfectly applied.

"That was a lovely service, Jeanette," Ann reached out and touched her arm. "Frank was a wonderful man."

"Thanks." Jeanette's eyes darted from Ann to the women at the table.

Who the hell were they? "Anything I can do to help in the next little while?" I said.

She looked at me, her eyes cold, almost hostile. "No. But thanks." The *No* had been a little too pronounced. She looked down and started picking at stuff on her jacket. "I'd better get back to my friends."

Ann started toward our table, but I followed Jeanette as she joined her two companions. I pulled a chair out for her then pulled one out for myself, sat down and hung my canes on the back. I extended my hand to the woman closest to me.

She looked at Jeanette then back at me. "Sylvia Kent," she said and held out her hand. Sylvia was round, grey-haired, and probably in her sixties. She wore no makeup or jewellery of any kind.

I smiled and introduced myself. "How do you know Frank?"

This time, when she looked at Jeanette, I did too. Her pink lips were pulled tight, eyes definitely hostile.

"I, um, didn't really know Frank," said Sylvia. "Jeanette and Marion and I have been friends for years."

I reached across the table. "You're Marion? Marshall Keene, an old friend of Frank's."

She rose slightly and shook my hand. Marion was thin and wore a ring on her left hand. The three women stared at me.

I sat back and smiled. "Well ladies, nice of you to come and support Jeanette. Frank was a favourite in our family." I looked around the table. "Can I get anyone anything from the buffet?"

Jeanette rose to her feet. "We need to circulate." She looked at the two women. "Syl, Marion, I want you to meet Frank's friends."

I'd been dismissed, except I was still sitting at the table. Jeanette knew damn well I was fishing for information. She was on guard, something I'd never seen before.

Sylvia and Marion exchanged glances, then obediently stood. With apologetic glances in my direction, they followed Jeanette across the room to a group of men holding plates of goodies and talking. I feigned texting again, took a photo of the group, retrieved my canes and returned to our table. Burton moved his chair to accommodate me. I picked up one of my two remaining sandwiches.

"Have you ever met those two women with Jeanette?" I said.

"No. I think maybe they're relatives from the East Coast," said Burton.

But they said they were friends. "Is that where Jeanette came from? How did she meet Frank?"

Burton frowned. "At a law convention in Montreal—she's a paralegal. Then she followed him here and convinced him that their combined skills would benefit the practice. You know all the rest. Frank never discussed her background."

She's a paralegal came out like a snarl. What did *all the rest* mean? I wasn't likely to find out today.

Nell and Eileen came our way. "We're leaving now," said Eileen. Nell's eyes were red and swollen, and she looked exhausted. She hugged me, waved to Burton, kissed Ann and promised to give us a call. Eileen embraced her daughter, then said goodbye to me and to Burton. Watching them walk away, he sighed and shook his head. I finished my sandwiches and started on the chocolate eclairs.

"Jeanette sure didn't want anything to do with me just now." I looked at Ann. "And I thought she'd be more pleasant to you. But she just stood picking stuff off her dress."

"Probably bird feathers," said Burton.

"What?" I said.

"Budgerigars." said Ann. "One of Frank's hobbies, he had two or three cages. Jeanette's stuck looking after them now, I guess."

Frank was a multi-talented guy—cars, horses, budgies, and blond women, except for Nell. We all stood and Burton went to say goodbye to Jeanette before we left the reception.

When he stopped his car in front of our house, I invited him in.

"I've got some Scotch tucked away. Why don't you come in for a drink?" I felt sorry for him going home alone, plus the journalist in me wanted to pick his brain. After a few drinks he might talk about Lund and his connections, and I might hear more about Jeanette Veale.

In the kitchen, Burton leaned against the counter, swirling his Scotch and looking out the back window. I stood beside him holding a beer.

"Guys, sit down," said Ann. "You're making me nervous. And you're getting in my way." She was bustling around the kitchen preparing ingredients for a bilious looking health drink she kept in the fridge—it even smelled green when she poured it out of the blender.

We obliged and sat at the table. "What did Jeanette have to say to you, Burton?"

"Not much. She avoided looking at me, but didn't seem to have any trouble socializing with other people."

"She always been standoffish with us," said Ann. "What did Frank see in her?"

"I told you, honey—her body. She probably blamed us that Nell was there."

Ann shrugged her shoulders. I took out my phone and brought up the pictures I'd taken. "Who are these guys? She left me sitting at the table and went over to talk to them. They were standing outside the church too."

Burton took the phone from my hand. He looked at the picture and shook his head. "No idea. Never seen them before, maybe Frank's friends from the racetrack." He scrolled through the other pictures. "These men are colleagues, and I think these are from the sports car club he belonged to. Undercover cops were at the funeral too."

"Yeah, they were obvious. Do you think they learned anything?"

Burton sat staring at me for a moment, then looked at Ann. "I don't know about today, but before I picked you up—and this is confidential information—I heard that Frank's gambling debt had been paid to the people he owed it to."

Wow. The big boys were looking after Burton again. Did he know anything else that he could share?

"Does that make things better or worse, Burton?" Then I answered my own question. "Thank God Frank's honour is intact. But who killed him? Why?"

"That's the big question." Burton shook his head. "By the way, Gary Lund will check in with you. I'm not happy with him, but right now he's the only lawyer in that office. I don't know what will happen to that practice, I had to sell out when I took the bench, and don't have any right to information."

"You hired Lund, though, so you can talk to him. I guess he's struck out so far finding Anderson," I said.

"Yes, he has." Burton sat swirling his Scotch. "I got rid of the detectives I hired—you found out more in one visit to that gym than they have since I hired them, Marshall."

I doubted Lund would call me—he'd have to kiss ass. He had plenty on his mind, like what was going to happen to the law practice? Burton was still a recognized force in judiciary circles. Lund should be smart enough to pay attention to that status in case he needed advice.

We sat quietly for a few moments. After Burton had downed half his Scotch, he decided it was time to go home.

When he left, I checked my messages. Don had sent the few changes he'd made to the story. They were trivial, but the boss had to be in control. Wetmore still hadn't called me back, meaning, I suppose, he had nothing to report on Anderson. I wouldn't bother calling—maybe I'd go to the station tomorrow.

Ann went to bed early. I stayed up playing Solitaire on my computer, feeling restless and uneasy. I couldn't shake a feeling of urgency. I'd gotten nowhere wondering *who'd* killed Frank so I started to think about *why*. There was always a reason for murder.

I thought about the people at Frank's Celebration of Life. I thought about everything I'd learned about him before and since his death, and went over recent scenarios involving him. I thought about the people closest to him. I started making implausible connections, sorting out possibilities.

Then it came to me. Made total sense. But what the hell could I do about it?

Chapter 27

I had to know. If I was right and waited until morning, it could be too late.

Jeanette Veale was at her husband's funeral today in body only. Those two women, Sylvia and Marion, were there as a shield. It didn't matter if they were friends or relatives—they had a job to do and followed Jeanette's orders. Alone, she'd have been vulnerable, forced into conversations she didn't want to have with people who knew and loved Frank.

Burton had learned that the two hundred grand was paid to the people Frank owed, so that was a closed issue. Except Frank was dead. And he'd joked to me about spousal connection the day before he died. The cops hadn't arrested Jeanette, but like the drug dealing Lancasters, they might not have anything solid on her.

It was worth a drive to the country. I'd never been to Frank's house and wanted to sniff the air in his space. I'd benefited from him in lawyer mode, and I'd enjoyed his friendship in social settings. I'd been at his funeral and heard how loved he was. I needed to get a picture of how he'd lived.

Ann was asleep and I didn't wake her. If I told her my plans, she'd say my curiosity was in overdrive. She had a scientist's brain—everything had to progress in a logical cause-and-effect sequence. My brain threw out random ideas and tried to make them light up.

With our new security system, Ann and our growing baby would be safe at home. If my calculations were correct, Anderson's threat would not be an issue. I pulled out my phone and texted Ann in case she woke up: *Couldn't sleep. Went for a drive to sort things out. Love you, babe.*

I grabbed my canes, and my clothes, and made my way into the front hall, dressed and put on my jacket. I reset the alarm, opened the door and locked it behind me. It was one a.m. Street lamps cast intermittent cones of light up and down our street. A raccoon scuttling along a neighbour's fence gave me a shiny-eyed glance before hurrying on its way.

Once inside the car, I leaned my canes against the passenger seat and punched Frank's address into my GPS. It would take at least twenty minutes to drive to his house—longer than I thought. He lived in what he'd referred to as *the country*. Ann and I had never been invited to his home—

all our gatherings had been at Young's house. According to Burton, Frank had moved there after his second wife left him. The house was old but sat on considerable acreage which Frank thought would have been ideal for a future subdivision. The property also had a large outbuilding in decent condition, a good place for his growing car collection.

Jeanette had moved into that house with him. I didn't know exactly when, but they were a couple when Ann and I had started dating six years ago. The closer I got to Frank's house, the more I questioned myself. It was the middle of the night. What did I think I'd find? But I kept driving and rationalizing. Jeanette hadn't even tried to fake being upset over her husband's death today. She acted as though she could hardly wait to get the reception over with.

So what, Keene? Did you think she'd greet you with a smile and a hug? She'd always had a chip on her shoulder the size of a Mack Truck.

Plus, Jeanette would've been pissed off seeing Nell there, and I'd be dog shit for sitting with her.

Why were Sylvia and Marion so guarded? If they had been pleasant, chatty even, taking the pressure off the widow Veale, I'd have come away with a different feeling.

Jeanette knew I didn't like her and didn't trust her. I wasn't the only one who felt that way.

The GPS genie interrupted my thoughts. *Your destination is six hundred metres on the right.*

The house, typical of an old farmhouse, was set well back from the road at the end of a plowed driveway. No lights were on inside, and a car, that could be Frank's Lincoln, was parked in the driveway. I rechecked the address. Yup, the number on the mailbox was 1255 and the street sign at the corner had said 5th Concession. It was one-twenty-two a.m.

I drove up the drive and got out. The parked car was Frank's. A double garage door was closed, the windows just low enough for me to look in. Two cars were inside. I used my phone but it didn't cast enough light to see much, just that one car was small and the other SUV size. I didn't know what Jeanette drove. Did they have three cars? I returned to the Mustang, backed down the driveway and onto the road.

About a hundred yards further along, I came to a much longer driveway. A large aluminum-sided drive shed stood at the end, an exterior light over the front entrance. This was probably where Frank kept his car collection.

I started toward the building. My tires crunched on the gravel drive, which was also well maintained with snow banked neatly on each side. Frank's domain was how I'd imagined it—orderly, bought with a future purpose in mind, useful for his current needs. I still felt wound up and decided to look around. First, I turned the car so it faced the road, then shut off the engine.

Except for the farmhouse, there wasn't another building in sight. I took my canes and got out. The night was still except for the odd gust of wind and skiff of blowing snow, the cold more intense in this open space.

My footsteps and canes echoed into the silence as I approached the door. It was locked, no window. I continued along the driveway to the back of the building, my canes and feet striking the ice with a cracking sound. An oversized metal garage door nearly filled the far end, certainly big enough to allow cars to go in and out. Close to the top of the door, a series of windows went from one side to the other, too high for me to look in. Lights were on inside, maybe part of a security system.

I tried to lift the door and it yielded to my touch. I heaved upward and it rose, sliding into place at the top of the rails. Odd that it was unlocked. I stepped inside. The interior was brightly lit, and security cameras were strategically placed along the ceiling. I wondered if I'd tripped an alarm, but didn't hear a siren.

Four cars were parked inside, two abreast, facing each other. Frank's prized collection— what was left of the original six. I knew he'd sold two to come up with part of the gambling money. He'd shown me pictures of the cars at one of our gatherings at Young's house, but in the flesh, they were much more impressive. The fire engine red '65 Corvette, the pale blue '59 Chevy convertible and the 1950 silver Cadillac Eldorado. The latest acquisition, a classic mustard yellow 2.4S Porsche. I didn't know the year. Huge money tied up in those babies.

I heard a door open and turned. Steven Anderson emerged from a darkened, glassed-in room to my right. "Well, well, Crip. You've saved me the trouble of coming to you."

My hunch was right. Then my heart leaped, and I felt light-headed. I took a breath and tightened my grip on the canes, keeping my eyes on Anderson's hands.

"Didn't expect to see me here, did you, Crip?"

"Actually, I did. Little birdies told me you were in Frank's house yesterday when your friend Trev made that call."

His eyes opened wider, then shifted to the room he'd come out of. "Thought you were smart tricking him into phoning me. You'll regret tracking me down. Or rather, your widow will."

Jeanette stepped out of the same room, pointing a gun, a crooked smirk on her face. She stopped when she reached Anderson's side.

"Good morning, Mrs. Veale," I said.

Anderson looked at her and laughed. "Think we didn't see you looking in the garage, then driving up here? You've just given us one more job tonight—nobody'll ever find a trace of you."

"Shut up, Steve," said Jeanette.

Her dark eyes pierced me. She held the gun like a pro, moved closer, then stopped. Probably wanting to make sure she did the job in one well-aimed shot. Anderson's eyes darted back and forth from Jeanette to me. The pair of them looked like two wolves about to pounce. She was the alpha. My mouth was so dry I couldn't swallow. Hold tight, Keene, and keep your eyes on the lady with the gun.

Her phone rang. She motioned to Anderson to take the gun then answered. "Yeah?"...

"Relax, everything's under control..." She hung up, thumbed a text and pocketed the phone. Anderson handed the gun back to her.

"Expecting someone else?" I said. "Like buyers for the cars? They coming on their own, or is there a third partner?"

A blast of wind and snow charged through the open overhead door, startling Jeanette and Anderson. He turned to look, and she glanced sideways. I stepped forward and lashed out. My right cane struck Jeanette under the chin, throwing her head backwards. The gun went off with a deafening blast. Anderson cringed as the bullet whizzed past us, shattering the windshield of the old Caddy. Jeanette staggered and fell back, her head striking the concrete floor with an audible thud. I couldn't see the gun. Maybe it was underneath her.

"You bastard!" Anderson knelt beside her. "Fuck! You've killed her!"

I stepped on the end of the cane I had dropped after hitting Jeanette, grabbing the handle as it popped up. Anderson shook both fists, his face red, teeth exposed in a snarl. "You son-of-a-bitch." Head down, he crouched and ran toward me.

I was no match for this raging animal, but my self-defence training kicked in. I managed to turn sideways before he plowed into me, deflecting a direct blow. He knocked me on my side and landed on top of me. My heavy coat cushioned the fall, but I heard a crunch as my shoulder hit the concrete. I'd feel that later, if I lived long enough to feel anything.

I swung my fist, but hardly touched Anderson as he rolled away and stood. I picked up my canes and pulled myself to my feet. "Surprised that I'm not such a cripple after all?"

He growled. An animal planning its next move. Behind him, Jeanette groaned and tried to sit up. Anderson turned to look at her.

"Go ahead and look for the gun, asshole," I said, and held one cane over my head. "I'll be right behind you."

He came at me, full on this time, without the crouch. I struck out, aiming at what seemed to be his lead hand, the left. But he was quick and grabbed at the cane. I held on. We played tug of war, yanking, yelling, shoving. I kept him at a distance with an outstretched arm, leaning forward to stay upright.

Jeanette pointed the gun again. She moved left and right in a boxer's dance, trying to get a clear shot, but keeping a safe distance this time.

Anderson pulled away and landed a crushing punch on my sore shoulder. When I yelled, he hesitated. I swung my left cane and caught the side of his head. He staggered and instinctively put a hand to his ear. I took a step back, lunged forward and swung my cane again. It connected on the other side of his head. He screamed, and with both hands, clutched his face. The cane we'd been fighting for crashed to the floor.

Jeanette stood about three feet away, pointing the gun. "Steve, get out of the way!"

I got behind him, planted my remaining cane, leaned in, and shoved him toward Jeanette. The gun went off, and he fell on top of her.

The force of my actions nearly toppled me, but I managed to stay on my feet. I caught my breath and reached down to grab the cane Anderson had dropped. Arms akimbo, his body covered hers. They both lay eerily still. I listened to my own breathing and counted to sixty, stepped closer, reached down and rolled him off her. Blood poured from a wound in his belly. If he wasn't dead, he soon would be. Beside Jeanette lay her cell phone. I picked it up and put it in my pocket, and was about to grab the gun from her hand when she came to.

At close range, it looked like a Beretta 92. Her eyes wide, she lay gasping for breath. The impact of Anderson's body had probably knocked the wind out of her. She held the gun, pointed to the ceiling. I planted one cane and kicked it out of her hand. It flew through the air, crashed into the side of the Porsche, and fell out of sight.

Jeanette seemed oblivious to her surroundings, unaware that I'd just relieved her of her protection. She sat and looked at me, then looked down at herself, watching Anderson's blood drip down her jacket. She touched the back of her head and recoiled at the sight of her own blood. Her straw-blond hair hung in limp strands, giving her an eerie costume party look.

She shook her head. "He killed Frank. He killed Frank."

"Yeah? Well now you've killed him."

I walked backwards to the Porsche, took my phone from my shirt pocket and dialled 911. "My name is Marshall Keene. I'm a journalist with the *Halton Register.* Please send the police and an ambulance to 1255- 5th Concession. A man's been shot. He could be dead, and the woman who shot him is injured. They are in the outbuilding beside the house."

"Are you injured, sir?"

"Yes, but not seriously."

"I'll stay on the line with you until help arrives, sir."

"Thanks."

I knew my call was being recorded. Anderson hadn't moved and I sure as hell wasn't about to check on him. Jeanette was in another world, shaking her head and muttering. Every few seconds the operator asked me if I was still there, if I was okay and if the injured parties were moving. It seemed like hours before I heard sirens approaching from a long way off.

I'd have to relinquish my phone and admit to taking Jeanette's, then hand it over. I dug it out of my pocket and tapped the face. The text she'd sent was still on the screen. *Minor stall will let you know when it's safe.* The text had been sent to Gary Lund.

I scrolled further back. Jeanette and Lund had been communicating all evening, confirming the logistics of their plan. He was bringing people to buy the cars, then he and Jeanette were catching a plane to Warsaw. Anderson wasn't mentioned.

Were those cars supposed to be leaving here tonight? What was going to happen to Anderson? Maybe they'd planned to kill him—after they killed me. Then they'd be gone, cash in hand.

Moments later, six cops ran in, two at a time, guns drawn. I propped myself against the Porsche, an ugly dent in its side where the gun had landed, and put my hands up. Two cops came over to me. One was Sergeant Reese. EMS ran in next. They took a brief look around and rushed over to Anderson, lying where I'd dragged him, blood from the wound forming a sizeable pool on the floor, glistening in the light.

Reese came over to me. "I hope you have a good explanation, Keene. You said you were injured?"

"My shoulder."

"Where's the gun?"

I pointed. "Probably under that car."

An officer beside him got down and looked under the Porsche. Seconds later he called for an evidence bag. Someone obliged, and the gun was dropped inside.

He glanced at Jeanette then back at me. "Where's your cell phone?"

I patted my shirt pocket.

"I'll take it." said Reese.

I handed it over. Christ, what if Ann tried to call?

"You might be interested in this one, too, Sergeant Reese."

He took Jeanette's phone. "How'd you get this?"

"She dropped it and I picked it up." Or something like that, I thought. "I kicked the gun out of her hand."

Reese patted me up and down. Did he really think I'd have a weapon? Too bad I hadn't thought to take pictures before I'd handed my phone over.

"Is that your Mustang out front?"

I nodded. "The keys are in my coat pocket."

"Take it off, please."

I pushed the coat off my injured shoulder and let it fall to the concrete floor. Reese picked it up and handed it and the phones to another officer who took them and left the building. There'd be blood splatter on my coat and clothes. Anderson's blood.

"Don't move. I'll be back," said Reese.

Where the hell could I go? Reese joined the team dealing with Anderson. He was lying on a stretcher, an I.V. already dripping into his arm. I hoped to God he lived to go to trial. Jeanette, now on her feet, was handcuffed. Somebody had found a chair and pulled it toward her. She sat, and one of the medics started to examine her head.

I looked up at the security cameras. For sure Anderson and Jeanette had disabled the system before they came into the building. They'd opened the drive-shed door, and were waiting for Lund to arrive with the prospective purchasers. Then I'd shown up and screwed up their plans. Thank God I got there before the rest of the guests appeared.

Anderson was wheeled out by two paramedics, accompanied by a cop. Reese motioned for me to join him. I grabbed my canes and tried to walk over. "You said your shoulder was injured?"

I nodded.

He called out to one of the medical team. "Can you take a look at this?"

A paramedic approached and asked me to take my shirt off. I undid the buttons and slipped my left arm out. Hurt like hell. He felt around. "Can you move your shoulder and raise your arm?"

I tried. "It hurts to move the shoulder. Really painful when I try to raise my arm."

"You need to have it examined in hospital, sir."

"I'll go to my doctor tomorrow."

"Are you refusing treatment?" said Reese.

"I'm refusing to go to the hospital right now." I knew damn well Reese would take me to the station. I didn't want to go to the hospital under police guard, wait for hours to be seen, then go on to the station for God knows how much longer.

"Your choice," said Reese. "We'd like you to come to the station, Mr. Keene."

"Am I being charged with something?"

He looked at me and didn't answer.

Reese knew our history with Steven Anderson, and knew Burton had pressed charges against him. The last time the cops interviewed me, Frank advised me just to answer questions and not provide any information.

"I'll come to the station, Sergeant Reese. But I want to call my wife."

He nodded. "Let's go." He turned and spoke to the cop next to him, ignoring my request. "We'll talk to the other two after they've been treated."

The cop handed me a blanket and I draped it around my shoulders.

"Just hold on a sec," said Reese walking over to guys taking pictures and picking up evidence.

Jeanette walked past, escorted by two cops, a wide bandage wound around her head. She stopped and looked at me with a snake-eye glare. I shot her a glare of my own.

I couldn't resist. "Lost your phone, Mrs. Veale?"

Reese finished his conversation, and the cop who'd given me the blanket took my arm. I told him I preferred to put my hand on his shoulder. I presumed my canes had been confiscated as evidence. We followed Reese to a cruiser, and I was ushered into the back seat. Reese and his colleague got into the front, and as soon as the engine came to life, we started down the long driveway. The ambulance had already left. When we drove past Frank's house, lights were on inside, and a couple of cruisers were parked in front. Were Sylvia and Marion there? Probably already gone back to wherever they came from.

Reese had the courtesy to crank up the heat in the squad car, and I wondered if there'd be anything left of my coat after forensics got finished with it. No one spoke during the ride except Reese, constantly giving instructions over the police radio. Nothing worthwhile—just back-and-forth conversations about who was where. When we reached the station, he parked in front, got out, and opened the back door. Before assisting me inside, he retrieved a couple of evidence bags out of the trunk.

"Can I have my cell?" I said.

"Later. Do you want coffee?"

A beer would have been better. "Thanks, double cream." I gave him the passwords to my phone. What the hell, I had nothing to hide.

I was led into an interrogation room. Twenty-five minutes passed before Reese came in and handed me a coffee and my phone.

"Thanks."

"Make your call," said Reese.

The wall clock said three-ten a.m. I dialled, and Ann picked up on the second ring. "Honey, it's me."

"Marsh! Where are you? What's going on?" I knew she was wide awake, her voice anxious.

"I'm at the police station."

"*What?*...Why? Your text didn't tell me anything. Then you didn't answer when I called."

"I drove out to Frank's house. I can't go into it all right now."

"Frank's? You sound funny. Are you okay?"

"Anderson punched me in the shoulder. The EMS think it might be dislocated."

"Steven? He's at the police station too?"

Why the hell did I say that? With each question, Ann's voice rose. "No, Anderson's not here. The police just want to ask me some questions. I'm fine. Make some tea. I'll be home as soon as I can."

"*Really*? First, I wake up and you're not in bed. Then I see you've gone for a drive in the middle of the night. And now you tell me you're at the police station and I should *make tea?*"

I'm sure Sergeant Reese heard every well-enunciated word. "We're not having a private conversation, honey. Please trust me."

"I don't like this, Marshall."

"I know, me either, but there's nothing I can do right now."

"Well, *I* can do something."

"What?"

"Why would I tell you?"

She hung up.

Shit. That went well. The adrenalin that had carried me for the last couple of hours disappeared. I couldn't think straight. My head was pounding, my shoulder was on fire, and all I wanted to do was lie down. I sat staring at my phone and took a sip of the coffee. God-awful. Instead of cream, they'd put in that white death powder.

Reese watched as I put the phone into my shirt pocket, a slight smile on his face. "Okay," he said. "Let's hear your story this time."

Chapter 28

Reese leaned across the table, studying my face. Another cop entered the room and sat beside him. His name tag said *Blair*. Two people staring at me, and they weren't smiling. I decided to follow Frank's advice and let them ask the questions.

Reese didn't waste any time. "Why were you at that location tonight, Mr. Keene?"

I took a deep breath. I felt like saying *what location* because he hadn't been specific, but that would be, as Frank might have said, inflammatory. "Because your officers weren't doing their job, Sergeant Reese."

He looked at me. I couldn't read his expression. "Can you enlighten me, Mr. Keene?"

I nodded. "Steven Anderson—the guy that was hauled away on a stretcher—was previously married to my wife. I left messages with two of your officers, Grant and Wetmore, asking for help after Anderson had been at our house when he knew my wife was alone. He threatened to kill us, including my in-laws." I paused and looked at Reese. "Don't you guys connect with each other?" His expression gave nothing away. "I contacted both those officers, left voicemail because they didn't pick up, then reported that Anderson was planning to leave the country. None of my calls were acknowledged or returned."

Reese leaned over the desk. "So, you sought out the guy that threatened to kill you and your wife."

Basically, yeah. I ignored his statement, and didn't answer.

"Mr. Keene, you put yourself in grave danger tonight."

I looked at him before speaking. "Sergeant Reese, I kept telling your officers that our family was in danger. They never responded—I should just sit back and wait for Anderson to come and kill us?"

I had nothing to hide and sent a silent plea to Frank. "Do I need a lawyer, Sergeant Reese? Are you charging me with a crime?" It was the second time in a week I'd mentioned a lawyer to the cops.

Reese shook his head. He and Blair sat silently. Moments later, there was a knock on the door. Blair got up to answer and stood aside as Burton walked in with a man I didn't know. They both carried briefcases. I assumed Ann had called her dad, but who was the second guy?

Mr. No-name spoke. "Sergeant Reese, I presume?"

Reese nodded.

"I'm Robert White, legal counsel to Mr. Marshall Keene, if necessary, and this is His Honour Burton Young."

Reese rose from his chair. "I'm familiar with His Honour."

White didn't introduce himself to Blair, and Reese didn't offer.

I knew I had a motive for shooting Anderson, and the cops had good reason to question me. Reese's nod moments before indicated he wasn't charging me. So, what the hell was going on? I smelled some kind of legal formality. Burton had probably come to spring me and had to bring another lawyer to avoid a conflict of interest. I knew question period was over.

In the coming days, forensics would report finding Anderson's blood on my canes and on my clothes. My fingerprints were not on the gun that shot Anderson, but scene cops had found it under the car where I'd been standing. I'd be a suspect until everything was sorted out.

"You're free to go, Mr. Keene," said Reese.

I looked at Burton and Mr. White for confirmation. When they nodded, I tried to stand. Wrong move. I had no canes and the pain in my shoulder nearly knocked me over.

Burton held his arm out. I pulled myself up, then transferred my hand to his shoulder. White led the way out of the interrogation room. We walked side by side past the front desk, Burton's pace steady, as though he was used to guiding me. Reese was nowhere in sight. The second cop, Blair, nodded as we left the station.

The Jag was parked close to the entrance. White held the car door open for me, and I lowered myself slowly into the passenger's seat. I thanked him for his part in whatever the hell had transpired. He smiled and closed the door.

White and Burton had a brief conversation then shook hands before he got into his car, started the engine and drove away. I didn't wait to ask questions.

"Did you wave a magic wand over Reese and his sidekick?"

He smiled. "The police might want to speak to you again, and you'll be called as a witness when this goes to trial."

"What did you say to them? I was so bloody glad when you walked in. They could have charged me with something. Where'd you get Mr. White from?"

Burton kept his eyes on the road. "He's…a colleague of mine. Let's wait until we get home and talk then. Ann's waiting. We've been up all night anyway—another hour won't hurt."

Was I being released because His Honour Burton Young was my father-in-law? Unlikely. For sure Mr. White was a legal boy, possibly one of Burton's sources.

I was too exhausted to think, and leaned my head against the seat. The next thing I heard was the car door opening, my wife speaking to her dad, then to me.

"Marsh?" Ann's hand was on my arm.

"Um? Oh, I guess I fell asleep."

"Let's go into the house," she said. I yelped as my shoulder brushed against the seat back. Ann put her arm around my waist and I put mine around hers, our usual way of walking when I wasn't using canes. The pain made me sweat, but I had to get inside. Burton followed, and I heard a beep as he locked the Jag.

Ann needed to know what was going on. How could I summon the energy to tell the story again? She was concerned right now, but would be so pissed when she found out what happened. We went into the front room and I sat in my wheelchair. If I'd gone for the couch, I would've fallen asleep immediately.

"Do you want anything, Marsh? How about you, Dad?"

Burton chose Scotch. Was it too early or too late for a beer? "I'll have a gallon of water, thanks."

While Ann got the drinks, I thanked Burton twice more.

"It's all worked out, Marshall," he said. He used the past tense. There was something I didn't know. A big something. Plus, rather than being annoyed, Burton seemed rather pleased. Ann handed him his Scotch. She put a jug full of ice water and a glass on the table in front of me, then sat on the couch beside her father.

I poured some water, and took a long drink. "Thank God I'm home."

"Marsh, why didn't you tell me where you were going tonight?"

I took a breath. "All I had were ideas after listening to people for the last couple of days. I couldn't stop thinking about the way Jeanette behaved at the funeral—like it was something she had to get out of the way. When Nell was here yesterday, she said something that struck me."

"What?" They both said.

"I asked her about Anderson—what she knew about him, what she thought of him. What others thought of him. She answered in a roundabout way, saying Jeanette didn't sneer at him the way she sneered at everyone else."

Burton pursed his lips and nodded. My wife frowned.

"After talking to Nell, I decided that Anderson and Jeanette had things in common. She knew Frank was having an affair with Nell—wives know these things. And she probably knew Frank was getting ready to dump her. For sure she knew about the cars, and that he'd sold two of them." I paused to pour more water. "And Anderson had one mission—money."

I looked at Burton. "You'd already refused him. It made sense that they'd joined forces. But I doubted Jeanette knew the combination to Frank's safe. No reason for her to have access to that.

"But she knew Frank was a gambler, and that he owed big money—otherwise why sell two of the cars? Or maybe she thought he was building a nest egg to live on after he dumped her. Either way, she wanted that cash.

"I figure that stealing the money out of the safe was a conspiracy. No one knew Frank had paid off his debt. I picked up Jeanette's phone when she dropped it tonight in that outbuilding and read her text—the third person was Gary Lund."

Ann took a deep breath and let it out. Burton nodded again.

I took another gulp of water. "After they missed grabbing the two hundred k, they were in deep trouble. Frank was dead and one of them killed him. They needed cash to get away. The four antique cars were their last hope."

"Gary Lund wasn't there tonight?" said Ann.

I shook my head.

"But…You knew all this before you went to Frank's?" said Ann.

I shook my head again. "I *suspected* what was going on, and needed confirmation." But I knew what she would say next.

"You *know* how dangerous Steven is. Why didn't you just call the police and tell them?" She looked down at her hands and twirled our wedding ring.

I repeated what I'd said to Sergeant Reese. "I *had* called the police, Ann, more than once. They ignored me." I let that sink in. "Anderson had to be stopped. I decided he and Jeanette were up to something together. Gary Lund had a daily pulse on Frank's practice.

"Nell said Jeanette liked Anderson. Maybe they saw themselves as wronged and wanted to get even. As the only other lawyer in the practice, Lund would have access to the safe. He'd have known about Frank's gambling problem, and Jeanette could've told him about the money from the sale of those two cars. Plus, we'd complained to Lund about Anderson, and I never got acknowledgement that anything was being done. I think all your dad heard was that Anderson had disappeared."

Burton's nod told me he agreed.

"Jeanette and Lund needed a fall guy to break into that safe. Anderson. When the money wasn't there, Anderson reported back to Lund, who decided it must be hidden somewhere, and he searched the office again."

I paused to think: Jeanette was in custody, and I presumed Stephen was in hospital under police guard. Did anyone know where Lund was?

"I needed proof that Anderson was in with Jeanette and Lund, then I could report something solid to the cops. I had to keep trying—Anderson said he'd kill us…that's what I focused on."

Ann didn't comment. She was probably just taking it all in.

Before I had a chance to continue, Burton turned to his daughter. "I suspected Jeanette too. After I found out the gambling debt had landed in the right hands, I wondered if she might try to cash in on those cars. I figured she and Lund were a pair, but I didn't think Anderson was involved." He looked at me. "Stroke of genius, my boy that you put all three together."

Ann volunteered some information of her own. "Nell was right—Jeanette was the only one who liked Steven. When we were married, he often told me he felt like an outsider."

I wondered if the Youngs considered Ann's marriage to me a step up.

Burton drained his drink and reached for the scotch. He tipped the bottle and the golden liquid slid down the side of his glass. How could anyone drink that stuff? I poured more water into my own glass, the half-melted ice cubes bashing against the side.

It seemed that we all felt a certain responsibility for how things had played out. I was back to being *my boy* in Burton's books. I sat up straighter hoping better posture would help me tell my wife the rest of the story. She hadn't asked who killed Frank, and I didn't jump in and offer my opinion. Not yet.

"There's something else you should know, Ann," I said. "Steven got shot tonight."

She looked at me, her eyes large and inquiring. "Oh, my God, Marsh, you didn't…."

"He died on the way to hospital," said Burton.

"*What*?" I said, "How'd you know?"

Ann looked back and forth between us. She thought I'd killed him. My gut felt like a quarry of rocks. Burton took a deep breath, reached over and placed a hand on Ann's.

"Okay, it's time you both know what I know." He picked up the Scotch bottle, thought better of it and placed it back on the table. "First—Marsh didn't shoot Steven—Jeanette did."

Ann gasped. "*Jeanette*?"

I was suddenly wide awake. How the hell did he know? Was my theory of events all wrong?

Before I dared ask, Burton jumped in. "Let me finish. I have to go back a bit. Those cars belonged to Frank and me. We bought them during the last few years—our little hobby. When he wanted to sell a couple of them a while ago, I agreed. He needed money for the gambling debt, and we got a good price for them. There's a dual security system in that outbuilding. We could call up a video stream anytime on our phones. A back-up system kicked in if the main one was faulty or turned off. I heard the secondary alarm tonight and knew something was wrong."

He stopped short of saying he watched while I was getting the shit kicked out of me.

"Good thing you had that back-up system, Dad. Does Mom know you and Frank own those cars?"

Burton looked at his daughter and shook his head. "When you called tonight, I'd already alerted the police and told Sergeant Reese about the video. He asked for a copy and I sent it to him."

Of course. That's why question period with the two cops wasn't question period. Without that security video, I would have been charged. I didn't know whether to be mad or glad.

Interesting that Eileen didn't know about the cars. First, the property ownership came to light after it burned, and now, the cars. But Burton's video had saved my ass tonight.

One thing was clear—Reese had played a game with me. Was he trying to teach me some kind of lesson? He knew damn well that I hadn't come to the station as ordered the night Lancaster was killed. So far, my decision to ignore that order had paid off. It pissed me off that he had already seen the video, and knew damn well that I was defending myself. He wanted to know why I'd gone to Frank's, and I told him. Fair enough. But would he investigate those two morons on the force who never called me back about Anderson? I'd probably never know.

Ann looked at her father, then at me. "So, what actually happened?"

"Do you want to see the video?" said Burton.

She took a deep breath and looked at me. "No thanks, I'll pass. All that really matters is that you didn't kill Steven, Marsh."

"There'll be no doubt that Jeanette shot him, Sweet t'ing," said Burton. "Marshall was defending himself."

Ann sighed. Her eyes closed momentarily…"Steven had a gun when we were married. I only saw it once—when he threatened to kill me. That was the day I came home to you and Mom." She got up, sat in my lap and put her arms around me. A stabbing pain shot through my shoulder, but I didn't let on and held her with my left arm. "I'm so relieved that you're okay, Marsh."

I winked at her. "Still love me?"

She smiled. "That was never in doubt."

Burton cleared his throat, eyed his empty glass, and told us he'd better be on his way, mumbling something about tomorrow being another day.

"Can you send me that video, Burton?"

"Sure."

He took out his phone and in seconds, the file landed in my inbox. He stood and called for an Uber. Our discussion was over. Steven was dead, according to Burton, and Jeanette had been arrested. Where was Lund?

Was it too soon for anyone to know? I was sure Burton would learn the details before the story hit the news. Ann didn't say anything more, and neither did I.

Ten minutes later Burton left, promising to come back for his car.

I thought about a shower, but just sat on the edge of the bed, threw my sweaty clothes into a corner and removed my prostheses. Ann and I lay close together. She was asleep before I'd hardly pulled the covers over us.

My mind went back to its staccato beat. Gregory Lancaster was in custody for the murder of Allan Wright. Check. Douglas Lancaster was dead, Steven Anderson was dead. Double check.

Was I right about who killed Frank?

Chapter 29

Every time I moved, stabbing pains in my shoulder woke me up. Finally, morning light outlined our bedroom blinds. I made a shaky transfer to the wheelchair, and left the room as soundlessly as possible, using my left hand to navigate. In the kitchen, I snapped on my prostheses, made coffee and wheeled into my office, anxious to read the accounts about the criminal goings-on in my hometown.

Last night's action with Anderson and company had been too late for any publication, so I mentally switched gears to the raid at Lancaster's the night before. For sure, that would be in print this morning. I logged on, went to the news website and brought up a dual screen—one half showing local news, the other the *Toronto Tribune* report.

Lakeville Man Arrested for Murder headlined the *Register* front page, and *Drugs and Firearms Seized* on the *Tribune* front page.

I was relieved that neither paper exposed my tussle with Douglas Lancaster. Both mentioned his death, the arrest of Gregory Lancaster and his two sidekicks, Gilardi and Jacobi. The *Register* wrote about the frantic chase through Lakeville streets before the criminals were finally apprehended. I wondered if those arrests put paid to the local gang.

The *Register* included the video I took of Lancaster running from the house and racing down Maple Street. The big Toronto daily had nothing like that. I congratulated myself for the brilliant coverage.

I read the articles about Operation Red Alert in both papers. The *Tribune* piece was boring as hell—droning on for a half-page about the Toronto raids and subsequent arrests. Totally lacking in sparkle, if such a word could be applied to guns, gangs and drugs. The *Register* detailed the Oakville raid, the shooting of Lancaster senior, and the arrests of his son, and the two sidekicks.

One thing made me smile—Don had inserted a picture of me in my wheelchair beside his editorial, even though I'd used canes that night. He credited me with the story of the year.

"How's the shoulder, Marsh?"

I jumped. “Jeeze, you snuck up on me! I’m not going in to work, it’s too damn sore.”

She refilled my coffee cup. “You tossed and turned all night. Let’s go to the Emerge. I’ve decided to just go in for a meeting later on.”

“I’m not going to argue. Do you think it’s broken?”

She shook her head. “It’s probably not a fracture—more likely a dislocation, from what I can tell. They’ll take x-rays, maybe do an MRI, and you’ll have to isolate it.”

“How?”

“They’ll tape it, and you’ll have to wear a sling to keep the shoulder immobile until it heals. You should have listened to me last night when I wanted you to ice it.”

I should have, but we were both exhausted. “Yeah, I guess you’re right,” I saluted her with my mug, slopping coffee on myself. I was shit with my left hand.

Ann helped me transfer from my chair onto the shower seat. We were afraid I’d fall and do more damage. She stuck around and helped me dry off and get back into my chair. While I shaved, combed my hair and snapped on the prostheses again, she went into the office and read the articles about the Lancasters.

I had to call her to button my shirt and help pull on my goddamn pants—just like after the accident when I couldn’t do anything for myself. On the way to the hospital, we discussed today’s news.

“I guess last night’s stuff about Jeanette and Steven happened too late…If it wasn’t for you, the police would never have caught the Lancasters,” said Ann. “I still can’t believe they haven’t acknowledged it.”

“During that press conference, Strathy referred to a tip from a citizen. And like I said, hon, they’d never reveal a source.”

She nodded. “Yeah…I guess.”

I reached over and patted her hand. “Glad you’re my biggest fan.”

She was on a roll. “I guess tomorrow’s papers will be full of Steven and Jeanette. I wonder if they got Gary Lund?” She paused and looked at me. “Even though last night was totally nuts—and don’t you ever to anything like that again—would the police ever have caught those two without you?”

She couldn’t let it go.

"And what about Uncle Frank? she said. "Was there any mention of him in any of the articles?"

I shrugged—wrong move. "The cops might know more than they're letting on. I think your dad will find out."

She took her eyes off the road momentarily to look at me. "Maybe Dad already knows who killed Uncle Frank."

"Or has suspicions." I didn't mention my own ideas.

I managed to text Don with my left hand and tell him I wouldn't be coming in. I'd have to take a cab home from the hospital. My car was probably still at Frank's outbuilding, and I wouldn't drive with just one arm anyway. I wondered if Don would ever find out how involved I'd been in last night's fiasco with Jeanette and Anderson. I sure as hell wouldn't offer the information.

Moments later, Ann parked the car and we entered the hospital. I looked around for Anderson. It would take time to get over worrying that he was stalking us.

I was determined to walk—you get treated differently, particularly in a hospital, if you were obviously disabled—and that meant using only one of my spare canes. It also meant using my left hand—awkward as hell. I had to keep stopping to maintain balance. It was easier if my feet were further apart than in my normal walking stride. Years ago, a physio had named it the tripod effect.

"I wish you'd stop being so stubborn and use the wheelchair, Marsh."

I grinned. "I love a challenge, honey."

Anderson's punch was not going to incapacitate me. I was sweating and weak by the time we entered the emergency department. Fortunately, one of Ann's friends was on triage. I described my injury and she ushered us into a treatment room. People who'd been there ahead of us frowned and shifted in their seats. As soon as I was comfortable in the cubicle, Ann left and went up to the fifth floor to get some work done before her meeting.

Hours later, after an MRI, x-rays and conversations with nurses and a doctor, I was diagnosed with rotator cuff injury. No surgery was recommended for now. In six months, after using ice and having therapy, plus wearing a brace to hold my shoulder in position, I should be back to normal. My wife was pretty much right.

Ann came down for the final word and agreed with the doctor that I should take pain meds. All I cared about was being able to type. She pushed me in a loaner wheelchair to a waiting cab—hospital policy, she claimed.

"You're not going to work now, are you?" she said.

"Nope. Going to bed. Wanna join me?"

She shook her head, but managed a grin. "I thought you were tired?"

"Seriously, honey," I said, "you didn't get much sleep either. Can't you just take the day off?"

"The meeting was late starting and is still going on. I'll get away as soon as I can."

On the way home, I checked my messages again. I'd been texting left-handed with Don and Munro all morning. When they asked if I was coming in to work, I gave them the same reply I'd given my wife, omitting the invitation.

Everything was in good order at the paper. Jeanette Veale had been charged with the murder of Steven Anderson, but my involvement was left out. I'd promised Don an exclusive when I was legally free to tell my side of the story, which wouldn't be until after her trial. My personal take was something no other publication could print, and would have greater impact when readers would put all the pieces together. Thinking about writing that future story made me feel more in control. But I'd risk pissing off my father-in-law. Again.

When the cab dropped me off, I was surprised to see Burton's car still parked in front. Why hadn't he picked up his precious Jag?

As I was getting into bed, a text dinged into my cell. Burton asked if he could come over around dinner time. He'd bring takeout. It seemed that lately all we'd eaten was restaurant food. I'd be glad when life returned to our routine, planning and cooking meals together.

I replied, "Sure, see you later," then turned off my cell phone and dragged the covers over myself.

I knew Burton. Something was going on. There was only one thing left—who killed Frank?

Chapter 30

What seemed like only a short time later, Ann got into bed beside me. "Glad you're home, honey. How was the meeting?"

"Routine, but I'm dead tired. I picked up your meds—how's the shoulder now?"

"Fine, as long as I lie on my back and don't move." I didn't acknowledge the painkillers.

"You know Dad's coming over around six, right? He's bringing dinner, thank God." She put her arm around my waist and sighed. "I don't want to think about what he has to tell us."

It had to be about Frank, Burton's best friend. Again, I wondered if I was correct about who killed him. But right now, we needed sleep.

The bedside clock said three p.m. I set my phone to vibrate at five-thirty and put it under my pillow.

**

Burton arrived well before six. He's early for everything. Fortunately, I was up and felt somewhat sensible after a few hours' sleep and a quick wash. He came through to the kitchen and placed a couple of bags on the counter, which I assumed was dinner. I couldn't smell anything, so we must be having sandwiches. I poured Burton a scotch, shoved a beer in my pocket, and we went into the front room. I silently congratulated myself for managing to navigate using only one cane. Maybe the Jag would be having another sleepover.

"How's your shoulder?" he said, eyeing the sling that held my right arm in place.

"Torn rotator cuff. Cramps my style."

He grinned. "You're young and healthy. It'll heal fast. My daughter will take excellent care of you."

Ann was still in bed. I hadn't wanted to disturb her, but moments later, she joined us. "I hope we didn't wake you up," I said.

She shook her head and kissed my cheek. "It's always been hard for me to sleep during the day." She kissed her father. "Hi, Dad."

"Hi, Sweet t'ing," he said. "Glad you got some rest."

"Did I mention that I filled the prescription for you, Marsh? It's in the bathroom."

I nodded. And she'd make sure I took those meds. After the car accident and my surgeries years ago, I'd refused most of the stuff they'd prescribed. I hated the dozy way pills made me feel.

Burton set his glass on the coffee table in front of him. He sat tall, regarding us with a commanding air. "This has been a crazy time. And it's nearly over."

I'd parked myself in the wheelchair. Ann moved her chair close to me. "I almost don't want to hear what you're going to say, Dad. I guess the police have found out what happened to Uncle Frank."

Burton picked up his scotch, took a sip and slowly lowered the glass to the table. "What I have to say cannot leave this room." His gaze rested on us, as if assessing our reliability. "Jeanette has been charged with the murder of Steven Anderson, which you probably know."

We nodded and leaned forward in our chairs. I wondered if the cops would charge her with attempted murder too, because she'd meant to kill *me*.

Burton pointed an index finger. "Remember—this is privileged information. I can't emphasise how important it is to keep it quiet."

We nodded again. In the telling, Burton would present each fact in strict order. Although he'd never get to try the guilty parties in court, Ann and I represented the judge and jury.

He shifted in his chair. "Jeanette, Steven Anderson and Gary Lund conspired to steal the money Frank had earmarked to pay off his gambling debt. You were right about that, Marshall. That plan failed and Frank was murdered.

Yup.

"Their next plan was selling the vintage cars Frank and I owned."

He'd skipped over who had killed Frank. Ann didn't comment.

"Marshall told us that he'd picked up Jeanette's phone, and Lund was the third party."

We both nodded.

"When Lund didn't hear back from Jeanette, he drove past the outbuilding. Police cars were there, he saw Marshall's car too, and knew the plan had gone wrong."

Who were Burton's informants? No ordinary cop would hand over that kind of information. Why take the chance? It was probably someone high up, untouchable, one of Burton's long-standing buddies. Maybe they'd traded favours back and forth, and the guy still owed him.

Ann fidgeted in her chair. "Dad, dad—who killed Uncle Frank?"

Burton stared at her. "*Please*…Everything in proper order…The police took Jeanette to the precinct. She blamed Steven Anderson for everything, including Frank's murder. Very clever, because she'd heard hospital personnel saying Anderson was dead. She said he'd tried to blackmail Eileen and I, which was the truth. I presume she wanted the police to think she was acting under threats from Anderson."

Yeah, the wronged, innocent party. I hadn't thought of that angle.

"Next, she told the police that Anderson tried to blackmail Frank. That has yet to be proven, and could be another lie. I know Frank never liked Anderson, and he certainly would have confided in me if he was being blackmailed." Burton hesitated, letting his words sink in.

What the hell would Anderson blackmail Frank for? Maybe stuff Anderson found out through Jeanette?

"Jeanette had it all figured out—that Anderson was friends with Frank's gambling buddies, and learned about the money through them," said Burton. "She claimed Anderson threatened to expose her affair with Gary Lund if she didn't give him the combination to the office safe."

I snorted and couldn't stop myself from commenting. "Anderson was friends with Frank's gambling buddies? Bull shit. And I can't believe that Jeanette knew the combo to that safe either." But she could have known about the money.

Burton grinned. "That was the first story Jeanette told last night. Sending that text was fatal. She panicked when you showed up, Marshall, and panicked when police read the text back to her. Then she implicated Gary Lund." He paused and looked at me. "If you hadn't been there, they might literally have gotten away with murder, and with selling the cars."

Ann fidgeted in her seat, but there was no hurrying her father. This was his day in court, and he was systematically proving his case by exposing the criminals who'd taken advantage of Frank Veale. Burton's oration was all about honour and respect.

He took off his jacket and wiped his face with an initialled handkerchief. "When I heard the secondary alarm, I took a look at the video. Thank God Marshall stalled Jeanette and Anderson."

Burton took a deep breath, then carried on with his story. "You already know that Jeanette's text told Lund to stall the buyers. She tripped over herself trying to explain that at the precinct." Burton looked at me. "What made you choose last night to go to Frank's?"

"Gut instinct," I said. "Things didn't sit well with me after the funeral. Like I said, Jeanette was just going through the motions—she didn't look like a grieving widow to me. I couldn't stop thinking about her and Anderson—that Nell told me he was the only person Jeanette seemed to like, the only person she didn't sneer at."

Burton's eyebrows rose. "Very astute, Marshall. *Sneer* is the right word to describe her reaction to most people. I didn't put her with Lund soon enough. Those cars were a now-or-never opportunity to get cash."

I nodded.

"Before I forget," said Burton, "that blue Honda Steven drove was inside the garage at Frank's house."

So far, I was A+ on guesses.

"The police have your Mustang. I'll have it picked up for you."

"Thanks, Burton, but I can't drive until this shoulder heals."

He took a deep breath. "Jeanette's second story came out after the police showed her the video. She didn't know Frank and I had installed that back-up, and she wasn't going to take all the heat, as you would say, Marshall. That's when she added Gary Lund."

"It sounded to me like she was protecting Gary by blaming Steven first," said Ann. "They were having an affair, then she dumps on him?"

Nell was right. Jeanette was *that bitch.*

Burton continued. "Jeanette accused Lund and Anderson of conspiring to steal Frank's two hundred grand. I presume Anderson had contacted her when he came back to Canada. She knew he hated the Young family, as well as Frank, and my guess is that he was willing to join their plan, particularly after I refused to give him money."

Why didn't Jeanette ask for a lawyer up front? She worked for one—her dead husband, and knew the importance of legal advice. Then I answered my own question—because she was Jeanette—curvy, blonde, beautiful, smart and a sweet-talker used to getting her own way. I'd watched her turn on the charm many times. At the station, she'd probably counted on mesmerizing the police into believing she was threatened at gunpoint by Anderson, that somehow, she'd managed to get the gun and shoot him. Clever of the cops to get her to talk before they showed her the back-up video.

Burton was still talking…

"After Anderson demanded money from me, I asked Frank to charge him with extortion and have him deported, which you both know. Frank, busy with a full caseload, referred the job to Lund, and I agreed, thinking the process would be as easy as last time."

Interesting that Burton left out that Eileen had paid Anderson off. Now it was obvious why Lund never returned my calls when I'd asked him to find Anderson too.

"Jeanette claimed that Lund gave Anderson the combination to the safe, and when he opened it, there was no money. Anderson reported back, and Lund decided to have a look around the office himself. He didn't expect Frank to come in and find him."

Burton refolded the handkerchief and wiped his face, then continued. "They probably argued, then fought…Lund killed Frank with my letter opener…the one I'd left behind when I took the bench."

I hated that I was right. Ann put her hands over her face.

"Oh, my God…I thought Steven killed him!" Ann thought for a moment. "We just saw Gary Lund at Frank's funeral! How could he show up and pretend—"

She stopped mid-sentence. I had nothing to add. Knowing my father-in-law's passion for order and truth, I didn't doubt his story. To honour Frank, Burton would make damn sure he had the facts before telling us.

It seemed fitting that Burton had capped off the story. "I have to thank you and Frank for installing that back-up system."

Burton nodded. "Remember, nothing has been proven in court. This chat is just amongst us."

He sagged in his chair. Ann slumped back after leaning forward for the whole oration.

I had huge admiration for Burton, trusting us to keep this quiet. He had outlined the horror of his best friend's murder—a compelling case, implicating three dangerous people. He'd delivered a prosecutor's dream argument.

"My God…" said Ann, again. "Did the police catch the people who were going to buy the cars?"

"Not yet," said Burton. "But knowing Jeanette, she'll name everyone who was part of their plan—she's not going down alone. The buyers could be totally innocent, of course."

Yeah right, I thought—doing a cash deal at two o'clock in the morning.

"Jeanette met Lund at Frank's office?" said Ann.

Burton nodded. "She worked part time. Frank told me he suspected she was having an affair with Lund. Maybe Lund knew Frank was suspicious, and maybe Jeanette knew Frank and Nell planned to live together, and she wanted to get even—plenty of *maybes*".

"Dad, did you think Lund had anything to do with Uncle Frank's murder?"

Burton dodged the question. "After the funeral, Frank's assistant, Gayle, told me that clients only wanted to deal with Frank. In hindsight, I guess Lund ignored my request to find Anderson. I wish I known he'd never returned your calls, Marshall."

He seemed to have forgotten we weren't talking to each other then.

Burton sighed. "The detectives I hired went to the gym you visited and came back with nothing. You interviewed that friend of Steven's—Trevor? Then you figured out Steven must have been at Frank's house when he took the call from Trevor. Now…as far as your newspaper is concerned."

"Certain things will become public knowledge," I said. "The papers will print everything they've learned. They'll love the story about Lund—a lawyer crossing to the dark side. They may even speculate that he killed Frank, but no information will come from me. To use your words, Burton, I'll recuse myself from the case."

"Much appreciated, Marshall."

"So how did Lund get picked up?" said Ann.

"Jeanette told the police he'd be catching a flight," said Burton. "In fact, she had a ticket in her pocket and planned to join him. He was arrested at the airport."

"I didn't clue in about Lund until Frank's funeral," I said. "He must have been the one arguing with Frank during our last phone conversation."

"But wouldn't the office admin, Gayle, have heard him yelling at Frank that day?" said Ann.

"She had the day off," said Burton.

"Oh, that makes sense," Ann nodded. "Maybe I'm biased, but I think you two did more than the police."

"There's nothing stronger than a *need to know,*" I said.

Burton nodded. "Absolutely right, Marshall."

"Well, I guess it *is* over." Ann shook her head. "I still can't believe Uncle Frank's gone…his kids will be so lost without him." She sighed and looked out the window.

I followed her gaze. Our neighbours were coming home from work after an ordinary day, on an ordinary night.

"Steven's dead. I hate to admit this, but I'm relieved," said Ann. "I don't have to worry about him anymore. But my peace of mind came at a terrible cost." She looked at her father, tears in her eyes. "You've lost your best friend, Dad. It's hard to believe things got so crazy."

No one had an answer to that. There were questions I wouldn't ask. Did Burton have any say in what happened to Frank's law practice? I seemed to remember him telling us he had to sell out when he took the bench. Would the practice just shut down? Burton owned the cottage property he'd bought for Frank. Would he continue to live next door, staring at that vacant lot every day?

The cop in me was satisfied with my role in exposing that trio. It takes a village, as the cliche says. I said a silent thank-you again to Burton and Frank for installing that back-up security…but Ann hadn't finished.

"I have a few questions, Dad. Why didn't you tell me more when I called you? I was worried about Marsh."

Burton opened his hands. "He was in a dangerous situation, Sweet, and I didn't want to worry you."

Ann knit her hands together. "But…"

Burton's words came quickly. "When I said dangerous, I meant legally as well as physically. I saw that back-up tape, called police, got dressed, and left the house in a hurry."

She looked at her father, saying nothing. I kept quiet, *very* glad he hadn't told her the police had been called, and even *worse*, that he'd seen me on that tape. What the hell good would that have done? She'd have freaked out.

Burton let out a shaky breath. "I knew the police would bring Marshall to the station. I sent Reese the video so they'd know exactly what was going on. I had to get there and bring support for Marshall if needed."

Ann looked at her father, but didn't speak.

Burton sighed. "Since my separation from your mother, the fire and Frank's death, I've felt so…unsettled. It started when Anderson tried to blackmail us. I thought it would be easy to charge him with extortion and have him deported. I should have realized he'd come to your house and threaten you." Burton sat for many moments without speaking. "I just didn't want to believe he was that dangerous." He shook his head. "We should have charged him years ago."

Burton still hadn't explained to Ann why he'd sat with his mouth shut when the cops asked if he'd known about Anderson's abuse. I left them alone, thinking that would be the next on her agenda. I wheeled into the kitchen, not anxious to wobble down the hall on one cane.

Their voices sounded edgy and elevated. The discussion between my wife and her father would remain private if she didn't choose to tell me. Finally, the voices softened. When they came into the kitchen, their expressions and posture were relaxed. Ann smiled and plugged in the kettle. Burton patted his pockets, and asked if he had time to go out on the porch for a smoke. He put his empty glass on the counter. I asked if he wanted a top-up.

"No, thanks, son. I don't want to call a cab two nights in a row."

Son.

"I'll just be a sec." He opened the back door and went out.

Ann came over, sat in my lap and put her arms around me. My right shoulder complained but I didn't listen. She let out a long breath and raised her face for a kiss. "Love you, millions," I said. "And soon we'll be a family."

"Oh, Marsh, I'm so glad you're the father of our baby."

As opposed to Stephen Anderson? I knew what she meant and didn't make a joke. I looked out the kitchen window. Burton had turned and was staring across the frozen lawn. He'd let us have our moment.

"What's for dinner?" said Ann.

"Macaroni pie, cold cuts and sweet bread. Fancy mustard."

"No salad? I'll make one."

If it wasn't for women, men would never eat anything green. While she chopped, I retrieved coats from the front hall and went out on the back porch. I handed Burton his, and winced as I slid mine over my left arm. He draped it around my shoulder then stood back, nodding slowly.

"Well, Marshall. I guess there's nothing you can't do. You've climbed over obstacles that would've stopped most people. You figured everything out, led the way, and persevered. But most important, my daughter is happy. I'm proud to have you as my son-in-law."

He took a last drag on the cigarette, dropped the butt on the deck and crushed it. I heard its final sizzle under his foot. He bent, picked it up and put it in his pocket. "And you'll be a fine father to my grandchild."

That was a son-in-law's job. Make the daughter happy and make the grandbaby happy. Bonus if the in-laws liked you too. Well, maybe one of the in-laws. It was a job that suited me, a life I wanted.

I looked at him, trying to compose my response "Family is everything, Burton, I learned that seven years ago. Without Ann, I'd be nothing. Thanks for welcoming me."

Ann opened the back door. "Come on guys, I'm starving."

EPILOGUE

I took a leave of absence after our adventures with Burton's gardener, Ann's ex-husband, Frank's wife, and his employee.

Ann and I needed to sort ourselves out and prepare for the birth of our first child.

My stiff shoulder was a reminder of those crazy two weeks. After months of therapy, it healed, and I started to feel like an ordinary person again.

Shortly after returning to work, I resigned from *The Halton Register.* Don tried to talk me out of leaving—I had such a bright future—he said. I'd keep my promise to write a personal account of the murder of Frank Veale after the trial was over.

Our beautiful daughter was born on Father's Day. We called her Lucy—a name not associated with anyone from the past—she had her own life to live. Lucy was eight pounds on the nose, tan skin, curly brown hair, blue eyes. I was so proud of my wife, and so in awe of our new human being.

When Ann's pregnancy leave ended, I became a full-time, work-from-home dad. My articles for *Able and Active* were picked up by five big dailies across Canada. The *Easy Up* portable ramps attracted buyers in all the major cities, including municipal and federal offices. My weekly blog, *WheelMaster,* appealed to readers of all stripes judging from responses in *Letters to the Editor,* and my website.

Except for the odd creak in my shoulder, I had no issues looking after our beautiful daughter while Ann was at work. I kept the wheelchair handy—Lucy loved it. I became an expert steering with one hand while holding her with the—the walls and door frames thanked me. Lucy and I whizzed around the house—she stopped crying the second we started rolling down the hall.

I'd never been so happy. There'd be sinkholes along the way—some deeper than others, but I had the tools to dig myself out. Ann and Lucy.

the end

ABOUT THE AUTHOR

Donna's first book, a non-fiction narrative, *Finding Matthew (A Child with Brain Damage, A Young Man with Mental Illness),* published in 2012, is still selling.

Donna's short stories have been published in *The Quick Brown Fox, Canadian Voices* Volume Two, *Ars Medica, Commuter Lit,* the *Daily American,* a U.S. newspaper, *The Desi Express,* to name a few publications.

Donna lives with her husband Ed, in Oakville, Ontario. They have three children, Matthew, Kelley and Joseph, daughter-in-law Crystal, and two granddaughters Sloane and Reese, who are perfect. Their son Matthew passed away in 2010, and their daughter Kelley passed away in 2021.

ALSO FROM MIDDLEROAD PUBLISHERS

MiddleRoad | Publishers

www.middleroadpublishers.ca

Making Literature See The Light Of Day

ALL BOOKS AVAILABLE AT AMAZON WORLDWIDE.

eBook versions available from all eBook channels

A TIME TO LOVE AN A TIME TO DIE

By Michael Joll

Finely drawn characters. Visually dramatic, tense and emotionally satisfying, this is one of the finest novels of the Great War. In this poignant story, the writing stands in stark contrast with the unvarnished brutality of trench warfare.

ATTITUDE

By Dave Moores

Fresh, gritty and laced with dry humour, Attitude is a fast-paced story readers of all ages won't want to put down. It's dead of winter and an outbreak of weird stuff, random acts of vandalism are unsettling the citizens of Southmead.

DANCING MY WAY TO 80

By Doris Naraine

Biography published privately and not available for sale.

DOWN INDEPENDENCE BOULEVARD AND OTHER STORIES

Winner: Guyana Prize For Literature 2022 (Fiction)

by Ken Puddicombe

"A brilliant collection of stories telling the tales of people forced to leave their homes...craving the past, escaping from racial conflicts and dictatorship..."—Judith Kopacsi Gelberger, author of *Heroes Don't Cry*.

FROM MY WINDOW

By Rena Flannigan

Rena was truly a Scots force of nature, a global whirlwind of activity, travelling the world and then setting it down in a flurry of missives and a storm of anecdotes.

GABRIELLE

By Michael Joll

Gabrielle transcends time and space, taking the reader on a journey to Poland, France, Holland and Israel as she searches for her identity.

GENERATIONS

Biography published privately and not available for sale.

HACKER

By Michael Joll

"The character Det. Inspector Richards could have been drawn from real life. My favourite character." David R. Vancouver, B.C.

I WENT TO THE END OF THE RAINBOW

by Pramita Chakraborty

A beautifully illustrated, captivating tale about a young child who can't sleep and embarks on a adventure through the colours of the rainbow.

JUNTA

By Ken Puddicombe

"A gripping story (of) an imperfect democracy...the tension...builds increasingly from page to page."—Rico Downer, author of *There Once Was a Little England*

LOVE HAS TWO MOONS

By Franklin Mohan

With humour, insight and sensitivity, Franklin Mohan peels back the subtle layers of prejudice and racism in North American and Caribbean society—Raymond Holmes, author of *Witnesses and other short stories*

MEET ME AT THE FOUR CORNERS

Anthology

Twenty-six stories, fiction and non-Fiction, some of them prize winning submissions from the writers of the Brampton Writers' Guild, are featured in this collection.

PEOPLE OF GUYANA

By Ian McDonald and Peter Jailall

"These beautifully crafted poems are shaped by their generosity of spirit and abundant capacity for empathy and fun..." —Clem Seecharan

PERFECT EXECUTION AND OTHER STORIES

by Michael Joll

"Michael Joll is a master of surprise endings, but they never seem forced. He always stays true to his characters and their worlds." —Nancy Kay Clark, author and editor, *CommuterLit.com*

PERSONS OF INTEREST

By Michael Joll

"Exotic and intriguing! Joll brilliantly captures the reader's interest with vivid imagery and a relentless sleuth." —Phyllis Humby, short story writer, poet and novelist.

POEMS FOR MARY

By Ian Mc Donald

"The garden which my wife has created, it is as much a work of art as a painting by a master spirit or a piece of perfect music by a composer."—Ian Mc Donald, author, poet.

RACING WITH THE RAIN

By Ken Puddicombe

"Puddicombe's brilliant novel...an historic political conflict in Guyana, during the Cold War and the cold cynicism and tragic irony of a state sacrificed to super-power hegemony." -Frank Birbalsingh, author of *Novels and The Nation: Essays in Canadian*

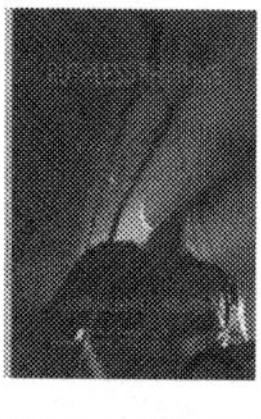

RUTHLESS RHYTHMS

By Judith Gelberger

If poetry is a window into the soul of the author, Judith Gelberger has opened one which illuminates some of the most painful emotions and experiences of human existence...—Raymond Holmes – Author of *Witnesses And Other Short Stories*

SCALING NEW HEIGHTS

Anthology

Forty-two pieces from the members of Pakaraima Writers Group are featured in this their first collection of poetry and non-fiction travel articles

---

SNAPSHOTS OF OUR LIVES

Anthology

Authors Ram Jagessar (Trinidad), Roop Misir and Kennard Ramphal (Guyana) combined their talents to produce a fifty-one-piece Collection of stirring anecdotes. These stories traverse *THE HOMELAND*, set in Trinidad and Guyana, and *THE IMMIGRANT EXPERIENCE* in Canada where they migrated as young men.

SPARKLES AND KARIM

By Dave Moores

Author Dave Moores follows up on his two novels: *ATTITUDE* and *WINDWARD LEGS* with an exciting novel set in Iraq 2014.

TASTE MY WORDS

By Lisa Freemantle

Freemantle's compositions are imbued with a highly poetic energy instilling in the reader a subtle, penetrating fever of contentment...." —Dr. Franklin Mohan, author *Love Has Two Moons and Other Stories*

THE DARKEST HOURS

By Michael Joll

***The Darkest Hours* is a novel of conflicts and contrasts set against the backdrop of WWII.**

THE GARDEN

By Ian McDonald

Ian McDonald's poems are full of light and love. His easy style about the beauty of nature connects with his readers.

TOWARDS THE PEBBLED SHORE

By Peter Jailall

"...thoughtfully conceived, expressed movingly and written with great clarity. I think this may be Peter's best book yet. It lifts the heart."

Ian McDonald, author The Garden and other works

TROPICAL SCENES

By Ken Puddicombe

Ken Puddicombe follows up on his first collection of poems: Unfathomable And Other Poems with another tribute to the land of his birth. "Each poem covers more ground than lengthy chapters." -Cherry Narula, author: Nona and Daniel, Goldfinch Sunshine Project

---

UNFATHOMABLE AND OTHER POEMS

by Ken Puddicombe

These poems cover a variety of themes, all connected to a childhood growing up in British Guiana, the rise of nationalism and the pre- and post-independence eras.

WEALTH THROUGH REAL ESTATE INVESTING

Manufactured by Amazon.ca
Bolton, ON

40205095R00149